W9-CYW-066

JOURNEY INTO THE UNKNOWN . . .

"COLLABORATING"—Michael Bishop

A young man born with two heads discovers that it's hard work competing for one body—especially when one of him falls in love. . . .

"FATE'S PURSE"—Russell Kirk

If money is the root of all evil, perhaps it is also the cause of terror? After all, people sometimes murder for money . . . why shouldn't spirits?

"RENT CONTROL"—Walter Tevis

An affluent New York couple realizes that they can make time stand still when they make love —with chilling consequences. . . .

"THE EXTRAORDINARY VOYAGES OF AMÉLIE BERTRAND"—Joanna Russ

A passenger in a French railway station, hurrying for his train, enters a passageway—and discovers the gateway to another world. . . .

FANTASY ANNUAL III

TERRY CARR, EDITOR

A TIMESCAPE BOOK
PUBLISHED BY POCKET BOOKS NEW YORK

This collection is comprised of works of fiction. Names, characters, places and incidents are either the product of the authors' imaginations or are used fictitiously, and any resemblance to actual persons, living or dead, events or locales is entirely coincidental.

Another *Original* publication of TIMESCAPE BOOKS

A Timescape Book published by
POCKET BOOKS, a Simon & Schuster division of
GULF & WESTERN CORPORATION
1230 Avenue of the Americas, New York, N.Y. 10020

Copyright © 1981 by Terry Carr

All rights reserved, including the right to reproduce
this book or portions thereof in any form whatsoever.
For information address Timescape Books, 1230
Avenue of the Americas, New York, N.Y. 10020

ISBN: 0-671-41272-8

First Timescape Books printing May, 1981

10 9 8 7 6 5 4 3 2 1

POCKET and colophon are trademarks of Simon & Schuster.

Printed in the U.S.A.

CREDITS

"The Crate" by Stephen King. Copyright © 1979 by Montcalm Publishing Corp. From *Gallery*, July 1979, by permission of the author and his agents, Kirby McCauley Ltd.

"Collaborating" by Michael Bishop. Copyright © 1979 by Lee Harding. From *Rooms of Paradise*, by permission of the author and his agent, Virginia Kidd.

"Fate's Purse" by Russell Kirk. Copyright © 1979 by Mercury Press, Inc. From *Fantasy and Science Fiction*, May 1979, by permission of the author and his agents, Kirby McCauley Ltd.

"The Things That Are Gods" by John Brunner. Copyright © 1979 by Davis Publications, Inc. From *Asimov's SF Adventure Magazine*, Fall 1979, by permission of Brunner Fact & Fiction Ltd.

"Flop Sweat" by Harlan Ellison. Copyright © 1977 by Harlan Ellison. From *Heavy Metal*, March 1979, by permission of, and by arrangement with, the author and the author's agent, Robert P. Mills, Ltd., New York. All rights reserved.

"Rent Control" by Walter Tevis. Copyright © 1979 by Omni Publications International Ltd. From *Omni*, October 1979, by permission of the author and his agent, Robert P. Mills Ltd.

"The Button Molder" by Fritz Leiber. Copyright © 1979 by Stuart David Schiff. From *Whispers*, October 1979, by permission of the author.

"The Extraordinary Voyages of Amélie Bertrand" by Joanna Russ. Copyright © 1979 by Mercury Press, Inc. From *Fantasy and Science Fiction*, September 1979, by permission of the author.

"Eumenides in the Fourth Floor Lavatory" by Orson Scott Card. Copyright © 1979 by Orson Scott Card. From *Chrysalis 4*, by permission of the author and his agent, The Barbara Bova Literary Agency.

"The White Horse Child" by Greg Bear. Copyright © 1979 by Terry Carr. From *Universe 9*, by permission of the author.

"Trill Coster's Burden" by Manly Wade Wellman. Copyright © 1979 by Stuart David Schiff. From *Whispers II*, by permission of the author and his agents, Kirby McCauley Ltd.

"Pie Row Joe" by Kevin McKay. Copyright © 1979 by Lee Harding. From *Rooms of Paradise*, by permission of the author.

"The Ancient Mind at Work" by Suzy McKee Charnas. Copyright © 1978 by Omni Publications International Ltd. From *Omni*, February 1979, by permission of the author and the author's agent, Virginia Kidd.

CONTENTS

INTRODUCTION

SCIENCE FICTION AND FANTASY ARE CONSIDered nearly identical genres by a great many people, but it's worthwhile to consider some of the important differences between them. I don't propose to worry about exact definitions here—obviously some stories, such as those by John Brunner and Suzy McKee Charnas in this volume, include elements of both genres and thus show that there's no hard and fast dividing line. Still, most stories occupy positions considerably farther from the middle of the spectrum: it would be difficult to classify *The Lord of the Rings* or *A Fine and Private Place* as science fiction, for instance, and *Rendezvous with Rama* certainly isn't a fantasy novel.

Generally speaking, a story that makes a serious attempt to justify its "impossible" events by scientific reasoning is science fiction, at least by intent; stories that present their marvels as inexplicable are fantasies. But there are differences much more important than those of definition.

One is the fact that most fantasy stories take place in milieux that are recognizably our "real" world of the present or known historical settings; fantastic beings or events that intrude in these ordinary worlds are striking by contrast and surprise. In such cases, the power of a story comes largely from the ability of writers to evoke backgrounds that are believable, even commonplace.

The writing techniques involved in such stories are identical with those of "mainstream" fiction writing: mentioning familiar details of the physical world and common types of actions of everyday people. This is a highly refined art in general fiction; such convincing details can be introduced with very few words because writers expect their readers to recognize brand names, for instance, or the meanings of social customs with which they've lived all their lives.

Science fiction writers are at a disadvantage in this respect because they must extrapolate artifacts and manners for their future worlds and explain them as briefly as possible in order not to have their stories bog down in undramatic exegeses.

So the writing of fantasy may be considered easier—but it really isn't. In order to induce readers to accept the incredible aspects of their stories, fantasy writers have to produce a "super-realistic" type of writing, one that will keep readers from stopping in disbelief. This is difficult; it requires imagination, art and craft of a high order.

Therefore, I'm convinced that the general level of writing in fantasy is higher than that in science fiction on the one hand and "mainstream" fiction on the other. In its necessary techniques, fantasy writing combines the demands of both—and interestingly, the people who write fantasy come from both camps.

Larry Niven is an accomplished science fiction writer who's done a number of delightful fantasies. Henry James was an excellent "realistic" writer whose *The Turn of the Screw* is a fantasy classic. Robert A. Heinlein's occasional fantasy stories are among his best; so are C. S. Lewis's fantasies.

There's an additional factor at work here: in this country at least, science fiction became ghettoized over fifty years ago when sf magazines proved to be its most profitable outlet. As a result, that genre developed specialized writers and "in-group" conventions such as faster-than-light travel, galactic empires, time travel and alternative worlds—things that soon didn't even need explanations for the hardcore readership of the sf magazines.

Despite the short-term success of several fantasy magazines, fantasy as a genre never quite went that route. There was always a large number of novels and stories produced by writers unfamiliar or unconcerned with the genre as such: people like James Branch Cabell, John Collier, Thorne Smith, Robert Nathan, Shirley Jackson, Jorge Luis Borges and Peter S. Beagle. Some of their stories, once these writers had drawn the attention of fantasy fans, were solicited by and published in fantasy magazines, but these writers and others hadn't begun as genre writers; they saw themselves simply as writers of general fiction.

The wider readership, those people who had never heard of specialized fantasy magazines, accepted them as such. Quite a number of their books became bestsellers; thus, they were "respectable" to the publishing community; thus, many other writers who'd have shuddered at the thought of submitting fiction to *Thrilling Wonder Stories* or *Unknown Worlds* happily produced fantasy stories year after year.

The auctorial gene-pool for fantasy has therefore always been larger than that for science fiction. Inevitably, the ideas, techniques and plots of fantasy have had a much wider range.

None of the foregoing is meant to suggest that fantasy is "better" than science fiction—that would be another case of comparing apples and oranges. But fantasy does have things to offer that current science fiction can seldom match. You'll find a number of them in this compilation of the finest fantasy stories published during 1979.

As usual, these stories display a high degree of writing skill, and some were originally published in magazines and books that are unfamiliar to most fantasy aficionados. The expected adventures, strangenesses and frights are all here . . . plus some quite unexpected things.

—TERRY CARR
April 23, 1980

~~~~~~

It's awfully hard to get rid of a monster forever, as the many returns of Dracula, Frankenstein's monster, the Werewolf, etc., have shown. Perhaps the best we can do is to imprison such a creature and hide it where it will never be found. But people in the grip of terror sometimes don't do the job thoroughly. . . .

Stephen King is the recognized master of the modern horror story. His latest novel is *Firestarter*.

THE CRATE

Stephen King

DEXTER STANLEY WAS SCARED. MORE; HE
felt as if that central axle that binds us to the state we
call sanity were under a greater strain than it had ever
been under before. As he pulled up beside Henry Northrup's house on North Campus Avenue that August night,
he felt that if he didn't talk to someone, he really would
go crazy.

There was no one to talk to but Henry Northrup. Dex
Stanley was the head of the Zoology Department, and
once might have been university president if he had been
better at academic politics. His wife had died twenty years
before, and they had been childless. What remained of his
own family was all west of the Rockies. He was not good
at making friends.

Northrup was an exception to that. In some ways, they
were two of a kind; both had been disappointed in the
mostly meaningless, but always vicious, game of university politics. Three years before, Northrup had made his
run at the vacant English Department chairmanship. He
had lost and one of the reasons had undoubtedly been his
wife, Wilma, an abrasive and unpleasant woman. At the
few cocktail parties Dex had attended where English people and Zoology people could logically mix, it seemed he
could always recall the harsh mule-bray of her voice, telling some new faculty wife to "call me Billie, dear, everyone does!"

Dex made his way across the lawn to Northrup's door
at a stumbling run. It was Thursday, and Northrup's un-

pleasant spouse took two classes on Thursday nights. Consequently, it was Dex and Henry's chess night. The two men had been playing chess together for the last eight years.

Dex rang the bell beside the door of his friend's house; leaned on it. The door opened at last, and Northrup was there.

"Dex," he said. "I didn't expect you for another—"

Dex pushed in past him. "Wilma," he said. "Is she here?"

"No, she left fifteen minutes ago. I was just making myself some chow. Dex, you look awful."

They had walked under the hall light, and it illuminated the cheesy pallor of Dex's face and seemed to outline wrinkles as deep and dark as fissures in the earth. Dex was sixty-one, but on that hot August night, he looked more like ninety.

"I ought to." Dex wiped his mouth with the back of his hand.

"Well, what is it?"

"I'm afraid I'm going crazy, Henry. Or that I've already gone."

"You want something to eat? Wilma left cold ham."

"I'd rather have a drink. A big one."

"All right."

"Two men dead, Henry," Dex said abruptly. "And I could be blamed. Yes, I can see how I could be blamed. But it wasn't me. It was the crate. And I don't even know what's in there!" He uttered a wild laugh.

"Dead?" Northrup said. "What is this, Dex?"

"A janitor. I don't know his name. And Gereson. A graduate student. He just happened to be there. In the way of . . . whatever it was."

Henry studied Dex's face for a long moment and then said, "I'll get us both a drink."

He left. Dex wandered into the living room, past the low table where the chess game had already been set up, and stared out the graceful bow window. That thing in his mind, the axle or whatever it was, did not feel so much in danger of snapping now. Thank God for Henry.

Northrup came back with two pony glasses choked with ice. Ice from the fridge's automatic ice maker, Stanley thought randomly. Wilma "just call me Billie, everyone does" Northrup insisted on all the modern conveniences

. . . and when Wilma insisted on a thing, she did so savagely.

Northrup filled both glasses with Cutty Sark. He handed one of them to Stanley, who slopped Scotch over his fingers, stinging a small cut he'd gotten in the lab a couple of days before. He hadn't realized until then that his hands were shaking. He emptied half the glass, and the Scotch boomed in his stomach, first hot, then spreading a steadying warmth.

"Sit down, man," Northrup said.

Dex sat, and drank again. Now it was a lot better. He looked at Northrup, who was looking levelly back over the rim of his own glass. Dex looked away, out at the bloody orb of moon sitting over the rim of the horizon, over the university, which was supposed to be the seat of rationality, the forebrain of the body politic. How did that jibe with the matter of the crate? With the screams? With the blood?

"Men are dead?" Northrup said at last. "Are you sure they're dead?"

"Yes. The bodies are gone now. At least, I think they are. Even the bones . . . the teeth . . . but the blood . . . the blood, you know . . ."

"No, I don't know anything. You've got to start at the beginning."

Stanley took another drink and set his glass down. "Of course I do," he said. "Yes. It begins just where it ends. With the crate. The janitor found the crate. . . ."

Dexter Stanley had come into Amberson Hall, sometimes called the Old Zoology Building, that afternoon at three o'clock. It was a blaringly hot day, and the campus looked listless and dead, in spite of the twirling sprinklers in front of the fraternity houses and the Old Front dorms.

The Old Front went back to the turn of the century, but Amberson Hall was much older than that. It was one of the oldest buildings on a university campus that had celebrated its tricentennial two years previous. It was a tall brick building, shackled with ivy that seemed to spring out of the earth like green, clutching hands. Its narrow windows were more like gun slits than real windows, and Amberson seemed to frown at the newer buildings with their glass walls and curvy, unorthodox shapes.

The new Zoology building, Cather Hall, had been completed eight months before, and the process of transition

4

would probably go on for another eighteen months. No one was completely sure what would happen to Amberson then. If the bond issue to build the new gym found favor with the voters, it would probably be demolished.

He paused a moment to watch two young men throwing a Frisbee back and forth. A dog ran back and forth between them, glumly chasing the spinning disc. Abruptly the mutt gave up and flopped in the shade of a poplar. A VW with a NO NUKES sticker on the back deck trundled slowly past, heading for the Upper Circle. Nothing else moved. A week before, the final summer session had ended and the campus lay still and fallow, dead ore on summer's anvil.

Dex had a number of files to pick up, part of the seemingly endless process of moving from Amberson to Cather. The old building seemed spectrally empty. His footfalls echoed back dreamily as he walked past closed doors with frosted glass panels, past bulletin boards with their yellowing notices and toward his office at the end of the first-floor corridor. The cloying smell of fresh paint hung in the air.

He was almost to his door, and jingling his keys in his pocket, when the janitor popped out of Room 6, the big lecture hall, startling him.

He grunted, then smiled a little shamefacedly, the way people will when they've gotten a mild zap. "You got me that time," he told the janitor.

The janitor smiled and twiddled the gigantic key ring clipped to his belt. "Sorry, Perfesser Stanley," he said. "I was hopin it was you. Charlie said you'd be in this after."

"Charlie Gereson is still here?" Dex frowned. Gereson was a grad student who was doing an involved—and possibly very important—paper on negative environmental factors in long-term animal migration. It was a subject that could have a strong impact on area farming practices and pest control. But Gereson was pulling almost fifty hours a week in the gigantic (and antiquated) basement lab. The new lab complex in Cather would have been exponentially better suited to his purposes, but the new labs would not be fully equipped for another two to four months . . . if then.

"Think he went over to the Union for a burger," the janitor said. "I told him myself to quit awhile and go get something to eat. He's been here since nine this morning.

5

Told him myself. Said he ought to get some food. A man don't live on love alone."

The janitor smiled, a little tentatively, and Dex smiled back. The janitor was right; Gereson was embarked upon a labor of love. Dex had seen too many squadrons of students just grunting along and making grades not to appreciate that . . . and not to worry about Charlie Gereson's health and well-being from time to time.

"I would have told *him,* if he hadn't been so busy," the janitor said, and offered his tentative little smile again. "Also, I kinda wanted to show you myself."

"What's that?" Dex asked. He felt a little impatient. It was chess night with Henry; he wanted to get this taken care of and still have time for a leisurely meal at the Hancock House.

"Well, maybe it's nothin," the janitor said. "But . . . well, this buildin is some old, and we keep turnin things up, don't we?"

Dex knew. It was like moving out of a house that has been lived in for generations. Halley, the bright young assistant professor who had been here for three years now, had found half a dozen antique clips with small brass balls on the ends. She'd had no idea what the clips, which looked a little bit like spring-loaded wishbones, could be. Dex had been able to tell her. Not so many years after the Civil War, those clips had been used to hold the heads of white mice, who were then operated on without anesthetic. Young Halley, with her Berkeley education and her bright spill of Farrah Fawcett-Majors golden hair, had looked quite revolted. "No antivivisectionists in those days," Dex had told her jovially. "At least not around here." And Halley had responded with a blank look that probably disguised disgust or maybe even loathing. Dex had put his foot in it again. He had a positive talent for that, it seemed.

They had found sixty boxes of *The American Zoologist* in a crawlspace, and the attic had been a maze of old equipment and moldering reports. Some of the impedimenta no one—not even Dexter Stanley—could identify. In the closet of the old animal pens at the back of the building, Professor Viney had found a complicated gerbil-run with exquisite glass panels. It had been accepted for display at the Museum of Natural Science in Washington.

But the finds had been tapering off this summer, and

Dex thought Amberson Hall had given up the last of its secrets.

"What have you found?" he asked the janitor.

"A crate. I found it tucked right under the basement stairs. I didn't open it. It's been nailed shut, anyway."

Stanley couldn't believe that anything very interesting could have escaped notice for long, just by being tucked away under the stairs. Tens of thousands of people went up and down them every week during the academic year. Most likely the janitor's crate was full of department records dating back twenty or twenty-five years. Or even more prosaic, a box of *National Geographics*.

"I hardly think—"

"It's a real crate," the janitor broke in earnestly. "I mean, my father was a carpenter, and this crate is built the way he was buildin em back in the Twenties. And he learned from *his* father."

"I really doubt if—"

"Also, it's got about four inches of dust on it. I wiped some off and there's a date. Eighteen thirty-four."

That changed things. Stanley looked at his watch and decided he could spare half an hour.

In spite of the humid August heat outside, the smooth tile-faced throat of the stairway was almost cold. Above them, yellow frosted globes cast a dim and thoughtful light. The stair levels had once been red, but in the centers they shaded to a dead black where the feet of years had worn away layer after layer of resurfacing. The silence was smooth and nearly perfect.

The janitor reached the bottom first and pointed under the staircase. "Under here," he said.

Dex joined him in staring into a shadowy, triangular cavity under the wide staircase. He felt a small tremor of disgust as he saw where the janitor had brushed away a gossamer veil of cobwebs. He supposed it was possible that the man had found something a little older than postwar records under there, now that he actually looked at the space. But 1834?

"Just a second," the janitor said, and left momentarily. Left alone, Dex hunkered down and peered in. He could make out nothing but a deeper patch of shadow in there. Then the janitor returned with a hefty four-cell flashlight. "This'll show it up."

"What were you doing under there anyway?" Dex asked.

The janitor grinned. "I was only standin here tryin to decide if I should buff that second-floor hallway first or wash the lab windows. I couldn't make up my mind, so I flipped a quarter. Only I dropped it and it rolled under there." He pointed to the shadowy, triangular cave. "I prob'ly would have let it go, except that was my only quarter for the Coke machine. So I got my flash and knocked down the cobwebs, and when I crawled under to get it, I saw that crate. Here, have a look."

The janitor shone his light into the hole. Motes of disturbed dust preened and swayed lazily in the beam. The light struck the far wall in a spotlight circle, rose to the zigzag undersides of the stairs briefly, picking out an ancient cobweb in which long-dead bugs hung mummified, and then the light dropped and centered on a crate about five feet long and two and a half wide. It was perhaps three feet deep. As the janitor had said, it was no knocked-together affair made out of scrap-boards. It was neatly constructed of a smooth, dark heavy wood. *A coffin,* Dexter thought uneasily. *It looks like a child's coffin.*

The dark color of the wood showed only in a fan-shaped wipe on the side. The rest of the crate was the uniform dull gray of dust. Something was written on the side —stenciled there.

Dex squinted but couldn't read it. He fumbled his glasses out of his breast pocket and still couldn't. Part of what had been stenciled on was obscured by the dust—not four inches of it, by any means, but an extraordinarily thick coating, all the same.

Not wanting to crawl and dirty his pants, Dex duck-walked under the stairway, stifling a sudden and amazingly strong feeling of claustrophobia. The spit dried in his mouth and was replaced by a dry, woolly taste, like an old mitten. He thought of the generations of students trooping up and down these stairs; all male until 1888, then in coeducational platoons, carrying their books and papers and anatomical drawings, their bright faces and clear eyes, each of them convinced that a useful and exciting future lay ahead . . . and here, below their feet, the spider spun his eternal snare for the fly and the trundling beetle, and here this crate sat impassively, gathering dust, waiting. . . .

A tendril of spidersilk brushed across his forehead and he swept it away with a small cry of loathing and an uncharacteristic inner cringe.

"Not very nice under there, is it?" the janitor asked sympathetically, holding his light centered on the crate. "God, I hate tight places."

Dex didn't reply. He had reached the crate. He looked at the letters that were stenciled there and then brushed the dust away from them. It rose in a cloud, intensifying that mitten taste, making him cough dryly. The dust hung in the beam of the janitor's light like old magic, and Dex Stanley read what some long-dead Chief of Lading had stenciled on this crate.

SHIP TO HORLICKS UNIVERSITY, the top line read. VIA JULIA CARPENTER, read the middle line. The third line read simply: ARCTIC EXPEDITION. Below that, someone had written in heavy black charcoal strokes: JUNE 19, 1834. That was the one line the janitor's hand-swipe had completely cleared.

ARCTIC EXPEDITION, Dex read again. His heart had begun to thump.

"So what do you think?" the janitor's voice floated in.

Dex grabbed one end and lifted it. Heavy. As he let it settle back with a mild thud, something shifted inside—he did not hear it but felt it through the palms of his hands, as if whatever it was had moved of its own volition. Stupid, of course. It had been an almost liquid feel, as if something not quite jelled had moved sluggishly.

ARCTIC EXPEDITION.

Dex felt the excitement of an antiques collector happening upon a neglected armoire with a twenty-five-dollar price tag in the back room of some hick-town junk shop . . . an armoire that just might be a Chippendale. "Help me get it out," he called to the janitor.

Working bent over to keep from slamming their heads on the underside of the stairway, sliding the crate along, they got it out and then picked it up by the bottom. Dex had gotten his pants dirty after all, and there were cobwebs in his hair.

As they carried it into the old-fashioned, train-terminal-sized lab, Dex felt that sensation of shift inside the crate again, and he could see by the expression on the janitor's face that he had felt it as well. They set it on one of the formica-topped lab tables. The next one over was littered with Charlie Gereson's stuff—notebooks, graph paper, contour maps, a Texas Instruments calculator.

The janitor stood back, wiping his hands on his double-pocket gray shirt, breathing hard. "Some heavy mother,"

9

he said. "That bastard must weigh two hunnert pounds. You okay, Perfesser Stanley?"

Dex barely heard him. He was looking at the end of the box, where there was yet another series of stencils:

PAELLA/SANTIAGO/SAN
FRANCISCO/CHICAGO/NEW
YORK/HORLICKS

"Perfesser ——"

"Paella," Dex muttered, and then said it again, slightly louder. He was seized with an unbelieving kind of excitement that was held in check only by the thought that it might be some sort of hoax. "Paella!"

"Paella, Dex?" Henry Northrup asked. The moon had risen in the sky, turning silver.

"Paella is a very small island south of Tierra del Fuego," Dex said. "Perhaps the smallest island ever inhabited by the race of man. A number of Easter Island-type monoliths were found there just after World War II. Not very interesting compared to their bigger brothers, but every bit as mysterious. The natives of Paella and Tierra del Fuego were stone-age people. Christian missionaries killed them with kindness."

"I beg your pardon?"

"It's extremely cold down there. Summer temperatures rarely range above the mid-forties. The missionaries gave them blankets, partly so they would be warm, mostly to cover their sinful nakedness. The blankets were crawling with fleas, and the natives of both islands were wiped out by European diseases for which they had developed no immunities. Mostly by smallpox."

Dex drank. The Scotch had lent his cheeks some color, but it was hectic and flaring—double spots of flush that sat above his cheekbones like rouge.

"But Tierra del Fuego—and this Paella—that's not the Arctic, Dex. It's the Antarctic."

"It wasn't in 1834," Dex said, setting his glass down, careful in spite of his distraction to put it on the coaster Henry had provided. If Wilma found a ring on one of her end tables, his friend would have hell to pay. "The terms subarctic, Antarctic, and Artarctica weren't invented yet. In those days there was only the north arctic and the south arctic.

"Okay."

"Hell, I made the same kind of mistake. I couldn't

figure out why Frisco was on that itinerary as a port of call. Then I realized I was figuring on the Panama Canal, which wasn't built for another eighty years or so."

"An Arctic expedition? In 1834?" Henry asked doubtfully.

"I haven't had a chance to check the records yet," Dex said, picking up his drink again. "But I know from my history that there were 'Arctic expeditions' as early as Francis Drake. None of them made it, that was all. They were convinced they'd find gold, silver, jewels, lost civilizations, God knows what else. The Smithsonian Institution outfitted an attempted exploration of the North Pole in, I think it was 1881 or '82. They all died. A bunch of men from The Explorers' Club in London tried for the South Pole in the 1850's. Their ship was sunk by icebergs, but three or four of them survived. They stayed alive by sucking dew out of their clothes and eating the kelp they caught on their boat, until they were picked up. They lost their teeth. And they claimed to have seen sea monsters."

"What happened, Dex?" Henry asked softly.

Stanley looked up. "We opened the crate," he said dully. "God help us, Henry, we opened the crate."

He paused for a long time, it seemed, before beginning to speak again.

"Paella?" the janitor asked. "What's that?"

"An island off the tip of South America," Dex said. "Never mind. Let's get this open." He opened one of the lab drawers and began to rummage through it, looking for something to pry with.

"Never mind that stuff," the janitor said. He looked excited himself now. "I got a hammer and chisel in my closet upstairs. I'll get em. Just hang on."

He left. The crate sat on the table's formica top, squat and mute.

It sits squat and mute, Dex thought, and shivered a little. Where had that thought come from? Some story? The words· had a cadenced yet unpleasant sound. He dismissed them. He was good at dismissing the extraneous. He was a scientist.

He looked around the lab just to get his eyes off the crate. Except for Charlie's table, it was unnaturally neat and quiet—like the rest of the university. White-tiled, subway-station walls gleamed freshly under the overhead

11

globes; the globes themselves seemed to be double-caught and submerged in the polished formica surfaces, like eerie lamps shining from deep quarry water. A huge, old-fashioned slate blackboard dominated the wall opposite the sinks. And cupboards, cupboards everywhere. It was easy enough—too easy, perhaps—to see the antique, sepia-toned ghosts of all those old zoology students, wearing their white coats with the green cuffs, their hairs marcelled or pomaded, doing their dissections and writing their reports. . . .

Footfalls clattered on the stairs and Dex shivered, thinking again of the crate sitting there—yes, squat and mute—under the stairs for so many years, long after the men who had pushed it under there had died and gone back to dust.

Paella, he thought, and then the janitor came back in with a hammer and chisel.

"Let me do this for you, Perfesser?" he asked, and Dex was about to refuse when he saw the pleading, hopeful look in the man's eyes.

"Of course," he said. After all, it was this man's find.

"Prob'ly nothin in here but a bunch of rocks and plants so old they'll turn to dust when you touch em. But it's funny; I'm pretty hot for it."

Dex smiled noncommittally. He had no idea what was in the crate, but he doubted if it was just plant and rock specimens. There was that slightly liquid shifting sensation when they had moved it.

"Here goes," the janitor said, and began to pound the chisel under the board with swift blows of the hammer. The board hiked up a bit, revealing a double row of nails that reminded Dex absurdly of teeth. The janitor levered the handle of the chisel down and the board pulled loose, the nails shrieking out of the wood. He did the same thing at the other end, and the board came free, clattering to the floor. Dex set it aside, noticing that even the nails looked different, somehow—thicker, squarer at the tip, and without that blued-steel sheen that is the mark of a sophisticated alloying process.

The janitor was peering into the crate through the long, narrow strip he had uncovered. "Can't see nothin," he said. "Where'd I leave my light?"

"Never mind," Dex said. "Go on and open it."

"Okay." He took off a second board, then a third. Six or seven had been nailed across the top of the box. He began on the fourth, reaching across the space he had already uncovered to place his chisel under the board, when the crate began to whistle.

It was a sound very much like the sound a teakettle makes when it has reached a rolling boil, Dex told Henry Northrup; no cheerful whistle this, but something like an ugly, hysterical shriek by a tantrumy child. And this suddenly dropped and thickened into a low, hoarse growling sound. It was not loud, but it had a primitive, savage sound that stood Dex Stanley's hair up on the slant. The janitor stared around at him, his eyes widening . . . and then his arm was seized. Dex did not see what grabbed it; his eyes had gone instinctively to the man's face.

The janitor screamed, and the sound drove a stiletto of panic into Dex's chest. The thought that came unbidden was: *This is the first time in my life that I've heard a grown man scream—what a sheltered life I've led!*

The janitor, a fairly big guy who weighed maybe two hundred pounds, was suddenly yanked powerfully to one side. Toward the crate. *"Help me!"* He screamed. *"Oh help doc it's got me it's biting me it's biting meeeee————"*

Dex told himself to run forward and grab the janitor's free arm, but his feet might as well have been bonded to the floor. The janitor had been pulled into the crate up to his shoulder. That crazed snarling went on and on. The crate slid backward along the table for a foot or so and then came firmly to rest against a bolted instrument mount. It began to rock back and forth. The janitor screamed and gave a tremendous lunge away from the crate. The end of the box came up off the table and then smacked back down. Part of his arm came out of the crate, and Dex saw to his horror that the gray sleeve to his shirt was chewed and tattered and soaked with blood. Smiling crescent bites were punched into what he could see of the man's skin through the shredded flaps of cloth.

Then something that must have been incredibly strong yanked him back down. The thing in the crate began to snarl and gobble. Every now and then there would be a breathless whistling sound in between.

At last Dex broke free of his paralysis and lunged creakily forward. He grabbed the janitor's free arm. He yanked . . . with no result at all. It was like trying to pull a man who has been handcuffed to the bumper of a trailer truck.

13

The janitor screamed again—a long, ululating sound that rolled back and forth between the lab's sparkling, white-tiled walls. Dex could see the gold glimmer of the fillings at the back of the man's mouth. He could see the yellow ghost of nicotine on his tongue.

The janitor's head slammed down against the edge of the board he had been about to remove when the thing had grabbed him. And this time Dex did see something, although it happened with such mortal, savage speed that later he was unable to describe it adequately to Henry. Something as dry and brown and scaly as a desert reptile came out of the crate—something with huge claws. It tore at the janitor's straining, knotted throat and severed his jugular vein. Blood began to pump across the table, pooling on the formica and jetting onto the white-tiled floor. For a moment, a mist of blood seemed to hang in the air.

Dex dropped the janitor's arm and blundered backward, hands clapped flat to his cheeks, eyes bulging.

The janitor's eyes rolled wildly at the ceiling. His mouth dropped open and then snapped closed. The click of his teeth was audible even below that hungry growling. His feet, clad in heavy black work shoes, did a short and jittery tap dance on the floor.

Then he seemed to lose interest. His eyes grew almost benign as they looked raptly at the overhead light globe, which was also blood-spattered. His feet splayed out in a loose V. His shirt pulled out of his pants, displaying his white and bulging belly.

"He's dead," Dex whispered. "Oh, Jesus."

The pump of the janitor's heart faltered and lost its rhythm. Now the blood that flowed from the deep, irregular gash in his neck lost its urgency and merely flowed down at the command of indifferent gravity. The crate was stained and splashed with blood. The snarling seemed to go on endlessly. The crate rocked back and forth a bit, but it was too well braced against the instrument mount to go very far. The body of the janitor lolled grotesquely, still grasped firmly by whatever was in there. The small of his back was pressed against the lip of the lab table. His free hand dangled, sparse hair curling on the fingers between the first and second knuckles. His big key ring glimmered chrome in the light.

And now his body began to rock slowly this way and that. His shoes dragged back and forth, not tap dancing now but waltzing obscenely. And then they did not drag.

They dangled an inch off the floor . . . then two inches . . . then half a foot above the floor. Dex realized that the janitor was being dragged into the crate.

The nape of his neck came to rest against the board fronting the far side of the hole in the top of the crate. He looked like a man resting in some weird Zen position of contemplation. His dead eyes sparkled. And Dex heard, below the savage growling noises, a smacking, rending sound. And the crunch of a bone.

Dex ran.

He blundered his way across the lab and out the door and up the stairs. Halfway up, he fell down, clawed at the risers, got to his feet, and ran again. He gained the first floor hallway and sprinted down it, past the closed doors with their frosted-glass panels, past the bulletin boards. He was chased by his own footfalls. In his ears he could hear that damned whistling.

He ran right into Charlie Gereson's arms and almost knocked him over, and he spilled the milk shake Charlie had been drinking all over both of them.

"Holy hell, what's wrong?" Charlie asked, comic in his extreme surprise. He was short and compact, wearing cotton chinos and a white T-shirt. Thick spectacles sat grimly on his nose, meaning business, proclaiming that they were there for the long haul.

"Charlie," Dex said, panting harshly. "My boy . . . the janitor . . . the crate . . . it whistles . . . *it whistles when it's hungry and it whistles again when it's full* . . . my boy . . . we have to . . . campus security . . . we . . . we . . ."

"Slow down, Professor Stanley," Charlie said. He looked concerned and a little frightened. You don't expect to be seized by the senior professor in your department when you had nothing more aggressive in mind yourself than charting the continued out-migration of sandflies. "Slow down, I don't know what you're talking about."

Stanley, hardly aware of what he was saying, poured out a garbled version of what had happened to the janitor. Charlie Gereson looked more and more confused and doubtful. As upset as he was, Dex began to realize that Charlie didn't believe a word of it. He thought, with a new kind of horror, that soon Charlie would ask him if he had been working too hard, and that when he did, Stanley would burst into mad cackles of laughter.

15

But what Charlie said was, "That's pretty far out, Professor Stanley."

"It's true. We've got to get Campus Security over here. We—"

"No, that's no good. One of them would stick his hand in there, first thing." He saw Dex's stricken look and went on. "If *I'm* having trouble swallowing this, what are *they* going to think?"

"I don't know," Dex said. "I . . . I never thought . . ."

"They'd think you just came off a helluva toot and were seeing Tasmanian devils instead of pink elephants," Charlie Gereson said cheerfully, and pushed his glasses up on his pug nose. "Besides, from what you say, the responsibility has belonged with Zo all along . . . like for a hundred and forty years."

"But . . ." He swallowed, and there was a click in his throat as he prepared to voice his worst fear. "But it may be out."

"I doubt that," Charlie said, but didn't elaborate. And in that, Dex saw two things: that Charlie didn't believe a word he had said, and that nothing he could say would dissuade Charlie from going back down there.

Henry Northrup glanced at his watch. They had been sitting in the study for a little over an hour; Wilma wouldn't be back for another two. Plenty of time. Unlike Charlie Gereson, he had passed no judgment at all on the factual basis of Dex's story. But he had known Dex for a longer time than young Gereson had, and he didn't believe his friend exhibited the signs of a man who has suddenly developed a psychosis. What he exhibited was a kind of bug-eyed fear, no more or less than you'd expect to see in a man who has had an extremely close call with . . . well, just an extremely close call.

"He went down, Dex?"

"Yes. He did."

"You went with him?"

"Yes."

Henry shifted position a little. "I can understand why he didn't want to get Campus Security until he had checked the situation for himself. But Dex, you knew you were telling the flat-out truth, even if he didn't. Why didn't *you* call?"

"You believe me?" Dex asked. His voice trembled. "You believe me, don't you, Henry?"

Henry considered briefly. The story was mad, no question about that. The implication that there could be something in that box big enough and lively enough to kill a man after some one hundred and forty years was mad. He didn't believe it. But this was Dex . . . and he didn't *disbelieve* it, either.

"Yes," he said.

"Thank God for that," Dex said. He groped for his drink. "Thank God for that, Henry."

"It doesn't answer the question, though. Why didn't you call the campus cops?"

"I thought . . . as much as I did think . . . that it might not *want* to come out of the crate, into the bright light. It must have lived in the dark for so long . . . so very long . . . and . . . grotesque as this sounds . . . I thought it might be potbound, or something. I thought . . . well, he'll see it . . . he'll see the crate . . . the janitor's body . . . he'll see the *blood* . . . and then we'd call Security. You see?" Stanley's eyes pleaded with him to see, and Henry did. He thought that, considering the fact that it had been a snap judgment in a pressure situation, that Dex had thought quite clearly. The blood. When the young graduate student saw the blood, he would have been happy to call in the cops.

"But it didn't work out that way."

"No." Dex ran a hand through his thinning hair.

"Why not?"

"Because when we got down there, the body was gone."

"It was *gone?*"

"That's right. And the crate was gone, too."

When Charlie Gereson saw the blood, his round and good-natured face went very pale. His eyes, already magnified by his thick spectacles, grew even huger. Blood was puddled on the lab table. It had run down one of the table legs. It was pooled on the floor, and beads of it clung to the light globe and to the white tile wall. Yes, there was plenty of blood.

But no janitor. No crate.

Dex Stanley's jaw dropped. "What the *fuck!*" Charlie whispered.

Dex saw something then, perhaps the only thing that allowed him to keep his sanity. Already he could feel that central axle trying to pull free. He grabbed Charlie's shoulder and said, "Look at the blood on the table!"

"I've seen enough," Charlie said.

His Adam's apple rose and fell like an express elevator as he struggled to keep his late lunch down.

"For God's sake, get hold of yourself," Dex said harshly. "You're a Zoology major. You've seen blood before."

It was the voice of authority, for that moment, anyway. Charlie did get hold of himself, and they walked a little closer. The random pools of blood on the table were not as random as they had first appeared. Each had been neatly straight-edged on one side.

"The crate sat there," Dex said. He felt a little better. The fact that the crate really *had* been there steadied him a good deal. "And look there." He pointed at the floor. Here the blood had been smeared into a wide, thin trail. It swept toward where the two of them stood, a few paces inside the double doors. It faded and faded, petering out altogether about halfway between the lab table and the doors. It was crystal clear to Dex Stanley, and the nervous sweat on his skin went cold and clammy.

It had gotten out.

It had gotten out and pushed the crate off the table. And then it had pushed the crate . . . where? Under the stairs, of course. Back under the stairs. Where it had been safe for so long.

"Where's the . . . the . . ." Charlie couldn't finish.

"Under the stairs," Dex said numbly. "It's gone back to where it came from."

"No. The . . ." He jerked it out finally. "The body."

"I don't know," Dex said. But he thought he did know. His mind would simply not admit the truth.

Charlie turned abruptly and walked back through the doors.

"Where are you going?" Dex called shrilly, and ran after him.

Charlie stopped opposite the stairs. The triangular black hole beneath them gaped. The janitor's big four-cell flashlight still sat on the floor. And beside it was a bloody scrap of gray cloth, and one of the pens that had been clipped to the man's breast pocket.

"Don't go under there, Charlie! Don't." His heartbeat whammed savagely in his ears, frightening him even more.

"No," Charlie said. "But the body . . ."

Charlie hunkered down, grabbed the flashlight, and shone it under the stairs. And the crate was there, shoved up against the far wall, just as it had been before, squat and mute. Except that now it was free of dust and three boards had been pried off the top.

The light moved and centered on one of the janitor's big, sensible work shoes. Charlie drew breath in a low, harsh gasp. The thick leather of the shoe had been savagely gnawed and chewed. The laces hung, broken, from the eyelets. "It looks like somebody put it through a hay baler," he said hoarsely.

"Now do you believe me?" Dex asked.

Charlie didn't answer. Holding on to the stairs lightly with one hand, he leaned under the overhang—presumably to get the shoe. Later, sitting in Henry's study, Dex said he could think of only one reason why Charlie would have done that—to measure and perhaps categorize the bite of the thing in the crate. He was, after all, a zoologist, and a damned good one.

"Don't!" Dex screamed, and grabbed the back of Charlie's shirt.

Suddenly there were two green-gold eyes glaring over the top of the crate. They were almost exactly the color of owls' eyes, but smaller. There was a harsh, chattering growl of anger. Charlie recoiled, startled, and slammed the back of his head on the underside of the stairs. A shadow moved from the crate toward him at projectile speed. Charlie howled. Dex heard the dry purr of his shirt as it ripped open, the click as Charlie's glasses struck the floor and spun away. Once more Charlie tried to back away. The thing began to snarl—then the snarls suddenly stopped. And Charlie Gereson began to scream in agony.

Dex pulled on the back of his white T-shirt with all his might. For a moment Charlie came backward and he caught a glimpse of a furry, writhing shape spread-eagled on the young man's chest, a shape that appeared to have not four but six legs and the flat bullet head of a young lynx. The front of Charlie Gereson's shirt had been so quickly and completely tattered that it now looked like so many crepe streamers hung around his neck.

Then the thing raised its head and those small green-gold eyes stared balefully into Dex's own. He had never seen or dreamed such savagery. His strength failed. His grip on the back of Charlie's shirt loosened momentarily.

A moment was all it took. Charlie Gereson's body was snapped under the stairs with grotesque, cartoonish speed.

Silence for a moment. Then the growling, smacking sounds began again.

Charlie screamed once more, a long sound of terror and pain that was abruptly cut off . . . as if something had been clapped over his mouth.

Or stuffed into it.   .

Dex fell silent. The moon was high in the sky. Half of his third drink—an almost unheard-of phenomenon—was gone, and he felt the reaction setting in as sleepiness and extreme lassitude.

"What did you do then?" Henry asked. What he hadn't done, he knew, was to go to Campus Security; they wouldn't have listened to such a story and then released him so he could go and tell it again to his friend Henry.

"I just walked around, in utter shock, I suppose. I ran up the stairs again, just as I had after . . . after it took the janitor, only this time there was no Charlie Gereson to run into. I walked . . . miles, I suppose. I think I was mad. I kept thinking about Ryder's Quarry. You know that place?"

"Yes," Henry said.

"I kept thinking that would be deep enough. If . . . if there would be a way to get that crate out there. I kept . . . kept thinking . . ." He put his hands to his face. "I don't know. I don't know anymore. I think I'm going crazy."

"If the story you just told is true, I can understand that," Henry said quietly. He stood up suddenly. "Come on. I'm taking you home."

"Home?" Dex looked at his friend vacantly. "But—"

"I'll leave a note for Wilma telling her where we've gone and then we'll call . . . who do you suggest, Dex? Campus Security or the state police?"

"You believe me, don't you? You believe me? Just say you do."

"Yes, I believe you," Henry said, and it was the truth. "I don't know what that thing could be or where it came from, but I believe you."

Dex Stanley began to weep.

"Finish your drink while I write my wife," Henry said, apparently not noticing the tears. He even grinned a little. "And for Christ's sake, let's get out of here before she gets back."

Dex clutched at Henry's sleeve. "But we won't go anywhere near Amberson Hall, will we? Promise me, Henry! We'll stay away from there, won't we?"

"Does a bear shit in the woods?" Henry Northrup asked. It was a three-mile drive to Dex's house on the outskirts of town, and before they got there, he was half asleep in the passenger seat.

"The state cops, I think," Henry said. His words seemed to come from a great distance. "I think Charlie Gereson's assessment of the campus cops was pretty accurate. The first one there would happily stick his arm into that box."

"Yes. All right." Through the drifting, lassitudinous aftermath of shock, Dex felt a dim but great gratitude that his friend had taken over with such efficiency. Yet a deeper part of him believed that Henry could not have done it if he had seen the things he had seen. "Just . . . the importance of caution . . ."

"I'll see to that," Henry said grimly, and that was when Dex fell asleep.

He awoke the next morning with August sunshine making crisp patterns on the sheets of his bed. Just a dream, he thought with indescribable relief. All some crazy dream.

But there was a taste of Scotch in his mouth—Scotch and something else. He sat up, and a lance of pain bolted through his head. Not the sort of pain you got from a hangover, though; not even if you were the type to get a hangover from three Scotches, and he wasn't.

He sat up, and there was Henry, sitting across the room. His first thought was that Henry needed a shave. His second was that there was something in Henry's eyes that he had never seen before—something like chips of ice. A ridiculous thought came to Dex; it passed through his mind and was gone. *Sniper's eyes. Henry Northrup, whose specialty is the earlier English poets, has got sniper's eyes.*

"How are you feeling, Dex?"

"A slight headache," Dex said. "Henry . . . the police . . . what happened?"

"The police aren't coming," Northrup said calmly. "As for your head, I'm very sorry. I put one of Wilma's sleeping powders in your third drink. Be assured that it will pass."

"Henry, what are you saying?"

Henry took a sheet of notepaper from his breast pocket.

"This is the note I left my wife. It will explain a lot, I think. I got it back after everything was over. I took a chance that she'd leave it on the table, and I got away with it."

"I don't know what you're———"

He took the note from Henry's fingers and read it, eyes widening.

> *Dear Billie,*
> *I've just had a call from Dex Stanley. He's hysterical. Seems to have committed some sort of indiscretion with one of his female grad students. He's at Amberson Hall. So is the girl. For God's sake, come quickly. I'm not sure exactly what the situation is, but a woman's presence may be imperative, and under the circumstances, a nurse from the infirmary just won't do. I know you don't like Dex much, but a scandal like this could ruin his career. Please come.*
>
> *Henry*

"What in God's name have you done?" Dex asked hoarsely.

Henry plucked the note from Dex's nerveless fingers, produced his Zippo, and set flame to the corner. When it was burning well, he dropped the charring sheet of paper into an ashtray on the windowsill.

"I've killed Wilma," he said in the same calm voice. "Ding. dong, the wicked bitch is dead." Dex tried to speak and could not. That central axle was trying to tear loose again. The abyss of utter insanity was below. "I've killed my wife, and now I've put myself into your hands."

Now Dex did find his voice. It had a sound that was rusty yet shrill. "The crate," he said. "What have you done with the crate?"

"That's the beauty of it," Henry said. "You put the final piece in the jigsaw yourself. The crate is at the bottom of Ryder's Quarry."

Dex groped at that while he looked into Henry's eyes. The eyes of his friend. Sniper's eyes. You can't knock off your own queen, that's not in anyone's rules of chess, he thought, and restrained an urge to roar out gales of rancid laughter. The quarry, he had said. Ryder's Quarry. It was over four hundred feet deep, some said. It was perhaps twelve miles east of the university. Over the thirty years that Dex had been here, a dozen people had drowned there, and three years ago the town had posted the place.

"I put you to bed," Henry said. "Had to carry you into your room. You were out like a light. Scotch, sleeping powder, shock. But you were breathing normally and well. Strong heart action. I checked those things. Whatever else you believe, never think I had any intention of hurting you, Dex.

"It was fifteen minutes before Wilma's last class ended, and it would take her another fifteen minutes to drive home and another fifteen to get over to Amberson Hall. That gave me forty-five minutes. I got over to Amberson in ten. It was unlocked. That was enough to settle any doubts I had left."

"What do you mean?"

"The key ring on the janitor's belt. It went with the janitor."

Dex shuddered.

"If the door had been locked—forgive me, Dex, but if you're going to play for keeps, you ought to cover every base—there was still time enough to get back home ahead of Wilma and burn that note.

"I went downstairs—and I kept as close to the wall going down those stairs as I could, believe me. . . ."

Henry stepped into the lab and glanced around. It was just as Dex had left it. He slicked his tongue over his dry lips and then wiped his face with his hand. His heart was thudding in his chest. *Get hold of yourself, man. One thing at a time. Don't look ahead.*

The boards the janitor had pried off the crate were still stacked on the lab table. One table over was the scatter of Charlie Gereson's lab notes, never to be completed now. Henry took it all in, and then pulled his own flashlight—the one he always kept in the glovebox of his car for emergencies—from his back pocket. If this didn't qualify as an emergency, nothing did.

He snapped it on and crossed the lab and went out the door. The light bobbed uneasily in the dark for a moment, and then he trained it on the floor. He didn't want to step on anything he shouldn't. Moving slowly and cautiously, Henry moved around to the side of the stairs and shone the light underneath. His breath paused, and then resumed again, more slowly. Suddenly the tension and fear were gone, and he only felt cold. The crate was under there, just as Dex had said it was. And the janitor's ball-point pen. And his shoes. And Charlie Gereson's glasses.

Henry moved the light from one of these artifacts to the next slowly, spotlighting each. Then he glanced at his watch, snapped the flashlight off and jammed it back in his pocket. He had half an hour. There was no time to waste.

In the janitor's closet upstairs he found buckets, heavy-duty cleaner, rags . . . and gloves. No prints. Just in case, he would leave no prints. He went back downstairs like the sorcerer's apprentice, a heavy plastic bucket full of hot water and foaming cleaner in each hand, rags draped over his shoulder. His footfalls clacked hollowly in the stillness. He thought of Dex saying, *It sits squat and mute.* And still he was cold.

He began to clean up.

"She came," Henry said. "Oh yes, she came. And she was . . . excited and happy."

"What?" Dex said.

"Excited," he repeated. "She was whining and carping the way she always did in that high, unpleasant voice, but that was just habit, I think. All those years, Dex, the only part of me she wasn't able to completely control, the only part she could never get completely under her thumb, was my friendship with you. Our two drinks while she was at class. Our chess. Our . . . our companionship."

Dex nodded. Yes, companionship was the right word. A little light in the darkness of loneliness. It hadn't just been the chess or the drinks; it had been Henry's face over the board, Henry's voice recounting how things were in his department, a bit of harmless gossip, a laugh over something.

"So she was whining and bitching in her best 'just call me Billie' style, but I think it was just habit. She was excited and happy, Dex. Because she was finally going to be able to get control over that last . . . little . . . bit." He looked at Dex calmly. "I knew she'd come, you see. I knew she'd want to see what kind of mess you had gotten yourself into, Dex."

"They're downstairs," Henry told Wilma. Wilma was wearing a bright yellow sleeveless blouse and green pants that were too tight for her. "Right downstairs." And he uttered a sudden, loud laugh.

Wilma's head whipped around, and her narrow face darkened with suspicion. "What are you laughing about?" She asked in her loud, buzzing voice. "Your best friend gets in a scrape with a girl and you're laughing?"

No, he shouldn't be laughing. But he couldn't help it. It was sitting under the stairs, sitting there squat and mute, just try telling that thing in the crate to call you Billie, Wilma—and another loud laugh escaped him and went rolling down the dim first-floor hall like a depth charge.

"Well, there is a funny side to it," he said, hardly aware of what he was saying. "Wait'll you see. You'll think ———"

Her eyes, always questing, never still, dropped to his front pocket, where he had stuffed the rubber gloves.

"What are those? Are those gloves?"

Henry began to spew words. At the same time he put his arm around Wilma's bony shoulders and led her toward the stairs. "Well, he's passed out, you know. He smells like a distillery. Can't guess how much he drank. Threw up all over everything. I've been cleaning up. Hell of an awful mess, Billie. I persuaded the girl to stay a bit. You'll help me, won't you? This is Dex, after all."

"I don't know," she said, as they began to descend the stairs to the basement lab. Her eyes snapped with dark glee. "I'll have to see what the situation is. You don't know anything, that's obvious. You're hysterical. Exactly what I would have expected."

"That's right," Henry said. They had reached the bottom of the stairs. "Right around here. Just step right around here."

"But the lab's that way——"

"Yes . . . but the girl . . ." And he began to laugh again in great, loonlike bursts.

"Henry, what *is* wrong with you?" And now that acidic contempt was mixed with something else—something that might have been fear.

That made Henry laugh harder. His laughter echoed and rebounded, filling the dark basement with a sound like laughing banshees or demons approving a particularly good jest. "The girl, Billie," Henry said between bursts of helpless laughter. "That's what's so funny, the girl, the girl has crawled under the stairs and won't come out, that's what's so funny, *ah-heh-heh-ha-hahahaaa*———"

And now the dark kerosene of joy lit in her eyes; her

25

lips curled up like charring paper in what the denizens of hell might call a smile. And Wilma whispered, "What did he *do* to her?"

"You can get her out," Henry babbled, leading her to the dark, triangular, gaping maw. "I'm sure you can get her out, no trouble, no problem." He suddenly grabbed Wilma at the nape of the neck and the waist, forcing her down even as he pushed her into the space under the stairs.

"What are you doing?" she screamed querulously. "What are you doing, Henry?"

"What I should have done a long time ago," Henry said, laughing. "Get under there, Wilma. Just tell it to call you Billie, you bitch."

She tried to turn, tried to fight him. One hand clawed for his wrist—he saw her spade-shaped nails slice down, but they clawed only air. "Stop it, Henry!" She cried. "Stop it right now! Stop this foolishness! I—I'll scream!"

"Scream all you want!" he bellowed, still laughing. He raised one foot, planted it in the center of her narrow and joyless backside, and pushed. "I'll help you, Wilma! Come on out! Wake up, whatever you are! Wake up! Here's your dinner! Poison meat! Wake up! Wake up!"

Wilma screamed piercingly, an inarticulate sound that was still more rage than fear.

And then Henry heard it.

First a low whistle, the sound a man might make while working alone without even being aware of it. Then it rose in pitch, sliding up the scale to an ear-splitting whine that was barely audible. Then it suddenly descended again and became a growl . . . and then a hoarse yammering. It was an utterly savage sound. All his married life Henry Northrup had gone in fear of his wife, but the thing in the crate made Wilma sound like a child doing a kindergarten tantrum. Henry had time to think: *Holy God, maybe it really is a Tasmanian devil . . . it's some kind of devil, anyway.*

Wilma began to scream again, but this time it was a sweeter tune—at least to the ear of Henry Northrup. It was a sound of utter terror. Her yellow blouse flashed in the dark under the stairs, a vague beacon. She lunged at the opening, and Henry pushed her back, using all his strength.

"Henry!" She howled. "*Hen-reeeee!*"

She came again, head first this time, like a charging

26

bull. Henry caught her head in both hands, feeling the tight, wiry cap of her curls squash under his palms. He pushed. And then, over Wilma's shoulder, he saw something that might have been the gold-glinting eyes of a small owl. Eyes that were infinitely cold and hateful. The yammering became louder, reaching a crescendo. And when it struck at Wilma, the vibration running through her body was enough to knock him backward.

He caught one glimpse of her face, her bulging eyes, and then she was dragged back into the darkness. She screamed once more.

Only once.

"Just tell it to call you Billie," he whispered.

Henry Northrup drew a great, shuddering breath.

"It went on . . . for quite a while," he said. After a long time, maybe twenty minutes, the growling and the . . . the sounds of its feeding . . . that stopped, too. And it started to whistle. Just like you said, Dex. As if it were a happy teakettle or something. It whistled for maybe five minutes, and then it stopped. I shone my light underneath again. The crate had been pulled out a little way. There was . . . fresh blood. And Wilma's purse had spilled everywhere. But it got both of her shoes. That was something, wasn't it?"

Dex didn't answer. The room basked in sunshine. Outside, a bird sang.

"I finished cleaning the lab," Henry resumed at last. "It took me another forty minutes, and I almost missed a drop of blood that was on the light globe . . . saw it just as I was going out. But when I was done, the place was as neat as a pin. Then I went out to my car and drove across campus to the English Department. It was getting late, but I didn't feel a bit tired. In fact, Dex, I don't think I ever felt more clearheaded in my life. There was a crate in the basement of the English Department. I flashed on that very early in your story. Associating one monster with another, I suppose."

"What do you mean?"

"Last year when Badlinger was in England—you remember Badlinger, don't you?"

Dex nodded. Badlinger was the man who had beaten Henry out for the English Department chair . . . partly because Badlinger's wife was bright, vivacious, and sociable, while Henry's wife was a shrew. Had been a shrew.

"He was in England on sabbatical," Henry said. "Had all their things crated and shipped back. One of them was a giant stuffed animal. Nessie, they call it. For his kids. I always wanted children, you know. Wilma didn't. She said kids get in the way.

"Anyway, it came back in this gigantic wooden crate, and Badlinger dragged it down to the English Department basement because there was no room in the garage at home, he said, but he didn't want to throw it out because it might come in handy someday. Meantime, our janitors were using it as a gigantic sort of wastebasket. When it was full of trash, they'd dump it into the back of the truck on trash day and then fill it up again.

"I think it was the crate Badlinger's damned stuffed monster came back from England in that put the idea in my head. I began to see how your Tasmanian devil could be gotten rid of. And that started me thinking about something else I wanted to be rid of. That I wanted so badly to be rid of.

"I had my keys, of course. I let myself in and went downstairs. The crate was there. It was a big, unwieldy thing, but the janitors' dolly was down there as well. I dumped out the little bit of trash that was in it and got the crate onto the dolly by standing it on end. I pulled it up-stairs and wheeled it straight across the mall and back to Amberson."

"You didn't take your car?"

"No, I left my car in my space in the English Department parking lot. I couldn't have gotten the crate in there, anyway."

For Dex, new light began to break. Henry would have been driving his MG, of course—an elderly sportscar that Wilma had always called Henry's toy. And if Henry had the MG, then Wilma would have had the Scout—a Jeep with a fold-down back seat. Plenty of storage space, as the ads said.

"I didn't meet anyone," Henry said. "At this time of year—and at no other—the campus is quite deserted. The whole thing was almost hellishly perfect. I didn't see so much as a pair of headlights. I got back to Amberson Hall and took Badlinger's crate downstairs. I left it sitting on the dolly with the open end facing under the stairs. Then I went back upstairs to the janitors' closet and got that long pole they use to open and close the windows. They only have those poles in the old buildings now. I went back

28

down and got ready to hook the crate—your Paella crate—out from under the stairs. Then I had a bad moment. I realized the top of Badlinger's crate was gone, you see. I'd noticed it before, but now I *realized* it. In my guts."

"What did you do?"

"Decided to take the chance," Henry said. "I took the window pole and pulled the crate out. I *eased* it out, as if it were full of eggs. No . . . as if it were full of Mason jars with nitroglycerine in them."

Dex sat up, staring at Henry. "What . . . what . . ."

Henry looked back somberly. "It was my first good look at it, remember. It was horrible." He paused deliberately and then said it again: "It was horrible, Dex. It was splattered with blood, some of it seemingly grimed right into the wood. It made me think of . . . do you remember those joke boxes they used to sell? You'd push a little lever and the box would grind and shake, and then a pale green hand would come out of the top and push the lever back and snap inside again. It made me think of that.

"I pulled it out—oh, so carefully—and I said I wouldn't look down inside, no matter what. But I did, of course. And I saw . . ." His voice dropped helplessly, seeming to lose all strength. "I saw Wilma's face, Dex. Her *face*."

"Henry, don't———"

"I saw her eyes, looking up at me from that box. Her glazed eyes. I saw something else, too. Something white. A bone, I think. And a black something. Furry. Curled up. Whistling, too. A very low whistle. I think it was sleeping.

"I hooked it out as far as I could, and then I just stood there looking at it, realizing that I couldn't drive knowing that thing could come out at any time . . . come out and land on the back of my neck. So I started to look around for something—anything—to cover the top of Badlinger's crate.

"I went into the animal husbandry room, and there were a couple of cages big enough to hold the Paella crate, but I couldn't find the goddamned keys. So I went upstairs and I still couldn't find anything. I don't know how long I hunted, but there was this continual feeling of time . . . slipping away. I was getting a little crazy. Then I happened to poke into that big lecture room at the far end of the hall—"

"Room 6?"

"Yes, I think so. They had been painting the walls. There was a big canvas dropcloth on the floor to catch the splatters. I took it, and then I went back downstairs, and I pushed the Paella crate into Badlinger's crate. Carefully! . . . You wouldn't believe how carefully I did it, Dex . . ."

When the smaller crate was nested inside the larger, Henry uncinched the straps on the English Department dolly and grabbed the end of the dropcloth. It rustled stiffly in the stillness of Amberson Hall's basement. His breathing rustled stiffly as well. And there was that low whistle. He kept waiting for 'it to pause, to change. It didn't. He had sweated his shirt through; it was plastered to his chest and back.

Moving carefully, refusing to hurry, he wrapped the dropcloth around Badlinger's crate three times, then four, then five. In the dim light shining through from the lab, Badlinger's crate now looked mummified. Holding the seam with one splayed hand, he wrapped first one strap around it, then the other. He cinched them tight and then stood back a moment. He glanced at his watch. It was just past one o'clock. A pulse beat rhythmically at his throat.

Moving forward again, wishing absurdly for a cigarette (he had given them up sixteen years before), he grabbed the dolly, tilted it back, and began pulling it slowly up the stairs.

Outside, the moon watched coldly as he lifted the entire load, dolly and all, into the back of what he had come to think of as Wilma's Jeep—although Wilma had not earned a dime since the day he had married her. It was the biggest lift he had done since he had worked with a moving company in Westbrook as an undergraduate. At the highest point of the lift, a lance of pain seemed to dig into his lower back. And still he slipped it into the back of the Scout as gently as a sleeping baby.

He tried to close the back, but it wouldn't go up; the handle of the dolly stuck out four inches too far. He drove with the tailgate down, and at every bump and pothole, his heart seemed to stutter. His ears felt for the whistle, waiting for it to escalate into a shrill scream and then descend to a guttural howl of fury, waiting for the hoarse rip of canvas as teeth and claws pulled their way through it.

And overhead the moon, a mystic silver disc, rode the sky.

"I drove out to Ryder's Quarry," Henry went on. "There was a chain across the head of the road, but I geared the Scout down and got around. I backed right up to the edge of the water. The moon was still up and I could see its reflection way down in the blackness, like a drowned silver dollar. I went around, but it was a long time before I could bring myself to grab the thing. In a very real way, Dex, it was three bodies . . . the remains of three human beings. And I started wondering . . . where did they go? I saw Wilma's face, but it looked . . . God help me, it looked all *flat*, like a Halloween mask. How much of them did it eat, Dex? How much *could* it eat? And I started to understand what you meant about that central axle pulling loose.

"It was still whistling. I could hear it, muffled and faint, through that canvas dropcloth. Then I grabbed it and I *heaved*. . . . I really believe it was do it then or do it never. It came sliding out . . . and I think maybe it suspected, Dex . . . because, as the dolly started to tilt down toward the water it started to growl and yammer again . . . and the canvas started to ripple and bulge . . . and I yanked it again. I gave it all I had . . . so much that I almost fell into the damn quarry myself. And it went in. There was a splash . . . and then it was gone. Except for a few ripples, it was gone. And then the ripples were gone, too."

He fell silent, looking at his hands.

"And you came here," Dex said.

"First I went back to Amberson Hall. Cleaned under the stairs. Picked up all of Wilma's things and put them in her purse again. Picked up the janitor's shoe and his pen and your grad student's glasses. Wilma's purse is still on the seat. I parked the car in our—in my—driveway. On the way there I threw the rest of the stuff in the river."

"And then did what? Walked here?"

"Yes."

"Henry, what if I'd waked up before you got here? Called the police?"

Henry Northrup said simply: "You didn't."

They stared at each other, Dex from his bed, Henry from the chair by the window.

Speaking in tones so soft as to be nearly inaudible, Henry said, "The question is, what happens now? Three people are going to be reported missing soon. There is no one element to connect all three. There are no signs of foul play; I saw to that. Badlinger's crate, the dolly, the painters' dropcloth—those things will be reported missing

31

too, presumably. There will be a search. But the weight of the dolly will carry the crate to the bottom of the quarry, and . . . there are really no bodies, are there, Dex?"

"No," Dexter Stanley said. "No, I suppose there aren't."

"But what are you going to do, Dex? What are you going to say?"

"Oh, I could tell a tale," Dex said. "And if I told it, I suspect I'd end up in the state mental hospital. Perhaps accused of murdering the janitor and Gereson, if not your wife. No matter how good your cleanup was, a state police forensic unit could find traces of blood on the floor and walls of that laboratory. I believe I'll keep my mouth shut."

"Thank you," Henry said. "Thank you, Dex."

Dex thought of that elusive thing Henry had mentioned —companionship. A little light in the darkness. He thought of playing chess perhaps twice a week instead of once. Perhaps even three times a week . . . and if the game was not finished by ten, perhaps playing until midnight if neither of them had any early morning classes, instead of having to put the board away (and as likely as not, Wilma would just "accidentally" knock over the pieces "while dusting," so that the game would have to be started all over again the following Thursday evening). He thought of his friend, at last free of that other species of Tasmanian devil that killed more slowly but just as surely—by heart attack, by stroke, by ulcer, by high blood pressure, yammering and whistling in the ear all the while.

Last of all, he thought of the janitor, casually flicking his quarter, and of the quarter coming down and rolling under the stairs, where a very old horror sat squat and mute, covered with dust and cobwebs, waiting . . . biding its time. . . .

What had Henry said? The whole thing was almost hellishly perfect.

"No need to thank me, Henry," he said.

Henry stood up. "If you got dressed," he said, "you could run me down to the campus. I could get my MG and go back home and report Wilma missing."

Dex thought about it. Henry was inviting him to cross a nearly invisible line, it seemed, from bystander to accomplice. Did he want to cross that line?

At last he swung his legs out of bed. "All right, Henry."

"Thank you, Dexter."

Dex smiled slowly. "That's all right," he said. "After all, what are friends for?"

"Monsters" come in all sizes and shapes; some of them aren't frightening at all. They might be, for instance, ordinary young men whose two heads share the same body—a situation that would pose more problems for them than for others. How might they cope with life . . . especially if one of them were to fall in love?

Michael Bishop writes few fantasy stories, but each is memorable. Best known in the science fiction field, he has written such novels as *Eyes of Fire* and *Catacomb Years*.

COLLABORATING

Michael Bishop

HOW DOES IT FEEL TO BE A TWO-HEADED man? Better, how does it feel to be two men with one body? Maybe we can tell you. We're writing this—though it's I, Robert, who am up at the moment—because we've been commissioned to tell you what it's like living inside the same skin another human being inhabits and because we have to have our say.

I'm Robert. My brother's name is James. Our adoptive surname is Self—without contrivance on our part, even if this name seems to mock the circumstances of our life. James and I call our body The Monster. Who owns The Monster is a question that has occupied a good deal of our time, by virtue of a straitjacketing necessity. On more than one occasion The Monster has nearly killed us, but now we have pretty much domesticated it.

James Self. Robert Self. And The Monster.

It's quite late. James, who sits on the right side of our shoulders, has long since nodded away, giving control to me. My brother has subdued The Monster more effectively than I, however. When he's up, we move with a catlike agility I can never manage. Although our muscle tone and stamina are excellent, when I'm up The Monster shudders under my steering, and shambles, and shifts anatomical gears I didn't even know we possessed. At six foot three I am a hulking man, whereas James at six foot four—he's taller through the temples than I—is a graceful one. And we share the same body.

As a result, James often overmasters me during the

day: I feel, then, like a sharp-witted invalid going the rounds in the arms of a kindly quarterback. Late at night, though, with James down in sleep and The Monster arranged propitiatingly on a leather lounge chair, even I can savor the animal potential of our limbs, the warmth of a good wine in our maw, the tingle of a privately resolvable sexual stirring. The Monster can be lived with.

But I'm leaping ahead. Let me tell you how we got this way, and what we look forward to, and why we persevere.

James and I were born in a southeastern state in 1951. (Gemini is our birth sign, though neither of us credits astrology.) A breech delivery, we've been told. I suppose we aligned ourselves buttocks first because we didn't know how to determine precedence at the opposite end. We were taken with forceps, and the emergence of James and Robert together, two perfect infant heads groggy from the general anesthetic they'd given our mother, made the obstetrics team draw back into a white huddle from which it regarded us with fear, scepticism, awe, incredulity. How could anyone have expected this? A two-headed infant has only one heartbeat to measure, and there'd been no X rays.

We were spirited away from the delivery room before our mother could recover and ask about us. The presiding physician, Dr. Larimer Self, then decreed that she would be told her child was stillborn. Self destroyed hospital records of the birth, swore his staff to silence and gave my biological father, an itinerant laborer following the peach and cotton crops, a recommendation for a job in Texas. Thus, our obstetrician became our father. And our real parents were lost to us forever.

Larimer Self was an autocrat—but a sentimental one. He raised James and me in virtual isolation in a small community seventeen miles from the tri-county hospital where we'd been born. He gave us into the daytime care of a black woman named Velma Bymer. We grew up in a two-story house surrounded by holly bushes, crape myrtle, nandin, and pecan trees. Two or three months ago, after attaining a notoriety or infamy you may already be aware of, we severed all connections with the outside world and returned to this big, eighty-year-old house. Neither Robert nor I know when we will choose to leave it again; it's the only real home we've ever had.

Velma was too old to wet-nurse us, and a bachelor woman besides, but she bottle-fed us in her arms, careful to alternate feedings between Robert's head and mine since we could not both take formula at once. She was forty-six when we came into her care, and from the beginning she looked upon us not as a snakish curse for her own barrenness, but as a holy charge. A guerdon for her piety. My memories of her focus on her raw-boned, purple hands and a voice like sweet water flowing over rocks. James says he remembers her instead for a smell like damp cotton mixed up with the odor of slowly baking bran rolls. Today Velma drives to Wilson & Cathet's for her groceries in a little blue Fiat and sits evenings in her tiny one-room house with the Bible open on her lap. She won't move from that house—but she does come over on Thursday afternoons to play checkers with James.

Larimer Self taught us how to read, do mathematics and reconcile our disagreements through rapid, on-the-spot bargaining. Now and again he took a strop to The Monster.

Most children have no real concept of "sharing" until well after three. James and I, with help from our stepfather, reached an earlier accommodation. We had to. If we wanted The Monster to work for us at all we had to subordinate self and cooperate in the manipulation of legs, arms, hands. Otherwise we did a Vitus dance, or spasmed like an epileptic, or crumpled into trembling stillness. Although I wrote earlier that James often "overmasters" me, I didn't mean to imply that his motor control is stronger than mine, merely better, and that I sometimes voluntarily give him my up time for activities like walking, lifting, toting, anything primarily physical. As children we were the same. We could neutralize each other's strengths, but we couldn't—except in rare instances of fatigue or inattention—impose our will on the other. And so at six or seven months, maybe even earlier, we began to learn how to share our first toy: the baby animal under our necks. We became that organizational anomaly, a team with two captains.

Let me emphasize this: James and I don't have a psychic link, or a telepathic hookup, or even a wholly trustworthy line to each other's emotions. It's true that when I'm depressed James is frequently depressed too; that when I'm exhilarated or euphoric James is the same. And why not? A number of feelings have biochemical determinants as well as psychological ones, and the biochemical state of Robert Self is pretty much the biochemical state of James Self. When James drinks, I get drunk. When I take smoke into our lungs, after a moment's delay James may well do the coughing. But we can't read each other's thoughts, and my brother—as I believe he could well say of me, too—can be as unpredictable as an utter stranger. By design or necessity we share many things, but our personalities and our thoughts are our own.

It's probably a little like being married, even down to the matter of sex. Usually our purely physical urges coincide, but one can put himself in a mental frame either welcoming or denying the satisfaction of that urge, whereupon, like husband and wife, James and Robert must negotiate. Of course, in our case the matter can be incredibly more complex than this. Legislation before congress, I suppose you could call some of our floor fights. But on this subject I yield to James, whose province the complexities are.

All right. What does being "up" mean if neither James nor I happen to be strong enough to seize The Monster's instrument panel and march it around to a goose step of our own? It means that whoever's up has almost absolute motor control, that whoever's down has willingly relinquished this power. Both James and I can give up motor control and remain fully aware of the world; we can—and do—engage in cognitive activity and, since our speech centers aren't affected, communicate our ideas. This ability has something Eastern and yogic about it, I'm sure, but we have developed it without recourse to gurus or meditation.

How, then, do we decide who's to be up, who's to be drown? Well, it's a "you first, Alphonse"/"after you, Gaston" matter, I'm afraid, and the only thing to be said in its favor is that it works. Finally, if either of us is sleeping, the other is automatically up.* The Monster gets only three or four hours of uninterrupted rest a night, but that, we have decided, is the price a monster must pay to preserve the sanity of its masters.

Of course there are always those who think that James and I are The Monster. Many feel this way. Except for nearly two years in the national limelight, when we didn't know what the hell we were doing, we have spent our life trying to prove these people wrong. We are human beings,

---

* This state can be complicated, however. James dreams with such intensity that The Monster thrashes out with barely restrainable, subterranean vehemence. Not always, but often enough.

James and I, despite the unconscionable trick played on us in our mother's womb, and we want everybody to know it.

Come, Monster. Come under my hand. Goodbrother's asleep, it's seven o'clock in the A.M., and you've had at least three long hours of shut-eye, all four lids fluttering like window shades in gusty May! Three hours! So come under my hand, Monster, and let's see what we can add to this.

There are those who think that James and I are The Monster.

O considerate brother, stopping where I can take off with a tail wind, even if The Monster is a little sluggish on the runway this morning. Robert is the man to be up, though; he's the one who taps this tipritter with the most authority, even if I am the high-hurdle man on our team. (He certainly wouldn't be mixing metaphors like this, goodbrother Robert.) Our editor wants both of us to contribute, however, and dissecting our monsterhood might be a good place for James to begin. Just let Robert snooze while you take my dictation, Monster, that's all I ask.

Yes. Many do see us as a monster. And somewhere in his introductory notes my goodbrother puts his hand to his mouth and whispers in an aside, "James is taller than me." Well, that's true—I am. You see, Robert and I aren't identical twins. (I'm better looking than Robert.) (And taller.) This means that a different genetic template was responsible for each goodbrother's face and features, and, in the words of a local shopkeeper: "That Just Don't Happen." The chromosomes must have got twisted, the genes multiplied and scrambled, and a monster set loose on the helical stairway of the nucleotides. What we are, I'm afraid, is a sort of double mutant. . . . That's right, you hear me clearly: a mutant.

M.U.T.A.N.T.

I hope you haven't panicked and run off to Bolivia. Mutants are scary, yes—but usually because they don't work very well or fit together like they ought. A lot of mutations, whether fruit flies or sheep, are stillborn, dead to begin with. Others die later. The odds don't favor creatures with abbreviated limbs and heads without skull caps. Should your code get bollixed, about the best you can hope for is an aristocratic sixth finger, one more pinky to lift away from your teacup. And everybody's seen those movies where radiation has turned picnicking ants or happy-go-lucky grasshoppers into ogres as big as frigates. Those are *mutants*, you know.

And two-headed men?

Well, in the popular media they're usually a step below your bona fide mutant, surgical freaks skulking through swamps, axe at the ready, both bottom lips adrool. Or, if the culprit *is* radiation—an after-the-bomb comeuppance for mankind's vanity—one of the heads is a lump capable only of going "la la, la la" and repeating whatever the supposedly normal head says. Or else the two heads are equally dumb and carry on like an Abbott and Costello comedy team, bumping noggins and singing duets. Capital crimes, all these gambits. Ha ha.

No one identifies with a two-headed man.

If you dare suggest that the subject has its serious side, bingo, the word they drop on you is: "morbid." Others in the avoidance arsenal? Try "Grotesque." "Diseased." "Gruesome." "Pathological." "Perverse." Or even this: "*Poly*perverse." But "morbid" is the mortar shell they lob in to break off serious discussion and the fragments corkscrew through you until even you are aghast at your depravity. People wonder why you don't kill yourselves at first awareness of your hideousness. And you can only wince and slink away, a morbid silver trail behind you. Like snail slime.

Can you imagine, then, what it's like being a (so-called) two-headed man in monocephalic America? Robert and I may well be the ultimate minority. Robert and I and The Monster, the three of us together.

Last year in St Augustine, Florida, at the Ripley museum, on tour with an Atlanta publicist, my brother and I saw a two-headed calf.

Stuffed. One head blind and misshapen, lolling away from the sighted head. A mutant, preserved for the delight and edification of tourists to the Oldest City in the USA. Huzza huzza.

In the crowded display room in front of this specimen our party halted. Silence snapped down like a guillotine blade. What were the Selfs going to do now, everyone wondered. Do you suppose we've offended them? Aw, don't worry about it, they knew what they were getting into. Yeah, but—

Sez I to brother, "This is a Bolshevik calf, Robert. The calf is undoubtedly no marcher in the procession of natural creatures. It's a Soviet sew-up. They did it to Man's Best Friend and now they've done it to a potential bearer of Nature's Most Perfect Food. Here's the proof of it, goodbrother, right here in America's Oldest City."

"Tsk, tsk," sez Robert. He sez that rather well.

"And how many Social Security numbers do you suppose our officialdom gave this calf before it succumbed? How many times did they let this moo-cow manqué inscribe in the local voting register?"

"This *commie* calf?"

"Affirmative."

"Oh, two, certainly. If it's a Soviet sew-up, James, it probably weasled its rights from both the Social Security apparatus and the voting registrar. Whereas we—"

"Upright American citizens."

"Aye," sez Robert. "Whereas we are but a single person in the eyes of the State."

"Except for purposes of taxation," sez I.

"Except for purposes of taxation," Robert echoes. "Though it is given to us to file a joint return."

We can do Abbott and Costello, too, you see. Larry Blackman, the writer, publicist, and "talent handler," wheezed significantly, moved in, and herded our party to a glass case full of partially addressed envelopes that—believe it or not—had nevertheless been delivered to the Ripley museum. One envelope had arrived safely with only a rip (!) in its cover as a clue to its intended destination.

"From rip to Zip," sez I, "and service has gotten worse."

Blackman coughed, chuckled, and tried to keep Robert from glancing over our shoulder at that goddamn calf. I still don't know if he ever understood just how bad he'd screwed up.

That night in our motel room Robert hung his head forward and wept. We were wracked with sobs. Pretty soon The Monster had ole smartass Jamebo doing it, too, just as if we were nine years old again and crying for Velma after burning a strawberry on our knobbly knees. James and Robert Self, in a Howard Johnson's outside St. Augustine, sobbing in an anvil chorus of bafflement . . . I only bring this up because the episode occurred toward the end of our association with Blackman and because our editor wanted a bit of "psychology" in this collaborative effort.

There it is, then: a little psychology. Make of it what you will.

Up, Monster! Get ye from this desk without awakening Robert and I'll feed ye cold peaches from the Frigidaire. Upon our shared life and my own particular palate, I will.

People wonder why you didn't kill yourselves at first awareness of your hideousness.

(James is reading over our chest as I write, happy that I've begun by quoting him. Quid pro quo, I say: tit for tat.)

Sex and death. Death and sex. Our contract calls upon us to write about these things, but James has merely touched on the one while altogether avoiding the other. Maybe he wishes to leave the harvesting of morbidities to me. Could that possibly be it?

("You've seen right through me, goodbrother," replies James.)

Leaving aside the weighty matter of taxes, then, let's talk about death and sex. . . . No, let's narrow our subject to death. I still have hopes that James will spare me a recounting of a side of our life I've allowed him, by default, to direct. James?

("Okay, Robert. Done.")

Very well. The case is this: When James dies, I will die. When I die, James will die. Coronary thrombosis. Cancer of the lungs. Starvation. Food poisoning. Electrocution. Snakebite. Defenestration. Anything fatally injurious to the body does us both in—two personalities are blotted out at one blow. The Monster dies, taking us with it. The last convulsion, the final laugh, belongs to the creature we will have spent our lives training to our wills. Well, maybe we owe it that much.

You may, however, be wondering: isn't it possible that James or Robert could suffer a lethal blow without causing his brother's death? A tumor? An embolism? An aneurysm? A bullet wound? Yes, that might happen. But the physical shock to The Monster, the poisoning of our bloodstream, the emotional and psychological repercussions for the surviving Self would probably bring about the other's death as a matter of course. We are not Siamese twins, James and I, to be separated with a scalpel or a medical laser and then sent on our individual ways, each of us less a man than before. Our ways have never been separate, and never will be, yet we don't find ourselves hideous simply because the fact of our interdependence has been cast in an inescapable anatomical metaphor. Just the opposite, perhaps.

At the beginning of our assault on the World of Entertainment two years ago (and, yes, we still receive daily inquiries from carnivals and circuses, both American and European), we made an appearance on the *Midnight Chatter*. This was Blackman's doing, a means of introducing us to the public without resorting to loudspeakers and illustrated posters. We were very lucky to get the booking, he told us, and it was easy to see that Blackman felt he'd pulled off a major show-business coup.

James and I came on at the tail end of a Wednesday's evening show, behind segments featuring the psychologist Dr. Irving Brothers, the playwright Kentucky Mann, and the actress Victoria Pate. When we finally came out from the backstage dressing rooms, to no musical accompaniment at all, the audience boggled and then timidly began to applaud. (James says he heard someone exclaim "Holy cow!" over the less than robust clapping, but I can't confirm this.) *Midnight Chatter*'s host, Tommy Carver, greeted us with boyish innocence, as if we were the Pope.

"I know you must, uh, turn heads where you go, Mr. Self," he began, gulping theatrically and tapping an unsharpened pencil on his desk. "Uh, *Misters* Self, that is. But what is it—I mean, what question really disturbs you the most, turns you off to the attention you must attract?"

"That one," James said. "That's the one."

The audience boggled again, not so much at this lame witticism as at the fact that we'd actually spoken. A woman in the front row snickered.

"Okay," Carver said, doing a shaking-off-the-roundhouse bit with his head, "I deserved that. What's your biggest personal worry, then? I mean, is it something common to all of us or something, uh, peculiar to just you?" That *peculiar* drew a few more snickers.

"My biggest worry," James said, "is that Robert will try to murder me by committing suicide."

The audience, catching on, laughed at this. Carver was looking amused and startled at once—the studio monitor had him isolated in a close-up, and he kept throwing coy glances at the camera.

"Why would Robert here—that's not a criminal face, after all—want to murder you?",

"He thinks I've been beating his time with his girl."

Over renewed studio laughter Carver continued to play his straight-man's role. "Now is *that* true, Robert?" I must have been looking fidgety or distraught—he wanted to pull me into the exchange.

"Of course it isn't," James said. "If he's got a date, I keep my eyes closed. I don't want to embarrass anybody."

It went like that right up to a commercial for dog food. Larry Blackman had written the routine for us, and James had practiced it so that he could drop in the laugh-lines even if the right questions weren't asked. It was all a matter, said Blackman, of manipulating the material. The *Midnight Chatter*'s booking agent had expected us to be a "people guest" rather than a performer—one whose appeal lies in what he is rather than the image he projects. But Blackman said we could be both, James the comedian, me the sincere human expert on our predicament. Blackman's casting was adequate, I suppose; it was the script that was at heart gangrenous. Each head a half. The audience liked the half it had seen.

("He's coming back to the subject now, folks," James says. "See if he doesn't.")

After the English sheepdog had wolfed down his rations, I said, "Earlier, James told you he was afraid I'd murder him by committing suicide—"

"Yeah. That took us all back a bit."

"Well, the truth is, James and I *have* discussed killing ourselves."

"Seriously?" Carver leaned back in his chair and opened his jacket.

"Very seriously. Because it's impossible for us to operate independently of each other. If I were to take an overdose of amphetamines, for instance, it would be *our* stomach they pumped."

Carver gazed over his desk at our midsection. "Yeah. I see what you mean."

"Or if James grew despondent and took advantage of his up time to slash our wrists, it would be both of us who bled to death. One's suicide is the other's murder, you see."

"The perfect crime," offered Victoria Pate.

"No," I replied, "because the act is its own punishment. James and I understand that very well. That's why we've made a pact to the effect that neither of us will attempt suicide until we've made a pact to do it together."

"You've made a pact to make a suicide pact?"

"Right," James said. "We're blood brothers that way. And that's how we expect to die."

Carver buttoned his jacket and ran a finger around the side of his collar. "Not terribly soon, I hope. I don't believe this crowd is up for that sort of *Midnight Chatter* first."

"Oh, no," I assured him. "We're not expecting to take any action for several more years yet. But who knows? Circumstances will certainly dictate what we do, eventually."

Afterward, viewers inundated the studio switchboard with calls. Negative reaction to our remarks on suicide ran higher than questions about how the cameramen had "done it." Although Blackman congratulated us both heartily, The Monster didn't sleep very well that night.

"He thinks I've been beating his time with his girl."

Well, strange types scuttled after us while Blackman was running interference for Robert and James Self. The Monster devoured them, just as if they were dog food. When it wasn't exhausted. We gave them stereophonic sweet nothings and the nightmares they couldn't have by themselves. Robert, for my and The Monster's sakes, didn't say nay. He indulged us. He never carped. Which has led to resentments on both sides, the right and the left. We've talked about these.

Before leaving town for parts north, west and glittering, Robert and I were briefly engaged to be married. And not to each other. She was four years older than us. She worked in the front office of the local power company, at a desk you could reach only by weaving through a staggered lot of electric ranges, dishwashers and hot-water heaters, most of them white, a few avocado.

We usually mail in our bill payments, or ask Velma to take them if she's going uptown—but this time, since our monthly charges had been fluctuating unpredictably, and we couldn't ring through on the phone, I drove us across the two-lane into our business district. (Robert doesn't have a license.) Our future fiancée—I'm going to call her X—was patiently explaining to a group of housewives and day laborers the rate hike recently approved by the Public Service Commission, the consumer rebates ordered by the PSC for the previous year's disallowed fuel tax, and the summer rates soon to go into effect. Her voice was quavering a little. Through the door behind her desk we could see two grown men huddling out of harm's way, the storeroom light off.

(Robert wants to know, "Are you going to turn this into a How-We-Rescued-the-Maiden-from-the-Dragon story?")

("Fuck off," I tell him.)

(Robert would probably like The Monster to shrug his indifference to my rebuke—but I'm the one who's up now and I'm going to finish this blood-sucking reminiscence.)

Our appearance in the power company office had its usual impact. We, uh, turned heads. Three or four people moved away from the payments desk, a couple of others pretended—not very successfully—that we weren't there at all, and an old man in overalls stared. A woman we'd met once in Wilson & Cathet's said, "Good morning, Mr. Self," and dragged a child of indeterminate sex into the street behind her.

X pushed herself up from her chair and stood at her desk with her head hanging between her rigid supporting arms. "Oh, shit," she whispered. "This is too much."

"We'll come back when you're feeling better," a biddy in curlers said stiffly. The whole crew ambled out, even the man in overalls, his cheeks a shiny knot because of the chewing tobacco hidden there. Nobody used the aisle we were standing in to exit by.

The telephone rang. X took it off the hook, hefted it as if it were a truncheon and looked at Robert and me without a jot of surprise.

"This number isn't working," she said into the receiver. "It's out of order." And she hung up.

On her desk beside the telephone I saw a battered paperback copy of The Thorn Birds. But X hadn't been able to read much that morning.

"Don't be alarmed," I said. X didn't look alarmed. "We're a lion tamer," I went on. "That's the head I stick into their mouths."

"Ha ha," Robert said.

A beginning. The game didn't last long, though. After we first invited her, X came over to Larimer Self's old house—our old house—nearly every night for a month, and she proved to be interested in us, both Robert and me, in ways that our little freak-show groupies never had any conception of. They came later, though, and maybe Robert and I didn't then recognize what an uncommon

45

woman this hip and straightforward X really was. She regarded us as people, X did.

We would sit in our candle-lit living room listening to the Incredible String Band sing "Douglas Traherne Harding," among others, and talking about old movies. (The candles weren't for romance; they were to spite, with X's full approval, the power company.) In the kitchen, The Monster, mindless, baked us chocolate-chip cookies and gave its burned fingers to Robert or me to suck. Back in the living room, all of us chewing cookies, we talked like a cage full of gibbering monkeys, and laughed giddily, and finally ended up getting serious enough to discuss serious things like jobs and goals and long-dreamt-of tomorrows. But Robert and I let X do most of the talking and watched her in rapt mystification and surrender.

One evening, aware of our silence, she suddenly stopped and came over to us and kissed us both on our foreheads. Then, having led The Monster gently up the stairs, she showed it how to coordinate its untutored mechanical rhythms with those of a different but complementary sort of creature. Until then, it had been a virgin.

And the sentient Selfs? Well, Robert, as he put it, was "charmed, really charmed." Me, I was glazed over and strung out with a whole complex of feelings that most people regard as symptomatic of romantic love. How the hell could Robert be merely—I think I'm going to be sick—"charmed"?

("The bitterness again?")

("Well, goodbrother, we knew it would happen. Didn't we?")

We discussed X, rationally and otherwise. She was from Ohio, and she had come to our town by way of a coastal resort where she had worked as a night clerk in a motel. The Arab oil embargo had taken that job away from her, she figured, but she had come inland with true resilience and captured another with our power company —on the basis of a college diploma, a folder of recommendations and the snow job she'd done on old Grey Bates, her boss. She flattered Robert and me, though, by telling us that we were the only people in town she could be herself with. I think she meant it, too, and I'm pretty certain that Robert also believed her. If he's changed his mind of late, it's only because he had to justify his own subsequent vacillation and sabotage.

("James, damn you!")

46

("All right. All right.")

About two weeks after X first started coming to our house in the evenings Robert and I reached an agreement. We asked her to marry us. Both of us. All three of us. There was no other way.

She didn't say yes. She didn't say no. She said she'd have to think about it, and both Robert and I backed off to keep from crowding her. Later, after we'd somehow managed to get past the awkwardness of the marriage proposal, X leaned forward and asked us how we supported ourselves. It was something we'd never talked about before.

"Why do you ask?" Robert snapped. He began to grind his molars—that kind of sound gets conducted through the bones.

"It's Larimer's money," I interjected. "So much a month from the bank. And the house and grounds are paid for."

"Why do you ask?" Robert again demanded.

"I'm worried about you," X said. "Is Larimer's money going to last forever? Because you two don't *do* anything that I'm aware of, and I've always been uptight about people who don't make their own way. I've always supported myself, you see, and that's how I am. And I don't want to be uptight about my—well, my husbands."

Robert had flushed. It was affecting me, too—I could feel the heat rising in my face. "No," Robert said. "Larimer's legacy to us won't last forever."

X was wearing flowered shorts and a halter. She had her clean bare feet on the dirty upholstery of our divan. The flesh around her navel was pleated enticingly.

"Do you think I want your money, Rob? I don't want your money. I'm just afraid you may be regarding marriage to me as a panacea for all your problems. It's not, you know. There's a world that has to be lived in. You have to make your way in it for yourselves, married or not. Otherwise it's impossible to be happy. Don't you see? Marriage isn't just a string of party evenings, fellows."

"We know," I said.

"I suppose you do," X acknowledged readily enough. "Well, I do, too. I was married in Dayton. For six years."

"That doesn't matter to us. Does it, goodbrother?"

Robert swallowed. It was pretty clear he wished that business about Dayton had come out before, if only between the clicks of our record changer. "No," he said gamely. "It doesn't matter."

"One light," the Incredible String Band said, *"the light that is one though the lamps be many."*

"Listen," X said earnestly. "If you have any idea what I'm talking about, maybe I *will* marry you. And I'll go anywhere you want to go to find the other keys to your happiness. I just need a little time to think."

I forget who was up just then, Robert or me. Maybe neither of us. Who cares? The Monster trucked us across the room with the clear intention of devouring X on the dirty divan. The moment seemed sweet, even if the setting wasn't, and I was close to tears thinking that Robert and I were practically *engaged* to this decent and compassionate woman.

But The Monster failed us that night. Even though X received the three of us as her lover, The Monster wasn't able to perform, and I knew with absolute certainty that its failure was Robert's fault.

"I'll marry you," X whispered consolingly. "There'll be other nights, other times. Sometimes this happens."

We *were* engaged! This fact, that evening, didn't rouse The Monster to a fever pitch of gentle passion—but me, at least, it greatly comforted. And on several successive evenings, as Robert apparently tried to acquiesce in our mutual good fortune, The Monster was as good as new again: I began to envision a home in the country, a job as a power company lineman, and, God help me, children in whose childish features it might be possible to see something of all three of us.

("A bevy of bicephalic urchins? Or were you going to shoot for a Cerberus at every single birth?")

("Robert, damn you, *shut up!*")

And then, without warning, Robert once again began sabotaging The Monster's poignant attempts to make it with X. Although capable of regarding its malfunctioning as a temporary phenomenon, X was also smart enough to realize that something serious underlay it. Sex? For the last week that Robert and I knew her, there wasn't any. I didn't mind that. What I minded was the knowledge that my own brother was using his power—a purely *negative* sort of power—to betray the both of us. I don't really believe that I've gotten over his betrayal yet. Maybe I never will.

So that's the sex part, goodbrother. As far as I'm concerned, that's the sex part. You did the death. I did the sex. And we were both undone by what you did and didn't do in both areas. At least that's how I see it. . . . I had intended to finish this—but to hell with it, Robert. You finish it. It's your baby. Take it.

All right. We've engaged in so many recriminations over this matter that our every argument and counterargument is annotated. That we didn't marry X is probably my fault. Put aside the wisdom or the folly of our even hoping to marry—for in the end we didn't. We haven't. And the fault is mine.

You can strike that "probably" I use up there.

James once joked—he hasn't joked much about this affair—that I got "cold foot." After all, he was willing, The Monster was amenable, it was only goodbrother Robert who was weak. Perhaps. I only know that after our proposal I could never summon the same enthusiasm for X's visits as I had before. I can remember her saying, "You two don't *do* anything that I'm aware of, and I've always been uptight about people who don't make their own way." I'll always believe there was something smug and condescending—not to say downright insensitive—in this observation. And, in her desire to know how we had managed to support ourselves, something grasping and feral. She had a surface frankess under which her ulteriority bobbed like a tethered mine, and James never could see the danger.

("Bullshit. Utter bullshit.")

("Do you want this back, Mr. Self? It's yours if you want it.")

(James stares out the window at our Japanese yew.)

X was alerted to my disenchantment by The Monster's failure to perform. Even though she persevered for a time in the apparent hope that James would eventually win me over, she was as alert as a finch. She knew that I had gone sour on our relationship. Our conversations began to turn on questions like "Want another drink?" and "How'd it go today?" The Monster sweated.

Finally, on the last evening, X looked at me and said, "You don't really want us to marry, do you, Robert? You're afraid of what might happen. Even in the cause of your own possible happiness, you don't want to take any risks."

It was put up or shut up. "No," I told her, "I don't

want us to marry. And the only thing I'm afraid of is what you might do to James and me by trying to impose your inequitable love on us in an opportunistic marriage."

"Opportunistic?" She made her voice sound properly disbelieving.

"James and I are going to make a great deal of money. We don't have to depend on Larimer's legacy. And you knew that the moment you saw us, didn't you?"

X shook her head. "Do you really think, Rob, that I'd marry"—here she chose her words very carefully—"two-men-with-one-body in order to improve my own financial situation?"

"People have undergone sex changes for no better reason."

"That's speculation," she said. "I don't believe it."

James, his head averted from mine, was absolutely silent. I couldn't even hear him breathing.

X shifted on the divan. She looked at me piercingly, as if conspicuous directness would `persuade me of her sincerity: "Rob, aren't you simply afraid that somehow I'll come between you and James?"

"That's impossible," I answered.

"Who assumed such a thing?" I demanded. "But I do know this. You'll never be able to love us both equally, will you? You'll never be able to bestow your heart's affection on me as you bestow it on James."

She looked at the ceiling, exhaled showily, then stood up and crossed to the chair in which The Monster was sitting. She kissed me on the bridge of my nose; turned immediately to James and favored him with a similar benediction.

"I would have tried," she said. "Bye, fellas."

James kept his head averted, and The Monster shook with a vehemence that would have bewildered me had I not understood how sorely I had disappointed my brother—even in attempting to save us both from a situation that had very nearly exploded in our faces.

X didn't come back again, and I wouldn't let James phone her. Three days after our final good-bye, clouds rolled in from the Gulf, and it rained as if in memory of Noah. During the thunderstorm our electricity went out. It didn't come back on all that day. A day later it was still out. The freezer compartment in our refrigerator began to defrost.

James called the power company. X wasn't there,

much to my relief. Bates told us that she had given notice the day before and walked out into the rain without her paycheck. He couldn't understand why our power should be off if we had paid our bills as conscientiously as we said. Never mind, though, he'd see to it that we got our lights back. The whole episode was tangible confirmation of X's pettiness.

It wasn't long after she had left that I finally persuaded James to let me write to Larry Blackman in Atlanta. We came out of seclusion. As X might have cattily put it, we finally got around to *doing* something. With a hokey comedy routine and the magic of our inborn uniqueness we threw ourselves into the national spotlight and made money hand over fist. James was so clever and cooperative that I allowed him to feed The Monster whenever the opportunity arose, and there were times, I have to admit, when I thought that neither it nor James was capable of being sated. But not once did I fail to indulge them. Not once—

All right. That's enough, goodbrother. I know you have some feelings. I saw you in that Howard Johnson's in St. Augustine. I remember how you cried when Charles Laughton fell off the cathedral of Notre Dame. And when King Kong plummeted from the Empire State Building. And when the creature from 20,000 fathoms was electrocuted under the roller coaster on Coney Island. And when I suggested to you at the end of our last road tour that maybe it was time to make the pact that we had so long ago agreed to make one day. You weren't ready, you said. And I am unable by the rules of both love and decency to make that pact and carry out its articles without your approval. Have I unilaterally rejected your veto? No. No, I haven't.

So have a little pity.

Midnight. James has long since nodded away, giving control to me. Velma called this afternoon. She says she'll be over tomorrow afternoon for checkers. That seemed to perk James up a little. But I'm hoping to get him back on the road before this month is out. Activity's the best thing for him now—the best thing for both of us. I'm sure he'll eventually realize that.

Lights out.

I brush my lips against my brother's sleeping cheek.

If money is the root of evil, might it not also be the cause of terror? People sometimes murder for money—but especially determined spirits might not be so easily separated from their fortunes. . . .

Russell Kirk is the author of many fine fantasy stories, including the novel *The Old House of Fear.*

FATE'S PURSE

Russell Kirk

Thy money perish with thee, because thou hast
thought that the gift of God may be purchased with
money.

—*Acts* VIII, 20, c. 75

FOUR MILES WEST OF BEAR CITY, CUBBY
Hasper splashed up the gravelly bed of Brownlee's Creek,
casting for trout. Although swift, the creek was very shallow this dry summer. It was a remote spot, the woods of
the Brownlee farmstead extending densely on either side
of the stream. Cubby, thirteen years old, trusted that he
wouldn't encounter old Fate Brownlee, who had a short
way with trespassers. Fate! It was a funny name to have
given a Brownlee baby—if one could imagine old Fate
as a baby—but as the man had turned out, the name was
suitable enough.

Rounding a bend, Cubby saw something curious. A
small tractor somehow had nosed down the low bank into
the creek and stood there silent and unmoving, the clear
water eddying round the fore part of it, as if the machine had given up the ghost. Cubby reeled in his line
and made his way to the tractor. Then he perceived what
turned him white and shaking all over.

Just under the surface of the fast-flowing water, shad-
owed by the branches of an ancient willow, a few feet
beyond the tractor's nose, lay a man's face. Cubby almost had stepped upon the dead thing. It was old Fate

54

Brownlee's face. Cubby screamed and turned and ran for home, falling into two or three creek-bed potholes on the way.

In the considered judgment of the coroner, Fate Brownlee's death, as an act of God, was a case for the judge of probate, not for the county prosecutor. Apparently the old miser had intended to cut yet more cords of firewood in preparation for winter—even though already there must have been a hundred cords stacked close beside his damp farmhouse, the earlier cut cords among them fungi-covered and rotting to punk. As best the circumstances might be reconstructed, it seemed that Fate must have driven his rusty tractor along the woods trail to the creek, intending to cross the stream at his ford and fell dead elms on the far side; his chain saw had been hanging upon the tractor when his body was taken from the water.

At the creek, something must have happened to the tractor, the coroner speculated—one of its treads snagged on a dead water-logged branch, perhaps. Old Fate, presumably, had waded into the creek to clear the way. Then his tractor, its engine left running, must have begun to move again when Fate had freed the tread; or else the tractor may have slid down the bank, unexpectedly, so pinning Fate Brownlee to the creek bed, cruelly imprisoned under great weight nearly to his waist, but his head and arms and chest free to flounder in the stream.

It had been a hard way to go. For it appeared that Fate may have lain alive and conscious in the creek for some time—possibly for hours. There had been lacerations on his hands, as if he had tried to hold his head above water by grasping willow twigs that strayed down from the vast old willow overhanging the ford; some willow branches had been broken off. But when Fate's strength had failed, and he had been able to grip the branches no longer, then his head had sunk beneath the shallow water.

The corpse may have lain there for as much as three days before little Cubby came upon it: Fate Brownlee, a loner, a bachelor all his life, sometimes had not gone into Bear City for weeks on end, and there had been no important reason why anyone should have bothered to seek him out. Fate's chickens, unfed, had scattered into the woods. His dog somehow had vanished altogether. The dead man's cattle had browsed unperturbed in the pastures, and the bees from his dozens of hives had buzzed about the honeysuckle hedges, at their business as usual. Few people in Bear City seemed more concerned at Fate's passing than had been the cows and the bees: in seventy years, Fate had made no friends, although he had accumulated (according to rumor) plenty of hard cash. "An act of God," the postmaster said in private, was just the right phrase for Fate's end.

Only one circumstance had puzzled the coroner a trifle: Fate's purse had been found nowhere. It had been a very big oldfangled leather change purse or pouch with steel fasteners at the mouth, from the time when everybody used silver dollars, and it had been in evidence when Fate had deposited money in the bank or had sold honey at people's doors. Although Fate had carried the purse with him always—it had been fastened to his overalls by a contraption of chain—that big purse had not been found on his body, nor near the tractor, nor in the decayed farmhouse. Could it have come loose from his overalls and have been washed down the creek? Cubby was an honest boy who wouldn't steal pennies off a dead man. Two neighbors had gone down the creek bed with rakes, at the coroner's request, but had not found the purse. Presumably there would have been only small change in it, anyway, for Fate had been popularly supposed to bury at least as much of his money as he put into the bank and not to lug cash about with him recklessly. An odd circumstance, this, but a small one: one of God's little jokes, conceivably, poetic justice. So much for Fate's fate. With that witticism, the coroner resigned the business to the county judge of probate.

Mr. Titus Moreton, sometime lieutenant colonel of cavalry in the Army of the United States, had been judge of probate in Pottawattomie County for more than a decade. He was a burly outdoor man, strong in defiance of his years, popular enough, who kept three horses, collected weapons, and understood how to manage young wards of the court competently and humorously. The judge had known Fate Brownlee slightly, as he knew most of the odd characters in Pottawattomie County. Niggardly old Fate, he suspected, must have stashed away a tolerable fortune somewhere: if a hard-fisted bachelor buys next to nothing for most of his life, and doesn't drink or smoke or treat, and owns a good farm and mortgages on other people's farms, and works his land as if somebody had him under the lash—why, in the nature of things, the money accumulates. The judge's wife couldn't believe that a ragged scarecrow in overalls like Fate Brownlee might have been by far the richest man in his rural township, but the judge could and did.

Judge Moreton had appointed as administrator of the estate of the late Fate Brownlee the township supervisor, Abe Redding, whose probity was undoubted: a sensible, lean man with a weathered face, jolly and resourceful. There might be a will in Fate's safety-deposit box at the bank. Undoubtedly there was an heir presumptive—the dead man's brother, Virgil Brownlee, who lived in the big city and sold real estate. The judge had not seen this Virgil, but Abe Redding said that the brother, who dressed well enough and had made plenty of money on his own, was nearly as miserly as Fate had been, except that Virgil had indulged himself in a spouse and a daughter. Fate and Virgil, Redding went on, had not been at all fond of each other, but the city miser had visited the country miser two or three times a year, according to the neighbors; perhaps he had felt some attachment to the old family farmstead, though the house was sufficiently bleak. If Fate had died intestate, the inheritance would go to Virgil, his wife and child; even had Fate made a will, Redding suggested, probably Virgil was the sole legatee.

"Why?" the judge wished to know. "If, as you say, the brothers fought every time they met. . . ."

"Because, Judge, Fate knew that Virgil would save his money."

"Save it for what?"

"Just to put a cool million into the hands of Virgil's daughter and Fate's niece, Judge—an ugly little thing called Dorcas."

"And what would the niece do with it, Abe?"

"Save it, if she's a chip off the old block, and she is."

The judge had snorted—he was open-handed to a fault himself—and had bought Abe a drink. "Here's to you, Administrator. If there's a will, it's up to you to unearth it. So far as I know, Fate had no lawyer. Do you think there's really a will?"

"Maybe, Judge. They say that after one or two fights

the brothers had, old Fate threatened to draw up a new last will and testament and leave money, farm and the whole kaboodle to the Salvation Army. He told Matt Heddle, at the post office, how he might do just that. Yet it wasn't in his nature: the Salvation Army would have spent the money on bums. Still, the talk of it was a good way to put the fear of God into Brother Virgil."

Fate and Virgil, the judge reflected—what incongruous names! The Brownlee parents, with such classical affectations in the backwoods, must have been as odd as their precious offspring. Fate—*fatum*—destiny; and Virgil, the poet of destiny, mission! The brothers had looked much alike, Abe said, but Virgil had been the younger by ten years.

As matters had turned out, there *had* been an old will in the safety-deposit box; and everything had been bequeathed to "my brother, Virgil H. Brownlee." Also it had turned out that Fate's savings account had been surprisingly small. Redding had contrived to track down certain very substantial investments of Fate in stocks and bonds, made late in his life, and there were also the mortgages on half the farms in the township. All this had made the deceased's estate plump and happy, as the judge had expected, Fate's lifelong woeful facade of desperate poverty notwithstanding. Yet Redding suspected, and the judge agreed, that very possibly there lay concealed in the farmhouse, or round about, currency and coin exceeding all the tangible and intangible assets which Redding had uncovered so far. Persistent and long-standing report among the neighbors had it so. And before ruling upon that old will from the safety-deposit box, the judge meant to find what—or at least part of what—lay behind those rumors.

The Brownlee farm, isolated and unguarded, was more than four miles distant from little Bear City. But happily an undersheriff, Buck Tuller, lived on a hardscrabble holding only half a mile distant from the dead man's house. Redding had prevailed upon Buck to keep an eye on the Brownlee place, feeding the cattle, taking the chickens into custody at his own chicken house, and making sure no rough boys might tip over the many beehives. (Redding had hinted to Tuller that perhaps the bee swarms might be given to him, on settlement day, as reward for these services.) Also, of course, Buck Tuller was to watch for any two-footed predators: two or three unoccupied lake cottages in the county had been plundered this season, a nocturnal burglary unsuccessfully attempted at the Bear City bank, and it was sufficiently notorious that old Fate had kept the green stuff and the silver dollars ready to hand. Money does not breed, but its proximity warms the cockles of miserly hearts that are too stingy to keep a fire burning on cold nights in a sooty old wood stove.

Still, Buck Tuller could not be always keeping a weather eye on the Brownlee place, around the clock; so some search of the premises ought to be made soon, Redding had declared. The judge had concurred. Mr. Virgil Brownlee, heir presumptive, had been invited to attend and witness on this occasion. On the appointed day, a Saturday, they had gathered at the Bear City post office to start out upon the formal search: Redding, the judge and Virgil Brownlee. Buck Tuller would be waiting for them at the gaunt farmhouse, and Buck would be armed. The judge thoughtfully brought along a long spade and wore in a holster at his belt his old army revolver. In these days, precautions were prudent even in farm townships. The gang which had looted the cottages and attempted the bank in recent months just conceivably might turn up at the Brownlee farm, and the judge was a practiced quick-draw man.

They drove out to the farm in Redding's car, Virgil Brownlee talking volubly. He was a long-nosed man, in physiognomy and figure nearly the spit and image of Fate, but clean-shaven and attired in black suit and black tie, as if in mourning. Mourning did not quite become Virgil. Now and again, this Virgil Brownlee bit his nails, but he smiled a great deal, even when speaking of his brother's untimely end and the melancholy character of it. And how Virgil did run on—a compulsive talker if ever there was one! He babbled of the dear boyhood intimacy between him and his brother.

"I suppose, Mr. Brownlee, that you two got along famously all your long lives, eh?" inquired the judge, a trifle dryly.

Virgil Brownlee looked sharply at him. "He left me everything, didn't he? Oh, brothers have their spats, you know, but deep down underneath, Judge Moreton, the bond lasted—right up to the end." Here Virgil sniffed and put his right hand over his eyes, as if in sharp sorrow, peering between his fingers at the judge.

Redding turned the car into a rutted driveway. "Here we are, gentlemen. You haven't seen the Brownlee place before, Judge?"

It was no delightful sight. The barns and sheds were well enough maintained; a perfectly astounding array of hives stood in long rows behind the chicken house, and fairly neat orchards stretched along either side of the honeysuckle-lined drive to the farmhouse. But that house itself was neither picturesque nor old, though it stood apparently upon the squared-boulder foundations of an earlier dwelling. The windows were uncurtained, and the afternoon sun glared back from their dull dirty panes. The chimney looked about ready to fall. It was a smallish house of a single story, the paint long ago peeled away from the warped siding.

"Your brother didn't bother much about appearances, Mr. Brownlee," Abe Redding offered.

"If you fix up the outside of a house, they raise your property taxes. My brother saved his money." Virgil spoke as if this retort were crushing. He kept up a flow of talk as they walked toward the house—having left their car near the road, the ruts of the farm lane being bone-bruising.

Meanwhile, the judge was surveying the orchards on either side of the track. Here and there, under one old apple tree or another, he noticed a little heap of stones, and touched Virgil's arm. "What do you suppose those stone piles are?"

"Just Fate's way of making it easier to plow," Virgil told him, smoothly. But it had passed through the judge's mind that these might be cairns marking—or some of them, only Fate knew which—burials of something of value.

Taking a ring of keys from his pocket, Redding unlocked the front door. "You first, friend, as next of kin," he told Virgil Brownlee, motioning toward the doorway. Brownlee hesitated, shook his head, again covering his eyes with the fingers of one hand.

"Let somebody else step in first; it's too sad for me."

What a rat's nest the place was! The judge had seen many filthy hovels in Pottawattomie County, but none so abominable as this. The four of them stared at the barren living room, with old newspapers pasted on the walls instead of regular wallpaper, no carpet or linoleum on the bare floorboards, the scanty cheap furniture damaged or broken. What had been meant for the dining room was perfectly empty. In the smeared, cheerless kitchen was the house's only source of heat, the battered wood range, looking as if it might explode were a fire lit. There was one fairly new, fairly serviceable thing: a big white freezer, doubtless acquired secondhand. Redding opened its lid: the freezer was full to its brim with loaves of store bread.

"Fate used to buy week-old bread cheap at the supermarkets in the county seat," Virgil commented, "and keep it here for a year or more. He said he didn't grudge eating it if it was a year old, even if he'd had to pay cash for it. Fate didn't waste." Virgil said this with fraternal pride.

To conceal anything in these squalid rooms, with their naked walls of unpainted plaster, would have been almost impossible, unless under the floorboards, which had many cracks; and besides, the judge ruminated, the place was a perilous firetrap, as even its owner must have perceived. Whatever Fate had hidden could not be above ground in this house.

The main bedroom was next for inspection, a dark hole. As they crowded in, some shape loomed at the foot of the bed. "O God!" Virgil Brownlee cried—yet recovered swiftly.

Fate had possessed but two outer garments aside from his ragged black overcoat, and those two identical: pairs of worn blue overalls. He had been buried in one pair, decently laundered for the ceremony by Mrs. Tuller. The remaining pair of overalls, caked with dried sweat and grime so that they were permanently filled out to their owner's proportions, hung suspended on a coat hanger from a ceiling hook, swaying slightly in the draft caused by the opening of the bedroom door. In the dimness, it had seemed as if Fate himself had been swaying there.

"Gives a man a turn, don't it?" Virgil sighed. Indeed it did.

On the cot bed's thin mattress lay a single frayed blanket and a pillow without a slip. A cheap straight chair stood beside the bed. Some grimy underclothing, socks and shirts lay on the floor of the closet. Otherwise the bedroom was empty. The man who had lived thus could have bought and sold nearly everybody in the county.

The house, though some light bulbs dangled from their cores, had no running water, let alone a bathroom. "Fate didn't complain about going out to the pump and using the backhouse," Virgil explained.

All the money they found in these rooms was contained in a glass jar atop the kitchen range: one dime, one nickel, two pennies. Perhaps even that sum had been left exposed there in the hope of persuading conceivable burglars that it was the whole of Fate's savings.

"There's nothing here," said Abe Redding. "Where'd we ought to look, Mr. Brownlee?"

"Why, I couldn't just say." Virgil's long nose twitched, and again he stared at the three of them through his fingers. "I don't have the least idea where my brother kept his money—supposing he had any, and I don't know that he did. But if I was you, I'd go down into the cellar."

It was an old Michigan cellar, surviving from the earlier farmhouse on this site—very deep and high-ceilinged, its walls in part rubble from the fields, in part packed earth rudely plastered over. As they went down the rickety stairs, the judge noticed here and there in the stone staircase walls certain patches which looked as if holes had been opened and then sealed up again: the mortar round the stones at these spots was newer and of a different hue. But they had no picks ready to hand, and it was uncertain how much authority even a judge of probate and a duly appointed administrator held, when causing actual damage to a house's fabric was in question.

This cellar had several rooms, and all but one of them crammed with rough shelving, and on the shelves lay food enough to feed a cavalry regiment for a whole month. There were hundreds, perhaps thousands, of glass jars of preserves—meat, fruit, berries, vegetables, fish, jellies, jams. Some of this unmistakably had spoiled, and growths of exotic tints oozed from beneath their jar lids. This must be an accumulation of decades. "Fate was the great one for home canning," Virgil offered. Into the judge's mind came the image of old Fate: a bag of bones in overalls, an effigy of Famine. What power of self-denial—or, rather, denial of the flesh; what lunacy!

Another cellar room contained tier upon tier of combs of honey, thick with dust, enough concentrated sweet to sicken every child in Pottawattomie County for a year at least. "Fate was handy with the bees," Virgil continued, "though he didn't eat much honey himself, except for reasons of health. He liked to see the stuff available here in case of need."

"About them bees," Buck Tuller broke in, awkwardly. "Now I could use the hives, and Mr. Redding here was suggestin'. . . ."

Virgil spoke with abrupt force and venom. "Yes, I sure heard what Abe Redding had in mind, and I can tell you, Buck Tuller. . . . Well, look at the thing this way. For my part, you'd be welcome to Fate's bees. But I don't know for sure yet that they belong to me; and even if I did know, there's others to consider—my wife, and our kid Dorcas, and I don't know who else. Now it wouldn't be fair of me to just give away other folks' property, would it? Anyway, Buck Tuller, them hives is going to stay just where they set, and I'm not going to have you lay hand on them, officer of the law though you be."

This at first surprised the judge. Giving Tuller the hives might have saved the estate the modest cash bill for services as watchman that Tuller could submit. But now it occurred to the judge—who kept his peace—that hives alive with stinging bees would be the last place which thieves might search for hidden money.

The four of them came to the last room in the cellar, a long narrow space running parallel with the front of the house. They had to use the flashlights that Redding and Tuller had brought. The floor here was of sand, and the room was empty of shelves or junk.

"I see you fetched a good spade, Judge Moreton," Virgil Brownlee commented. "Now, like I say, I don't have no notion as to where Fate buried his money, if he had any." His speech has grown hurried and blurred, and his grammar rougher. "But if I was you, Judge, I'd dig *right over there*." He indicated the northern end of the room.

The judge thrust his spade into the sand. At the second spadeful of earth, the sharp spade-edge struck against something that rang. Bending down, the judge extracted from the sand a sealed glass jar. It was packed tight with little cylinders of something, sewn up neatly in newspaper. Redding held the jar, and the judge thrust in his spade afresh, again successfully. Altogether, he dug up some twenty-nine jars, buried fairly close together. Spade where he would in the rest of the cellar, he could discover no more.

They carried the jars to the living room and set them

on a pine table. Strong in his fingers, the judge screwed open the first jar and extracted the several cylinders and cut them carefully with his pocket knife. Underneath the integument of stitched newspaper was a tight roll of hundred-dollar bills.

The judge let Abe Redding open the other jars. Not all contained hundred-dollar bills, but there was nothing so small as a one-dollar bill. All were currency issued during the Twenties and Thirties.

But when Redding removed the newspaper wrapping from the cylinders in the ninth jar, there were no notes inside. Instead the jar was packed with dry corncobs, sewn up as neatly as the rolls containing money.

"I'll be a monkey's uncle," Buck Tuller declared. "Now why did Fate save them old corncobs?"

Virgil Brownlee, previously so loquacious, had fallen silent, and his face was expressionless. But he did not seem really astonished or chagrined. The judge wondered cynically whether this fellow, years ago, might not have got into this cellar when his brother had been absent for a few hours, say, and have made substitutions not easy to detect, so many as he dared.

Only eight of the jars contained corncobs; the rest were stuffed with bills. Putting all the jars on the floor, Redding proceeded to count their take, jotting down the contents of each jar in his notebook. He had opened his mouth to announce the grand total when the boards of the porch floor creaked, and something rattled the knob of the front door.

"For Christ's sake, don't let him in!" Virgil Brownlee shrieked.

What Virgil meant, the judge did not know; for his own part, he thought immediately of the gang who had attempted the bank. Visions of an autumnal glory suffused his judicial imagination; he could see the headline in the county daily—"Probate Judge Wipes Out Robber Band."

Faster than Bat Masterson, as the front door swung inward and Virgil fled to the inner rooms, Judge Moreton had his pistol out and was thumbing back the hammer. A gray bulk occupied the doorway.

"Hold it, please, Judge!" Buck Tuller implored him. "That's a federal man!"

So it was. With a slight sigh, the judge slid his gun

back into its holster, not fancying a headline like "Probate Judge Slaughters IRS Agent."

"I was just seeing what might be up," the federal man muttered apologetically. "Afternoon, everybody. Judge, did you know that Fate Brownlee, for years back, had written 'no income' on his federal returns?"

Virgil, his composure recovered, had returned from the back of the house. "What you see here ain't income," he put in, tartly. "It's capital, and it's old money. And I don't need to tell you that there's a three-year limit on investigating income-tax returns."

"I know that," the federal man admitted, not happily. "Judge Moreton, you're going to give this house a real thorough search?"

The judge, like other judges of probate whose authority is indefinite but ample, was easily put on his mettle; and he was zealous for state and local powers. "You're intervening in the proceedings of a duly constituted court of probate," he retorted in his colonel's tones of yesteryear, "and I'll not allow it. You go out that door and sit on that porch until we've finished our business, or I might find you in contempt."

The federal man having obeyed, Virgil Brownlee clapped the judge approvingly on the shoulder. "That's the way to handle them meddlers, Judge."

"Take your hand off me," the judge said. "Abe Redding, what's your total?"

In those glass jars there had been found the sum of $17,490. "Deposit it in the bank under a special account for the estate, Abe," the judge told Redding. "Brownlee, don't stand so close to that table."

Whatever might lie still behind those patches in the stone walls or under orchard cairns or in hives—why, this was a clammy house, a presence brooding over it, and already the sun was going down. And why should the Treasury get its fingers, through arrears of income tax or extortionate inheritance tax, upon the hoard for which dead old Fate has sacrificed comfort, pleasure, friends, even true humanity? Fate had paid for his ignoble treasure. Why, should he linger longer in this deathly house, the judge thought, he might turn miser himself.

As they left, Redding locking the door behind them, the judge told the waiting federal man, "Unless you have a warrant, keep off this property, or I'll warrant *you*. Scat, now! Mr. Redding's in charge of all this."

They waited in their car until the federal man had driven off. Behind them, against its background of neglected woods, the farmhouse looked lonely enough to give anyone the shivers.

"You being in real estate, Mr. Brownlee," Abe Redding said as they parted at the Bear City post office, "I guess you'll be selling the old place once it's settled that it's all yours."

"Wouldn't think of selling." Virgil informed him. "Not a farm that's been in the family a hundred years! Why, the wife and daughter may not care for the place, but I might spend a good deal of time up here by myself, just loafing around, thinking of dad and mom and—and Fate."

"It has a hold on you, Brownlee?" The judge did not shake his hand. "I can imagine why. Well, if Abe's work goes along smoothly, we should be able to settle this estate about a month from now. My clerk will send you a notice in sufficient time. Meanwhile, stay off that property. Keep everybody else off it, Tuller. It's not a healthy place to be alone."

On the day of the settlement in September, everyone concerned with the Fate Brownlee estate met at the judge's chambers in the courthouse. The chambers were paneled in old oak, and portraits—well, photographs, mostly—of earlier judges of probate hung on the walls, in heavy frames, high up; and there was set into one wall the splendid painted cast-iron door of the old strongroom. The judge felt majestic here.

Virgil's wife and daughter were present along with Virgil, the judge noticed; also a scruffy-looking lawyer whom Virgil Brownlee had fetched from the big city. The judge secretly regretted having to turn over so much money and land to such dubious-looking characters.

Fate's will was valid, no later will having been discovered, and everything was to pass to Virgil Brownlee, after any charges against the estate had been paid in full. Abe Redding's labors as administrator had turned up a respectable fortune for the heir, quite as the judge had anticipated—a fortune subject to federal and state inheritance taxes, necessarily. Virgil very privily might turn up a second fortune for himself, clear of taxes, mining that ancestral farmstead so dear to Virgil's sentimental heart. But the judge spoke no word of that. A curious thought came casually into his head, just before he opened the proceedings: why hadn't they found Fate's purse anywhere at all? It had been a big, rather conspicuous thing.

Virgil's city lawyer sat close beside his client as bills against the estate were presented for settlement. Fate had paid for everything by cash or check, lifelong; so the only charges against the patrimony were those incurred since Fate's drowning. Abe Redding, as administrator, presented his bill for a sum very tidy indeed—yet only the minimum fee authorized by statute for so substantial an estate. The judge rather had expected Virgil and his household to protest so whopping a deduction from their inheritance; but Virgil sat wooden-faced, allowing the bill to be approved; presumably his lawyer had advised him that Redding could have made bigger charges, had he been greedy, with an excellent chance for approval of the court; let well enough alone, Mr. Brownlee.

Buck Tuller's modest wage for watching over the farm, too, slipped by undiminished: Virgil did open his mouth, as if meaning to say something indignant, but throught better of it. Perhaps he recollected that he could have let Buck take the hives, by way of compensation, and did not care to have that alternative raised afresh.

And then Frank McCullough, who kept the garage and auto-parts emporium at Bear City, submitted his account for payment. Fate had been a customer of his ever since Frank had opened his garage—though not a very profitable patron. Once Fate had driven coughingly up to Frank's station and asked if Frank could repair his dragging ragged muffler. Frank had inspected it solemnly.

"I don't think so, Fate," he had pronounced. "Now I could sell you a new one. . . ."

"O Lord Jesus, man, don't say that!" Fate had ejaculated in anguish. "Just give it a hit with a board or something, and maybe it'll be all right."

Now Frank McCullough's bill went to the judge's desk. It had been Frank who had pulled the tractor off Fate Brownlee's corpse in the creek, had taken the murderous thing to his garage, had put it back in working order, and had returned it to the Brownlee barn. For these services he requested the compensation of twenty-nine dollars and seventy cents.

At that demand, Mr. Virgil Brownlee rose up in wrath, ignoring his city lawyer. "Outrageous!" he shouted. "Scandalous! We can't pay that much! Why, a bill like that just shows you what people won't do for money."

Nearly a month after Virgil Brownlee had entered upon possession of his brother's goods and chattels, the judge, in an idle hour, decided to pay a visit to the Brownlee farm. It was his custom, nearly every Sunday, to saddle one of his horses and take a long ride along the back roads and sand trails of Pottawattomie County, often exchanging some pleasant words with farmers and pensioners he passed along the way—a tactic useful for one who meant to be re-elected judge of probate, term upon term. It had been more than a year since he had ridden the country west of Bear City, and he felt a hankering to see what Virgil might have done with his tangible inheritance. If the judge himself had owned both the Brownlee farm and Hell, he would have rented out the Brownlee place and lived in Hell. He put into his pocket a detailed map of the county.

As he saddled his mare Diane, his wife came out to hand him a thermos of coffee for the ride on this brisk fall day. "Titus, you silly," said Charlotte, "you've put on that nasty pistol of yours. You'd look a fool, and what if you fell off Diane and the gun shot you?"

It was the judge's long sorrow that Charlotte disliked horses and guns. "There's a safety on it, my darling, and a hard trigger pull." But not being quite sure why he had happened to belt on the revolver, anyway, the judge put the gun back on the shelf in his bedroom. Sometimes he called Charlotte by the pet appellation of Ozymandia, Queen of Queens—"Look on my works, ye mighty, and despair."

She supplied him with a sandwich well wrapped, an orange, and a chocolate bar, and compelled him to don a heavy riding jacket, and would have thrust more impedimenta upon him, until he protested that she meant to make him look like the White Knight. She demanded to know what way he was bound, and he told her that he would ride to Brownlee's.

"Why do you want to see that smirking Virgil Brownlee?"

"I don't want to see him, my darling; it's just that I want a long ride, and I might have a glance at what he's done to that sad house. They say he comes up alone from the city on weekends. I hear he's sold the herd and rents out the pastures and most of the fields, but threatens trespassers, like Fate before him."

"Don't quarrel with him, if he's there; a judge is supposed to be above that. You're so aggressive and domineering, Titus."

"Yes, my darling."

Then the uxorious judge, astride Diane, went on his cheerful way to the west of Bear City, occasionally putting the mare to a canter or a trot, keeping to the gravel roads and sand trails, greeting an elector or an electress now and again—but not many, this township being scantily peopled. Halfway to his destination, he tied Diane to a tree, sat upon a stump, ate his sandwich and drank his coffee, and read an old pocket edition of Cicero's *Offices*—he had retained classical tastes from college— for more than half an hour.

He rode on. Finding himself about a mile, presumably, from the Brownlee homestead, he consulted his map and ascertained that he could approach the place by a forgotten lumbermen's road which must cross Brownlee's Creek a few hundred rods to the rear of the farmstead.

Kept open at all only by venturesome hunters and fishermen, this track was overgrown. Now he could hear the rippling of the creek, and he emerged upon a ford of sorts overhung by a giant willow. Why, this must be the very spot where old Fate had drowned; he never had happened upon it before.

Without warning, Diane neighed, and shied so violently that she almost threw him, inveterate rider though he was. Close at hand on his left, something fairly big retreated through the thickets, more heard than glimpsed. A deer it must be, or just possibly a large raccoon. "Easy, Diane!"

But the mare was behaving badly, almost hysterical. She reared and plunged; she did not mean to cross that ford. Ordinarily as gentle with good horses as with good women, the judge refrained from using his full strength on Diane's mouth. "Why, girl! Easy, easy!" She tried to swing back toward the trail by which they had come.

He might as well humor her this once, as he humored

Charlotte. Dismounting with some difficulty, he led Diane a hundred yards back from the creek and fastened her to a silver birch; he patted her, and she seemed more at ease away from the ford. It would be only a short walk to the farmstead.

In his riding boots, he crossed the creek without trouble and strolled up the track toward the Brownlee place. He ascended a low hogback; the woods ended on the far side of that ridge; and standing in scrub at the edge of the tangle, head and shoulders above a thick clump of wild blackberry bushes, he had a good view of the farm. On his ride he carried field glasses, and now he took these from their case at his belt and surveyed the field between him and the farm buildings.

He could see a part of one of the orchards; he thought he could make out piles of fresh earth under some trees. He could see very clearly that a number of the beehives back of the chicken house had been overturned and lay on the ground. Then across his line of vision a man moved: a man in old overalls, gaunt, with a rifle in his hand. He saw him in profile and was not perceived himself. For a silly instant, the judge took the man for Fate Brownlee *redivivus;* then he knew it must be Virgil. He was startled when the man abruptly brought the stock up to his shoulder and fired toward a sugarbush grove to the north. The rifle crack echoed mightily over the desolation.

What might Virgil be hunting with a rifle in October —deer out of season? The judge could not trust a city man's discretion or aim, and he didn't mean to be taken for a buck; he must make his presence known. "Virgil!" the judge shouted, hoarsely.

The man started conspicuously, swung around, hastily took aim, and pulled the trigger before the judge grasped his intention. The judge felt a swift stinging blow, reeled, and fell forward to earth, among the bushes.

If he had fainted, it could have been only for a moment. He had been hit in the head: Virgil Brownlee was a crack shot, or a lucky one. How badly? Half dazed, the judge sensed that blood was running thickly down his right cheek and his chin. He thought that he could have stood up, but he didn't mean to try it; for the moment he was invisible behind the blackberry bushes. He remembered, relevantly, how last December one deer hunter had fired at another, taking him for game; and when the wounded man had screeched, stood up, and tried to run, the whiskey-swigging first hunter had pumped bullet after bullet into him, blind with hunter's lust.

The judge heard a shrill voice, happily still some distance off. "Come on out! Come on out of there, Fate!"

The judge had been wounded twice in New Guinea, and on one of those occasions had played possum while the Japanese poked about the jungle to finish him off. Four of his own men had come to his rescue then, but no one could help him here. He felt his bloody head with his right hand: there was a flesh wound in his cheek, and the cheekbone must be broken, and the lobe of his right ear was missing. As yet, the pain was surprisingly endurable, but the bleeding was profuse. Confound darling Charlotte for depriving him of his pistol! There was not even a stick or a big stone ready to hand—nothing to defend him against Virgil Brownlee's damned rifle. The judge wouldn't sing out a second time, not he. Would Virgil come into the brush after his trophy?

He would. Close now, too close, there came a second wild shout: "Fate, you in there? You come on out of there, or I'll give it to you in your belly like I gave it to your dog after you got caught in the creek. I ain't scared of you, live or dead!" It was a maniac shriek.

There was a trampling in the brush; and peering eagerly through the lower part of the bushes without raising his head or stirring a finger, the judge could see a pair of muddy farm boots only a few yards distant from him. But he judged from the boots' angle that the man was staring somewhat to his left, his rifle at the ready. The judge held his breath.

"Fate," the frantic voice cried, "it's all mine now, by law. You think you can scare me out of it by peeking in windows and rattling knobs? You can't take it with you, Fate!"

At that moment, there occurred some slight noise in the woods off to the left, and perhaps some slight movement, too; Virgil heard and perhaps saw, or thought he saw, and swung in that direction, crouching, so that his back was fully turned upon the judge. Staring at the man's boot heels, the judge tensed himself for action.

"Fate," the shriek came, "you let me off, I'll let you off. Hell, I didn't start up the tractor; all I done was walk away after you got caught. Fate, I wouldn't of done that if you hadn't said you'd give the whole shebang to them Salvationers. I ain't scared to look at you in daylight—come on out and show your dirty old face. Come on out, now, or I'll give it to you in the belly!"

Nobody answered. The judge rose on hands and knees, most stealthily. Blood was streaming down his arm and his side.

After what seemed like an hour but must have been seconds, the shouting was resumed. "What you after, Fate? You want what I took off you in the creek? All right—take it, then!"

Something must have been flung toward the grove of maples, for there was a faint clinking thud. Then came a second rustling of bushes—from that deer or coon which had frightened Diane at the ford? "And take this, Fate!" Pow! The rifle cracked again and again and again.

Rising desperately to his feet, the judge hurled himself through the bushes and rushed at Virgil's back. He made it. Flinging all his weight upon the man, he hit Virgil's spine with his knee and clamped his blood-dripping hands over Virgil's averted face. In a voice that seemed like someone else's, the judge roared, "Got you, Virgil!"

The man collapsed, the judge tumbling upon him, and the rifle fell just beyond Virgil's head. The judge pounded Virgil's face against the earth, and then he poked the lunatic. "Get up, Brownlee: I'm taking you to jail."

Virgil did not stir. Another possum? The judge tore off his own necktie and bound Virgil's wrists behind his back; still no resistance. Virgil's hands felt cold. "Get up, you brother-killer!"

No movement at all. The judge rolled the man over and ripped open his clothes: he could detect no heartbeat, no breathing. Virgil's unattractive face was close to his, and the fixed, open eyes were sightless. No possum! In his time, the judge had seen many dead men, but all the others had borne wounds.

Buck Tuller's house stood less than half a mile distant, the judge contrived to recollect in his confusion, and he thought he might get there before fainting from loss of blood. He had clapped his handkerchief to ear and cheek. Ride Diane? No, he was in no shape to force her across the creek. He must foot it to Tuller's, even if already his legs quivered ominously under him.

Keeping his handkerchief pressed hard against his cheek and ear, he took three or four steps; and then his foot struck something. Part of it glittered. It was Fate's old steel-mouthed purse, lying among ferns: this was what Virgil had flung out as bait to the invisible. Virgil must have taken it from his brother trapped in the creek, perhaps while Fate still had clung to the willow-branches and begged for life. The judge nudged the thing with his foot; coins clinked inside.

Let it lie, for the moment: if he bent over, giddiness might undo him. Let it lie, for more reasons than one. Two months before, at the Brownlee house, there had come upon him the sense of a hungry presence; that sense descended again upon him now, more powerful and more malign, and he enfeebled. Was he alone with one corpse and two dead things?

Did those woods creatures stir again at the edge of the field? Deer or raccoon, of course; keep telling yourself that, Titus Moreton: coon or deer. Let the purse lay where it had fallen.

Come on, Titus: you walked out of the jungle at Buna, with grenade-fragments in both arms, and even now you can walk as far as Tuller's. Walk as fast as you can, not showing fear. Pay no heed to that deer, or that coon, or whatever it may be, scrunching somewhere behind you. A bullet to the head can inflict hallucinations even upon a steady-nerved man. Don't look back: walk!

Buck's eldest son and Buck's wife drove the judge to the hospital, and Buck Tuller and his second boy took the panel truck and went after Virgil Brownlee's body. It was there, all right, cold stone dead, clad in the pair of overalls that Virgil had inherited from his brother. Then Buck and his boy searched in the ferns and elsewhere for Fate's purse, the judge having said it was a piece of evidence. They did pick up the judge's binoculars, fallen when he was shot, but no purse. They looked until sundown, glancing over their shoulders often, but they could not find it. Buck gave up when his son's teeth began to chatter.

When, a fortnight later, the judge had mended sufficiently, Charlotte drove him out to the Brownlee place, and he poked through the scrub for two hours or more, kicking aside masses of fallen maple leaves. He was perfectly sure of the spot. Defying Ozymandia's commands and entreaties, he went down on his hands and knees, feeling all over for the purse. No luck. With the coins in it, the purse would have been too heavy and awkward for any squirrel to carry off. Yet the thing had been taken, and no pack rats live in Pottawattomie County.

Charlotte now had grown as skittish as Diane had been at the ford, glancing back and forth from the judge among the leaves to the house so silent and derelict. "Give it up, silly," she demanded, almost *sotto voce*. "Is anybody in that house?"

The judge straightened up and joined her at the car. "Ask me what songs the sirens sang, darling."

"Who wants that old purse, anyway?"

"I won't speak his name here, Charlotte, if you'll excuse me. I suppose he has his heart's desire, and the iron in his soul withal."

"You make me angry when you're so obscure, Titus." She started up their car. "Oh! What's that toward the creek?" She stepped hard on the gas, and the car bounced so over the ruts that the alert judge, his head craned backward, could make out nothing.

"Did you see anything, darling?"

"Not exactly." Her hands trembled on the wheel.

"I suppose it was some obscure hungry thing, Ozymandia, needing an obol or two for Charon. It was a poor thing; let it fade."

≈≈≈≈≈≈≈≈≈≈≈≈≈≈≈≈≈≈≈≈≈≈≈≈≈

A Being living near the beginning of time, charged with the task of bringing order out of chaos—but forced to fulfill any wish he hears: that's the Traveller in Black, who in this story comes upon a town whose people follow a witch who knows less than she thinks. In such a situation, odd wishes might be made, with surprising results.

John Brunner's previous tales in this series were collected in the book *The Traveller in Black*. The present story, Brunner's only Traveller in Black tale in over a decade, requires no knowledge of the earlier ones.

THE THINGS THAT ARE GODS

John Brunner

> *Lo how smothe and curvit be these rockes that in
> the creacion weren jaggit, for that they haf ben
> straikit by myriades of thickheidit folk hither ycom-
> men in peregrinage, beggarlie criand after Mirac-
> ula. And I say one at the leste wis granted 'em.
> Was't not a marveil and a wonder, passand
> credence, that they helden dull ston for more puis-
> saunt than your quicke man, the which mought
> brethe and dreme and soffre and fede wormes?*
>
> —A Lytel Boke Againste Folie

I

TIPPING BACK THE HOOD OF HIS BLACK
cloak, leaning on his staff of curdled light, the traveller
contemplated the land where he had incarcerated the
elemental called Litorgos. That being hated both salt and
silt; accordingly, here had been a most appropriate
choice.

Half a day's walk from the edge of the sea the land
reared up to form a monstrous irregular battlemented
cliff twenty times the height of a tall man, notched where
a river cascaded over the rim of the plateau above.
Thence it spilled across a wedge-shaped plain of its
own making and developed into a narrow delta, following sometimes this and sometimes that main channel. In
principle such land should have been fertile. Opposite
the river's multiple mouths, however, a dragon-backed

island created a swinge such that, at spring tide, ocean-water flooded ankle-deep over the soil, permeating it with salt. Therefore, only hardy and resistant crops could be grown here, and in a bad year might be overtaken by the salty inundation before they were ready to harvest.

This had not prevented the establishment of cities. One had been founded close to the waterfall, and flourished awhile on trade with the plateau above. A crude staircase had been carved out of the living rock, up which slaves daily toiled bearing salt, dried fish and baskets of edible seaweed, to return with grain and fruit and sunflower oil. Then the elemental slumbering below stretched to test the firmness of his intangible bonds; they held him, but the staircase crumbled and the city disappeared.

More recently a port had been built on wooden piles at the mouth of the main channel; the island opposite was thickly forested. With the clearance of the woodland, marble was discovered. Cutting and polishing it, exporting it on rafts poled along the coastal shallows, the inhabitants grew rich enough to deck their own homes with marble and with colorful tiles in patterns each of which constituted a charm against ill fortune. But now the marble was exhausted, and so was most of the timber, and the city Stanguray, which had once been famous, was reduced to a village. Its present occupants lived in the attics and lofts of the old town, and as they lay down to sleep could listen to the chuckle of water rippling within the lower part of their homes. To get from one surviving building to another even toddlers deftly walked along flimsy rope bridges, while the needs of the elderly and better-off—for there were still rich and poor in Stanguray—were met by bearers of reed-mat palankeens, adept at striding down the waterways and across the mudflats on stilts taller than themselves. This mode of transport had no counterpart elsewhere.

And it was entirely fitting, the traveller reflected, that this should be so. For once the river, which here met the ocean, had run under the ramparts of Acromel, and was known as Metamorphia. No longer did it instantly change whatever fell or swam in its waters, it having been decreed that after a certain span of altering the nature of other things, it must amend its own. Yet and still a trace of what had gone before remained, and would forever in the work of all rivers: they would erode mountains, create plains, cause the foundation and destruction of countless cities.

Moreover, in all the settlements along it, including those around Lake Taxhling on the plateau above—the first earnest of the inevitable change in the river's nature, for there it spread out and grew sluggish and reed-fringed before it ultimately spilled over the cliffs and became the opposite, violent and fast and sparkling—the residual magic of Metamorphia had led to schools of enchantment. Of no very great import, admittedly, nothing to compare with the traditions of Ryovora or Barbizond or the Notorious Magisters of Alken Cromlech, but dowered nonetheless with a certain potency.

Such matters being of the keenest interest to him, the traveller set forth along riverside paths toward this paradoxical village of marble columns and tiled pilasters. It was dawn; the clouds in the east were flushing scarlet and rose and vermilion, and fisherfolk were chanting melodiously as they carried their night's catch ashore in reed baskets and spilled them into marble troughs, once destined for the watering of noblemen's horses, where women and children busily gutted them. The smell of blood carried on the wind. It was acute in the traveller's nostrils when he was still a quarter-hour's walk distant.

And then it occurred to him that in fact there was only a slight breeze, and that it was at his back: blowing off the land, toward the sea.

Moreover, he perceived of a sudden that it was not just the light of dawn which was tinting pink the water in the channels either side of the crude causeway he was following.

There must have been an astonishing slaughter.

The traveller sighed. Last time he had seen a river literally running red in this manner, it had been because of a battle: one of dozens, all indecisive, in the constant war between Kanishmen and Kulyamen. But that matter was regulated pretty well to his satisfaction, and, in any case, this was not human blood.

If it were a precedented event, the inhabitants of Stanguray would presumably be able to inform him concerning this tainting of their river. The ground being impregnated with salt, one could not sink a sweet-water well; rainfall, moreover, was exiguous and seasonal hereabouts. Consequently folk were much dependent on the river's cleanliness.

More disturbed by the situation than seemed reasonable, the traveller lengthened his strides.

II

When the fish guts had been thrown to the gulls the people of Stanguray went their various ways: the poorest to the beach, where they made fires of twigs and scorched a few of the smaller fish, sardines and pilchards, and gobbled them down with a crust of bread left over from yesterday's baking; the most prosperous, including naturally all those who owned an entire fishing smack with a reliable charm on it, to their homes where breakfast awaited them; and the middling sort to the town's only cookshop, where they handed over a coin or a portion of their catch against the privilege of having their repast grilled on the public fire. Fuel was very short in Stanguray.

The said cookshop was the upper part of what had formerly been a temple, extended under the sky by a platform of creaky scantlings, water-worn and boreworm-pierced, salvaged from a wreck or a building long submerged.

Here a thin-faced, sharp-nosed, sharp-tongued young woman in a russet gown and a long apron supervised a fire on a block of slate whose visible sides were engraved with curlicues and runes. It would have been the altar when the temple's cult still thrived. Presiding over it like any priestess, she deigned to dispense hunks of griddle cake and char or stew vegetables brought by those lucky enough to own a farmable patch of ground, as well as cooking fish, while a hunchbacked boy, who never moved fast enough to please her, meted out rations of pickled onions, vinegar and verjuice to add a quicker relish to the oily food.

A public fire, plainly, was a profitable operation, for everything about the shop was better appointed than one might have predicted. Though the external platform was fragile, though the variety of the food was wholly dependent on who brought what, nonetheless the woman's gown was of excellent quality, and the walls were ornamented with numerous precious relics such as one would rather have expected to find in the homes of wealthy fishing-boat owners. Also, at least for those who paid in money, not only beer but even wine was to be had. The hunchback, lashed on by the woman's shouted order, rushed them by the mugful to the customers.

It was clear that at least one more waiter was not only affordable, but urgently needed.

However, that—to the traveller's way of thinking— was not the most curious aspect of this cookshop.

Having sated their bellies, the homeless poor plodded up from the beach carrying clay jars which they had filled at the point where the estuary water turned from brackish to drinkable . . . or should have done. Not long after, a string of children, bearing by ones and twos full leathern buckets they could scarcely stand under the weight of, also assembled.

The woman in charge seemed not to notice them for a long while. The delay grated on the patience of one girl, some twelve or thirteen years old, and finally she called out.

"Crancina, don't you know it's a foul-water day?"

"What of it?" the woman retorted, rescuing the roasted turnip from the flames, not quite in time.

"We had salt eels this morning, and we're clemmed!"

"Tell your mother to learn better," was the brusque reply, and Crancina went on serving her other customers.

Finally, several minutes later, she stood back from the fire and dusted her hands. Instantly, the people waiting rushed toward her. The poorer got there first, being adult and desperate; nonetheless, they contrived to offer at least a copper coin, which she took, bit and dropped in the pocket of her apron, while pronouncing a cantrip over their water jugs. Forced to the rear by those larger and stronger, the children from wealthier homes had no lack of cash, but they cautiously tasted the water after the spell had been spoken, as though fearing that much repetition might weaken it. All satisfied, they wended homeward.

"Are you curious concerning what you see, sir?" a thin voice said at the traveller's elbow. He had taken pains, as ever, not to be conspicuous, but it was time now to make more direct inquiries.

Turning, he found the hunchbacked boy perched on a table, for all the world like a giant frog about to take a leap. His sly dark eyes peered from under a fringe of black hair.

"I own that I'm intrigued," the traveller said.

"I thought you would be, seeing as I don't recall noticing you before. A pilgrim, are you? Cast ashore by
some rascally sea captain because contrary winds made
it too expensive to carry you all the way to the shrine
you booked your passage for?" The boy grinned hugely,
making his face as well as his body resemble a frog's.

"Do you meet many castaway pilgrims here, then?"

A crooked shrug. "Never! But even that would vary
the monotony of my existence. Every day is more or less
the same for all of us. Why otherwise would this en-
chanting of water be so remarkable?"

"Ah, then magic is at work."

"What else? Crancina has a sweet-water spell from
granny, all she left when she died, and so whenever the
water pinkens, they all come here. It's making a nice
little pile for her, naturally."

"She charges everybody?"

"Indeed, yes! She claims that performing the rite tires
her out, so she must be recompensed."

"What of those—for there must be some such—who
have no money to pay for her services?"

"Why, she says they may wait for rain!" The boy es-
sayed a laugh, which became more of a croak immediately.

"I deduce you are Crancina's brother," the traveller
said after a pause.

"How so?" The boy blinked.

"You spoke of 'granny,' as though you shared her."

A grimace. "Well, half brother. I often wonder
whether it was granny's curse that twisted me, for I know
she disapproved of our mother's second marriage. . . .
However that may be!" His tone took on sudden urgency.
"Will not you instruct me to bring you something, if only
a hunk of bread? For I should by now have cooked and
brought her the choicest of last night's catch, rich with
oil and fragrant with herbs, and grilled to perfection on
the best of our scant supply of logs. Any moment now
she will tongue-lash me until it stings like a physical
castigation—at which, I may say, she is even more
adept! Would you inspect my bruises?"

"There seems to be little love lost between you," the
traveller observed.

"Love?" The hunchback cackled. "She wouldn't know
the meaning of the word! So long as my father survived, and before our mother became bedridden, I made

the most of life despite my deformity. Now she's my sole commander, mine's a weary lot! I wish with all my heart that someday I may find means to break free of her tyranny and make my own way in the world, against all odds!"

Prompt to his prediction Crancina shouted, "Jospil, why have you not set my breakfast on the embers? There's costly wood going up in smoke, and all the customers are served!"

Her shrill reprimand quite drowned out the traveller's reflexive murmur: "As you wish, so be it."

Cringing, the boy regained the floor and scurried toward her. "Not so, sister!" he pleaded. "One remains unfed, and I did but inquire what he would order."

Abruptly noticing the traveller, Crancina changed her tone to one of wheedling deference. "Sir, what's your pleasure? Boy, make him room and bring clean dishes and a mug at once!"

"Oh, I'll not trouble you to cook for me," the traveller answered, "seeing as how your brother explained your spell leaves you fatigued, and you must need sustenance yourself. I'll take a bit of fish from pickle, bread and beer."

"You're courteous, sir," Crancina sighed, dropping on a nearby bench. "Yes, in truth these foul-water days are an accursed nuisance. Over and over I've proposed that a band of well-armed men be sent out, to trace the trouble to its source, but it's on the high plateau, seemingly, and these fainthearts hold that to be a place of sorcerers none can oppose. Monsters, too, if you believe them."

"Maybe it's the one slaughtering the other," Jospil offered as he set mug and platter before the traveller. "There must come an end of that, when all expire!"

"It's not a joking matter!" snapped Crancina, raising her fist and then reluctantly unballing it, as though belatedly aware she was being watched by a stranger. But she continued, "By all the powers, I wish I knew what use there is in spilling so much blood! Maybe then I could turn it to my own account for a change, instead of having to pander to the wants of these cajoling idiots, fool enough—*you* heard the girl, sir, I'll warrant!—fool enough to eat salt eels for breakfast when their noses must advise 'em there'll be nothing sweet to quench their thirst. Would you not imagine they could keep a day or two's supply that's fit to drink? If they can't afford a coopered barrel, surely there are enough old marble urns to be had for the trouble of dragging them to the surface. But they can't or won't be bothered. They're so accustomed to leaning out the window and dipping in the stream—and sending their ordures the same way, to the discomfort of us who live closer to the sea—they regard it as a change in the proper order of the world, never to be resisted, which will come right of itself."

"They pay you for performing your spell," the traveller said, munching a mouthful of the pickled fish Jospil had brought and finding it savory. "There's a compensation."

"I admit it," said Crancina. "In time I may grow rich, as wealth is counted in this miserable place. Already two widowers and two middle-aged bachelors are suing for my hand—and half a share in this cookshop, of course. . . . But that is not what I want!" —with sudden fierceness. "I've told you what I want! I'm accustomed to being in charge, and I want that with all my heart and soul, and I'm seeking a way of securing my fate while this dismal half-ruined town crumbles about me!"

So long ago there was not means to measure it, the traveller had accepted conditions pertaining to his sundry and various journeys through the land, imposed on him when a quartet of crucial planets cycled to a particular configuration in the sky.

The granting of certain wishes formed an essential element in the conditions circumscribing him . . . though it was true that the consequences of former wishes were gradually limiting the previous totality of possibilities. Some now were categorically unimplementable.

But even as he muttered formal confirmation—"As you wish, so be it!"—he knew one thing beyond peradventure. This was not one of those.

III

Once it had been permitted him to hasten the seasons of the year and even alter their sequence. But that power belonged to the ages when the elementals still roved abroad, their random frenzy entraining far worse divagations of the course of nature. Tamed and pent—like Litorgos under the delta of the river which no longer merited the name of Metamorphia—they were little able to affect the world. Events were ending, in the prescribed manner, toward that end which Manuus the enchanter had once defined as "desirable, perhaps, but appallingly dull." The day would break when all things would have but one nature, and time would have a stop, for the last randomness of the chaos existing in Eternity would have been eliminated.

To make way for a new beginning? Possibly. If not, then—in the very strictest sense—*no matter, never mind* . . .

Until then, however, the elementals did still exist and fretted away with their enfeebled force, like Fegrim beating at the cap of cold lava which closed the crater of the volcano wherein perforce he now dwelt. Not a few had discovered that human practitioners of magic were, without having chosen to be, their allies. But there was a penalty attached to such collaboration, and the most minor of them had paid it long ago; they were reduced to activating hearth-charms. No doubt this was the fate which had overtaken Litorgos; no doubt it was he who drew the blood from the foul water, though he was in no position to benefit thereby. Blood had its place in magic, but it could never free an elemental.

But the traveller did not want so much as to think about Litorgos, or Stanguray, until the remainder of his business was completed. Nonetheless, he did wish—and withal wished he could grant himself that wish, as he must grant those of others—that he could whirl the planets around to the conformation which would mark the conclusion of his journey, and thereby enable a return to that place which, with every pace he took, seemed more and more likely to become the focus of terrible and inexplicable events.

Making haste was pointless. The orderly succession of time which he himself had been responsible for, as riversilt had created land at Stanguray, now held him tight in its grip. Some relief from his apprehension might be obtained, however, by overoccupying himself. Accordingly, on his journey he made a point of visiting not only those places familiar to him from aforetime—and sometimes from before time—but also newer locations.

One such was known by the name of Clurm. Here in the shadow of great oaks a lordling, who held his birthright to have been usurped, planned with a group of fanatical followers to create such a city as would lure anyone to remove thither on hearing news of it. Now they shivered in tents and ate half-raw game and wild mushrooms, but this new city was to have towers that touched the clouds, and streets wide enough for a hundred to march abreast, and brothels with the fairest of women to attract spirited youths, and a treasury overflowing with gold and gems to pay their fee, and an army would be forged from them to overthrow the usurper, and magicians would be hired to make them unquestioningly loyal, and all in the upshot would be as this wild dreamer pictured it.

Except that after a year of exile his little band had not erected so much as a log cabin, deeming manual labor beneath their dignity.

"But the new Clurm will be of such magnificence!" asserted the lordling, seated as ever closest to the warmth of their tiny campfire; they dared not build a larger one, for fear of being spotted by the usurper's forces, who roamed free in the countryside while they hid among trees, being less beloved of the common folk. "It will be . . . it will be . . . Oh, I can see it now! Would you too could see its wonders! Would I could make you believe in its existence!"

"As you wish, so be it," said the traveller, who stood a little apart, leaning on his staff.

Next day the inevitable happened. In the morning they awoke, convinced that their city was real, for they saw it all about them. Joyful, bent on their leader's errand, they set out for all points of the compass and returned with eager young followers, just as he had predicted.

Who thereupon, not finding the grand city which members of the band believed they could see, set about them with cudgels and bound them hand and foot and committed them for lunatics. The lordling was not exempted from this treatment.

But the traveller, departing, found himself unable to avoid thinking about Stanguray.

Therefore, he turned aside from the road which led to Wocrahin, and made his way to a green thicket in the midst of a perfectly circular expanse of hard clay, which neither rain nor thawing after snow could turn to mud. Here was imprisoned Tarambole, with sway over dryness, as Karth formerly over cold in the land called Eyneran: a being to whom the gift had not been granted to tell lies.

Within the thicket, concealed from sight of passers-by —which was as well, since lately the people of the region had taken much against magic—the traveller resigned himself to the performance of a ceremony none but he and Tarambole recalled. It gained him the answer to a single question, and it was not what he had looked forward to.

No, it was not, so Tarambole declared, an elemental ranged against him which drew his mind back and back, and back again to thoughts of Stanguray.

"Would that I might consult with Wolpec," murmured the traveller. But he knew not where that strange, coy, harmless spirit bided now; he had yielded too early to the blandishments of humans, and by his own volition had wasted his power to the point where it was needless to imprison him. He chose his own captivity. Much the same be said for Farchgrind, who once or twice had provided intelligence for the traveller and indeed for countless others.

There remained, of course, those whom he had only banished: Tuprid and Caschalanva, Quorril and Lry. . . . Oh, indubitably they would know what was happening! It was quite likely they had set this train of events in motion. But to call on them, the most ancient and powerful of his enemies, when he was in this plight, weakened by puzzlement . . .

Had they set out to undermine him, knowing they could not meet him in fair fight?

Yet Tarambole, who could not lie, had said his disquiet was not due to the opposition of an elemental.

The gravely disturbing suspicion burgeoned in the traveller's mind that for the first (and the next word might be taken literally in both its senses) *time* a new enemy had arrayed against him.

New.

Not an opponent such as he had vanquished over and over, but something original, foreign to his vast experience. And if it were not the Four Great Ones who had contrived so potent a device . . .

Then only one explanation seemed conceivable, and if it were correct, then he was doomed.

But his nature remained single, and it was not in him to rail against necessity. Necessarily he must continue on his way. He retrieved his staff and with its tip scattered the somewhat disgusting remains of what he had been obliged to use in conjuring Tarambole, and headed once more toward Wocrahin.

Where, in a tumbledown alley, a smith whose forge blazed and roared and stank yelled curses at his neighbors as he hammered bar-iron into complex shapes. His only audience was his son, a boy of ten, who hauled on the chain of the great leather bellows which blew his fire.

"Hah! They want me out of here because they don't like the noise, they don't like the smell, they don't like me. . . . That's what it boils down to, they don't like me because my occupation's not genteel! But they buy my wares, don't they? Boy, answer when you're spoken to!"

But the boy had been at his work three years, and the noise had made him deaf, and inhalation of foul smokes had affected his brain, so he could only either nod or shake his head by way of answer. Fortuitously, this time he did the proper thing; he nodded.

Thus assuaged, his father resumed his complaining.

"If they don't care to live hard by a forge, let 'em club together and buy me a house outside the town, with a stream beside it to turn a trip-hammer. Let 'em do something to help me, as I help them! After all, a forge must be built somewhere, right? They should see what it's like to live without iron, shouldn't they, boy?"

This time, by alternation, the youngster shook his head. Infuriated, the smith flung down his tools and bunched his fists.

"I'll teach you and the rest of 'em to make mock of me!" he roared. "Oh, that they could see what life is like without iron!"

"As you wish," the traveller said from a smoky corner, "so be it."

Whereupon the iron in the smithy rusted all at once: the anvil, the hammerheads, the tongs, the nails, the cramps that held the massy wooden portion of the bellows, even the horseshoes waiting on the wall. The smith let out a great cry, and the neighbors came running. Such was their laughter that shortly the phrase, "like a smith

87

without iron," entered the common parlance of Wocra-hin. Indeed, he taught them to make mock. . . .

But the traveller was ill pleased. This was not like his customary regulation of affairs. It was clumsy. It was more like the rough-and-ready improvisations of the times before Time.

And he could not cure himself of thinking about Stanguray.

In Teq, they still gambled to the point of insanity, and might supplanted right among its decadent people.

"No, you may not waste time in playing!" a woman scolded her son, dragging him back from a sandpit where a score of children were amusing themselves. "You're to be the greatest winner since Fellian and support me in my old age. Ah, would I knew how to make you understand what I plan for you!"

"As you wish," sighed the traveller, who had taken station in the square where formerly the statue of Lady Luck upreared—where now greedy, unscrupulous landlords sold a night's lodging in squalid hovels to those who believed sleeping here would bring good fortune.

The boy's eyes grew round, and a look of horror spread across his face. Then he sank his teeth into his mother's arm, deep enough to draw blood, and took to his heels screaming, to scrape a living as best he could among the other outcasts of this now dismal city, the better for his freedom.

Yet that also was unbefitting, in the traveller's view, and still he could not rid his mind of thoughts of Stanguray.

In Segrimond, folk no longer tended a grove of ash trees. They had been felled to make a fence and grandstand around an arena of pounded rocks where, for the entertainment of the wealthy, savage beasts were matched with one another and against condemned criminals, armed or unarmed according to the gravity of their offense and the certainty of the jury which had heard the evidence. Today witnessed the bloody demise of a girl who had charged her respectable uncle with raping her.

"Now this," the traveller said under his breath, "is not as it should be. It smacks more of chaos, this indecision, than of the proper unfolding of Time. When all things have but a single nature, there will be no room for the doubt which requires settlement in this manner."

He waited. In a little the dead girl's uncle, resplendent in satin trimmed with fur, came weeping from the vantage point reserved for privileged onlookers. "Ah, if you but knew," he cried to fawning hangers-on, "how much it cost me to accuse my darling niece!"

"So be it," said the traveller, and by nightfall the people did indeed know what it had cost him, in bribes to perjured witnesses. On the morrow he was kicked to death by a wild onager.

Yet and still the traveller felt himself infected with the foulness of the world and could not release his mind from thinking about Stanguray.

Like Teq, Gryte was no longer rich, and on the marches of its land a new town had grown up called Amberlode. To it had removed the more enterprising of the old families from Gryte; against it the less enterprising were mouthing curses.

But the powers on which they called were petty compared to those which carried Ys back across the boundary of Time and into Eternity—albeit briefly—so their impact on Amberlode was minimal. Realizing this, a man who hated his younger brother for seizing an opportunity he had rejected cried aloud, and said, "Would it were I rather than he who enjoyed that fine new house in the new city!"

"As you wish," murmured the traveller, who had accepted the hospitality this man accorded grudgingly to travellers in order to acquire virtue against some misty hereafter.

And it was so; and because the younger brother under any circumstances was the more enterprising and talented and, moreover, understood how to hate, his cursing was efficacious, and the fine new house collapsed to its occupants' vast discomfiture.

And that was wrong!

The realization brought the traveller up short. There should have lain neither blame nor suffering on the brother who had chosen aright, yet here it came, and with brutal force. For as far back as he could recall it had been his intention that the literal interpretation he placed on the wishes he granted should be a means of ensuring justice. The suffering must be confined to those who had richly earned it. What was awry?

The constellations had not yet wheeled to the configuration marking the conclusion of his journey. By rights he should have continued in prescribed sequence from one stage of it to the next, to the next, to the next. . . .

But he found he could not. If it were true that some hitherto unencountered foe, neither human nor elemental, now ranged against him, that implied a fundamental shift in the nature of all the realities. Beyond that, it hinted at something so appalling that he might as well abandon his task at once. He had believed his assignment binding, forever and forever, within and outside Time. But it was possible, to the One for Whom all things were possible . . .

He canceled that thought on the instant. Completion of it would of itself wipe him from the record of what was, what might be and what was as though it had never been. His status was, as he well knew, at best precarious.

Which made him think of the rope-walking children at Stanguray.

Which made him think on what he had said and done there.

Which made him take the most direct route thither, and immediately.

Which taught him the most painful lesson of his existence.

IV

Initially, around Lake Taxhling there had been only reed huts wherein dwelt fisherfolk who well understood how to charm their way safely across its waters, and distinguish by simple conjuration those natural fishes which were safe to eat from those which had been transformed by the river Metamorphia and on which a geas lay.

Certain onerous duties bought them this privilege, but in general they regarded their prime deity Frah Frah as being exigent but not unkind.

Time wore on, though, and by degrees they quit performance of the rituals which had purchased their livelihood; in particular, they no longer ceremonially burned down and rebuilt their homes twice annually.

By then it was no longer so essential to tell the nature of one's catch; the river's power was waning. Now and then someone died through carelessness—generally a child or an oldster—but the survivors shrugged it off.

Then, as the river's magic diminished further, certain nomads followed it downstream: traders and pilgrims, and people who had so ill-used their former farms that the topsoil blew away, and criminal fugitives as well. Finding that on the far side of Lake Taxhling there was a sheer enormous drop, they decided to remain, and the original inhabitants—being peaceable—suffered them to do so.

Henceforward, the reed huts were not burned because there were none; the newcomers preferred substantial homes of timber, clay and stone. Henceforward, the shrines dedicated to Frah Frah were increasingly neglected. Henceforward, meat figured largely in the local diet, as fish had formerly; herds of swine were established in the nearby woodlands and grew fat in autumn on acorns and beechmast, while sheep and goats were let loose on the more distant slopes, though the grazing was too poor for cattle. The way of life around Lake Taxhling was transformed.

There followed a succession of three relatively gentle invasions, by ambitious conquerors, each of which endowed the area with a new religion not excessively dissimilar from the old one. It was a reason for children to form gangs and stage mock battles on summer evenings, rather than a cause for adult strife, that some families adhered to Yelb the Comforter and others to Ts-graeb the Everlasting or Honest Blunk. They coexisted with fair mutual tolerance.

Altogether, even for someone like Orrish whose stock was unalloyed pre-conquest, and whose parents maintained a dignified pride in their seniority of residence, life on the edge of Taxhling was not unpleasant.

Or rather, it had not been until lately. Oh, in his teens —he had just turned twenty—he had been mocked because he confessed to believing in the fables told to children about a town below the waterfall with which there had once been trade, but he was strong and supple and could prove his point by scaling the ruined stairs both ways, demonstrating that the idea was not wholly out of the question.

That, therefore, was endurable. So too was the military service imposed by the region's current overlord, Count Lashgar, on all between eighteen and twenty-one. It was a nuisance, but it was imperative if one wished to marry, and it enabled youngsters to break free of their parents, which could not be bad. Because the count had no territorial ambitions and spent his time poring over ancient times, the most dangerous duties assigned to his troops consisted in keeping track of goats on hilly pastures, and the most unpleasant, in the monthly shambles. There were too many people now for fish to feed them all, so the latest invader, Count Lashgar's grandfather, had exhibited a neat sense of household economy by decreeing that the slaughter of animals should henceforth be an army monopoly, thereby tidily combining weapons training (they were killed with sword and spear) with tax collection (there was a fixed charge based on weight and species, which might be commuted by ceding one sheep of seven, one goat of six and one hog of five), with religious duty (the hearts were saved to be offered on the altar of his preferred deity, Ts-graeb the Everlasting), and with—as he naïvely imagined—an increase in the fish supply. It seemed reasonable to expect that by establishing a shambles in the shallows of the lake one could contrive to give them extra nourishment.

The lake being sluggish, however, the stench grew appalling; moreover, it was the only source of drinking- and cooking-water. His son peremptorily removed the shambles to the very edge of the plateau, and his grandson Lashgar saw no grounds for disturbing this arrangement. Now and then in the old days, one had seen, on the delta below, people shaking fists and shouting insults, but they were too far away to be heard, and none had the temerity to climb the ancient stairs and argue. Not since before Orrish was born had it been deemed advisable to maintain double guards along the rim of the cliffs.

Maybe if that old custom had been kept up . . .

Perhaps, yes, things would not have taken such a horrifying turn around Taxhling. He would naturally not have been able to do what he was doing—deserting his post by night—without killing his companion or persuading him to come along; on the other hand, the necessity would not have arisen. . . .

Too late for speculation. Here he was, scrambling down the cliff, repeating under cover of darkness his climb of five years ago, wincing at every pebble he dislodged, for the steps rocked and tilted, and some had vanished for five or ten feet together. His muscles ached abominably, and though the night was frosty, rivulets of perspiration made him itch all over. However, there was no turning back. He must gain the safety of the level ground below. He must let the people of Stanguray know what enormities one of their number was perpetrating, rouse them to anger and to action!

Under his cold-numbed feet a ledge of friable rock abruptly crumbled. Against his will he cried out as he tumbled into blackness. His memory of the climb he had made when he was fifteen was not so exact that he knew how high he was, but he guessed he fell no more than twenty feet.

But he landed on a heap of small boulders, frost-fractured from the cliff, and felt muscles and sinews tearing like wet rags.

How now was he to bear a warning to Stanguray? And if not he, then who?

There was nothing else for it. Despite his agony, he must crawl onward. Even though the witch Crancina had been spawned among them, the people of Stanguray did not deserve the fate she planned. They had at least, presumably, had the sense to drive her out, instead of—like that damned fool Count Lashgar!—welcoming her and giving in to every one of her foul demands.

V

Autumn had begun to bite when the traveller returned to Stanguray. It was a clear though moonless night. Mist writhed over the marshes. The mud was stiff with cold, and here and there a shallow puddle was sufficiently free from salt to have formed a skim of ice.

Despite the chill, the reek of blood was dense in the air.

But in the village of marble pillars and gaudy tilework there was no sign of life, save for suspicious birds and rats.

Unable at first to credit that the place was totally deserted, the traveller slacked the grip of the forces which held together his staff of curdled light. A radiance bright as the full moon's revealed it was only too true. Everywhere doors and shutters stood ajar. No chimney, even on the wealthiest homes, uttered smoke. The boats were gone from the quay, and some few poor household items lay on it, abandoned.

Yet this did not smack of a raid. There was no sign of violence—no fires had been started, no dead bodies lay untidy on the ground. This had been a planned and voluntary departure.

Moreover, as he abruptly realized, something else was wrong. He was immune to the night's freezing air, but not to the chill of dismay which this discovery evoked in him.

Litorgos was no longer penned between salt and silt. The elemental too was absent from this place.

Until this moment he had believed that in all of space and all of time none save he had been granted the power to bind and loose the elemental spirits. Could it be that to another the inverse of his gift had been assigned? Surely the One Who . . .

But if that were so, then Tarambole had lied. And if that were so, then the universe would become like the pieces on a game board, to be tipped randomly back into their box and played again with different rules. There was no sign of such a catastrophe: no comets, no eruptions, no dancing stars.

A new enemy.

More at a loss than ever before, he pondered and reviewed his knowledge, standing so still that hoarfrost had the chance to form on the hem of his black cloak. With all his powers of reasoning he was still far from an answer when he heard a thin cry, weak as a child's but far too bass.

"Help! Help! I can go no further!"

Half in, half out of a muddy channel, some three or four hundred paces toward the escarpment, he came upon the one who had shouted: a young man in leather jerkin, breeches and boots, whimpering against his will for the pain of torn ligaments in his leg.

"Who are you?" the traveller challenged.

"Orrish of Taxhling," came the faint reply.

"And your mission?"

"To warn the folk of Stanguray what doom's upon them! I never dreamed such horrors could be hatched in a human brain, but———— Ow, ow! Curses on my hurt leg! But for it, I'd have been there long ere now!"

"To small avail," the traveller said, bending to haul the man clear of the icy water. "They're gone. All of them."

"Then my errand of mercy was in vain?" Orrish said blankly. And of a sudden he began to laugh hysterically.

"Not so," the traveller returned, touching with his staff the injured leg. At every contact a light shone forth, the color of which humans had no name for. "There, how does it feel?"

Sobered by astonishment, Orrish rose incredulously to his feet, testing the damaged limb. "Why—why, it's a miracle!" he whispered. "Who are you, that you can work such magic?"

"I have many names, but a single nature. If that means aught to you, so be it; if not, and increasingly I find it does not, well and good. . . . With a name like Orrish, I take you to be of ancient Taxhling stock."

"You know our people?"

"I daresay I've known them longer than you," the traveller admitted. "What's amiss, that sent you on your desperate mission?"

"They've gone insane! A witch has come among us, dedicated to the service of Ts-graeb—or so she says— claiming to know how to make our lord Count Lashgar live forever! Now me, I hold no brief against the worshippers of Ts-graeb, or anyone else, although in truth . . ." Orrish's tongue faltered.

With a hint of his customary dry humor the traveller said, "In truth you adhere to the cult of Frah Frah, and you wear his amulet in the ancient and invariable place, and because your belt has come adrift from your breeches, the fact is plainly discernible. I am pleased to learn Frah Frah is not wholly devoid of followers; his ceremonies were often very funny, in a coarse way, and among his favorite offerings was a hearty laugh. Am I not right?"

Frantically making good the deficiencies in his garb, Orrish said in awe, "But that was in my grandfather's day!"

"More like your three-times-great-grandfather's day," the traveller said matter-of-factly. "But you still haven't told me why you were so desperate to warn the folk of Stanguray."

Piecemeal, then, he extracted the whole story and thereby learned that Tarambole, while of course he could not lie, had access to the power of ambiguity.

That discovery was a vast relief. But it still left a wholly unprecedented situation to resolve.

"This witch is called Crancina," Orrish said. "She came among us recently—last spring—and brought with her a familiar in the guise of a hunchbacked boy. They hailed from Stanguray, and at once everybody was prepared to accept them as marvel workers, for in living memory none but I has attempted to scale the face of yon escarpment.

"We'd always regarded Count Lashgar as a harmless, bookish fellow. In shops and taverns one might hear people say with knowing nods and winks, 'One could do worse than live under such an overlord!' Confessedly, I've said and believed the same.

"Little did we know that he plotted with his books and incantations to find a means of outliving us all! But *she* did, the witch Crancina, and she came to him and said she knew what use could be made of the blood spilled from the beasts we kill each month at the dark of the moon. She said that once there was enough blood in the water of the lake . . . Sir, are you well?"

For the traveller had fallen silent and stock-still, gazing into the past.

In a little he roused himself enough to answer. "No! No, my friend, I am not well, nor is anything well! But at least I now comprehend what is the nature of my unprecented enemy."

"Explain, then!" pleaded Orrish.

"She made out that once enough blood was in the water, it would turn to an elixir of long life, is that the case?"

"Why, yes! Moreover, she declared it should be ample for all to drink, giving each of us an extra span of years!"

"In that she lied," the traveller said, flat-voiced.

"I have suspected so." Orrish bit his lip. "I won't presume to ask how you know—that you're a strange and powerful personage, my well-healed leg declares. . . . Would, though, I might give her the lie direct, on your authority! For what they propose up yonder, in my name, is so ghastly, so awful, so disgusting . . . !"

"It was this that drove you to desert your post?"

The young man gave a miserable nod. "Indeed, indeed. For, lacking as much blood as she maintained was requisite, they began to say, 'Are there not those who bleed at Stanguray? Did not Orrish clamber down and up the cliffs? And must not human blood be more effective? Let us set forth and capture them and drag them hither and cut their throats to make the magic work!' "

"And what said Count Lashgar to this mad scheme?"

"Unless Crancina's rites succeed today, he'll give his soldiers orders for the mission."

"Who's making rope?"

The question took Orrish aback for a second; then he caught on and burst out laughing, not as before—halfway to hysteria—but with honest mirth, making an offering to Frah Frah.

"Why, I'm as dumb and blind as they! Surely it will call for miles of rope to fetch hundreds of unwilling captives over level ground, let alone drag them up the cliffs!"

"Such work is not in hand?"

"Why, no! Drunk on promises, the people care only for butchery. Now it's at such a stage, those who set snares by night are ordered to bring their catch, still living, to be included in the daily ceremony. And woe betide those whose rabbits and hares and badgers are already dead!"

"I understand," the traveller said somberly, and thought on an ancient ceremony, practiced when the forces of chaos were more biddable than now. Then, one had taken a shallow bowl, ideally of silver, incised with the character harst, midmost of those in the Yuvallian script, and filled it with water, and laid therein the germ of a homunculus, and cut one's finger and let three drops fall to mingle with the water, and thereupon the homunculus set forth to do one's bidding. Kingdoms had been overthrown that way.

What would betide when the ceremony was expanded to a whole great lake?

And particularly and essentially: this lake of all . . . !

"Sir," Orrish ventured anxiously, "you spoke just now of some enemy of yours. Is that the witch—is your enemy the same as ours? May we count you for an ally?"

The traveller parried the question. "What drove you to climb down the cliff by night? Fear that you, not worshiping Ts-graeb, would be excluded from the universal benefit of immortality?"

"No—no, I swear on my father's honor!" Orrish was sweating; the faint light of the false dawn glistened on his forehead. "But—well, in the cult of the god I have been raised to worship, it is said that pleasure bought at the cost of another's suffering is no pleasure at all. So it seems to me with this pretended immortality—even given that that is the goal of those cruel ceremonies, which you contest. How can a life worth living be purchased at the expense of so much viciousness?"

"Then let us return together to Taxhling," the traveller said with decision. "Your wish is granted. You shall give the witch the lie direct."

"But *is* she your enemy?" Orrish persisted.

"No, my friend. No more than you are."

"Then—who . . . ?"

Because the question was posed with an honest need to know, the traveller was constrained to answer, after long reluctance.

"That which is against me is within me."

"You speak in riddles!"

"So be it! I had rather not let it be noised abroad that I overlooked so crude a truth: this is my fault. For the first time, I set forth to fight *myself*."

VI

Blessedly warm in the room assigned to her at Count Lashgar's residence—for here on the plateau they could afford to be prodigal with fuel, and a log fire had burned all night two steps away from her bed—Crancina woke with a sudden sense of excitement such as she had only felt once before: back in the spring, when it had suddenly dawned on her what use could be made of all that blood fouling Stanguray's river.

A servingmaid drowsed on a stool in the chimney corner. Shouting to rouse her, Crancina threw aside the thick coverlet of her bed.

Today, yes today, her efforts were sure to be rewarded! Then let that slimy count go whistle for his dreamed-of immortality! He was on all fours with the greedy men who had demanded her hand in marriage back at Stanguray, when what they wanted was not her, but the profits of her cookshop and her sweet-water spell.

Today would teach him, and tomorrow would teach the world, a lesson never to be forgotten.

Humming a merry tune, she wrapped herself snug in a sheepskin cape against the chill early morning air.

"My lord! My lord! Wake up!" whispered the serving-man whose duty it was to rouse Count Lashgar. "Mistress Crancina is certain of success today, and sent her girl to tell me so!"

Muzzily peering from among high-piled pillows, the count demanded, "What's worked the trick, then? The extra animals I ordered to be brought in from snares and traps?"

"My lord, I'm not party to your high councils," was the reproachful answer. "But surely in one of your books the secret's explained?"

"If it had been," Lashgar sighed, forcing himself to sit up, "I'd not have waited this long for the fulfillment of my lifetime dreams."

Through the mists which haunted the edges of the lake a band of shivering soldiers marched with drums and gongs, and on hearing them, people turned out enthusiastically, forgoing breakfast save for a hasty crust and a mouthful of strong liquor. In the old days the morning of a shambles was one to be avoided; now, miraculously, it had been transformed into the signal event of the month . . . today more than ever, for the rumors had already taken rise.

"Today's the day! Crancina told the count—it's bound to work today! Just think! Maybe some of us, maybe all of us, will be deathless by tonight!"

Only a few cynical souls were heard to wonder aloud what would happen if it proved there was power enough in the bloody water to make one person live forever, and no more. Who would get it, if it weren't the witch?

But those were generally of the aboriginal lakeside stock, whose ancestors had had their fill of magic long ago. Those who worshiped Ts-graeb the Everlasting, as Lashgar did—and his adorers had grown vastly more numerous since the witch arrived—clamored loudly for the favor of their deity, and arrived at the lake's shore singing and clapping their hands.

They raised a vast cheer when Lashgar and Crancina appeared, preceded by the image of Ts-graeb in the guise of an old and bearded wiseacre, which was borne on the shoulders of six men-at-arms. The procession was flanked by the priests and priestesses of Yelb the Comforter, portrayed as having nipples all over her naked bulk from toes to hairline, and the handful who still adhered to Honest Blunk, whose image and symbol was a plain white sphere. No believers in Frah Frah were bold enough to parade their creed, and indeed, scarcely any remained.

But, bringing up the very tail, here came a hunchbacked boy in jester's garb, with bells on hat and heels, capering and grimacing as he feigned to strike the onlookers with his wand of office; a pig's bladder on a rod tied with gaudy ribbons. Even the followers of Honest Blunk were glad to crack a smile at sight of him, for a bitter wind soughed over the plateau.

"And where," the traveller murmured, as he contrived to fall in beside the jester, "did you get that particolored finery?"

"It's not stolen, if that's what you're thinking!" came the sharp reply. "It belonged to the jester whom Count Lashgar's grandfather kept, and I have been given it by one of the count's retainers. Who are you that you put such a question to me? Why, I recall *you,* and only too well." At once the boy ceased his awkward parody of a dance. "It was the very day after you spoke with her that my sister took this crazy notion into her head, and forced me hither up the cliffs! More than once I thought I would die, but my deformity has luckily left my torso light enough for my arms to bear the weight of, and where she almost fell, I could cling on for us both. . . . But often I feel I'd rather have let her fall than be condemned to my present lot!"

"Is it no better than at Stanguray?"

"Perhaps by a hair's breadth, now I've appropriated these clothes and wand." Jospil struck the traveller with it, scowling. "But they made me out to be Crancina's familiar at first, and wanted to feed me on hot coals and *aqua regia*. Besides, they have no sense of humor, these people! If they did, would they not long ago have laughed Crancina out of countenance?"

"You are absolutely correct," the traveller agreed solemnly. "And therein lies the key to fulfillment of a wish you made in my hearing. Do you recall it?"

The hunchback gave his usual crooked shrug. "It would have been the same as what I say to everybody, except of course my sister: that one day I should find a means of freeing myself from her."

"And making your way in the world against all odds?"

"Yes, I've said that over and over, and doubtless to you."

"Meaning it?"

Jospil's eyes flashed fire. "Every word!"

"Today, then, is your chance to make the most of your jester's rôle and achieve your ambition simultaneously."

Jospil blinked. "You speak so strangely," he muttered. "Yet you came to the hearth like anybody, and you were politer to my sister than she deserved, and . . . yes, it was precisely from the moment of your visit that she took these crazy notions into her head, and . . . I don't know what to make of you, I swear I don't."

"Count yourself fortunate," the traveller said dryly, "that you are not called on to do so. But remember that there is magic abroad today, if not the kind Count Lashgar is expecting, and that you are a crux and focus of it. Sir Jester, I bid you good morning!"

And with a deep-dipping bow, and an inclination of his staff, and a great flapping swirl of his black cape, the traveller was gone about his business.

VII

How it was that he was back at his guard post in time to reclaim his spear and shield and greet his dawn relief before his absence was noticed, Orrish could afterward never quite recall—nor what had become of his mysterious companion once they were on the plateau.

But he did remember one thing with perfect clarity. He had been promised the chance to give the witch the lie direct. Anxious, he awaited his opportunity. There seemed little chance of its happening, though, for immediately on returning to barracks he had been cornered by a sergeant with a squad lacking one man, to collect the night's trapped animals and bring them to the lakeside to have their life's blood let. In all their various tones they squeaked and whimpered, and their cries made a hideous cacophony along with the bleating and grunting of the few remaining domestic animals, pent in folds of hurdles within scent of the bloody water. At this rate of slaughter, though there would be more pickled meat than their barrels could hold, and more smoked meat than hooks to hang it on, which would see the community through the winter, there would be no breeding stock to start again in the summer. Orrish shook his head dolefully, detesting the assignment he had been given almost as much as he loathed the notion of kidnapping and killing the people of Stanguray.

That at least, if the traveller was to be trusted, was no longer a possibility.

But where was the traveller? Orrish searched the vicinity with worried eyes. Like all those who came of the ancient Taxhling stock, he had been raised to distrust magic and its practitioners, and the way his leg had been healed left no room for doubt that the man in the black cloak trafficked in such arts. Was he—like the witch Crancina—deceitful and self-serving . . . ?

Orrish started a little. How did he know the witch was defrauding the people? Why, because the traveller in black had told him so. Maybe he should believe what the rest of his folk believed, rather than taking the word of a stranger?

Biting his lip in terrible confusion, he was distracted by a shout from the sergeant, calling the soldiers to attention at the appearance of Count Lashgar. Numbly obeying, Orrish wished desperately that the traveller would come back; everything had seemed so simple in his company.

Along with the other young conscripts, he awaited the order to butcher the pitiable beasts.

There were obligatory cheers and shouts; they did not last long, however, because everybody was too eager to hear what Crancina proposed to do today. Graciously bowing from side to side as he took station on a kind of dais erected over the water, Lashgar addressed his subjects in a surprisingly large voice for so slim and short a man.

"We are promised marvels!" he declared. "You want to see them as much as I do! I'll waste no time on speechifying, therefore, but let Mistress Crancina have her way!"

Everybody brightened at the brevity of his introduction. And then quieted and shivered. Even while Lashgar was speaking, Crancina had thrown aside her thick sheepskin cape and begun to make passes in the air, muttering to herself the while. The words could not be made out even at close quarters, yet there was such a resonance to them that if one caught their slightest echo it could send a tremor down the spine.

Now and then she felt in a pouch hung at her girdle and tossed a pinch of powder into the water, rather as though she were seasoning a soup.

Along with all the rest the traveller was mightily impressed. This was the first occasion in more of his visits to this world than he cared to try and count, when he had witnessed a genuinely new magic rite. Even though the change might be classed as more quantitative than qualitative, the purpose Crancina was putting her work to was radically different from anything he could recall.

Now and then in the past he had wondered whether cookery, where the practitioner might begin with something not only unpalatable but actually poisonous, and conclude with something not only digestible but delicious, might not be the ultimate destiny of temperaments which in earlier ages would have led people to meddle in magic. He made a firm resolve to keep a careful eye on cooks in future.

For this recipe, at least, was working fine.

Much as though it were milk being curdled by rennet, the water of Lake Taxhling was solidifying. Instead of the random patterns made by wind and wave, shapes were discernible on the surface, and though they jostled and shifted, they did not break up any longer. The onlookers oohed and aahed, while Count Lashgar, barely disguising his incredulity, tried not to jump up and down for joy.

The shapes were not altogether comfortable to look at; however, they were visible, and little by little they were beginning to stand up from the surface, first as shallowly as ripples, then with more and more protuberance. Also, they enlarged. Somewhat separated from each other, they numbered altogether a thousand or two, and their forms were strange beyond description. If this one was reminiscent of a claw-tipped fern frond, its neighbor hinted at a dishmop with vastly enlarged tentacles; if another called to mind a hog's head with holes in it, the next resembled a mouse with twenty legs.

The only thing they had in common, barring their present almost stillness, was their coloration. They were the gray of common pumice stone, and bobbed on the now oily surface of the lake, which had congealed to form them, with a motion as sluggish as though time had slowed to a twentieth of its regular rate.

"Magic!" murmured the onlookers, delighted. "Magic indeed!"

"But she is a liar—she *is!*" came a sudden cry from the direction of the stock pens, where soldiers were dutifully readying the last of the animals to be killed. *"The witch Crancina is a liar!"*

Everyone reacted, especially Lashgar and Crancina herself; the count shouted an order to the sergeant to quiet the man who had called out, while she shot one nervous glance in that direction and kept on with her recital of cantrips, faster and faster. The images forming on the lake wavered, but grew firm again.

"Silence that man!" the sergeant bellowed, and two of his companions tried to take Orrish by the arms. He shoved his shield in the face of one, breaking his nose, and winded the other with the butt end of his spear, on his way to the nearest point of vantage, the shambles stone—formerly at the far end of the lake near the water-fall, but lately brought back to this spot in the interests of conserving the spilled blood. It was a block of granite with channels cut in the upper face for the blood to drain from. Taking stance on it, Orrish waved his spear across the waters of the lake.

"How did she expect to get away with it?" he roared. "We know what these apparitions are!"

They wavered again, but remained solid, and were now stock-still, as rigid as glass, and as fragile.

Suddenly, cautiously, a few of the watchers—mostly elderly—nodded. Realizing they were not alone, they drew themselves proudly upright and did it again more vigorously.

"And *we* know they have nothing to do with immortality!" Orrish yelled at the top of his lungs. *"Get* away!" —kicking out at the sergeant who was trying to snare him by the ankles. "I don't mean *you* or your blockhead of a master, the Count! I mean *us,* who've been here long enough not to be cheated by the witch! Look at her! Look at her! Can't you read fear and terror on every line of her face?"

Crancina was wildly shouting something, but the wind had risen in the past minute or two, and the words were carried away. Beside her, paling, Count Lashgar was signaling to his bodyguard to close in; the priests of Blunk and Yelb and Ts-graeb were likewise huddling together for comfort.

Meantime, the images formed on the lake remained unmoving.

"And for the benefit of you who weren't lucky enough to be brought up like me in a household where they still know about this kind of thing," Orrish blasted, "I'll explain! In the remote and distant past our superstitious ancestors believed that the weird and unique objects which came down the river—those which had been of a sinking nature floated, obviously!—all these objects were divine and deserving of worship. So they set up shrines and made offerings, and called on them when reciting hearth spells, and the rest of it. But at last a sensible teacher arose among us and asked why we had so many petty deities when we could contrive one with all their best attributes and none of their worst. The people marveled and wondered and agreed, and that was how we came to worship Frah Frah! And when we had all consented to the change, the old gods were carried to the lake and thrown back in, to lie on the bottom until the end of the world. And so would they have done, but for Crancina! Ask her now what they have to do with immortality for us, or even her and Lashgar!"

"This is all a falsehood!" Crancina gasped. "I know nothing of ancient gods such as you describe!"

"But do you know of immortality?" Lashgar demanded. Seizing a sword from the nearest of his guardsmen, he leveled it at her breast.

"Of course she doesn't!" came a crowing voice. "She's fit to run a cookshop and no more, and that's what she did in Stanguray! Hee-hee-hee-hee-hee-*haw!*"

And Jospil in his jester's guise frog-hopped toward his sister with a donkey-loud bray of laughter.

Startled, about to launch another broadside of invective, Orrish high on his rock checked and looked toward Jospil and against all his best intentions had to grin. The grin turned to a chuckle; the chuckle became a roar of merriment, and he had to lean on his spear for support as he rocked back and forth with tears streaming from his eyes. The mirth was so contagious that, without knowing what was funny, small children echoed it, and tending them, their parents could not help but giggle, at the least, and that also spread. While Lashgar and Crancina and the more pompous of the attendant priests—of whichever denomination—looked scandalized and shouted orders which went disregarded by their subordinates, the entire crowd was caught up in one monstrous eruption of hilarity. The eldest of the onlookers, hobbling and toothless, who were as much at a loss about the proceedings as the babes in arms, cackled along with the rest, until the welkin seemed to ring with the sound.

And it did.

Echoed, re-echoed, amplified, the laughter started to resonate. There was a sort of buzzing which filled the air, making it denser than was normal. The vibrations fed on one another; they became painful to the ears; they set the teeth on edge; they shrilled and rasped and ground. Here and there among the throng people looked frightened and cast about for a way of escape. But there was none. The whole huge bowl which constituted the plateau of Lake Taxhling had become a valley of echoes, where sound—instead of dying away—increased in volume, and intensity, and harshness.

All this while the accidental creations of the river once known as Metamorphia, conjured back to the surface of the lake, stood utterly still . . . until they began to tremble under the impact of the noise.

Suddenly a thing like a walrus with a flower for a head crackled sharply across. A sprinkling of fine powder drifted into the air, dancing in time with the vibrations.

Then a curiously convoluted object, half slender and half bulky as though a giant dragonfly had miscegenated with a cart horse, shattered into tiny fragments. At once there was a rush into the vacancy from either side. Something not unlike a colossal fist, with feathery excrescences, collided with a great hollow structure and reduced it to tinkling shards.

The laughter took on a rhythmical pattern. Now it could be discerned that whenever it reached a certain pitch of intensity another of the objects Crancina had conjured forth broke apart; each such breaking entailed another, and then others. The watchers, who for a moment had been frightened, found this also very amusing, and their mirth redoubled until all were gasping for breath.

Into dust vanished the last relics of articles cast long ago from the citadel of Acromel; into sparkling crystals and

VIII

"It is not given to many to enjoy their heart's desire," murmured the traveller. "Did you enjoy it?"

"I . . ." Not knowing quite whether he was speaking, nor whether he was speaking to somebody, Orrish licked his lips. "I guess I'm glad to have made the proper offering to Frah Frah. But as for tomorrow . . ." He shrugged. "Things can never be the same."

"Interesting," said the traveller. "One might say the same about Chaos, yet here we are at a point where its forces so much wane that laughter serves to defeat them. . . . Nonetheless, in times to come you will be remembered, and even honored, as the man who gave the witch the lie direct. And you, Jospil, even though you are not likely to be revered, you may henceforward pride yourself on having broken free of the witch's tyranny to make your way in the world against all odds."

"If that be so," answered the hunchback sharply, "I reckon little of it. Was my sister a witch before you came to us at Stanguray?"

The traveller perforce was discreetly silent for a while; then said at last, "I should like you to know: it is an earnest of the fulfillment of my task that you relish my aid so much less than what you have previously accomplished on your own."

"Oh, it's not that," sighed Jospil. "It's . . . well, I don't honestly understand! What was Crancina up to when she forced me to quit our home in search of Count Lashgar?"

"She had made a wish, and I was bound to grant it."

"A wish . . . ?" Jospil's eyes grew round. "Of course! I'd half-forgotten! To know what use might be made of all the blood being spilled up here!"

"Your memory is exact."

"And she discovered, or worked out, that it could be used to revive those strange and ancient things from the bottom of the lake. . . . How?"

"Yes, how?" chimed in Orrish. "And to what end?"

"Jospil knows the answer to half that question," said the traveller with a wry smile.

"You mean . . . ?" The hunchback bit his thumb, pondering. "Ah! We only spoke of half her wish just now. The other part concerned her being in charge."

"As you say."

"But if part was granted, why is the other part not? Why is she not in charge completely, of everything, which I'm sure would suit her perfectly?"

"Because you wished to break free of her against all odds," the traveller answered. "And it so happens that those conflicting wishes which I grant tend to be loaded in favor of whoever cares less for himself, or herself, in the upshot." He added sternly, "But in your case, boy, it was a close call!"

Jospil gave his sly frog's grin. "Well, at least I have a trade now"—he slapped the traveller with his bauble—"and there will be a great dispersion from Taxhling, in all directions. From Lashgar's retainer who gave me this jester's outfit I've learned that a comedian at court may be a man of influence; certainly my involuntary benefactor was, who served Lashgar's grandfather until he was beheaded."

"You're prepared to run that risk?" Orrish demanded, aghast.

"Why not?" Jospil said, spreading his hands. "It's better than some risks we take for granted, isn't it? A moment of glory redeems an age of suffering. . . . But one more thing, sir, if I may trespass on your patience. What did my sister hope to achieve, if it was not to make herself immortal?"

"To re-enact a certain ceremony formerly involving a homunculus."

Jospil blinked. "That means nothing to me!" he objected. "Nor would it have done to her when you called at our cookshop that time! But for your intrusion, we might still be there, and—"

"And she might still be pronouncing her sweet-water cantrip at every dark of the moon."

"Exactly!" Jospil rose awkwardly to his feet. "Sir, I hold you entirely to blame for the predicament we're all cast into!"

"Even though you so much desired to be rid of your sister's tyranny, and you are?"

"Yes—*yes!*"

"Ah, well" —with a sigh. "I deserve the reproaches, I admit. Since but for me your sister would never have known how reviving the strange creations of Metamorphia and imbuing them with blood could have made her mistress of the world."

Orrish's jaw dropped; a second later, Jospil clutched the hem of the traveller's cloak.

"She could have done *that?*"

"Why, beyond a peradventure! What magic is left nowadays is residual, by and large, and the bed of Lake Taxhling was the repository of an enchantment such as few contemporary wizards would dare risk."

"I could have been half-brother to the ruler of the world?" Jospil whispered, having paid no attention to the last statement.

"Indeed you could," the traveller said calmly, "if you genuinely believed that a moment of glory redeems an age of suffering—and, I assure you, had she become ruler of the world she would have understood how to inflict suffering."

Frowning terribly, Jospil fell silent to reflect on what had been said, and Orrish ventured, "Sir, will you stay with us to rectify the consequences of your actions?"

There was a long, dead pause; the traveller hunched gradually further and further into the concealment of his hood and cloak.

Finally he said, as from a vast distance, "The consequences of my actions? Yes! But never the consequences of yours."

There followed a sudden sense of absence, and in a little while Jospil and Orrish felt impelled to go and join the rest of the people, clearing the debris left by the earthquake.

Which, of course, was all that had really happened . . . wasn't it?

IX

"Litorgos!" said the traveller in the privacy of his mind, as he stood on a rocky outcrop overlooking the salt-and-silt delta being transformed by the outgush of water from on high. Already the pillars of Stanguray were tilting at mad angles; marble slabs and tiled façades were splashing into the swollen river. "Litorgos, you came closer to deceiving me than any elemental in uncounted eons!"

Faint as wind soughing in dry branches, the answer came as though from far away.

"But you knew. You knew very well."

And that was true. Silent awhile, the traveller reflected

on it. Yes indeed: he had known, though he had not paid attention to the knowledge that when he granted Crancina her wish, he was opening the bonds which held Litorgos. For the sole and solitary and unique fashion in which the blood spilled into the river at Taxhling might be turned to the purpose Crancina had in view was by the intervention of an elemental. So much blood had been spilled the world over, another few thousand gallons of it was trivial, except . . .

And therefore Tarambole had told the truth. It was not an elemental working against the traveller which called him back to Stanguray.

It was an elemental working with him.

For otherwise the wish could never have been granted.

"There was a time," the traveller said in this confessional, "when I was ready to believe that the One Who—"

"She does not change Her mind," came the sharp retort.

"She has not done so," the traveller corrected. "But as the One to Whom all things are possible . . ."

"Then if that may prove to be the case, reward me straight away, before the unthinkable occurs!"

"Reward you? For deceiving me?"

"For working with you, instead of against you!"

The traveller considered awhile; then he said, "I find that while I am not constrained to grant the wish of an elemental, I have done it in the past and am therefore not debarred from doing so. Besides, I am inclined to favor you, inasmuch as you foresaw the need for the people of Stanguray to evacuate their homes and contrived that they should do so before the flood came pouring down from Taxhling. What then is your wish?"

"I would cease!"

The fury behind the message made the ruined plateau tremble one more time, and people rescuing their belongings from half-wrecked houses redoubled their efforts.

"Once I and all were free, and we could play with the totality of the cosmos! Once we could roam at large and transform galaxies at our whim, breaking the rope of time and making it crack like a whip! Then we were caught and bound, and pent as you pent me, and I know, in the very core and centre of my being, this imprisonment will never cease.

"So let *me* cease!"

For a long, long moment the traveller remained impassive, reflecting on what a change Litorgos had just wrought. Now the balance had been tipped; now the triumph he looked forward to was certain—always excepting the intervention of the Four Great Ones whom he could only banish, who might return.

But who would be insane enough to open a door for Tuprid and Caschalanva, Quorril and Lry—even if anybody remembered their existence?

With a great sigh of contentment the traveller said aloud, "In Eternity the vagaries of Chaos permit even death to be reversed. In Time the certainties of reason insist that even elementals may be . . . *dead.*"

For another hour the flood continued to wash away both sand and silt from the area where Litorgos had been and was no longer.

Later, the settlements which had surrounded Lake Taxhling were overthrown by further earth movements, and at last there was a vast slumping of the escarpment, such that half the old delta was hidden under scree and mud.

And in due time, when people came and settled thereabouts, ignorant of what cities had stood on the same site before—though not wholly the same, for the coastline also changed—it was held to be a pleasant and fortunate ground, where generations prospered who knew nothing about magic, or elemental spirits, or rivers running stinking-red with blood.

Anyone who's ever listened to nighttime radio talk shows knows that they attract some very strange phone calls. This is, of course, the very stuff of fantasy: night, and strangeness. What if one of those callers were not only odd, but . . . frightening?

Harlan Ellison, a master of the fantasy short story, tells how this story came to be written.

These remarks are prompted by the Editor's concern that readers will note a 1977 original copyright date on this story and wonder how it could be included in a collection of the best of the year from 1979. Easily explained. Not usual, but easily expained. To whit:

In December of 1977, I was contacted in Los Angeles by a radio talk show host named Carole Hemingway. I had done her program a number of times and had apparently been sufficiently weird for her vast audience to ask for return engagements. Several of these listeners remarked on my having written new stories in bookstore windows and mentioned that I had even written a story over the radio for the Pacifica outlet here in L.A. She was intrigued, and asked me if I would repeat the act on her show.

But with the enormous number of commercial interruptions on her show, it was obvious to me that even with a two-hour format, I wouldn't be able to write anything coherent and still be able to carry on a conversation. So an alternate *modus operandi* was devised. She would announce my forthcoming appearance for a number of days preceding, and as early as possible on the morning of the day I was to be her guest, she would call me and give me a specific thing she wanted me to write about. I would take that situation or plot-element or *whatever* and write the story that day, completely that day, and have it ready to read when we went on the air at 8:00 P.M.

Well, one should never rely on non-writers for this kind of thing. She didn't call till one in the afternoon, and when she did, her idea of an original idea to use as impetus for the story was this: "Write a story about a female talk show host." I think I groaned. Not only was it incredibly banal and self-serving, but it had been so many years since I'd done any radio interviewing myself, I wasn't sure I could write it with any degree of verisimilitude. But I accepted the challenge and sat down and started plotting. In a few minutes I had the basic idea and started typing "Flop Sweat."

In the course of typing as fast as I could (I do 120 words a minute on an Olympia office manual, two fingers only), I found I needed some data I didn't have here in my library. So I called her liaison at the station, Fred Harris, and asked him to describe the physical setup of the broadcast booth, how many and what kinds of telephone lines they had (it's a call-in show), and how many commercials per minute. And more. That kind of stuff.

The dominant news story during that period here in Los Angeles was, if you'll remember, the mystery of the Hillside Strangler. I decided to use that as one of the basic elements in the piece, and I sat here writing the story wih Ms.

Hemingway's station blasting away so I'd get the cadence of talk-to-commercials that would make the story read realistically.

I wrote all day, and by 7:30 that night had completed 4500 words, wasting myself in the process. But I then had to shower, get dressed (I'd been working in a bathrobe all day), get in the car, and drive all the way across Los Angeles to the station. The show went on the Los Angeles ABC affiliate, KABC, at 8:00. Fortunately, the top of the hour is given over to a five minute news roundup that's fed from ABC New York. That was all the slack time I needed. In the car, speeding at eighty mph down the Santa Monica Freeway, I heard Carole Hemingway on the car radio saying, "Harlan Ellison isn't here yet, but as you listeners know, he's a most unusual person, and I'm sure he'll rush into the control booth at any moment."

Which is what happened. I dashed into KABC–AM at 8:16 P.M. and proceeded to scare the shit out of many thousands of radio listeners with the story you're about to read.

So the explanation of why a story written and performed on December 21, 1977, appears in a collection of the best fantasies of 1979 is simply that to protect the story for its world premiere reading, it had to be copyright at that time. But when I sold it for publication to *Heavy Metal* magazine, it didn't appear in print until March 1979, even though it bore the 1977 copyright.

Which ought to get Terry Carr off the hook. On the other hand, perhaps I'm just lying, having made all of this lunacy up on the spur of the moment; in which case my friend Terry is still suspect. Ah me. Ain't Life difficult! But then, as I'm fond of saying, if Life were easy, everybody'd be doing it.

—HARLAN ELLISON
Los Angeles
4 January 1980

FLOP SWEAT

Harlan Ellison

HER FIRST GUEST OF THE EVENING SAT across the table from her, there in the tiny broadcast booth, staring at her with unreadable green eyes showing through the mask. She was dead certain he was crazy as a thousand battlefields; but he was, without a doubt, one of the best interviews she'd ever had on the program. She knew it without a doubt because her hands were soaking wet with perspiration, and her upper lip above the glossed line of Ultima II was dewy with sweat.

When she had been in the theater, in the years before she had found that hosting a talk show was easier and steadier work, she had come to understand what the perspiration meant. In show biz they called it "flop sweat," the physical manifestation of nervousness just before going on stage. And during the seven years here at KDID the flop sweat had dampened her palms and upper lip every time she'd had a dynamite show. It was a certain barometer of something happening.

But to call this strange man, dressed all in black, wearing a cheap K-Mart domino mask, the kind children wear at Halloween, a "happening" was to fling oneself face-forward into understatement. Brother Michael Darkness was more than a happening; he was a force of nature, a powerful presence, a disturbing reality; even if he was obviously a certifiable nut-case, a card-carrying whacko, a psychotic in the top one-tenth of the top percentile of emotional walking woundeds with whom she shared air-space.

"Reverend Darkness," she said, "it's almost the top of the hour, and we have to break now for the network news, but—"

"*Brother* Darkness," he said, cutting her off.

She was nonplussed for a moment. His voice. It had the deep, warm, musky timbre of secrets whispered in dark rooms. When he spoke she thought of a stick of butter, squeezed through a fist. "Yes, of course; I'm sorry. You've told me several times you're not a minister. I'll try to remember, *Brother* Darkness." He nodded politely. She could not read his expression around the mask. He disturbed her fluid ease behind the mike. That didn't happen very often. Seven years at this gig had made her almost unflappable. "What I was about to suggest, Brother Darkness, is that we break for the news and you come back for the second hour of the show. My next guest is Dr. Jacob Theiss, a very well known psychiatrist who works with the Los Angeles police; he'll be coming on to talk about this epidemic of razor-blade killings . . . and I think some of what you've been saying about evil in our times might be very interesting to have him comment on."

"I'd be pleased to stay, Miss Ketchum."

The way he said it, made Theresa Ketchum almost regret she had suggested it. He made his acceptance sound as if they had entered into some kind of unholy alliance. But she signaled to Jerry, the engineer in the control room, and he turned up the network feed pot, and the news rushed in with drums and trumpets and the voice of the sixty-thousand-dollar-a-year announcer from New York.

Now she was alone with Brother Darkness. The on-air studio in which they sat was a claustrophobic box, fifteen by ten, with two windowed walls: one side looked into the control room; the other looked into the waiting room where Millie sat taking and screening phone calls from the general public. The studio seemed somehow smaller than usual, and throat-cloggingly filled with menace. And it had started out being such a *lovely* day.

She took off her earphones and racked them. She stood up, smoothing her skirt, and was suddenly aware of Brother Darkness looking at her not as a dispassionate "communicaster," but as an attractive woman, thirty-four years old, body tanned and well toned from afternoons at the Beverly Hills Health Club, nose bobbed exquisitely by Dr. Parks, auburn hair coddled and cozened just so at

Jon Peters' parlor in the Valley. She had a momentary flash of regret at not having worn something bulky and concealing. The blouse was too sheer, the skirt too tight, the whole image too provocative. But she had dressed for *after* the broadcast, for the party CBS was hosting that night at the Bonaventure to promote its new mid-season sitcom. The party at which she would use the sensual good looks, the tanned and well-toned body, the exquisite nose and brushfire hair to play some ingratiating politics; to move herself out of a seven-year rut on local talk radio and into a network job. Dressing with care this afternoon, before coming into the station, she had given no thought to the effect on her guests, only to how she would present herself at the party. Attention where it mattered.

But Brother Michael Darkness was staring at her the way men stared at her in the Polo Lounge or in the meat-rack pickup bar of the Rangoon Racquet Club. And she wished she were wearing a kaftan, a fur-lined parka, a severe three-piece tweed pantsuit.

"Would you like a cup of coffee?" She heard her voice coming thickly and distantly. Not at all the liquid honey tone she used as the trademark of an audial sex object when broadcasting.

"No thank you, Miss Ketchum. I'll just sit here, if that's all right."

She nodded. "Yes, of course. That'll be fine. I'll go get Dr. Theiss and be right back. We have five minutes before we're back on the air." And she escaped into the corridor quickly, finding herself leaning against the sea-green wall and breathing very deeply.

Over the station speakers in the hall the newscaster was headlining the Los Angeles razor-blade slayings, commenting on the discovery that morning of an eleventh young woman, nude and with throat sliced open, in the bushes near the Silverlake off-ramp of the Hollywood Freeway. She heard the voice, but paid no attention.

She stepped into the waiting room beside the studio. Jake Theiss was leaning against the wall sipping coffee from a paper cup. The telephone switchboard was lit from one end to the other, all ten lines strobing with urgency. Millie looked up from the log and rolled her eyes. "Jesus, Terri, you've got a live one tonight. They're crawling down the wires to talk to him."

She felt her heart racing. "Keep the best ones on hold; I'll try to get to them after I introduce Jake."

Then she turned to Jake Theiss, who smiled at her, and it was as if someone had returned her stolen security blanket. He had been on the show a dozen times before, and they had even gone out several evenings. His mere presence reassured her.

"Theresa," he said, stepping away from the wall and taking her hand, "you look a trifle whiplashed."

She hugged him and kissed his cheek. "My God, Jake, have you been *listening* to him?"

The psychiatrist nodded slowly. "I have indeed. But it's not so much *what* he says, as the way he says it. A little de Sade, a little Gilles de Rais, echoes of Proterius, a smidgeon of Cotton Mather and some direct quotes from the *Evangelium Nicodemi,* if memory serves well. All made contemporary by the addition of Jung, Freud, Adler and Werner Erhard's look-out-for-number-one. Nothing particularly spectacular there; most modern demonologists plunder the same bag. But your Brother Michael in there has a sense of the dramatic, and a voice to match, and a nasty way of bringing in current events that . . . well . . . I can't say I'm looking forward to sharing a microphone with him."

She drew a deep breath. "Jake, *stop it!* This flake does a good enough job scaring the hell out of me on his own. I mean, it's like *Exorcist* time in there. When he starts talking about the return of the devils I swear to God I can *feel* the slimy things in that booth. And I never thought a kid's Halloween mask could chill me, but each time he looks at me with those green eyes I feel every part of my body trying to run away and leave my head behind."

Millie handed her a Kleenex from the box. "Your lip," she said. Theresa took the tissue and blotted herself.

"Okay, don't worry about it," Jake said, setting down the empty coffee cup. "I'll come on like the voice of rationality."

She smiled wanly, feeling like a fool. This was hardly professional behavior.

They walked back into the on-air studio just as the news was ending. Theresa moved to the console and flipped the toggle switch on the intercom. "Jerry, let's do the Southern California Buick Dealers, Pacific Telephone and Roto-Rooter. Is there a live tag on the Roto-Rooter commercial?"

The tinny voice of Jerry from the other side of the control room glass filled the booth. "Yeah. Ten seconds."

He ran up the cartridges and for a moment, before she turned down the sound in the booth, the Buick announcer's voice filled the air. When she turned back to her guests, Jake Theiss had already seated himself at the empty third mike, to the right of her swivel chair. She drew a deep breath and sat down. "Jake, this is Brother Michael Darkness; Brother Darkness, Dr. Jacob Theiss." She watched them shake hands. She studied Jake's face closely, but if he reacted to the touch of Brother Michael's hand, as she had reacted the first time he had touched her, the *only* time he had touched her, earlier that evening, the psychiatrist concealed the fact. Jake did not shiver. He smiled at Brother Michael and said, "I've been listening to the interview. Pretty strong medicine for a lay audience just around dinnertime, wouldn't you say?"

Brother Michael's face was impassive. "If you think I'm a fraud, Dr. Theiss, why not just come out with it. Mendacity is unappealing in someone who professes to being a man of science. Even such an alleged science as the study of the mind."

Theresa's heart beat faster. It was as though she had just received two separate and powerful electrical shocks, so close together they seemed one: outrage and fear at the antagonism of the man in black, which might lead in a (moment) to a thrown punch; and delight at the instant animus between Jake and the Brother, guaranteeing a controversial second hour for the show. She hated herself for feeling pleasure, but it was always this way when something terrible but promotable happened on the show.

"I didn't know you also read minds, Brother Darkness," Jake said, swallowing the affront. "If I wanted to call you a fraud, I'd certainly wait till we were on the air."

Brother Michael's tone softened. He knew he wasn't going to get a fight. Not now, at any rate. "I'm pleased to know you recognize the apocryphal texts. Too few practitioners of what you call 'the healing arts' familiarize themselves with the black documents of antiquity."

Theresa was lost.

"I beg your pardon, what do you mean?" Jake said.

"I mean: you were correct in recognizing my quote from the *Evangelium Nicodemi.*"

A chill spread its web across Theresa's back. Jake had said that in the waiting room. How could Brother Michael have heard it? She reached over and flipped the toggle for Millie. "Did we leave the intercom feed open?" Millie shook her head no. Theresa stared at her through the glass. The chill spread deeper and farther. She looked at Jake with confusion.

He caught the look. "A condemned document dating from the third century. It describes Christ's descent into hell and a session of Satan's sanhedrin, his court."

The Roto-Rooter jingle was just ending, and Theresa held up a hand for silence as she riffled through the sheaf of tags for commercials and simultaneously punched the square red button that gave her a live microphone.

"So say good-bye forever to clogged drains caused by those tree roots that've grown into pipes. Get to the *root* of your problem by calling your Roto-Rooter service representative. . . ." She conversationalized the written tag, reading it with warmth and friendly understatement, but all the while keeping her eye on her guests.

"Well, we're back with Brother Michael Darkness, the head of the Euchite Sect, a group we're told has no affiliation with any orthodox or recognized religious denomination; a man who says he represents those who believe in the return of the dark forces that once ruled the Earth. And we're being joined now by Dr. Jacob Theiss, M.D., Ph.D., a member of the governing board of the American Psychiatric Association, he's on the staff at the UCLA Medical Center, and the winner of many prestigious awards in the field of human behavior. Dr. Theiss, have you been listening to the interview so far?"

"Yes, Theresa. And I'm most intrigued by Brother Darkness and what he's been saying. But I think you're mistaken when you say that the Euchites are an unrecognized sect.

"Brother Darkness, correct me if I'm wrong, but weren't the Euchites an early Christian sect who believed that each man had a congenital devil that could be expelled only by constant prayer? They were supposed to have repudiated the sacraments and moral law, to have worshiped Lucifer as the oldest son of the Creator, isn't that right? About twelfth century, if I remember correctly."

Brother Michael leaned forward till his face almost touched the microphone. "Very good, Dr. Theiss. I'm

123

pleased and surprised at your erudition. Quite correct, on every point."

"And you're reviving this sect here in Los Angeles, in the middle of The Age of Plastic?"

"When better? The time is right."

"What do you mean by that?" Theresa said.

"Just look around," Brother Michael said softly. "Everywhere a belief in the irrational and the obscure takes greater hold daily. Films tell us we are being watched by aliens from other worlds or that demons infest the night; there is a frenzied rush to believe in astrology, in demonology and assassination conspiracies, in superstition and magic: we seek messiahs on all sides; Atlantis, the Bermuda Triangle, lost worlds at the center of the earth, spirits speaking from the grave; Eastern mysticism . . . they dominate our every waking moment and plunge through our dreams at night. Do you think this is accidental? No, I'm sure you don't. You may be confused and frightened by it all, but in some secret part of your mind and your soul you understand that is the first clarion call of the ancient devils, come again to rule us. As is only right and proper."

And they were off. Theresa barely had time to get in the live commercials required by the log and the FCC. She had to run them in clusters, knowing her listeners were pounding furiously on the busy telephone lines. Jake and the Brother went at it fiercely, with Jake trying to hold a line of logic and sanity against the ferocious dynamics of Brother Darkness's statements.

The first of the calls came in at twenty after the hour.

"Okay, let's take a break from this for a moment," Theresa said. "Wheeew! You two make my head spin. Let's hear what our listeners have to say. Dr. Theiss, Brother Darkness, if you'll use those headsets you'll be able to hear the caller. Okay. Hello, this is Theresa Ketchum and you're on KDID talk radio. Who's this?"

The voice that came across the line was strangely unisexual, neither male nor female, identifiable neither as young nor old. It seemed to be coming from a great distance, though it was clear and precise. "This is someone all of Los Angeles wants to know," the voice said. "I'm responsible for the razor-blade cleansings. You call them slayings, but I assure you, they're cleansings."

Through the glass, Millie's face filled with horror.

She grabbed for the private line and dialed. Theresa

saw her frantic movements and knew at once she was dialing the police emergency number, 911. Thank God Millie was on tonight, and not Charlie, who was so slow on the uptake that he often patched through rambling dingbats.

"Come on, whoever you are," Theresa said, stalling for time so the police could trace back across the phone company's machinery to the line on which this self-proclaimed killer was speaking, "we know there are enough cuckoos out there who like to confess to crimes to fill The Forum. Why should we believe you're the razor-blade killer?"

"It isn't necessary that you believe. But here's a bit of information the police have been holding back: when I perform my cleansing operations, I always cut a pentacle into the sole of the left foot of my sacrifices."

He went on speaking, but Theresa saw Jake signaling her frantically. She hit the green button killing the live mike, and Jake gasped, "It's him! Or her! I can't tell which! But that's even been kept out of the coroner's reports."

"How do you know?"

"For God's sake, Terri. I'm *working* with the LAPD on this! It's the killer, I tell you!"

She punched the mike to life. "Why are you calling us?"

The voice went on carefully, very steadily, "I just wanted to say it would serve you to listen to what Brother Darkness is saying. He's right you know."

The most violent reaction came from Brother Michael Darkness. He grabbed the boom on the mike and pulled the instrument to him. "Whoever you are . . . you've got to stop this . . . it's awful . . . it's not right . . . you're a sick person. . . ."

But the line went dead. The dial tone came over the open mike.

They sat there in silence, knowing that all over Los Angeles pandemonium was gripping the thousands of listeners to this program; knowing that if the station management was listening, they were already calling in on the private lines to find out why the 4½-second time-delay intercept hadn't been used; knowing that the police were on their way to the station; knowing that out there somewhere a lunatic was being primed to kill again. Surely that was what this portended. Another slaughter.

She didn't know what to say. For the first time in seven years she was too terrified and too stunned to let her sense of theatrics override her shock. But Jake had already jumped in.

"Brother Michael, do you know that person?"

"I swear to you, I have never heard that voice. I don't want you to think that my beliefs or the sect I represent have anything to do with murder."

"But that person, male or female I can't tell which, that person says your doctrine is correct. That speaker was an adherent of what you profess. *Now* do you see what your insane, your profane doctrine leads to? Chaos! Lunacy! It makes it all right for madmen to kill innocent people!"

And Millie was waving frantically from the other side of the glass, signaling Theresa to pick up line three.

She punched up line three and started to say, "You're on KDID talk radio . . ." but the voice from the night came once again. "Don't try to trace me; you'll have no luck. I just want you to know that it all begins and ends tonight."

Theresa heard herself gasp, and then she barely managed to say, "What do you mean?"

And the voice said, "It's all coming together tonight. Have you looked out at the moon. It's full tonight. And everything you people believe, all the mad things, all the terrible things, all the things Brother Darkness calls 'the irrational' come together. Belief in the dark things, the ancient fears, the crazy things you all believe in your souls *really* move the universe . . . all of it has become strong enough for the end of my cleansing labors . . . and the beginning of the Apocalypse."

And the mike went dead again.

Theresa cut in Millie's intercom. "Where did that come from?"

Millie was crying. "That was line three, from Orange County. But the first one was an LA line. It can't be!"

Jake's face was white with fear. "Oh, my God," he said, very quietly, the words trembling with terror.

Brother Michael was babbling, saying over and over, "I had nothing to do with it, nothing . . . I don't know him . . . I swear I didn't mean any harm. . . ."

And as the hour wore to a close, there were two more calls. One on a line from Long Beach, the other on a line originating in Glendale. It was impossible for anyone to get from one of those far areas to another in the space of minutes; yet it was the same voice, and it happened.

And when the police came they took Brother Michael

away. And Jake went with them, to help coordinate the mobilization of every available cop in the city. And when the hour ended Theresa was left sitting in the booth, shaking with terror.

Party tonight? No, not possible. No party tonight. Perhaps no party *any* night. That voice, the calm in the words, the certainty. Tonight: the Apocalypse. And one word from the razor-blade killer's last message: Armageddon. The final battle between good and evil, the last battle between the forces of the Creator and the dark demons who had been banished before man walked the earth.

"Terri, I'm going home now."

It was Millie's voice from the other side of the glass. The control room was empty. Jerry had gone. Theresa looked up dazedly, nodded once, and tried to rise. She found she had lost the strength to leave this terrible little box, at least for the moment. "Go ahead, Millie; I'll see you tomorrow." She let her hand lie on the console after releasing the toggle. Millie left.

She knew there were other people in the building. In other studios, KDID was carrying on; even in the face of what had gone out over the air tonight. She found that she was too frightened to leave, to go out through the corridors, past the security desk, into the parking lot with its high wire fence, to get into her car all alone, and to drive across town to her apartment. No. She would stay here. Safe in the booth. Locked away from whatever might happen tonight.

There was a faint light in the empty control room.

She looked through the glass, strained forward to see what it was, moving toward her. A faint purple light, soft and blurred, like a fading bruise on battered flesh. And now another light, in the glass of the waiting room on the other side of the studio. She stared from one to another, watching them moving slowly toward the glass partitions. Now another light in the control room. And another. Two more in the waiting room.

There was a rumbling beneath her feet. The studio trembled with the reverberation of an impact in the earth. Through the soundproof walls came the dull roar of explosions. Temblors rippled the floor; the vinyl tiles buckled around her feet.

The faint lights moved closer. Figures coming toward the glass. Stopping to stare in at her. Figures in long black garments, with drawn cowls that covered their faces. And strange, sickly purple light, the faintest, most terrible glow, shining out from beneath the cowls. They stared in at her. She could see no eyes: but they were staring in at her.

They raised their arms slightly, slowly, and the sleeves of their black robes fell back revealing their hands. Theresa found that she could not breathe, that her chest was convulsing with the pain of her wildly beating heart.

Their fingers did not end in flesh. Metal. Sharp, cold metal; thin and final. This was the answer to how phone calls from the same person could come from distant sources.

There was the sound of movement just outside the door of the studio. The walls shook with the echoes of the cataclysm outside. The roaring was louder now.

And in the moment before the door opened she had the final, petrifying thought that she had been part of it all, had spread the doctrine of irrationality and superstition every night for seven years, had given a platform to every demented True Believer whose wild fantasies might build her audience.

And now her worshipers had come to sacrifice their very own prophet. She felt cold and dead already, could feel the chill slice of the thin, metal fingertips. Her palms were soaked with sweat in expectation of the final performance.

The door opened, and they filed in to fill the studio. They stood staring at her as she felt her life clog up in her throat and arteries. They raised their arms and the sleeves fell back from pale flesh and metal fingertips. She waited for the first touch.

And they sank to their knees, lifting their arms in supplication. She began to tremble with the rictus of a scream shaking her like a fever. Now she knew the worst, now she understood.

She was not to die. She had broadcast the word for them, every night for seven years, and she was not to die. She would be their dark priestess. Like the others who had done their spadework, like the others who had spread the word, she was to be kept alive; perhaps forever.

Dark priestess in a world of desolation, ruled by devils, cleansed of humanity. She would not die!

More ruinous than death: to rule forever in Hell. Lovelessly alive; worshiped by eaters of the darkness. To live on, coated always with a cold sweat, through a final performance that had no curtain, no exit lines.

Her scream could have shattered glass, but it didn't; it merely resonated against the metal fingertips of her subjects, her masters.

From the burning world beyond the studio came the wind whisper of the plague of locusts.

~~~~~~

When you're in love, time seems to stop, you step outside reality, all things become possible. Maybe that's literally true, at least sometimes. If you found it had become true for you, perhaps you'd act as do the lovers in this story. (But maybe reality is better.)

Walter Tevis is the author of *The Hustler* and *The Man Who Fell to Earth*, both of which were made into successful movies. His latest novel, *Mockingbird*, is another science fiction extrapolation.

RENT CONTROL

Walter Tevis

"MY GOD," EDITH SAID, "THAT WAS THE MOST *real* experience of my life." She put her arms around him, put her cheek against his bare chest, and pulled him tightly to her. She was crying.

He was crying, too. "Me, too, darling," he said, and he held his arms around her. They were in the loft bed of her studio apartment on the East Side. They had just had orgasms together. Now they were sweaty, relaxed, blissful. It had been a perfect day.

Their orgasms had been foreshadowed by their therapy. That evening, after supper, they had gone to Harry's group as always on Wednesdays, and somehow everything had focused for them. He had at last shouted the heartfelt anger he bore against his incompetent parents; she had screamed her hatred of her sadistic mother, her gutless father. And their relief had come together there on the floor of a New York psychiatrist's office. After the screaming and pounding of fists, after the real and potent old rage in both of them was spent, their smiles at each other were radiant. They went afterwards to her apartment, where they had lived together half a year, climbed up the ladder into her bed, and began to make love slowly, carefully. Then frenetically. They were picked up bodily by it and carried to a place where they had never been before.

Now, afterward, they were settling down in that place, huddled together. They lay silently for a long time. Idly she looked toward the ledge next to the mattress, where

132

she kept cigarettes, a mason jar with miniature roses, a Japanese ashtray, and an alarm clock.

"The clock must have stopped," she said.

He mumbled something inarticulate. His eyes were closed.

"It says nine-twenty," she said, "and we left Harry's at nine."

"Hmmm," he said, without interest.

She was silent for a while, musing. Then she said, "Terry, what time does your watch say?"

"Time time," he said. "Watch watch." He shifted his arm and looked. "Nine-twenty," he said.

"Is the second hand moving?" she asked. His watch was an Accutron, not given to being wrong or stopping.

He looked again. "Nope. Not moving." He let his hand fall on her naked behind, now cool to his touch. Then he said, "That is funny. Both stopping at once." He leaned over her body toward the window, pried open a space in her Levolor blinds, and looked out. It was dark outside, with an odd shimmer to the air. Nothing was moving. There was a pile of plastic garbage bags on the sidewalk opposite. "It can't be eleven yet. They haven't taken the garbage from the Toreador." The Toreador was a Spanish restaurant across the street; they kept promising they would eat there sometime but never did.

"It's probably about ten-thirty," she said. "Why don't you make us an omelet and turn the TV on? Make mine with cheddar. And three eggs."

"Sure, honey," he said. He slipped on his bikini briefs and eased himself down the ladder. Barefoot, he went to the tiny Sony near the fireplace, turned it on, and padded over to the stove and sink at the other end of the room. He heard the TV come on as he located the omelet pan, which he had bought her, under the sink, nestling between the Bon Ami and the Windex. He got eggs out, cracked one, looked at his watch. It was running. It said nine-twenty-six. "Hey, honey," he called out. "My watch is running."

After a pause she said, her voice slightly hushed, "So is the clock up here."

He shrugged and put butter in the pan and finished cracking the eggs, throwing the shells into the sink. He whipped the eggs with a fork, then turned on the fire under the pan and walked back to the Sony for a moment.

A voice was saying, ". . . nine-thirty." He looked at his watch. Nine-thirty. *"Jesus Christ!"* he exclaimed.

But he had forgotten about it by the time he cooked the omelets. His omelets had been from the beginning one of the things that made them close. He had learned to cook them before leaving his wife, and it meant independence to him. He made omelets beautifully—tender and moist—and Edith was impressed. They had fallen in love over omelets, had called themselves the Cholesterol Kids, eating them after making love, eating them on Sundays. He cooked lamb chops, too, and bought things like frozen cappelletti from expensive shops, but omelets were central.

They were both thirty-five years old, both youthful, good-looking, smart. They were both Pisces, with birthdays three days apart. Both had good complexions, healthy dark hair, clear eyes. They both bought clothes at Bergdorf Goodman and Saks and Bloomingdale's; they both read the Sunday *Times,* spoke fair French, and watched *Nova,* and each had read *The Stories of John Cheever.* He was a magazine illustrator, she a lawyer; they could have afforded a bigger place, but her studio was rent-controlled and had a terrific Midtown address. It was too much of a bargain to give up. *"Nobody* ever leaves a rent-controlled apartment," she told him. So they lived in one and a half rooms together, and money piled up in their bank accounts.

They were terribly nervous lovers at first, too unsure of everything to enjoy it, full of explanations and self-recriminations. He had trouble staying hard; she would not lubricate and could excite herself only with his hands on her. She was afraid of him and made love dutifully, often with resentment. He was embarrassed by his unreliable member, sensed her withdrawal from his ardor, was afraid to tell her so. Often they were miserable.

But she had the good sense to take him to her therapist, and he had the good sense to go. Finally, after six months of private sessions and of group, it had worked. They had had the perfect orgasm, the perfect release from tension, the perfect intimacy.

Now they ate their omelets in bed from Spode plates, using his mother's silver forks. Sea salt and Java pepper. Their legs were entwined as they ate.

They lay silent for a while afterwards. He looked out the window. The garbage was still there; there was no movement in the street; no one was on the sidewalk. There was a flatness to the way the light shone on the buildings across from them, as if they were painted—some kind of a backdrop.

He looked at his watch. It said nine-forty-one. The second hand wasn't moving. "Shit!" he said, puzzled.

"What's that, honey?" Edith said. "Did I do something wrong?"

"No, sweetie," he said. "You're the best thing that ever happened. I'm crazy about you." He patted her ass with one hand and gave her his empty plate with the other.

She set the two plates on the ledge, which was barely wide enough for them. She glanced at the clock. "Jesus," she said, "that sure is strange . . ."

"Let's go to sleep," he said. "I'll explain the theory of relativity in the morning."

But when he woke up, it wasn't morning. He felt refreshed, thoroughly rested; he had the sense of a long and absolutely silent sleep, with no noises intruding from the world outside, no dreams, no complications. He had never felt better.

When he looked out the window, the light from the streetlamp was the same and the garbage bags were still piled in front of the Toreador and—he saw now—what appeared to be the same taxi stood motionless in front of the same green station wagon in the middle of Fifty-first Street. He looked at his watch. It said nine-forty-one.

Edith was still asleep, on her belly, with one arm across his waist, her hip against his. Not waking her, he pulled away and started to climb down from the bed. On an impulse he looked again at his watch. It was nine-forty-one still, but now the second hand was moving.

He reached out and turned the electric clock on the ledge to where he could see its face. It said nine-forty-one also, and when he held it to his ear, he could hear its gears turning quietly inside. His heart began to beat stronger, and he found himself catching his breath.

He climbed down and went to the television set and turned it on again. The same face appeared as before he had slept, wearing the same oversized glasses, the same bland smile.

Terry turned the sound up, seated himself on the sofa, lit a cigarette, and waited.

It seemed a long time before the news program ended and a voice said, "It's ten o'clock."

He looked at his watch. It said ten o'clock. He looked out the window; it was dark—evening. There was no way it could be ten in the morning. But he knew he had slept a whole night. He knew it. His hand holding the second cigarette was trembling.

Slowly and carefully he put out his cigarette, then climbed back up the ladder to the loft bed. Edith was still asleep. Somehow he knew what to do. He laid his hand on her leg and looked at his watch. As he touched her the second hand stopped. For a long moment he did not breathe.

Still holding her leg, he looked out the window. This time there was a group of people outside; they had just left the restaurant. None of them moved. The taxi had gone and with it the station wagon, but the garbage was still there. One of the people from the Toreador was in the process of putting on his raincoat. One arm was in a sleeve and the other wasn't. There was a frown on his face visible from the third-story apartment where Terry lay looking at him. Everything was frozen. The light was peculiar, unreal. The man's frown did not change.

Terry let go of Edith, and the man finished putting on his coat. Two cars drove by in the street. The light became normal.

Terry touched Edith again, this time laying his hand gently on her bare back. Outside the window everything stopped, as when a switch is thrown on a projector to arrest the movement. Terry let out his breath audibly. Then he said, "Wake up, Edith. I've got something to show you."

They never understood it, and they told nobody. It was relativity, they decided. They had found, indeed, a perfect place together, where subjective time raced and the external world stood entirely still.

It did not work anywhere but in her loft bed—and only when they touched. They could stay together there for hours or days, although there was no way they could tell how long the "time" had really been; they could make love, sleep, read, talk, and no time passed whatever.

They discovered, after a while, that only if they quarreled did it fail, and then the clock and watch would run even though they were touching. It required intimacy, even of a slight kind—the intimacy of casual touching for it to work.

They adapted their lives to it quickly, and at first it extended their sense of life's possibilities enormously. It bathed them in a perfection of the lovers' sense of being apart from the rest of the world and better than it.

Their careers improved; they had more time for work and for play than anyone else had. If one of them was ever under serious pressure—of job competition, of the need to make a quick decision—one could get the other in bed and they would have all the time necessary to decide, to think up the speech, to plan the magazine cover, or to review the details of the case going to trial.

Sometimes they took what they called Weekends, buying and cooking enough food for five or six meals, and just staying in the loft bed, touching, while reading or meditating or making love or working. He had his art supplies in shelves over the bed now, and she had reference books and note pads on the ledge. He had put mirrors on two of the walls and on the ceiling, partly for sex, partly to make the small place seem bigger, less confining.

The food was always hot, unspoiled; no time had passed for it between their meals. They could not watch television or listen to records while in suspended time; no machinery worked while they touched.

Sometimes for fun they would watch people out the window and stop and start them up again comically, but that soon grew tiresome.

They both got richer and richer, earning promotions and higher pay, and the low rent helped them to save plenty of money. Of course there was now truly no question of leaving the apartment; there was no other bed in which they could stop time—no other place.

For about a year they would always stay later at parties than anyone else; they would taunt acquaintances and colleagues when they were too tired to accompany them to all-night places for scrambled eggs or a final drink. Sometimes they annoyed colleagues by showing up bright-eyed and rested in the morning, no matter how late the party had gone on, no matter how many drinks had been drunk, no matter how loud and fatiguing the revelry. They were always buoyant, healthy, awake, and just a bit smug.

But after the first year they tired of partying, grew bored with friends, and went out less often. Somehow they had come to a place that they were never bored with,

Edith referred to it as "our little loft bed." The center of their lives had become a king-sized foam mattress with a foot-wide ledge and a few inches of head and foot room at each end. They were never bored when in that small space.

What they had to learn was not to quarrel, not to lose the modicum of intimacy that their relativity phenomenon required. But that came easily, too; without discussing it, each learned to give only a small part of self to intimacy with the other, to cultivate a state of mind that was distant, remote enough to be safe from conflict, yet with a controlled closeness. They practiced yoga for body and spirit and Transcendental Meditation. They never told each other their mantra. Often they found themselves staring at different mirrors. Now they seldom looked out the window.

It was Edith who made the second major discovery. One day when Terry was in the bathroom shaving, and his watch was running, he heard her shout to him, in a kind of cool playfulness. "Quit dawdling in there, Terry. I'm getting older for nothing." There was some kind of urgency in her voice, and he caught it. He rinsed his face off in a hurry, dried, and walked to the bedroom. "What do you mean?" he asked.

She didn't look at him. "Get on up here, Dum-dum," she said, still in that controlled, playful voice. "I want you to touch me."

He climbed up and laid a hand on her shoulder. Outside the window a walking man froze in mid-stride and the sunlight darkened as if a shutter had been placed over it.

"What do you mean, 'older for nothing'?" he asked.

She looked at him thoughtfully. "It's been about five years now, in the real world," she replied. The "real world" for them meant the time lived by other people. "But we must have spent five years in suspended time here in bed. More than that. And we haven't been aged by it."

He looked at her. "How could . . . ?"

"I don't know," she said. "But I know we're not any older than anybody else."

He turned toward the mirror at her feet and stared at himself in it. He was still youthful, firm, clearcomplexioned. Suddenly he smiled, at himself. "Maybe I can fix it so I can shave in bed."

Their Weekends became longer. Although they could not measure their special time, the number of times they slept and the times they made love could be counted; both those numbers increased once they realized the time in bed together was "free"—that they did not age while touching in the loft bed, while the world outside was motionless and the sun neither rose nor set.

Sometimes they would pick a time of day and a quality of light they both liked, and they'd stop their time there: at twilight, with empty streets and a soft ambience of light. They would allow for the slight darkening effect, and then they'd touch and stay touching for eight or ten sleeping periods, six or eight orgasms, fifteen meals.

They had stopped the omelets because of the real time it took to prepare them. Now they bought pizzas and prepared chickens and ready-made desserts and quarts of milk and coffee and bottles of good wine and cartons of cigarettes and cases of Perrier water, and they filled shelves at each side of the window with them. The hot food would never cool as long as Edith and Terry were touching each other in the controlled intimacy they now had learned as second nature. They could look at themselves in their own mirror and not even think about the other in a conscious way, but if their fingertips were so much as touching, as if the remote sense of the other was unruffled by anger or anxiety, then the pizzas on the shelf would remain hot, the Perrier cold, the vehicles in the street motionless, and the sky and weather without change forever. No love was needed now, no feeling whatever—only the lack of unpleasantness and the slightest of physical contact.

The world outside became less interesting for them. They both had large bank accounts, and both had high-level yet undemanding jobs; her legal briefs were prepared by assistants; three young men in his studio made the illustrations that he designed, on drawing pads, in the loft bed. Often the nights were a terrible bore, and they had to let go of each other if they wanted morning to come —just so they could go to work, a change of pace.

But less and less did either of them want the pace to change. Each had learned to spend "hours" motionless, staring at a mirror or out of the window, preserving his or her youth against the ravages of real time and real movement. Each became obsessed, without sharing the obsession, with a single idea: immortality. They could live forever, young and healthy and fully awake, in this loft bed. There was no question of interestingness or of boredom; they had moved, deeply in their separate souls, far beyond that distinction, that rhythm of life. Deep in themselves they had become a pharaoh's dream of endless time; they had found the pyramid that kept the flow of the world away.

One autumn morning that had been like two weeks for them he looked at her, after waking, and said, "I don't want to leave this place. I don't want to get old."

She looked at him before she spoke. Then she said, "There's nothing I want to do outside."

He looked away from her, smiling. "We'll need a lot of food," he said.

They had already had the apartment filled with shelves, and a bathroom was installed beneath the bed. Using the bathroom was the only concession to real time; to make the water flow, it was necessary for them not to touch.

They filled the shelves that autumn afternoon with hundreds of pounds of food—cheeses and hot chickens and sausages and milk and butter and big loaves of bread and precooked steaks and pork chops and hams and bowls of cooked vegetables, all prepared and delivered by a wondering caterer and five assistants. They had cases of wine and beer and cigarettes. It was like an efficient, miniature warehouse.

When they got into bed and touched, she said, "What if we quarrel? The food will all spoil."

"I know," he said. Taking a deep breath, he added, "What if we just don't talk?"

She looked at him for a long time. Then she said, "I've been thinking that, too."

So they stopped talking, and they turned toward their own mirror and thought of living forever, back to back, touching.

No friend found them, for they had no friends. But when the landlord came in through the empty shelves on what was for him the next day, he found them in the loft bed, back to back, each staring into a different mirror. They were perfectly beautiful, with healthy, clear complexions, youthful figures, dark and glistening hair. But they had no minds at all. They were not even like beautiful children; there was nothing there but prettiness.

The landlord was shocked at what he saw. But he recognized soon afterward that they would be sent somewhere and that he would be able to charge a profitable rent, at last, from someone new.

Strange things encountered in ordinary circumstances are usually even more frightening than they would be if we ran into them in dark old mansions: it's the difference between surprise and shock. But what if you're a calm, settled man who's studied phantasms long enough to be quite sure they're not real? In fact, imagine you're Fritz Leiber, and then . . . something happens.

Fritz Leiber has been a major writer of fantasy for forty years. His fantasy novels include *Conjure Wife* and *Our Lady of Darkness.*

THE BUTTON MOLDER

Fritz Leiber

I DON'T RIGHTLY KNOW IF I CAN CALL THIS figure I saw for a devastating ten seconds a ghost. And *heard* for about ten seconds just before that. These durations are of course to a degree subjective judgments. At the time they seemed to be lasting forever. Ten seconds can be long or short. A man can light a cigarette. A sprinter can travel a hundred yards, sound two miles, and light two million. A rocket can launch, or burn up inside. A city can fall down. It depends on what's happening.

The word "ghost," like "shade" or "wraith" or even "phantom," suggests human personality and identity, and what this figure had was in a way the antithesis of that. Perhaps "apparition" is better, because it ties it in with astronomy, which may conceivably be the case in a farfetched way. Astronomers speak of apparitions of the planet Mercury, just as they talk of spurious stars (novas) and occultations by Venus and the moon. Astronomy talk can sound pretty eerie, even without the help of any of the witching and romantic lingo of astrology.

But I rather like "ghost," for it lets me bring in the theory of the Victorian scholar and folklorist Andrew Lang that a ghost is simply a short waking dream in the mind of the person who thinks he sees one. He tells about it in his book *Dreams and Ghosts,* published in 1897. It's a praiseworthily simple and sober notion (also a very polite one, typically English!—"I'd never suggest you were lying about that ghost, old boy. But perhaps you dreamed it, not knowing you were dreaming?") And a theory easy to believe, especially if the person who sees the ghost is fatigued and under stress and the ghost something seen in the shadows of a dark doorway or a storm-lashed window at night or in the flickering flames of a dying fire or in the glooms of a dim room with faded tapestries or obscurely patterned wallpaper. Not so easy to credit for a figure seen fully illuminated for a double handful of long seconds by someone untired and under no physical strain, yet I find it a reassuring theory in my case. In fact, there are times when it strikes me as vastly preferable to certain other possibilities.

The happening occurred rather soon after I moved from one six-story apartment building to another in downtown San Francisco. There were a remarkable number of those put up in the decades following the quake and fire of 1906. A lot of them started as small hotels, but transformed to apartments as the supply of cheap menial labor shrank. You can usually tell those by their queer second floors, which began as mezzanines. The apartment I was moving from had an obvious one of those, lobby-balcony to the front, manager's apartment and some other tiny ones to the rear.

I'd been thinking about moving for a long time, because my one-room-and-bath was really too small for me and getting crammed to the ceiling with my files and books, yet I'd shrunk from the bother involved. But then an efficient, "savvy" manager was replaced by an ineffectual one, who had little English, or so pretended to save himself work, and the place rather rapidly got much too noisy. Hi-fi's thudded and thumped unrebuked until morning. Drunken parties overflowed into the halls and took to wandering about. Early on the course of deterioration the unwritten slum rule seemed to come into effect of "If you won't call the owner (or the cops) on me. I won't call him on you." (Why did I comply with this rule? I hate rows and asserting myself.) There was a flurry of mail box thefts and of stoned folk setting off the building's fire alarm out of curiosity, and of nodding acquaintances whose names you didn't know hitting you for small loans. Pets and stray animals multiplied—and left evidence of themselves, as did the drunks. There were more than the usual quota of overdosings and attempted suicides and incidents of breaking down doors (mostly by drunks who'd lost their keys) and series of fights that were, perhaps unfortunately, mostly racket, and at least one rape. In the end the halls came to be preferred for every sort of socializing. And if the police were at last summoned, it was generally just in time to start things up again when they'd almost quieted down.

I don't mind a certain amount of stupid noise and even hubbub. After all, it's my business to observe the human condition and report on it imaginatively. But when it comes to spending my midnight hours listening to two elderly male lovers shouting horrendous threats at each other in prison argot, repeatedly slamming doors on each other and maddeningly whining for them to be reopened, and stumbling up and down stairs menacing each other with a dull breadknife which is periodically wrested in slow-motion from hand to hand, I draw the line. More important, I am even able to summon up the energy to get myself away from the offensive scene forever.

My new apartment building, which I found much more easily than I'd expected to once I started to hunt, was an earthly paradise by comparison. The *occupants stayed out of the halls* and when forced to venture into them traveled as swiftly as was compatible with maximum quiet. The walls were thick enough so that I hadn't the faintest idea of what they did at home. The manager was a tower of resourceful efficiency, yet unobtrusive and totally uninquisitive. Instead of the clanking and groaning monster I'd been used to, the small elevator (I lived on six in both places) was a wonder of silent reliability. Twice a week the halls roared softly and briefly with a large vacuum cleaner wielded by a small man with bowed shoulders who never seemed to speak.

Here the queer second-floor feature hinting at hotel-origins took the form of three private offices (an architect's, a doctor's, and a CPA's), instead of front apartments, with stairway of their own shut off from the rest of the building, while the entire first floor except for the main entrance and its hall was occupied by a large fabrics or yard-goods store, which had in its display window an item that intrigued me mightily. It was a trim lay figure, life-size, made of ribbed white cotton material and stuffed. It had mitts instead of hands (no separate fingers or toes) and an absolutely blank face. Its position and attitude were altered rather frequently, as were the attractive materials displayed with it—it might be standing or reclining, sitting or kneeling. Sometimes it seemed to be pulling fabrics from a roller, or otherwise arranging them, things like that. I always thought of it as female, I can't say why; although there were discreet suggestions of a bosom and a pubic bump, its hips were narrow; perhaps a woman would have thought of it as male. Or perhaps my reasons for thinking of it as feminine were as simple as its small life-size (about five feet tall) or (most obvious) its lack of any external sex organ. At any rate, it rather fascinated as well as amused me, and at first I fancied it was standing for the delightfully quiet, unobstrusive folk who were my new fellow-tenants as opposed to the noisy and obstreperous quaints I had endured before. I even thought of it for a bit as the "faceless" and unindividualized proto-human being to which the Button Molder threatens to melt down Peer Gynt. (I'd just re-read that classic of Ibsen's—really, Peer stands with Faust and Hamlet and Don Quixote and Don Juan as one of the great fundamental figures of western culture.) But then I became aware of its extreme mute expressiveness. If a face is left blank, the imagination of the viewer always supplies an expression for it—an expression which may be more intense and "living" because there are no lifeless features for it to clash with.

(If I seem to be getting off on sidetracks, please bear with me. They really have a bearing. I haven't forgotten my ghost, or apparition, or those agonizing ten seconds I want to tell you about. No indeed.)

My own apartment in the new building was almost too good to be true. Although advertised as only a studio, it contained four rooms in line, each with a window facing east. They were, in order from north to south (which would be left to right as you entered the hall: bathroom, small bedroom (its door faced you as you entered from the outside hall), large living room, and (beyond a low arched doorway) dinette-kitchen. The bathroom window was frosted; the other three had Venetian blinds. And besides two closets (one half the bedroom long) there were seventeen built-in cupboards with a total of thirty-one shelves—a treasure trove of ordered emptiness, and all, all, mine alone! To complete the pleasant picture, I had easy access to the roof—the manager assured me that a few of the tenants regularly used it for sunbathing. But I wasn't interested in the roof by day.

The time came soon enough when I eagerly supervised the transfer to my new place of my luggage, boxes, clothes, the few articles of furniture I owned (chiefly bookcases and filing cabinets), and the rather more extensive materials of my trade of fiction-writing and chief avocation of roof-top astronomy. That last is more important to me than one might guess. I like cities, but I'd hate to live in one without having easy access to a flat roof. I'd had that at my old apartment, and it was one of the features that kept me there so long—I'd anticipated difficulties getting the same privilege elsewhere.

I have the theory, you see, that in this age of mechanized hive-dwelling and of getting so much input from necessarily conformist artificial media such as TV and newspapers, it's very important for a person to keep himself more directly oriented, in daily touch with the heavens or at least the sky, the yearly march of the sun across the stars, the changing daily revolution of the stars as the world turns, the crawl of the planets, the swift phases of the moon, things like that. After all, it's one of the great healing rhythms of nature like the seas and the winds, perhaps the greatest. Stars are a pattern of points upon infinity, elegant geometric art, with almost an erotic poignancy, but all, all nature. Some psychologists say that people stop dreaming if they don't look out over great distances each day, "see the horizon," as it were, and that dreams are the means by which the mind keeps its conscious and unconscious halves in balance, and I certainly agree with them. At any rate I'd deliberately built up the habit of rooftop observing, first by the unaided eye, then with the help of binoculars, and, finally, a small refracting telescope on an equatorial mounting.

Moreover—and especially in a foggy city like San Francisco!—if you get interested in the stars, you inevitably get interested in the weather if only because it so often thwarts you with its infinitely varied clouds and winds (which can make a telescope useless by setting it trembling), its freaks and whims and its own great allover rhythms. And then it gives you a new slant on the city itself. You become absorbed into the fascinating world of roofs, a secret world above the city world, one mostly uninhabited and unknown. Even the blocky, slablike highrises cease to be anonymous disfigurements, targets of protests. They become the markers whence certain stars appear or whither they trend, or which they graze with twinkling caress, and which the sun or moon touch or pass behind at certain times of the year or month, exactly like the menhirs at Stonehenge which primitive man used similarly. And through the gaps and narrow chinks between the great highrises, you can almost always glimpse bits and pieces of the far horizon. And always once in a while there will be some freakish sky or sky-related event that will completely mystify you and really challenge your imagination.

Of course, roof-watching, like writing itself, is a lonely occupation, but at least it tends to move outward from self, to involve more and more of otherness. And in any case, after having felt the world and its swarming people much too much with me for the past couple of years (and in an extremely noisy, sweaty way!) I was very much looking forward to living alone by myself for a good long while in a supremely quiet environment.

In view of that last, it was highly ironic that the first thing to startle me about my new place should have been *the noise*—noise of a very special sort, the swinish grunting and chomping of the huge garbage trucks that came rooting for refuse every morning (except Sunday) at four A.M. or a little earlier. My old apartment had looked out on a rear inner court in an alleyless block, and so their chuffing, grinding sound had been one I'd been mostly spared. While the east windows of my new place looked sidewise down on the street in front and also into a rather busy alley—there wasn't a building nearly as high as mine in that direction for a third of a block. Moreover, in moving the three blocks between the two apartments, I'd moved into a more closely supervised and protected district—that of the big hotels and theaters and expensive stores—with more police protection and enforced tidiness —which meant more garbage trucks. There were the yellow municipal ones and the green and gray ones of more than one private collection company, and once at three thirty I saw a tiny white one draw up on the sidewalk beside an outdoor phone booth and the driver get out and spend ten minutes rendering it pristine with vacuum, sponge, and squeegee.

The first few nights when they waked me I'd get up and move from window to window, and even go down the outside hall to the front fire escape with its beckoning red light, the better to observe the racketty monsters and their hurrying attendants—the wide maws into which the refuse was shaken from clattering cans, the great revolving steel drums that chewed it up, the huge beds that would groaningly tilt to empty the drums and shake down the shards.

(My God, they were ponderous and cacophonous vehicles!)

But nothing could be wrong with my new place—even these sleep-shattering mechanical giant hogs fascinated me. It was an eerie and mysterious sight to see one of them draw up, say, at the big hotel across the street from me and an iron door in the sidewalk open upward without visible human agency and four great dully gleaming garbage cans slowly arise there as if from some dark hell. I found myself comparing them also (the trucks) to the Button Molder in *Peer Gynt*. Surely, I told myself, they each must have a special small compartment for discarded human souls that had failed to achieve significant individuality and were due to be melted down! Or perhaps they just mixed in the worn-out souls with all the other junk.

At one point I even thought of charting and timing the trucks' exact routes and schedules, just as I did with the planets and the moon, so that I'd be better able to keep tabs on them.

That was another reason I didn't mind being waked at four—it let me get in a little rooftop astronomy before the morning twilight began. At such times I'd usually just take my binoculars, though once I lugged up my telescope for an apparition of Mercury when he was at his greatest western elongation.

Once, peering down from the front fire escape into the dawn-dark street below, I thought I saw a coveralled attendant rudely toss my fabric-store manikin into the rear-end mouth of a dark green truck, and I almost shouted down a protesting inquiry . . . and ten minutes later felt sorry I hadn't—sorry and somehow guilty. It bothered me so much that I got dressed and went down to check out the display window. For a moment I didn't see her, and I felt a crazy grief rising, but then I spotted her peeping up at me coyly from under a pile of yardage arranged so that she appeared to have pulled the colorful materials down on herself.

And once at four A.M. in the warm morning of a holiday I was for variety awakened by the shrill, argumentative cries of four slender hookers, two black, two white, arrayed in their uniform of high heels, hotpants, and long-sleeved lacy blouses, clustered beneath a streetlight on the far corner of the next intersection west and across from an all-hours nightclub named the Windjammer. They were preening and scouting about at intervals, but mostly they appeared to be discoursing, somewhat less raucously now, with the unseen drivers and passengers of a dashing red convertible and a slim white hardtop long as a yacht, which were drawn up near the curb at nonchalant angles across the corner. Their customers? Pimps more likely, from the glory of their equipages. After a bit the cars drifted away and the four lovebirds wandered off east in a loose formation, warbling together querulously.

After about ten days I stopped hearing the garbage trucks, just as the manager told me would happen, though most mornings I continued to wake early enough for a little astronomy.

My first weeks in the new apartment were very happy ones. (No, I hadn't encountered my ghost yet, or even got hints of its approach, but I think the stage was setting itself and perhaps the materials were gathering.) My writing, which had been almost stalled at the old place, began to go well, and I finished three short stories. I spent my afternoons pleasantly setting out the stuff of my life to best advantage, being particularly careful to leave most surfaces clear and not to hang too many pictures, and in expeditions to make thoughtful purchases. I acquired a dark blue celestial globe I'd long wanted and several maps to fill the space above my filing cabinets: one of the world, a chart of the stars on the same mercator projection, a big one of the moon, and two of San Francisco, the city and its downtown done in great detail. I didn't go to many shows during this time or see much of any of my friends— I didn't need them. But I got caught up on stacks of unanswered correspondence. And I remember expending considerable effort in removing the few blemishes I discovered on my new place: a couple of inconspicuous but unsightly stains, a slow drain that turned out to have been choked by a stopper-chain, a venetian blind made cranky by twisted cords, and the usual business of replacing low wattage globes with brighter ones, particularly in the case of the entry light just inside the hall door. There the ceiling had been lowered a couple of feet, which gave the rest of the apartment a charmingly spacious appearance, as did the arched dinette doorway, but it meant that any illumination there had to come down from a fixture in the true ceiling through a frosted plate in the lowered one. I put in a 200-watter, reminding myself to use it sparingly. I even remember planning to get a thick rubber mat to put under my filing cabinets so they wouldn't indent and perhaps even cut the heavy carpeting too deeply, but I never got around to that.

Perhaps those first weeks were simply too happy, perhaps I just got to spinning along too blissfully, for after finishing the third short story, I suddenly found myself tempted by the idea of writing something that would be more than fiction and also more than a communication addressed to just one person, but rather a general statement of what I thought about life and other people and history and the universe and all, the roots of it, something like Descartes began when he wrote down, "I think, therefore I am." Oh, it wouldn't be formally and certainly not stuffily philosophical, but it would contain a lot of insights just the same, the fruits of one man's lifetime experience. It would be critical yet autobiographical, honestly rooted in me. At the very least it would be a testimonial to the smooth running of my life at a new place, a way of honoring my move here.

I'm ordinarily not much of a nonfiction writer. I've done a few articles about writing and about other writers I particularly admire, a lot of short book reviews, and for a dozen or so years before I took up full-time fiction, I edited a popular science magazine. And before that I'd worked on encyclopedias and books of knowledge.

But everything was so clear to me at the new place, my sensations were so exact, my universe was spread out around me so orderly, that I knew that now was the time to write such a piece if ever, and so I decided to take a chance on the new idea, give it a whirl.

At the same time at a deeper level in my mind and feelings, I believe I was making a parallel decision running something like this: *Follow this lead. Let all the other stuff go, ease up, and see what happens.* Somewhere down there a control was being loosened.

An hour or so before dawn the next day I had a little experience that proved to be the pattern for several subsequent ones, including the final unexpected event. (You see, I haven't forgotten those ten seconds I mentioned. I'm keeping them in mind.)

I'd been on the roof in the cool predawn to observe a rather close conjunction (half a degree apart) of Mars and Jupiter in the east (they didn't rise until well after midnight), and while I was watching the reddish and golden planets without instrument (except for my glasses, of course) I twice thought I saw a shooting star out of the corner of my eye, but didn't get my head around in time to be sure. I was intrigued because I hadn't noted in the handbook any particular meteor showers due at this time and also because most shooting stars are rather faint and the city's lights tend to dim down everything in the sky. The third time it happened I managed to catch the flash and for a long instant was astounded by the sight of what appeared to be three shooting stars traveling fast in triangular formation like three fighter planes before they whisked out of sight behind a building. Then I heard a faint bird-cry and realized they had been three gulls winging quite close and fast overhead, their white underfeathers illumined by the upward streaming streetlights. It was really a remarkable illusion, of the sort that has to be seen to be fully believed. You'd think your eye wouldn't make that sort of misidentification—three sea birds for three stars—but from the corner of your eye you don't see shape or color or even brightness much, only pale movement whipping past. And then you wouldn't think three birds would keep such a tight and exact triangular formation, very much like three planes performing at an air show.

I walked quietly back to my apartment in my bathrobe and slippers. The stairway from the roof was carpeted. My mind was full of the strange triple apparition I'd just seen. I thought of how another mind with other anticipations might have seen three UFOs. I silently opened the door to my apartment, which I'd left on the latch, and stepped inside.

I should explain here that I always switch off all the lights when I leave my apartment and am careful about how I turn them on when I come back. It's partly thrift and citizenly thoughts about energy, the sort of thing you do to get gold stars at grown-ups' Sunday school. But it's also a care not to leave an outward glaring light to disturb some sleeper who perhaps must keep his window open and unshuttered for the sake of air and coolth; there's a ten-storey apartment building a quarter block away overlooking my east windows, and I've had my own sleep troubled by such unnecessary abominable beacons. On the other hand, I like to look out open windows myself; I hate to keep them wholly shaded, draped, or shuttered, but at the same time I don't want to become a target for a sniper—a simply realistic fear to many these days. As a result of all this I make it a rule never to turn on a light at night until I'm sure the windows of the room I'm in are fully obscured. I take a certain pride, I must admit, in being able to move around my place in the dark without bumping things—it's a test of courage too, going back to childhood, and also a proof that your sensory faculties haven't been dimmed by age. And I guess I just like the feeling of mysteriousness it gives me.

So when I stepped inside I did *not* turn on the 200-watt light above the lowered ceiling of the entry. My intention was to move directly forward into the bedroom, assure myself that the venetian blinds were tilted shut, and then switch on the bedside lamp. But as I started to do that, I heard the beginning of a noise to my right and I glanced toward the living room, where the street lights striking upward through the open venetian blinds made pale stripes on the ceiling and wall and slightly curving ones on the celestial globe atop a bookcase, and into the dinette beyond, and I saw a thin dark figure slip along the wall. But then, just as a feeling of surprise and fear began, almost at the same moment but actually a moment later, there came the realization that the figure was the black frame of my glasses, either moving as I turned my head or becoming more distinct as I switched my eyes that way, more likely a little of both. It was an odd mixture of sensation and thought, especially coming right on top of the star-birds (or bird-stars), as if I were getting almost simultaneously the messages *My God, it's an intruder, or ghost, or whatever* and *It isn't any of those, as you know very well from a lifetime's experience. You've just been had again by appearances.*

I'm pretty much a thoroughgoing skeptic, you see, when it comes to the paranormal, or the religious supernatural, or even such a today-commonplace as telepathy. My mental attitudes were formed in the period during and just after the first world war, when science was still a right thing, almost noble, and technology was forward-looking and labor-saving and progressive, and before folk wisdom became so big and was still pretty much equated with ignorance and superstition, no matter how picturesque. I've never seen or heard of a really convincing scrap of evidence for ancient or present-day astronauts from other worlds, for comets or moons that bumped the earth and changed history, or for the power of pyramids to prolong life or sharpen razor blades. As for immortality, it's my impression that most people do or don't do what's in them and then live out their lives in monotonous blind alleys, and what would be the point in cluttering up another world with all the worn-out junk? And as for God, it seems to me that the existence of one being who knew everything, future as well as past, would simply rob the universe of drama, excuse us all from doing anything. I'll admit that with telepathy the case is somewhat different, if only because so many sensible, well-educated, brilliant people seem to believe in some form of it. I only know I haven't experienced any as far as I can tell; it's almost made me jealous—I've sometimes thought I must be wrapped in some very special insulation against thought-waves, if there be such. I *will* allow that the mind (and also mental suggestions from outside) can affect the body, even affect it greatly—the psychosomatic thing. But that's just about all I will allow.

So much for the first little experience—no, wait, what did I mean when I wrote, "I heard the beginning of a noise"? Well, there are sounds so short and broken-off that you can't tell what they are going to be, or even for sure just how loud they were, so that you ask yourself if you imagined them. It was like that—a tick without a tock, a ding without the dong, a creak that went only halfway, never reaching that final *kuh* sound. Or like a single footstep that started rather loud and ended muted down to nothing—very much like the whole little experience itself, beginning with a gust of shock and terror and almost instantly reducing to the commonplace. Well, so much for that.

The next few days were pleasant and exciting ones, as I got together materials for my new project, assembling the favorite books I knew I'd want to quote (Shakespeare and the King James Bible, *Moby Dick* and *Wuthering Heights,* Ibsen and Bertrand Russell, Stapledon and Heinlein), looking through the daybooks I've kept for the past five years for the entries in black ink, which I reserve for literary and what I like to call metaphysical matters, and telling my mind (programming it, really) to look for similar insights whenever they happened to turn up during the course of the day—my chores and reading, my meals and walks—and then happily noting down those new insights in turn. There was only one little fly in the ointment: I knew I'd embarked on projects somewhat like this before—autobiographical and critical things—and failed to bring them to conclusions. But then

I've had the same thing happen to me on stories. With everything, one needs a bit of luck.

My next little experience began up on the roof. (They all did, for that matter.) It was a very clear evening without a moon, and I'd been memorizing the stars in Capricorn and faint Aquarius and the little constellations that lie between those and the Northern Cross: Sagitta, Delphinus, and dim Equuleus. You learn the stars rather like you learn countries and cities on a map, getting the big names first (the brightest stars and star groups) and then patiently filling in the areas between—and always on the watch for striking forms. At such times I almost forget the general dimming effect of San Francisco's lights since what I'm working on is so far above them.

And then, as I was resting my eyes from the binoculars, shut off by the roof's walls and the boxlike structure housing the elevator's motor from the city's most dazzling glares (the big, whitely fluorescent streetlights are the worst, the ones that are supposed to keep late walkers safe) I saw a beam of bright silver light strike straight upward for about a second from the roof of a small hotel three blocks away. And after about a dozen seconds more it came again, equally brief. It really looked like a sort of laser-thing: a beam of definite length (about two storys) and solid-looking. It happened twice more, not at regular intervals, but always as far as I could judge in exactly the same place (and I'd had time to spin a fantasy about a secret enclave of extra-terrestrials signaling to confederates poised just outside the stratosphere) when it occurred to me to use my binoculars on it. They solved the mystery almost at once: It wasn't a light beam at all, but a tall flagpole painted silver (no wonder it looked solid!) and at intervals washed by the roving beam of a big arc light shooting upward from the street beyond and swinging in slow circles—the sort of thing they use to signalize the opening of movie houses and new restaurants, even quite tiny ones.

What had made the incident out of the ordinary was that most flagpoles are painted dull white, not silver, and that the clearness of the night had made the arc light's wide beam almost invisible. If there'd been just a few wisps of cloud or fog in the air above, I'd have spotted it at once for what it was. It was rather strange to think of all that light streaming invisible up from the depths of the city's reticulated canyons and gorges.

I wondered why I'd never noted that flagpole before. Probably they never flew a flag on it.

It all didn't happen to make me recall my three starbirds, and so when after working over once more this night's chosen heavenly territory, including a veering aside to scan the rich starfields of Aquila and the diamond of Altair, one of Earth's closest stellar neighbors, I was completely taken by surprise again when on entering my apartment, the half a noise was repeated and the same skinny dark shape glided along the wall across the narrow flaglike bands of light and dark. Only this time the skeptical, deflating reaction came a tiny bit sooner, followed at once by the almost peevish inner remark, *Oh, yes, that again!* And then as I turned on the bedside light, I wondered, as one will, how I would have reacted if the half step had been completed and if the footsteps had gone on, getting louder as they made their swift short trip and there peered around the side of the doorway at me . . . what? It occurred to me that the nastiest and most frightening thing in the world must differ widely from person to person, and I smiled. Surely in man's inward lexicon, the phobias outnumber the philias a thousand to one!

Oh, I'll admit that when I wandered into the living room and kitchen a bit later, shutting the blinds and turning on some lights, I did inspect things in a kind of perfunctory way, but noted nothing at all out of order. I told myself that all buildings make a variety of little noises at night, waterpipes especially can get downright loquacious, and then there are refrigerator motors sighing on and off and the faint little clicks and whines that come from electric clocks, all manner of babble—that half a noise might be anything. At least I knew the identity of the black glider—the vaguely seen black form always at the corner of my eye when I had on my glasses and most certainly there now.

I went on assembling the primary materials for my new project, and a week later I was able to set down, word by mulled-over word, the unembroidered, unexemplified, unproven gist of what I felt about life, or at least a first version of it. I still have it as I typed it from a penciled draft with many erasures, crossings out, and interlineations:

There is this awareness that is I, this mind that's me, a little mortal world of space and time, which glows and aches, which purrs and darkens, haunted and quickened by the ghosts that are memory, imagination, and thought, forever changing under urgings from within and proddings from without, yet able to hold still by fits and starts (and now and then refreshed by sleep and dreams), forever seeking to extend its bounds, forever hunting for the mixture of reality and fantasy—the formula, the script, the scenario, the story to tell itself or others—which will enable it to do its work, savor its thrills, and keep on going.

A baby tells itself the simplest story: that it is all that matters, it is God, commanding and constraining all the rest, all otherness. But then the script becomes more complicated. Stories take many forms: a scientific theory or a fairy tale, a world history or an anecdote, a call to action or a cry for help—all, all are stories. Sometimes they tell of our love for another, or they embody our illusioned and illusioning vision of the one we love—they are courtship. But every story must be interesting or it will not work, will not be heard, even the stories that we tell ourselves. And so it must contain illusion, fantasy. No matter how grim its facts, it must contain that saving note, be it only a surpassing interesting bitter, dry taste.

And then there are the other mortal minds I know are there, fellow awarenesses, companion consciousnesses, some close, a very few almost in touching space (but never quite), most farther off in almost unimaginable multitudes, each one like mine a little world of space and time moment by moment seeking its story, the combination of illusion and hard fact, of widest waking and of deepest dreaming, which will allow it to create, enjoy, survive. A company of loving, warring minds, a tender, rough companioning of tiny cosmoses forever telling stories to each other and themselves—that's what there is.

And I know that I must stay aware of all the others, listening to their stories, trying to understand them, their sufferings, their joys, and their imaginings, respecting the thorny facts of both their inner and their outer lives, and nourishing the needful illusions at least of those who are closest to me, if I am to make progress in my quest.

Finally there is the world, stranger than any mind or any story, the unknown universe, the shadowy scaffolding holding these minds together, the grid on which they are mysteriously arrayed, their container and their field, perhaps (but is there any question of it?) all-powerful yet quite unseen, its form unsensed, known only to the companion minds by the sensations it showers upon them and pelts them with, by its cruel and delicious proddings and graspings, by its agonizing and ecstatic messages (but never a story), and by its curt summonses and sentences, including death. Yes, that is how it is, those are the fundamentals: There is the dark, eternally silent, unknown universe; there are the friend-enemy minds shouting and whispering their tales and always seeking the three miracles—that minds should really touch, or that the silent universe should speak, tell minds a story, or (perhaps the same thing) that there should be a story that works that is all hard facts, all reality, with no illusions and no fantasy; and lastly there is lonely, story-telling, wonder-questing, mortal me.

As I re-read that short statement after typing it out clean, I found it a little more philosophical than I'd intended and also perhaps a little more overly glamorized with words like "ecstatic" and "agonizing," "mysteriously" and "stranger." But on the whole I was satisfied with it. Now to analyze it more deeply and flesh it out with insights and examples from my own life and from my own reflections on the work of others!

But as the working days went on and became weeks (remember, I'd pretty much given up all other work for the duration of this project) I found it increasingly difficult to make any real progress. For one thing, I gradually became aware that in order to analyze that little statement much more deeply and describe my findings, I'd need to use one or more of the vocabularies of professional philosophy and psychology—which would mean months at least of reading and reviewing and of assimilating new advances, and I certainly didn't have the time for that. (The vocabularies of philosophies can be *very* special—Whitehead's, for instance, makes much use of the archaic verb "prehend," which for him means something very different from "comprehend" or "perceive.")

Moreover, the whole idea had been to skim accumulated insights and wisdom (if any!) off my mind, not become a student again and start from the beginning.

And I found it was pretty much the same when I tried to say something about other writers, past and contemporary, beyond a few obvious remarks and memorable quotations. I'd need to read their works again and study their lives in a lot more detail than I had ever done, before I'd be able to shape statements of any significance, things I really believed about them.

And when I tried to write about my own life, I kept discovering that for the most part it was much too much like anyone else's. I didn't want to set down a lot of dreary dates and places, only the interesting things, but how tell about those honestly without bringing in the rest? Moreover, it began to seem to me that all the really interesting subjects, like sex and money, feelings of guilt, worries about one's courage, and concern about one's selfishness were things one wasn't supposed to write about, either because they were too personal, involving others, or because they were common to all men and women and so quite unexceptional.

This state of frustration didn't grip me all the time, of course. It came in waves and gradually accumulated. I'd generally manage to start off each day feeling excited about the project (though it began to take more and more morning time to get my head into that place, I will admit); perhaps some part of my short statement would come alive for me again, like that bit about the universe being a grid on which minds are mysteriously arrayed, but by the end of the day I would have worried all the life out of it and my mind would be as blank as the face of my manikin in the fabric shop window downstairs. I remember once or twice in the course of one of our daily encounters shaking my head ruefully at her, almost as if seeking for sympathy. She seemed to have a lot more patience and poise than I had.

I was beginning to spend more time on the roof too, not only for the sake of the stars and astronomy, but just to get away from my desk with all its problems. In fact my next little experience leading up to the ghostly one began shortly before sunset one day when I'd been working long, though fruitlessly. The sky, which was cloudless from my east windows, began to glow with an unusual violet color and I hurried up to get a wider view.

All day long a steady west wind had been streaming out the flags on the hotels and driving away east what smog there was, so that the sky was unusually clear. But the sun had sunk behind the great fog bank that generally rests on the Pacific just outside the Golden Gate. However, he had not yet set, for to the south, where there were no tall buildings to obstruct my vision, his beams were turning a few scattered clouds over San Jose (some thirty miles away) a delicate shade of lemon yellow that seemed to be the exact complement of the violet in the sky (just as orange sunset clouds tend to go with a deep blue sky).

And then as I watched, there suddenly appeared in the midst of that sunset, very close to the horizon in a cloudless stretch, a single yellow cloud like a tiny dash. It seemed to appear from nowhere, just like that. And then as I continued to watch, another cloud appeared close beside the first at the same altitude, beginning as a bright yellow point and then swiftly growing until it was as long as the first, very much as if a giant invisible hand had drawn another short dash.

During the course of the next few minutes, as I watched with a growing sense of wonder and a feeling of giant release from the day's frustrations, eight more such mini-clouds (or whatever) appeared at fairly regular intervals, until there were ten of them glowing in line there, fluorescent yellow stitches in the sky.

My mind raced, clutching at explanations. Kenneth Arnold's original flying saucers thirty years ago, which he'd glimpsed from his light plane over the American northwest, had been just such shining shapes in a row. True, his had been moving, while mine were hovering over a city, having appeared from nowhere. Could they conceivably have come from hyperspace? my fancy asked.

And then, just as the lemon sunset began to fade from the higher clouds, an explanation struck me irresistibly. What I was seeing was skywriting (which usually we see above our heads) from way off to one side, viewed edgewise. My ten mystery clouds (or giant ships!) were the nine letters—and the hyphen—of Pepsi-Cola. (Next day I confirmed this by a telephone call to San Jose; there had been just such an advertising display.)

At the time, and as the giant yellow stitches faded to gray unsewn sky-cloth, I remember feeling very exhilarated and also slightly hysterical at the comic aspect of the event. I paced about the roof chortling, telling myself that the vision I'd just witnessed outdid even that of the Goodyear blimp acrawl with colored lights in abstract patterns that had welcomed me to this new roof the first night I'd climbed up here after moving in. I spent quite a while quieting myself, so that the streetlights had just come on when I went downstairs. But somehow I hadn't thought of it being very dark yet in my apartment, so that was perhaps why it wasn't until I was actually unlocking the door that, remembering the Starbirds and the Silver Laser (and now the Mystery of the Ten Yellow Stitches!), I also remembered the events that had followed them. I had only time to think *Here we go again* as I pushed inside.

Well, it *was* dark in there and the pale horizontal bands were on the wall and the skeleton black figure slipped along them and I felt almost instantly the choked-off gust of terror riding atop the remnants of my exhilaration, all of this instantly after hearing that indefinable sound which seemed to finish almost before it began. That was one thing characteristic of all these preliminary incidents—they ended so swiftly and so abruptly that it was hard to think about them afterwards, the mind had nothing to work with.

And I know that in trying to describe them I must make them sound patterned, almost prearranged, yet at the time they just happened and somehow there was always an element of surprise.

Unfortunately the exhilaration I'd feel on the roof never carried over to the next morning's work on my new project. This time, after sweating and straining for almost a week without any progress at all, I resolutely decided to shelve it, at least for a while, and get back to stories.

But I found I couldn't do that. I'd committed myself too deeply to the new thing. Oh, I didn't find that out right away, of course. No, I spent more than a week before I came to that hateful and panic-making conclusion. I tried every trick I knew of to get myself going: long walks, fasting, starting to write immediately after waking up when my mind was hypnogogic and blurred with dream, listening to music which I'd always found suggestive, such as Holst's *The Planets,* especially the "Saturn" section, which seems to capture the essence of time—you hear the giant footsteps of time itself crashing to a halt— or Williams's *Sinfonia Antarctica* with its lonely wind-machine finish, which does the same for space, or Berlioz's *Funeral March for the Last Scene of Hamlet*, which reaches similarly toward chaos. Nothing helped. The more I'd try to work up the notes for some story I had already three-quarters planned, the less interesting it would become to me, until it seemed (and probably was) all cliche. Some story ideas are as faint and insubstantial as ghosts. Well, all of *those* I had just got fainter as I worked on them.

I hate to write about writer's block; it's such a terribly childish, yes, frivolous seeming affliction. You'd think that anyone who was half a human being could shake it off or just slither away from it. But I couldn't. Morning after morning I'd wake with an instant pang of desperation at the thought of my predicament, so that I'd have to get up right away and pace, or rush out and walk the dawn-empty streets, or play through chess endings or count windows in big buildings to fill my mind with useless calculations—anything until I grew calm enough to read a newspaper or make a phone call and somehow get the day started. Sometimes my desk would get to jumping in the same way my mind did and I'd find myself compulsively straightening the objects on it over and over until I'd spring up from it in disgust. Now when the garbage trucks woke me at four (as they began to do again), I'd get up and follow their thunderous mechanical movements from one window or other vantage point to another, anxiously tracing the course of each can-lugging attendant—anything to occupy my mind.

Just to be doing something, I turned to my correspondence, which had begun to pile up again, but after answering three or four notes (somehow I'd pick the least important ones) I'd feel worn out. You see, I didn't want to write my friends about the block I was having. It was such a bore (whining always is) and besides, I was *ashamed*. At the same time I couldn't seem to write honestly about anything without bringing my damn block in.

I felt the same thing about calling up or visiting my friends around me in the city. I'd have nothing to show them, nothing to talk about. I didn't want to see anyone. It was a very bad time for me.

Of course I kept on going up to the roof, more than ever now, though even my binoculars were a burden to me and I couldn't bear to lug up my telescope—the weary business of setting it up and all the fussy adjustments I'd have to make made that unthinkable. I even had to *make* myself study the patterns of the lesser stars when the clear nights came, that had formerly been such a joy to me.

But then one evening just after dark I went topside and immediately noticed near Cygnus, the Northern Cross, a star that shouldn't have been there. It was a big one, third magnitude at least. It made a slightly crooked extension of the top of the cross as it points toward Cassiopeia. At first I was sure it had to be an earth satellite (I've spotted a few of those)—a big one, like the orbiting silvered balloon they called Echo. Or else it was a light on some weird sort of plane that was hovering high up. But when I held my binoculars on it, I couldn't see it move at all—as a satellite would have done, of course. Then I got really excited, enough to make me bring up my telescope (and *Norton's Star Atlas* too) and set it up.

In the much smaller and more magnified field of that instrument, it didn't move either, but glared there steadily among the lesser points of light, holding position as it inched with the other stars across the field. From the atlas I estimated and noted down its approximate co-ordinates (right ascension 21 hours and 10 minutes, north declination 48 degrees) and hurried downstairs to call up an astronomer friend of mine and tell him I'd spotted a nova.

Naturally I wasn't thinking at all about the previous ghostly (or whatever) incidents, so perhaps this time the strange thing was that, yes, it did happen again, just as before though with even more brevity, and I sort of went through all the motions of reacting to it, but very unconcernedly, as if it had become a habit, part of the routine of existence, like a step in a stairway that always creaks when your foot hits it but nothing more ever comes of it. I recall saying to myself with a sort of absent-minded lightheartedness *Let's give the ghost E for effort, he keeps on trying.*

I got my astronomer friend and, yes, it was a real nova; it had been spotted in Asia and Europe hours earlier and all the astronomers were very busy, oh, my, yes.

The nova was a four-days' wonder, taking that long to fade down to naked-eye invisibility. Unfortunately my own excitement at it didn't last nearly that long. Next morning I was confronting my block again. Very much in the spirit of desperation, I decided to go back to my new project and make myself finish it off somehow, force myself to write no matter how bad the stuff seemed to be that I turned out, beginning with an expansion of my original short statement.

But the more I tried to do that, the more I reread those two pages, the thinner and more dubious all the ideas in it seemed to me, the junkier and more hypocritical it got. Instead of adding to it, I wanted to take stuff away, trim it down to a nice big nothing.

To begin with, it was so much a writer's view of things, reducing everything to stories. Of course! What could be more obvious?—or more banal? A military man would explain life in terms of battles, advances and retreats, defeats and victories, and all their metaphorical analogues, presumably with strong emphasis on courage and discipline. Just as a doctor might view history as the product of great men's ailments, whether they were constipated or indigestive, had syphillis or TB—or of subtle diseases that swept nations; the fall of Rome?—lead poisoning from the pipes they used to distribute their aqueducted water! Or a salesman see everything as buying and selling, literally or by analogy. I recalled a 1920s' book about Shakespeare by a salesman. The secret of the Bard's unequalled dramatic power? He was the world's greatest salesman! No, all that stuff about stories was just a figure of speech and not a very clever one.

And then that business about illusion coming in everywhere—what were illusions and illusioning but euphemisms for lies and lying? We had to nourish the illusions of others, didn't we? That meant, in plain language, that we had to flatter them, tell them white lies, go along with all their ignorance and prejudices—very convenient rationalizations for a person who was afraid to speak the truth! Or for someone who was eager to fantasize everything. And granting all that, how had I ever hoped to write about it honestly in any detail?—strip away from myself and others, those at all close to me at least, all our pretenses and boasts, the roles we played, the ways we romanticized ourselves, the lies we agreed to agree on, the little unspoken deals we made ("You build me up, I'll build you up"), yes, strip away all that and show exactly what lay underneath: the infantile conceits, the suffocating selfishness, the utter unwillingness to look squarely at the facts of death, torture, disease, jealousy, hatred, and pain—how had I ever hoped to speak out about all that, I an illusioner?

Yes, how to speak out the truth of my real desires? that

were so miserably small, so modest. No vast soul-shaking passions and heaven-daunting ambitions at all, only the little joy of watching a shadow's revealing creep along an old brick wall or the infinitely delicate diamond-prick of the first evening star in the deepening blue sky of evening, the excitement of little discoveries in big dictionaries, the small thrill of seeing and saying, "That's not the dark underside of a distant low narrow cloudbank between those two buildings, it's a TV antenna," or "That's not a nova, you wishful thinker, it's Procyon," the fondling and fondlings of slender, friendly, cool fingers, the hues and textures of an iris seen up close—how to admit to such minuscule longings and delights?

And getting still deeper into this stories business, what was it all but a justification for always *talking* about things and never *doing* anything? It's been said, "Those who can, do; those who can't, teach." Yes, and those who can't even teach, what do they do? Why, they tell stories! Yes, always talking, never acting, never being willing to dirty your fingers with the world. Why, at times you had to drive yourself to pursue even the little pleasures, were satisfied with fictional or with imagined proxies.

And while we were on that subject, what was all this business about minds never touching, never being quite able to? What was it but an indirect, mealy-mouthed way of confessing my own invariable impulse to flinch away from life, to avoid contact at any cost—the reason I lived alone with fantasies, never made a friend (though occasionally letting others, if they were forceful enough, make friends with me), preferred a typewriter to a wife, talked, talked, and never did? Yes, for minds, read bodies, and then the truth was out, the secret of the watcher from the sidelines.

I tell you, it got so I wanted to take those thumbed-over two grandiose pages of my "original short statement" and crumple them together in a ball and put that in a brown paper sack along with a lot of coffee grounds and grapefruit rinds and grease, and then repeat the process with larger and larger sacks until I had a Chinese-boxes set of them big around as a large garbage can and lug that downstairs at four o'clock in the morning and when the dark truck stopped in front personally hurl it into that truck's big ass-end mouth and *hear* it all being chewed up and ground to filthy scraps, the whole thing ten times louder than it ever sounded from the sixth floor, knowing that my "wisdom"-acorn of crumpled paper with all its idiot notions was in the very midst and getting more masticated and befouled, more thoroughly destroyed, than anything else (while my manikin watched from her window, inscrutable but, I felt sure, approving)—only in that way, I told myself, would I be able to tear myself loose from this whole damn minuscule, humiliating project, kill it inside my head.

I remember the day my mind generated that rather pitiful grotesque vision (which, incidentally, I half seriously contemplated carrying into reality the next morning). The garbage trucks had wakened me before dawn and I'd been flitting in and out most of the day, unable to get down to anything or even to sit still, and once I'd paused on the sidewalk outside my apartment building, visualizing the truck drawing up in the dark next morning and myself hurling my great brown wad at it, and I'd shot to my manikin the thought *Well, what do you think of it? Isn't it a good idea?* They had her seated cross-legged in a sort of Lotus position on a great sweep of violet sheetings that went up behind her to a high shelf holding the bolt. She seemed to receive my suggestion and brood upon it enigmatically.

Predictably, I gravitated to the roof soon after dark, but without my binoculars and not to study the stars above (although it was a clear evening) or peer with weary curiosity at the window-worlds below that so rarely held human figures, or even hold still and let the lonely roof-calm take hold of me. No, I moved about restlessly from one of my observation stations to another, rather mechanically scanning along the jagged and crenellated skyline, between the upper skyey areas and the lower building-bound ones, that passed for a horizon in the city (though there actually were a couple of narrow gaps to the east through which I could glimpse, from the right places on my roof, very short stretches of the hills behind smoky transbay Oakland). In fact, my mind was so little on what I was doing and so much on my writing troubles that I tripped over a TV-antenna cable I'd known was there and should have avoided. I didn't fall, but it took me three plunging steps to recover my balance, and I realized that if I'd been going in the opposite direction I might well have pitched over the edge, the wall being rather low at that point.

The roof world can be quite treacherous at night, you

see. Older roofs especially are apt to be cluttered with little low standpipes and kitchen chimneys and ventilators,
things very easy to miss and trip over. It's the worst on
clear moonless nights, for then there are no clouds to reflect the city's lights back down, and as a result it's dark
as pitch around your feet. (Paradoxically, it's better when
it's raining or just been raining for then there's streetlight
reflected by the rainclouds and the roof has a wet glisten
so that obstructions stand out.) Of course, I generally
carry a small flashlight and use it from time to time, but
more important, I memorize down to the last detail the
layout of any roof visited by night. Only this time that
latter precaution failed me.

It brought me up short to think of how my encounter
with the TV cable could have had fatal consequences. It
made me see just how very upset I was getting from my
writer's block and wonder about unconscious suicidal im-
pulses and accidentally-on-purpose things. Certainly my
stalled project was getting to the point where I'd have to
do something drastic about it, like seeing a psychiatrist or
getting drunk . . . or something.

But the physical fear I felt didn't last long, and soon I
was prowling about again, though a little less carelessly. I
diidn't feel comfortable except when I was moving. When
I held still, I felt choked with failure (my writing project). And yet at the same time I felt I was on the verge of
an important insight, one that would solve all my problems if I could get it to come clear. It seemed to begin
with "If you could sum up all you felt about life and crystallize it in one master insight . . ." but where it went from
there I didn't know. But I knew I wasn't going to get an
answer sitting still.

Perhaps, I thought, this whole roof-thing with me ex-
presses an unconscious atavistic faith in astrology, that I
will somehow find the answer to any problem in the stars.
How quaint of skeptical me!

On the roof at my old place, one of my favorite sights
had been the Sutro TV Tower with its score or so of wink-
ing red lights. Standing almost a thousand feet high on a
hill that is a thousand already, that colorful tripod tower
dominates San Francisco from its geographical center and
is a measuring rod for the altitude of fogs and cloud
banks, their ceilings and floors. One of my small regrets
about moving had been that it couldn't be seen from this
new roof. But then only a couple of weeks ago I'd dis-

covered that if you climb the short stairway to the locked door of the boxlike structure hiding the elevator's motor, you see the tops of the Tower's three radio masts poking up over and two miles beyond the top of the glassy Federal Building. Binoculars show the myriad feathery white wires guying them that look like sails—they're nylon so as not to interfere with the TV signals.

This night when I got around to checking the three masts out by their red flashes, I lingered a bit at the top of the skeleton stairs watching them, and as I lingered I saw in the black sky near them a tremorous violet star wink on and then after a long second wink off. I wouldn't have thought of it twice except for the color. Violet is an uncommon color for a light on a building or plane, and it's certainly an uncommon color for a star. All star colors are very faint tinges, for that matter. I've looked at stars that were supposed to be green and never been able to see it.

But down near the horizon where the air is thicker, anything can happen, I reminded myself. Stars that are white near the zenith begin to flash red and blue, almost any color at all, when they're setting. And suddenly grow dim, even wink out unexpectedly. Still, violet, that was a new one.

And then as I was walking away from the stars and away from Sutro Tower too, diagonally across the roof toward the other end of it, I looked toward the narrow, window-spangled slim triangle of the Trans-American Pyramid Building a half mile or so away and I saw for a moment, just grazing its pinnacle, what looked like the same mysteriously pulsing violet star. Then it went off or vanished—or went behind the pinnacle, but I couldn't walk it into view again, either way.

What got me the most, perhaps, about that violet dot was the way the light had seemed to *graze* the Pyramid, coming (it was my impression) from a great distance. It reminded me of the last time I'd looked at the planet Mercury through my telescope. I'd followed it for quite a while as it moved down the paling dawn sky, flaring and pulsing (it was getting near the horizon) and then it had reached the top of the Hilton Tower where they have a room whose walls are almost all window, and for almost half a minute I'd continued my observation of it through the glassy corner of the Hilton Hotel. Really, it had seemed most strange to me, that rare planetary light linking me to another building that way, and being tainted by that building's glass, and in a way confounding all my ideas as to what is close and what is far, what clean and what unclean. . . .

While I was musing, my feet had carried me to another observation place, where in a narrow slot between two close-by buildings I can see the gray open belfry towers of Grace Cathedral on Nob Hill five blocks off. And there, through or *in* one of the belfry's arched openings, I saw the violet star again resting or floating.

A star leaping about the sky that way?—absurd! No, this was something in my eye or eyes. But even as I squeezed my eyes shut and fluttered the lids and shook my head in short tight arcs, my neck muscles taut, to drive the illusion away, that throbbing violet star peered hungrily at me from the embrasure wherein it rested in the gray church's tower.

I've stared at many a star, but never before with the feeling that it was glaring at me.

But then (something told me) you've never seen a star that came to earth, sliding down that unimaginable distance in a trice and finding itself a niche or hiding hole in the dark world of roofs. The star went out, drew back, was doused.

Do you know that right after that I was afraid to lift my head? or look up at anything? for fear of seeing that flashing violet diamond somewhere it shouldn't be? And that as I turned to move toward the door at the head of the stairs that led down from the roof, my gaze inadvertently encountered the Hilton Tower and I ducked my head so fast that I can't tell you now whether or not I saw a violet gleam in one of that building's windows?

In many ways the world of roofs is like a vast, not too irregular games board, each roof a square, and I thought of the violet light as a sort of super-chess piece making great leaps like a queen (after an initial vast one) and crookedly sidewise moves like a knight, advancing by rushings and edgings to checkmate me.

And I knew that I wanted to get off this roof before I saw a violet glow coming from behind the parapet of one of the airshafts or through the cracks around the locked door to the elevator's motor.

Yet as I moved toward the doorway of escape, the door down, I felt my face irresistibly lifted from between my hunched shoulders and against my neck's flinching opposition until I was peering through painfully winced eye-slits at the cornice of the next building east, the one that overlooked the windows of my apartment.

At first it seemed all dark, but then I caught the faintest violet glint or glimmer, as of something spying down most warily.

From that point until the moment I found myself facing the door to my apartment, I don't remember much at all except the tightness with which my hands gripped the stair-rails going down . . . and continued to grip railings tightly as I went along the sixth-storey hall, although of course there are no railings there.

I got the door unlocked, then hesitated.

But then my gaze wavered back the way I'd come, toward the stair from the roof, and something in my head began to recite in a little shrill voice, *I met a star upon the stair, A violet star that wasn't there. . . .*

I'd pressed on inside and had the door shut and double locked and was in the bedroom and reaching for the bedside light before I realized that this time it *hadn't* happened, that at least I'd been spared the half sound and the fugitive dark ghost on this last disastrous night.

But then as I pressed the switch and the light came on with a tiny fizzing crackle and a momentary greenish glint and then shone more brightly and whitely than it should (as old bulbs will do when they're about to go—they arc) something else in my head said in a lower voice, *But of course when the right night came it wouldn't make its move until you were safely locked inside and unable to retreat. . . .*

And then as I stared at the bright doorway and the double-locked door beyond, there came from the direction of the dinette-kitchen a great creaking sound like a giant footstep, no half-sound but something finished off completely, very controlled, very *deliberate*, neither a stamp nor a tramp, and then another and a third, coming at intervals of just about a second, each one a little closer and a little louder, inexorably advancing very much like the footsteps of time in the "Saturn" section of *The Planets*, with more instruments coming in—horns, drums, cymbals, huge gongs and bells—at each mounting repetition of the beat.

I went rigid. In fact, I'm sure my first thought was *I must hold absolutely still and watch the doorway*, with perhaps the ghost comment riding on it, *Of course! the panic reaction of any animal trapped in its hole.*

171

And then a fourth footstep and a fifth and sixth, each one closer and louder, so that I'm sure my second real thought was, *The noise I'm hearing must be more than sound, else it would wake the city.* Could it be a physical vibration? Something was resounding deeply through my flesh, but the doorway wasn't shaking visibly as I watched it. Was it the reverberation of something mounting upward from the depths of earth or my subconscious mind, taking giant strides, smashing upward through the multiple thick floors that protect surface life and daytime consciousness? Or could it be the crashing around me in ruins of my world of certainties, in particular the ideas of that miserable vaunting project that had been tormenting me, all of them overset and trodden down together?

And then a seventh, eighth, ninth footstep, almost unbearably intense and daunting, followed by a great grinding pause, a monstrous hesitation. Surely something must appear now, I told myself. My every muscle was tight as terror could make it, especially those of my face and, torus-like, about my eyes (I was especially and rather fearfully conscious of their involuntary blinking). I must have been grimacing fearfully. I remember a fleeting fear of heart attack, every part of me was straining so, putting on effort.

And then there thrust silently, rather rapidly, yet gracefully into the doorway a slender, blunt-ended, sinuous leaden-gray, silver-glistening arm (or other member, I wondered briefly), followed immediately and similarly by the remainder of the figure.

I held still and observed, somehow overcoming the instant urge to flinch, to not-see. More than ever now, I told myself, my survival depended on that, my very life.

How describe the figure? If I say it looked like (and so perhaps was) the manikin in the fabrics shop, you will get completely the wrong impression; you will think of that stuffed and stitched form moving out of its window through the dark and empty store, climbing upstairs, etc., and I knew from the start that that was certainly not the case. In fact, my first thought was, *It is not the manikin, although it has its general form.*

Why? How did I know that? Because I was certain from the first glimpse that it was *alive,* though not in quite the way I was alive, or any other living creatures with which I am familiar. But just the same, that leaden-gray, silver-misted integument was skin, not sewn-fabric—there *were* no sewn seams, and I knew where the seams were on the manikin.

How different *its* kind of life from mine? I can only say that heretofore such expressions as "dead-alive," "living dead," and "life in death" were horror-story cliches to me; but now no longer so. (Did the leaden hue of its skin suggest to me a drowned person? I don't think so—there was no suggestion of bloat and all its movements were very graceful.)

Or take its face. The manikin's face had been a blank, a single oval piece of cloth sewn to the sides and top of the head and to the neck. Here there was no edgestitching and the face was not altogether blank, but was crossed by two very faint, fine furrows, one vertical, the other horizontal, dividing the face rather like a mandala or the symbol of the planet Earth. And now, as I forced myself to scan the horizontal furrow, I saw that it in turn was not altogether featureless. There were two points of violet light three inches apart, very faint but growing brighter the longer I watched them and that moved from side to side a little without alteration in the distance between them, as though scanning me. *That* discovery cost me a pang not to flinch away from, let me tell you!

The vertical furrow in the face seemed otherwise featureless, as did the similar one between the legs with its mute suggestion of femininity. (I had to keep scanning the entire figure over and over, you see, because I felt that if I looked at the violet eyepoints too long at any one time they would grow bright enough to blind me, as surely as if I were looking at the midday sun; and yet to look away entirely would be equally, though not necessarily similarly disastrous.)

Or take the matter of height. The window manikin was slenderly short. Yet I was never conscious of looking down at this figure which I faced, but rather a little up.

What else did I glean as this long nightmarish moment prolonged itself almost unendurably, going on and on and on, as though I were trapped in eternity?

Any other distinguishing and different feature? Yes. The sides and the top of the head sprouted thick and glistening black "hair" that went down her back in one straight fall.

(There, I have used the feminine pronoun on the figure, and I will stick with that from now on, although it is a judgment entirely from remembered feeling, or instinct, or whatever, and I can no more point to objective evidence for it than I can in the case of the manikin's imagined gender. And it is a further point of similarity between the two figures although I've said I *knew* they were different.)

What else, then, did I feel about her? That she had come to destroy me in some way, to wipe me out, erase me —I felt a calmer and colder thing than "kill," there was almost no heat to it at all. That she was weighing me in a very cool fashion, like that Egyptian god which weighs the soul, that she was, yes (And had her leaden-hued skin given me a clue here?), the Button Molder, come to reduce my individuality to its possible useful raw materials, extinguish my personality and melt me down, recycle me cosmically, one might express it.

And with that thought there came (most incidentally, you might say—a trifling detail) the answer I'd been straining for all evening. It went this way: *If you could sum up all you felt about life and crystallize it in one master insight, you would have said it all and you'd be dead.*

As that truism(?) recited itself in my mind, she seemed to come to a decision and she lithely advanced toward me two silent steps so she was barely a foot away in the arcing light's unnatural white glare, and her slender mitten-hands reached wide to embrace me, while her long black "hair" rose rustlingly and arched forward over her head, in the manner of a scorpion's sting, as though to enshroud us both, and I remember thinking, *However fell or fatal, she has style.* (I also recall wondering why, if she were able to move silently, the nine footsteps had been so loud? Had those great crashes been entirely of mind-stuff, a subjective earthquake? Mind's walls and constructs falling?) In any case her figure had a look of finality about it, as though she were the final form, the ultimate model.

That was the time, if ever (when she came close, I mean), for me to have flinched away or to have shut tight my eyes, but I did not, although my eyes were blurred— they had spurted hot tears at her advance. I felt that if I touched her, or she me, it would be death, the extinguishment of memory and myself (if they be different), but I still clung to the faith (it had worked thus far) that if I didn't move away from and continued to observe her, I might survive. I tried, in fact, to tighten myself still further, to make myself into a man of brass with brazen head and eyes (the latter had cleared now) like Roger Bacon's robot. I was becoming, I thought, a frenzy of immobility and observation.

But even as I thought "immobility" and "touching is death" I found myself leaning a little closer to her (although it made her violet eye-points stingingly bright) the better to observe her lead-colored skin. I saw that it was poreless, but also that it was covered by a network of very fine pale lines, like crazed or crackled pottery, as they call it, and that it was this network that gave her skin its silvery gloss . . .

As I leaned toward her, she moved back as much, her blunt arms paused in their encirclement, and her arching "hair" spread up and back from us.

At that moment the filament of the arcing bulb fizzled again and the light went out.

Now more than ever I must hold still, I told myself.

For a while I seemed to see her form outlined in faintest ghostly yellow (violet's compliment) on the dark and hear the faint rustle of "hair," possibly falling into its original position down her back. There was a still fainter sound like teeth grating. Two ghost-yellow points twinkled a while at eye-height and then faded back through the doorway.

After a long while (the time it took my eyes to accommodate, I suppose) I realized that white fluorescent street light was flooding the ceiling through the upward-tilted slats of the blind and filling the whole room with a soft glow. And by that glow I saw I was alone. Slender evidence, perhaps, considering how treacherous my new apartment had proved itself. But during that time of waiting in the dark my feelings had worn out.

Well, I said I was going to tell you about those ten endless seconds and now I have. The whole experience had fewer consequences and less aftermath than you might expect. Most important for me, of course, my whole great nonfiction writing project was dead and buried, I had no inclination whatever to dig it up and inspect it (all my feelings about it were worn out too), and within a few days I was writing stories as if there were no such thing as writer's block. (But if, in future, I show little inclination to philosophize dogmatically, and if I busy myself with trivial and rather childish activities such as haunting game stores and amusement parks and other seedy and picturesque localities, if I write exceedingly fanciful even frivolous fiction, if I pursue all sorts of quaint and curious people restlessly, if there is at times something frantic in my desire for human closeness, and if I seem occasionally to head out toward the universe, anywhere at all in it, and dive in—well, I imagine you'll understand.)

What do I think about the figure? How do I explain it (or her)? Well, at the time of her appearance I was absolutely sure that she was real, solid, material, and I think the intentness with which I observed her up to the end (the utterly unexpected silvery skin-crackle I saw at the last instant!) argues for that. In fact, the courage to hold still and fully observe was certainly the only sort of courage I displayed during the whole incident. Throughout, I don't believe I ever quite lost my desire to *know,* to look into mystery. (But why was I so absolutely certain that my life depended on *watching* her? I don't know.)

Was she perhaps an archetype of the unconscious mind somehow made real? the Anima or the Kore or the Hag who lays men out (if those be distinct archetypes)? Possibly, I guess.

And what about the science fiction suggestiveness about her? that she was some sort of extraterrestrial being? That would fit with her linkage with a very peculiar violet star, which (the star) I do *not* undertake to explain in any way! Your guess is as good as mine.

Was she, *vide* Lang, a waking dream?—nightmare, rather? Frankly, I find that hard to believe.

Or was she really the Button Molder? (who in Ibsen's play, incidentally, is an old man with pot, ladle, and mold for melting down and casting lead buttons). That seems just my fancy, though I take it rather seriously.

Any other explanations? Truthfully, I haven't looked very far. Perhaps I should put myself into the hands of the psychics or psychologists or even the occultists, but I don't want to. I'm inclined to be satisfied with what I got out of it. (One of my author friends says it's a small price to pay for overcoming writer's block.)

Oh, there was one little investigation that I did carry out, with a puzzling and totally unexpected result which may be suggestive to some, or merely baffling.

Well, when the light went out in my bedroom, as I've said, the figure seemed to fade back through the doorway into the small hallway with lowered ceiling I've told you about and there fade away completely. So I decided to have another look at the ceilinged-off space. I stood on a chair and pushed aside the rather large square of frosted glass and (somewhat hesitantly) thrust up through the opening my right arm and head. The space wasn't altogether empty, as it had seemed when I changed the bulb originally. Now the 200-watt glare revealed a small figure lying close behind one of the 4-by-4 beams of the false ceiling. It was a dust-filmed doll made (I later discovered) of a material called Fabrikoid and stuffed with kapok—it was, in fact, one of the Oz dolls from the 1920's; no, not the Scarecrow, which would surely be the first Oz character you'd think of as a stuffed doll, but the Patchwork Girl.

What do you make of that? I remember saying to myself, as I gazed down at it in my hand, somewhat bemused, *Is this all fantasy ever amounts to? Scraps? Rag dolls?*

Oh, and what about the lay figure in the store window? Yes, she was still there the next morning same as ever. Only they'd changed her position again. She was standing between two straight falls of sheeting, one black, one white, with her mitten hands touching them lightly to either side. And she was bowing her head a trifle, as if she were taking a curtain call.

Jules Verne was one of the most influential writers in the history of imaginative fiction, yet modern writers have ignored his legacy except through fourth- and fifth-hand use of his ideas and techniques. Here's a story that returns to the source to pay tribute to Verne, in an account of strange voyages told as Verne himself might have written it.

Joanna Russ is one of the foremost stylists and thinkers of science fiction and fantasy. She's written mostly science fiction, such as the novels *And Chaos Died* and *The Female Man*, but also some fine fantasy, such as *Kittatinny*.

THE EXTRAORDINARY VOYAGES OF AMÉLIE BERTRAND

Joanna Russ

Hommage à Jules Verne

IN THE SUMMER OF 192- THERE OCCURRED to me the most extraordinary event of my life.

I was traveling on business and was in the French countryside, not far from Lyons, waiting for my train on a small railway platform on the outskirts of a town I shall call Beaulieu-sur-le-Pont. (This is not its name.) The weather was cool, although it was already June, and I shared the platform with only one other passenger: a plump woman of at least forty, by no means pretty but respectably dressed, the true type of our provincial *bonne bourgeoise,* who sat on the bench provided for the comfort of passengers and knitted away at some indeterminate garment.

The station at Beaulieu, like so many of our railway stops in small towns, is provided with a central train station of red brick through which runs an arch of passageway, also of red brick, which thus divides the edifice of the station into a ticket counter and waiting room on one side and a small café on the other. Thus, having attended one's train on the wrong side of the station (for there are railroad tracks on both sides of the edifice), one may occasionally find oneself making the traversal of the station in order to catch one's train, usually at the last minute.

So it occurred with me. I heard the approach of my

train, drew out my watch, and found that the mild spring weather had caused me to indulge in a reverie not only lengthy but at a distance from my desired track; the two-fifty-one for Lyons was about to enter Beaulieu, but I was wrongly situated to place myself on board; were I not quick, no entrainment would take place.

Blessing the good fathers of Beaulieu-sur-le-Pont for their foresight in so dividing their train depot, I walked briskly but with no excessive haste towards the passage. I had not the slightest doubt of catching my train. I even had leisure to reflect on the bridge which figures so largely in the name of the town and to recall that, according to my knowledge, this bridge had been destroyed in the time of Caractacus; then I stepped between the buildings. I noticed that my footsteps echoed from the walls of the tunnel, a phenomenon one may observe upon entering any confined space. To the right of me and to the left were walls of red brick. The air was invigoratingly fresh, the weather sunny and clear, and ahead was the wooden platform, the well-trimmed bushes, and the potted geraniums of the other side of the Beaulieu train station.

Nothing could have been more ordinary.

Then, out of the corner of my eye, I noticed that the lady I had seen knitting on the platform was herself entering the passage at a decorous distance behind me. We were, it seems, to become fellow passengers. I turned and raised my hat to her, intending to continue. I could not see the Lyons train, but to judge by the faculty of hearing, it was rounding the bend outside the station. I placed my hat back upon my head, reached the center of the tunnel, or rather, a point midway along its major diameter—

Will you believe me? Probably. You are English; the fogs and literature of your unfortunate climate predispose you to marvels. Your winters cause you to read much; your authors reflect to you from their pages the romantic imagination of a *refugé* from the damp and cold, to whom anything may happen if only it does so outside his windows! I am the product of another soil; I am logical, I am positive, I am French. Like my famous compatriot, I cry, "Where is this marvel? Let him produce it!" I myself do not believe what happened to me. I believe it no more than I believe that Phineas Fogg circumnavigated the globe in 187- and still lives today in London with the lady he rescued from a funeral pyre in Benares.

Nonetheless I will attempt to describe what happened.

The first sensation was a retardation of time. It seemed to me that I had been in the passage at Beaulieu for a very long time, and the passage itself seemed suddenly to become double its length, or even triple. Then my body became heavy, as in a dream; there was also a disturbance of balance as though the tunnel sloped *down* towards its farther end and some increase in gravity were pulling me in that direction. A phenomenon even more disturbing was the peculiar *haziness* that suddenly obscured the forward end of the Beaulieu tunnel, as if Beaulieu-sur-le-Pont, far from enjoying the temperate warmth of an excellent June day, were actually melting in the heat—yes, heat!—a terrible warmth like that of a furnace, and yet humid, entirely unknown to our moderate climate even in the depths of summer. In a moment my summer clothing was soaked, and I wondered with horror whether I dared offend customary politeness by opening my collar. The noise of the Lyons train, far from disappearing, now surrounded me on all sides as if a dozen trains, and not merely one, were converging upon Beaulieu-sur-le-Pont, or as if a strong wind (which was pushing me forward) were blowing. I attempted to peer into the mistiness ahead of me but could see nothing. A single step farther and the mist swirled aside; there seemed to be a vast spray of greenery beyond—indeed, I could distinctly make out the branches of a large palm tree upon which intense sunlight was beating—and then, directly crossing it, a long, thick, sinuous, gray serpent which appeared to writhe from side to side, and which then fixed itself around the trunk of the palm, bringing into view a gray side as large as the opening of the tunnel itself, four gray columns beneath, and two long ivory tusks.

It was an elephant.

It was the roar of the elephant which brought me to my senses. Before this I had proceeded as in an astonished dream; now I turned and attempted to retrace my steps but found that I could hardly move *up* the steep tunnel against the furious wind which assailed me. I was aware of the cool, fresh, familiar spring of Beaulieu, very small and precious, appearing like a photograph or a scene observed through the diminishing, not the magnifying end, of an opera glass, and of the impossibility of ever attaining it. Then a strong arm seized mine, and I was back on the platform from which I had ventured—it seemed now so long ago!—sitting on the wooden bench while the good bourgeoise in the decent dark dress inquired after my health.

I cried, "But the palm tree—the tropical air—the elephant!"

She said in the calmest way in the world, "Do not distress yourself, monsieur. It was merely Uganda."

I may mention here that Madame Bertrand, although not in her first youth, is a woman whose dark eyes sparkle with extraordinary charm. One must be an imbecile not to notice this. Her concern is sincere, her manner *séduisante,* and we had not been in conversation five minutes before she abandoned the barriers of reserve and explained to me not only the nature of the experience I had undergone, but (on the café of the train station at Beaulieu, over a lemon ice) her own extraordinary history.

"Shortly after the termination of the Great War" (said Madame Bertrand) "I began a habit which I have continued to this day: whenever my husband, Aloysius Bertrand, is away from Beaulieu-sur-le-Pont on business, as often happens, I visit my sister-in-law in Lyons, leaving Beaulieu on one day in the middle of the week and returning on the next. At first my visits were uneventful. Then, one fateful day only two years ago, I happened to depart from the wrong side of the train station after purchasing my ticket, and so found myself seeking to approach my train through that archway or passage where you, monsieur, so recently ventured. There were the same effects, but I attributed them to an attack of faintness and continued, expecting my hour's ride to Lyons, my sister-in-law's company, the cinema, the restaurant, and the usual journey back the next day.

"Imagine my amazement—no, my stupefaction—when I found myself instead on a rough wooden platform surrounded on three sides by the massive rocks and lead-colored waters of a place entirely unfamiliar to me! I made inquiries and discovered, to my unbounded astonishment, that I was on the last railway stop or terminus of Tierra del Fuego, the southernmost tip of the South American continent, and that I had engaged myself to sail as supercargo on a whaling vessel contracted to cruise the waters of Antarctica for the next two years. The sun was low, the clouds massing above, and behind me (continuing the curve of the rock-infested bay) was a jungle of squat pine trees, expressing by the irregularity of their trunks the violence of the climate.

"What could I do? My clothing was Victorian, the ship ready to sail, the six months' night almost upon us. The next train was not due until spring.

"To make a long story short, I sailed.

"You might expect that a lady, placed in such a situation, would suffer much that was disagreeable and discommoding. So it was. But there is also a somber charm to the far south which only those who have traveled there can know: the stars glittering on the ice fields, the low sun, the penguins, the icebergs, the whales. And then there were the sailors, children of the wilderness, young, ardent, sincere, especially one, a veritable Apollo with a broad forehead and golden mustachios. To be frank, I did not remain aloof; we became acquainted, one thing led to another, and *enfin* I learned to love the smell of whale oil. Two years later, alighting from the railway train I had taken to Nome, Alaska, where I had gone to purchase my *trousseau* (for having made telegraphic inquiries about Beaulieu-sur-le-Pont, I found that no Monsieur Bertrand existed therein and so considered myself a widow) I found myself, not in my Victorian dress in the bustling and frigid city of Nome, that commercial capital of the North with its outlaws, dogs, and Esquimaux in furs carrying loads of other furs upon their sleds, but in my old, familiar visiting-dress (in which I had started from Beaulieu so long before) on the platform at Lyons, with my sister-in-law waiting for me. Not only that, but in the more than two years I had remained away, no more time had passed in what I am forced to call the real world than the hour required for the train ride from Beaulieu to Lyons! I had expected Garance to fall upon my neck with cries of astonishment at my absence and the strangeness of my dress; instead she inquired after my health, and not waiting for an answer, began to describe in the most ordinary manner and at very great length the roast of veal which she had purchased that afternoon for dinner.

"At first, so confused and griefstricken was I, that I thought I had somehow missed the train for Nome, and that returning at once from Lyons to Beaulieu would enable me to reach Alaska. I almost cut my visit to Lyons short on the plea of ill-health. But I soon realized the absurdity of imagining that a railway could cross several thousand miles of ocean, and since my sister-in-law was already suspicious (I could not help myself during the visit and often burst out with a *'Mon cher Jack!'*) I controlled myself and gave vent to my feelings only on the return trip to Beaulieu—which, far from ending in Nome, Alaska, ended at the Beaulieu train station and at exactly the time predicted by the railway timetable.

"I decided that my two-years' holiday had been only what the men of psychological science would entitle an unusually complete and detailed dream. The ancient Chinese were, I believe, famous for such vivid dreams; one of their poets is said to have experienced an entire lifetime of love, fear, and adventure while washing his feet. This was my case exactly. Here was I not a day—nay not an hour—older, and no one knew what had passed in the Antarctic save I myself.

"It was a reasonable explanation, but it had one grave defect, which rendered it totally useless.

"It was false.

"Since that time, Monsieur, I have gone on my peculiar voyages, my holidays, *mes vacances,* as I call them, not once but dozens of times. My magic carpet is the railway station at Beaulieu, or to be more precise, the passageway between the ticket office and the café at precisely ten minutes before three in the afternoon. A traversal of the passage at any other time brings me merely to the other side of the station, but a traversal of the passage at this particular time brings me to some far, exotic corner of the globe. Perhaps it is Ceylon with its crowds of variegated hue, its scent of incense, its pagodas and rickshaws. Or the deserts of Al-Iqah, with the crowds of Bedawi, dressed in flowing white and armed with rifles, many of whom whirl round about one another on horseback. Or I will find myself on the languid islands of Tahiti, with the graceful and dusky inhabitants bringing me bowls of *poi* and garlands of flowers whose beauty is unmatched anywhere else in the tropical portion of the globe. Nor have my holidays been entirely confined to the terrestrial regions. Last February I stepped through the passage to find myself on the sands of a primitive beach under a stormy, gray sky; in the distance one could perceive the roarings of saurians and above me were the giant saw-toothed, purple leaves of some palmaceous plant, one (as it turned out) entirely unknown to botanical science.

"No, monsieur, it was not Ceylon; it was Venus. It is true that I prefer a less overcast climate, but still one can hardly complain. To lie in the darkness of the Venerian night, on the silky volcanic sands, under the starry leaves of the *laradh,* while imbibing the million perfumes of the night-blooming flowers and listening to the music of the *karakh*—really, one does not miss the blue sky. Although only a few weeks ago I was in a place that also pleased me: imagine a huge, whitish-blue sky, a desert with giant mountains on the horizon, and the lean, hard-bitten water-prospectors with their dowsing rods, their high-heeled boots, and their large hats, worn to protect faces already tanned and wrinkled from the intense sunlight.

"No, not Mars, Texas. They are marvelous people, those American pioneers, the men handsome and laconic, the women sturdy and efficient. And then one day I entrained to Lyons only to find myself on a railway platform that resembled a fishbowl made of tinted glass, while around me rose mountains fantastically slender into a black sky where the stars shone like hard marbles, scarcely twinkling at all. I was wearing a glass helmet and clothes that resembled a diver's. I had no idea where I was until I rose, and then to my edified surprise, instead of rising in the usual manner, I positively bounded into the air!

"I was on the Moon.

"Yes, monsieur, the Moon, although some distance in the future, the year two thousand eighty and nine, to be precise. At that date human beings will have established a colony on the Moon. My carriage swiftly shot down beneath one of the Selenic craters to land in their principal city, a fairy palace of slender towers and domes of glass, for they use as building material a glass made from the native silicate gravel. It was on the Moon that I gathered whatever theory I now have concerning my peculiar experiences with the railway passage at Beaulieu-sur-le-Pont, for I made the acquaintance there of the principal mathematician of the twenty-first century, a most elegant lady, and put the problem to her. You must understand that on the Moon *les nègres, les juifs* even *les femmes* may obtain high positions and much influence; it is a true republic. This lady introduced me to her colleague, a black physicist of more-than-normal happenings, or *le paraphysique* as they call it, and the two debated the matter during an entire day (not a Selenic day, of course, since that would have amounted to a time equal to twenty-eight days of our own). They could not agree, but in brief, as they told me, either the railway tunnel at Beaulieu-sur-le-Pont has achieved infinite connectivity or it is haunted. To be perfectly sincere, I regretted leaving the Moon. But one has one's obligations. Just as my magic carpet here at Beaulieu is of the nature of a railway tunnel, and just as I always find myself in *mes vacances* at first situated on a railway platform, thus my return must also be effected by that so poetically termed road of iron; I placed myself into the railway that connects two of the principal Selenic craters, and behold!—I alight at the platform at Lyons, not a day older.

"Indeed, monsieur" (and here Madame Bertrand coughed delicately) "as we are both people of the world, I may mention that certain other of the biological processes also suspend themselves, a fact not altogether to my liking, since my dear Aloysius and myself are entirely without family. Yet this suspension has its advantages; if I had aged as I have lived, it would be a woman of seventy who speaks to you now. In truth, how can one age in worlds that are, to speak frankly, not quite real? Though perhaps if I had remained permanently in one of these worlds, I too would have begun to age along with the other inhabitants. That would be a pleasure on the Moon, for my mathematical friend was age two hundred when I met her, and her acquaintance, the professor of *le paraphysique*, two hundred and five."

Here Madame Bertrand, to whose recital I had been listening with breathless attention, suddenly ceased speaking. Her lemon ice stood untouched upon the table. So full was I of projects to make the world acquainted with this amazing history that I did not at first notice the change in Madame Bertrand's expression, and so I burst forth:

"The National Institute—the Académie—no, the universities, and the newspapers also—"

But the charming lady, with a look of horror, and risen from the table, crying, "Mon dieu! My train! What will Garance think? What will she say? Monsieur, not a word to anyone!"

Imagine my consternation when Madame Bertrand here precipitously departed from the café and began to cross the station towards that ominous passageway. I could only postulate, "But, madame, consider! Ceylon! Texas! Mars!"

"No, it is too late," said she. "Only at the former time in the train schedule. Monsieur, remember, please, not a word to anyone!"

Following her, I cried, "But if you do not return—" and she again favored me with her delightful smile, saying rapidly, "Do not distress yourself, monsieur. By now I have developed certain sensations—a *frisson* of the neck and shoulder blades—which warns me of the condition of the passageway. The later hour is always safe. But my train—!"

And so Madame Bertrand left me. Amazing woman! A traveler not only to the far regions of the earth but to those of imagination, and yet perfectly respectable, gladly fulfilling the duties of family life, and punctually (except for this one time) meeting her sister-in-law, Mademoiselle Garance Bertrand, on the train platform at Lyons.

Is that the end of my story? No, for I was fated to meet Amélie Bertrand once again.

My business, which I have mentioned to you, took me back to Beaulieu-sur-le-Pont at the end of that same summer. I must confess that I hoped to encounter Madame Bertrand, for I had made it my intention to notify at least several of our great national institutions of the extraordinary powers possessed by the railway passage at Beaulieu, and yet I certainly could not do so without Madame Bertrand's consent. Again it was shortly before three in the afternoon; again the station platform was deserted. I saw a figure which I took to be that of Madame Bertrand seated upon the bench reserved for passengers and hastened to it with a glad cry—

But it was not Amélie Bertrand. Rather it was a thin and elderly female, entirely dressed in the dullest of black and completely without the charm I had expected to find in my fellow passenger. The next moment I heard my name pronounced and was delighted to perceive, issuing from the ticket office, Madame Bertrand herself, wearing a light-colored summer dress.

But where was the gaiety, the charm, the pleasant atmosphere of June? Madame Bertrand's face was closed, her eyes watchful, her expression determined. I would immediately have opened to her my immense projects, but with a shake of her head the lady silenced me, indicating the figure I have already mentioned.

"My sister-in-law, Mademoiselle Garance," she said. I confess that I nervously expected that Aloysius Bertrand himself would now appear. But we were alone on the platform. Madame Bertrand continued: "Garance, this is the gentleman who was the unfortunate cause of my missing my train last June."

Mademoiselle Garance, as if to belie the reputation for loquacity I had heard applied to her earlier in the summer, said nothing, but merely clutched to her meager bosom a small train case.

Madame Bertrand said to me, "I have explained to Garance the occasion of your illness last June and the manner in which the officials of the station detained me. I am glad to see you looking so well."

This was a clear hint that Mademoiselle Garance was to know nothing of her sister-in-law's history; thus I merely bowed and nodded. I wished to have the opportunity of conversing with Madame Bertrand more freely, but I could say nothing in the presence of her sister-in-law. Desperately I began: "You are taking the train today—"

"For the sake of nostalgia," said Madame Bertrand. "After today I shall never set foot in a railway carriage. Garance may if she likes, but I will not. Aeroplanes, motor cars, and ships will be good enough for me. Perhaps like the famous American, Madame Earhart, I shall learn to fly. This morning Aloysius told me the good news: a change in his business arrangements has enabled us to move to Lyons, which we are to do at the end of the month."

"And in the intervening weeks—?" said I.

Madame Bertrand replied composedly, "There will be none. They are tearing down the station."

What a blow! And there sat the old maid, Mademoiselle Garance, entirely unconscious of the impending loss to science! I stammered something—I know not what—but my good angel came to my rescue; with an infinitesimal movement of the fingers, she said:

"Oh, monsieur, my conscious pains me too much! Garance, would you believe that I told this gentleman the most preposterous stories? I actually told him—seriously, now—that the passageway of this train station was the gateway to another world! No, many worlds, and that I had been to all of them. Can you believe it of me?" She turned to me. "Oh, monsieur," she said, "you were a good listener. You only pretended to believe. Surely you cannot imagine that a respectable woman like myself would leave her husband by means of a railway passage which has achieved infinite connectivity?"

Here Madame Bertrand looked at me in a searching manner, but I was at a loss to understand her intention in so doing and said nothing.

She went on, with a little shake of the head. "I must confess it; I am addicted to storytelling. Whenever my dear Aloysius left home on his business trips, he would say to me, '*Occupe-toi, occupe-toi, Amélie!*' and alas, I have occupied myself only too well. I thought my romance might divert your mind from your ill-health and so presumed to tell you an unlikely tale of extraordinary voyages. Can you forgive me?"

I said something polite, something I do not now recall. I was, you understand, still reeling from the blow. All that merely a fable! Yet with what detail, what plausible circumstance Madame Bertrand had told her story. I could only feel relieved I had not actually written to the National Institute. I was about to press both ladies to take some refreshment with me, when Madame Bertrand (suddenly putting her hand to her heart in a gesture that seemed to me excessive) cried, "Our train!" and turning to me, remarked, "Will you accompany us down the passage?"

Something made me hesitate; I know not what.

"Think, monsieur," said Madame Bertrand, with her hand still pressed to her heart, "where will it be this time? A London of the future, perhaps, enclosed against the weather and built entirely of glass? Or perhaps the majestic, high plains of Colorado? Or will we find ourselves in one of the underground cities of the moons of Jupiter, in whose awesome skies the mighty planet rises and sets with a visual diameter more than that of the terrestrial Alps?"

She smiled with humor at Mademoiselle Garance, remarking, "Such are the stories I told this gentleman, dear Garance; they were a veritable novel," and I saw that she was gently teasing her sister-in-law, who naturally did not know what any of this was about.

Mademoiselle Garance ventured to say timidly that she "liked to read novels."

I bowed.

Suddenly I heard the sound of the train outside Beaulieu-sur-le-Pont. Madame Bertrand cried in an utterly prosaic voice, "Our train! Garance, we shall miss our train!" and again she asked, "Monsieur, will you accompany us?"

I bowed, but remained where I was. Accompanied by the thin, stooped figure of her sister-in-law, Madame Bertrand walked quickly down the passageway which divides the ticket room of the Beaulieu-sur-le-Pont station from the tiny café. I confess that when the two ladies reached the midpoint of the longitudinal axis of the passageway, I involuntarily closed my eyes, and when I opened them, the passage was empty.

What moved me then I do not know, but I found myself quickly traversing the passageway, seeing in my mind's eye Madame Bertrand boarding the Lyons train with her sister-in-law, Mademoiselle Garance. One could certainly hear the train; the sound of its engine filled the whole station. I believe I told myself that I wished to exchange one last polite word. I reached the other side of the station—

And there was no Lyons train there.

There were no ladies on the platform.

There is, indeed, no two-fifty-one train to Lyons whatsoever, not on the schedule of any line!

Imagine my sensations, my dear friend, upon learning that Madame Bertrand's story was true, all of it! It is true, all too true, all of it is true, and my Amélie is gone forever!

"My" Amélie I call her; yet she still belongs (in law) to Aloysius Bertrand, who will, no doubt, after the necessary statutory period of waiting is over, marry again, and thus become a respectable and unwitting bigamist.

That animal could never have understood her!

Even now (if I may be permitted that phrase) Amélie Bertrand may be drifting down one of the great Venerian rivers on a gondola, listening to the music of the *karakh;* even now she may perform acts of heroism on Airstrip One or chat with her mathematical friend on a balcony that overlooks the airy towers and flower-filled plazas of the Selenic capitol. I have no doubt that if you were to attempt to find the places Madame Bertrand mentioned by looking in the Encyclopedia or a similar work of reference, you would not succeed. As she herself mentioned, they are "not quite real." There are strange discrepancies.

Alas, my friend, condole with me; by now all such concern is academic, for the train station at Beaulieu-sur-le-Pont is gone, replaced by a vast erection swarming with workmen, a giant *hangar* (I learned the name from one of them), or edifice for the housing of aeroplanes. I am told that large numbers of these machines will soon fly from *hangar* to *hangar* across the country.

But think: these aeroplanes, will they not in time be used for ordinary business travel, for scheduled visits to resorts and other places? In short, are they not even now the railways of the new age? Is it not possible that the same condition, whether of infinite connectivity or of hauntedness, may again obtain, perhaps in the same place where the journeys of my vanished angel have established a precedent or predisposition?

My friend, collude with me. The *hangar* at Beaulieu will soon be finished, or so I read in the newspapers. I shall go down into the country and establish myself near this *hangar*. I shall purchase a ticket for a ride in one of the new machines, and then we shall see. Perhaps I will enjoy only a pleasant ascension into the air and a similar descent. Perhaps I will instead feel that *frisson* of the neck and shoulder blades of which Madame Bertrand spoke; well, no matter: my children are grown, my wife has a generous income, the *frisson* will not dismay me. I shall walk down the corridor or passageway in or around the *hangar* at precisely nine minutes before three and into the space between the worlds; I shall again feel the strange retardation of time, I shall feel the heaviness of the body, I shall see the haziness at the other end of the tunnel, and then through the lashing wind, through the mistiness which envelops me, with the rushing and roaring of an invisible aeroplane in my ears, I shall proceed. Madame Bertrand was kind enough to delay her own holiday to conduct me back from Uganda; she was generous enough to offer to share the traversal of the passage with me a second time. Surely such kindness and generosity must have its effect! This third time I will proceed. Away from my profession, my daily newspaper, my chess games, my *digestif*—in short, away from all those habits which, it is understood, are given us to take the place of happiness. Away from the petty annoyances of life I shall proceed, away from a dull old age, away from the confusions and terrors of a Europe grown increasingly turbulent, to—

—*What?*

The above copy of a letter was found in a volume of the Encyclopedia (U-Z) in the Bibliothèque National. *It is believed from the evidence that the writer disappeared at a certain provincial town (called "Beaulieu-sur-le-Pont" in the manuscript) shortly after purchasing a ticket for a flight in an aeroplane at the flying field there, a pastime popular among holiday makers.*

He has never been seen again.

Our sins return upon us, even if we don't think we believe that. Even if we don't remember our sins. Yet they remain, and they're as real as mathematics, and eventually each of us is forced to confront them—perhaps in malignant forms we also didn't think we knew. . . .

Orson Scott Card's imaginative and emotion-filled stories have attracted a large audience in the few years he's been writing. His novels include *Hot Sleep* and *A Planet Called Treason*.

EUMENIDES IN THE
FOURTH-FLOOR LAVATORY

Orson Scott Card

LIVING IN A FOURTH-FLOOR WALK-UP WAS PART
of his revenge, as if to say to Alice, "Throw me out
of the house, will you? Then I'll live in squalor in a
Bronx tenement, where the toilet is shared by four apartments! My shirts will go unironed, my tie will be perpetually awry. *See what you've done to me?*"

But when he told Alice about the apartment, she only
laughed bitterly and said, "Not anymore, Howard. I
won't play those games with you. You win every damn
time."

She pretended not to care about him anymore, but
Howard knew better. He knew people, knew what they
wanted, and Alice wanted *him*. It was his strongest card
in their relationship—that she wanted him more than he
wanted her. He thought of this often: at work in the offices of Humboldt and Breinhardt, Designers; at lunch in
a cheap lunchroom (part of the punishment); on the sub-
way home to his tenement (Alice had kept the Lincoln
Continental). He thought and thought about how much
she wanted him. But he kept remembering what she had
said the day she threw him out: If you ever come near
Rhiannon again I'll kill you.

He could not remember why she had said that. Could
not remember and did not try to remember because that
line of thinking made him uncomfortable and one thing
Howard insisted on being was comfortable with himself.
Other people could spend hours and days of their lives

chasing after some accommodation with themselves, but Howard was accommodated. Well adjusted. At ease. I'm okay, I'm okay, I'm okay. Hell with you. "If you let them make you feel uncomfortable," Howard would often say, "you give them a handle on you and they can run your life." Howard could find other people's handles, but they could never find Howard's.

It was not yet winter but cold as hell at three A.M. when Howard got home from Stu's party. A "must attend" party, if you wished to get ahead at Humboldt and Breinhardt. Stu's ugly wife tried to be tempting, but Howard had played innocent and made her feel so uncomfortable that she dropped the matter. Howard paid careful attention to office gossip and knew that several earlier departures from the company had got caught with, so to speak, their pants down. Not that Howard's pants were an impenetrable barrier. He got Dolores from the front office into the bedroom and accused her of making life miserable for him. "In little ways," he insisted. "I know you don't mean to, but you've got to stop."

"What ways?" Dolores asked, incredulous yet (because she honestly tried to make other people happy) uncomfortable.

"Surely you knew how attracted I am to you."

"No. That hasn't—that hasn't even crossed my mind."

Howard looked tongue-tied, embarrassed. He actually was neither. "Then—well, then, I was—I was wrong. I'm sorry, I thought you were doing it deliberately—"

"Doing what?"

"Snub—snubbing me—never mind, it sounds adolescent, just little things, hell, Dolores, I had a stupid schoolboy crush—"

"Howard, I didn't even know I was hurting you."

"God, how insensitive," Howard said, sounding even more hurt.

"Oh, Howard, do I mean that much to you?"

Howard made a little whimpering noise that meant everything she wanted it to mean. She looked uncomfortable. She'd do anything to get back to feeling right with herself again. She was so uncomfortable that they spent a rather nice half hour making each other feel comfortable again. No one else in the office had been able to get to Dolores. But Howard could get to anybody.

He walked up the stairs to his apartment feeling very, very satisfied. Don't need you, Alice, he said to himself.

Don't need nobody, and nobody's who I've got. He was still mumbling the little ditty to himself as he went into the communal bathroom and turned on the light.

He heard a gurgling sound from the toilet stall, a hissing sound. Had someone been in there with the light off? Howard went into the toilet stall and saw nobody. Then looked closer and saw a baby, probably about two months old, lying in the toilet bowl. Its nose and eyes were barely above water; it looked terrified; its legs and hips and stomach were down the drain. Someone had obviously hoped to kill it by drowning—it was inconceivable to Howard that anyone could be so moronic as to think it would fit down the drain.

For a moment he thought of leaving it there, with the big city temptation to mind one's own business even when to do so would be an atrocity. Saving this baby would mean inconvenience: calling the police, taking care of the child in his apartment, perhaps even headlines, certainly a night of filling out reports. Howard was tired. Howard wanted to go to bed.

But he remembered Alice saying. "You aren't even human, Howard. You're a goddamn selfish monster." I am not a monster, he answered silently, and reached down into the toilet bowl to pull the child out.

The baby was firmly jammed in—whoever had tried to kill it had meant to catch it tight. Howard felt a brief surge of genuine indignation that anyone could think to solve his problems by killing an innocent child. But thinking of crimes committed on children was something Howard was determined not to do, and besides, at that moment he suddenly acquired other things to think about.

As the child clutched at Howard's arms, he noticed the baby's fingers were fused together into flipperlike flaps of bone and skin at the end of the arm. Yet the flippers gripped his arms with an unusual strength as, with two hands deep in the toilet bowl, Howard tried to pull the baby free.

At last, with a gush, the child came up and the water finished its flushing action. The legs, too, were fused into a single limb that was hideously twisted at the end. The child was male; the genitals, larger than normal, were skewed off to one side. And Howard noticed that where the feet should be were two more flippers, and near the tips were red spots that looked like putrifying sores. The child cried, a savage mewling that reminded Howard of a dog he had seen in its death throes. (Howard refused to be reminded that it had been he who killed the dog by throwing it out in the street in front of a passing car just to watch the driver swerve; the driver hadn't swerved.)

Even the hideously deformed have a right to live, Howard thought, but now, holding the child in his arms, he felt a revulsion that translated into sympathy for whoever, probably the parents, had tried to kill the creature. The child shifted its grip on him, and where the flippers had been Howard felt a sharp, stinging pain that quickly turned to agony as it was exposed to the air. Several huge, gaping sores on his arm were already running with blood and pus.

It took a moment for Howard to connect the sores with the child, and by then the leg flippers were already pressed against his stomach, and the arm flippers already gripped his chest. The sores on the child's flippers were not sores; they were powerful suction devices that gripped Howard's skin so tightly that it ripped it away when the contact was broken. He tried to pry the child off, but no sooner was one flipper free than it found a new place to hold even as Howard struggled to break the grip of another.

What had begun as an act of charity had now become an intense struggle. This was not a child, Howard realized. Children could not hang on so tightly, and the creature had teeth that snapped at his hands and arms whenever they came near enough. A human face, certainly, but not a human being. Howard threw himself against the wall, hoping to stun the creature so it would drop away. It only clung tighter, and the sores where it hung on him hurt more. But at last Howard pried and scraped it off by levering it against the edge of the toilet stall. It dropped to the ground, and Howard backed quickly away, on fire with the pain of a dozen or more stinging wounds.

It had to be a nightmare. In the middle of the night, in a bathroom lighted by a single bulb, with a travesty of humanity writhing on the floor, Howard could not believe that it had any reality.

Could it be a mutation that had somehow lived? Yet the thing had far more purpose, far more control of its body than any human infant. The baby slithered across the floor as Howard, in pain from the wounds on his body, watched in a panic of indecision. The baby reached the wall and cast a flipper onto it. The suction held and the baby began to inch its way straight up the wall. As it climbed, it defecated, a thin drool of green tracing down the wall behind it. Howard looked at the slime following the infant up the wall, looked at the pus-covered sores on his arms.

What if the animal, whatever it was, did not die soon of its terrible deformity? What if it lived? What if it were found, taken to a hospital, cared for? What if it became an adult?

It reached the ceiling and made the turn, clinging tightly to the plaster, not falling off as it hung upside down and inched across toward the light bulb.

The thing was trying to get directly over Howard, and the defecation was still dripping. Loathing overcame fear, and Howard reached up, took hold of the baby from the back, and, using his full weight, was finally able to pry it off the ceiling. It writhed and twisted in his hands, trying to get the suction cups on him, but Howard resisted with all his strength and was able to get the baby, this time headfirst, into the toilet bowl. He held it there until the bubbles stopped and it was blue. Then he went back to his apartment for a knife. Whatever the creature was, it had to disappear from the face of the earth. It had to die, and there had to be no sign left that could hint that Howard had killed it.

He found the knife quickly, but paused for a few moments to put something on his wounds. They stung bitterly, but in a while they felt better. Howard took off his shirt; thought a moment, and took off all his clothes, then put on his bathrobe and took a towel with him as he returned to the bathroom. He didn't want to get any blood on his clothes.

But when he got to the bathroom, the child was not in the toilet. Howard was alarmed. Had someone found it, drowning? Had they, perhaps, seen him leaving the bathroom—or worse, returning with his knife? He looked around the bathroom. There was nothing. He stepped back into the hall. No one. He stood a moment in the doorway, wondering what could have happened.

Then a weight dropped onto his head and shoulders from above, and he felt the suction flippers tugging at his face, at his head. He almost screamed. But he didn't want to arouse anyone. Somehow the child had not drowned after all, had crawled out of the toilet, and had waited over the door for Howard to return.

Once again the struggle resumed, and once again Howard pried the flippers away with the help of the toilet stall, though this time he was hampered by the fact that the child was behind and above him. It was exhausting work. He had to set down the knife so he could use both hands, and another dozen wounds stung bitterly by the time he had the child on the floor. As long as the child lay on its stomach, Howard could seize it from behind. He took it by the neck with one hand and picked up the knife with the other. He carried both to the toilet.

He had to flush twice to handle the flow of blood and pus. Howard wondered if the child was infected with some disease—the white fluid was thick and at least as great in volume as the blood. Then he flushed seven more times to take the pieces of the creature down the drain. Even after death, the suction pads clung tightly to the porcelain; Howard pried them off with the tip of the knife.

Eventually, the child was completely gone. Howard was panting with the exertion, nauseated at the stench and horror of what he had done. He remembered the smell of his dog's guts after the car hit it, and he threw up everything he had eaten at the party. Got the party out of his system, felt cleaner; took a shower, felt cleaner still. When he was through, he made sure the bathroom showed no sign of his ordeal.

Then he went to bed.

It wasn't easy to sleep. He was too keyed up. He couldn't take out of his mind the thought that he had committed murder (not murder, not murder, simply the elimination of something too foul to be alive). He tried thinking of a dozen, a hundred other things. Projects at work . . . but their faces turned to the intense face of the struggling monster he had killed. Alice . . . ah, but Alice was harder to think of than the creature.

At last he slept, and dreamed, and in his dream remembered his father, who had died when he was ten. Howard did not remember any of his standard reminiscences. No long walks with his father, no basketball in the driveway, no fishing trips. Those things had happened, but tonight, because of the struggle with the monster, Howard remembered darker things that he had long been able to keep hidden from himself.

"We can't afford to get you a ten-speed bike, Howie. Not until the strike is over."

"I know, Dad. You can't help it." Swallow bravely.

"And I don't mind. When all the guys go riding around after school, I'll just stay home and get ahead on my homework."

"Lots of boys don't have ten-speed bikes, Howie."

Howie shrugged, and turned away to hide the tears in his eyes. "Sure, lots of them. Hey, Dad, don't you worry about me. Howie can take care of himself."

Such courage. Such strength. He had gotten a ten-speed within a week. In his dream, Howard finally made a connection he had never been able to admit to himself before. His father had a rather elaborate ham radio setup in the garage. But about that time he had become tired of it, he said, and he sold it off and did a lot more work in the yard and looked bored as hell until the strike was over and he went back to work and got killed in an accident in the rolling mill.

Howard's dream ended madly, with him riding piggyback on his father's shoulders as the monster had ridden on *him,* tonight—and in his hand was a knife, and he was stabbing his father again and again in the throat.

He awoke in early morning light, before his alarm rang, sobbing weakly and whimpering, "I killed him, I killed him, I killed him."

And then he drifted upward out of sleep and saw the time. Six-thirty. "A dream," he said. And the dream had awakened him early, too early, with a headache and sore eyes from crying. The pillow was soaked. And, as was his habit, he got up and went to the window and opened the curtain.

On the glass, suction cups clinging tightly, was the child.

It was pressed close, as if by sucking very tightly it would be able to slither through the glass without breaking it. Far below were the honks of early morning traffic, the roar of passing trucks, but the child seemed oblivious of its height far above the street, with no ledge to break its fall. Indeed, there seemed little chance it would fall. The eyes looked closely, piercingly, at Howard.

Howard had been prepared to pretend that the night before had been another terribly realistic nightmare.

He stepped back from the glass, watched the child in fascination. It lifted a flipper, planted it higher, pulled itself up to a new position where it could stare at Howard eye to eye. And then, slowly and methodically, it began beating on the glass with its head.

The landlord was not generous with upkeep on the

building. The glass was thin, and Howard knew that the child would not give up until it had broken through the glass so it could get to Howard.

He began to shake. His throat tightened. He was terribly afraid. Last night had been no dream. The fact that the child was here today was proof of that. Yet he had cut the child into small pieces. It could not possibly be alive. The glass shook and rattled with every blow the child's head struck.

The glass slivered in a starburst from where the child had hit it. The creature was coming in. And Howard picked up the room's one chair and threw it at the child, threw it at the window. Glass shattered, and the sun dazzled on the fragments as they exploded outward like a glistening halo around the child and the chair.

Howard ran to the window, looked out, looked down and watched as the child landed brutally on the top of a large truck. The body seemed to smear as it hit, and fragments of the chair and shreds of glass danced around the child and bounced down into the street and the sidewalk.

The truck didn't stop moving; it carried the broken body and the shards of glass and the pool of blood on up the street, and Howard ran to the bed, knelt beside it, buried his face in the blanket, and tried to regain control of himself. He had been seen. The people in the street had looked up and had seen him in the window. Last night he had gone to great lengths to avoid discovery, but today discovery was impossible to avoid. He was ruined. And yet he could not, could never have, let the child come into the room.

Footsteps on the stairs. Stamping up the corridor. Pounding on the door. "Open up! Hey in there!"

If I'm quiet long enough, they'll go away, he said to himself knowing it was a lie. He must get up, must answer the door. But he could not bring himself to admit that he ever had to leave the safety of his bed.

"Hey, you son-of-a-bitch—" The imprecations went on but Howard could not move until, suddenly, it occurred to him that the child could be under the bed, and as he thought of it he could feel the tip of the flipper touching his thigh, stroking and getting ready to fasten itself—

Howard leaped to his feet and rushed for the door. He flung it wide, for even if it was the police come to arrest him, they could protect him from the monster that was haunting him.

It was not a policeman at the door. It was the man on the first floor who collected rent. "You son-of-a-bitch irresponsible pig-kisser!" the man shouted, his toupe only approximately in place. "That chair could have hit somebody! That window's expensive! Out! Get out of here, right now, I want you out of this place, I don't care how the hell drunk you are——"

"There was——there was this thing on the window, this creature——"

The man looked at him coldly, but his eyes danced with anger. No, not anger. Fear. Howard realized the man was afraid of him.

"This is a decent place," the man said softly. "You can take your creatures and your booze and your pink stinking elephants and that's a hundred bucks for the window, a hundred bucks right now, and you can get out of here in an hour, an hour, you hear? Or I'm calling the police, you hear?"

"I hear." He heard. The man seemed careful to avoid touching Howard's hands, as if Howard had become, somehow, repulsive. Well, he had. To himself, if to no one else. He closed the door as soon as the man was gone. He packed the few belongings he had brought to the apartment in two suitcases and went downstairs and called a cab and rode to work. The cabby looked at him sourly, and wouldn't talk. It was fine with Howard, if only the driver hadn't kept looking at him through the mirror ——nervously, as if he was afraid of what Howard might do or try. I won't try anything, Howard said to himself, I'm a decent man. Howard tipped the cabby well and then gave him twenty to take his bags to his house in Queens, where Alice could damn well keep them for a while. Howard was through with the tenement——that one or any other.

Obviously it had been a nightmare, last night and this morning. The monster was only visible to him, Howard decided. Only the chair and the glass had fallen from the fourth floor, or the manager would have noticed.

Except that the baby had landed on the truck, and might have been real, and might be discovered in New Jersey or Pennsylvania later today.

Couldn't be real. He had killed it last night and it was whole again this morning. A nightmare. I didn't really kill anybody, he insisted. (Except the dog. Except Father, said a new, ugly voice in the back of his mind.)

Work. Draw lines on paper, answer phone calls, dictate letters, keep your mind off your nightmares, off your family, off the mess your life is turning into. "Hell of a good party last night." Yeah, it was, wasn't it? "How are you today, Howard?" Feel fine, Dolores, fine—thanks to you. "Got the roughs on the IBM thing?" Nearly, nearly. Give me another twenty minutes. "Howard, you don't look well." Had a rough night. The party, you know.

He kept drawing on the blotter on his desk instead of going to the drawing table and producing real work. He doodled out faces. Alice's face, looking stern and terrible. The face of Stu's ugly wife. Dolores's face, looking sweet and yielding and stupid. And Rhiannon's face.

But with his daughter Rhiannon, he couldn't stop with the face.

His hand started to tremble when he saw what he had drawn. He ripped the sheet off the blotter, crumpled it, and reached under the desk to drop it in the wastebasket. The basket lurched, and flippers snaked out to seize his hand in an iron grip.

Howard screamed, tried to pull his hand away. The child came with it, the leg flippers grabbing Howard's right leg. The suction pad stung, bringing back the memory of all the pain last night. He scraped the child off against a filing cabinet, then ran for the door, which was already opening as several of his co-workers tumbled into his office demanding, "What is it! What's wrong! Why did you scream like that!"

Howard led them gingerly over to where the child should be. Nothing. Just an overturned wastebasket, Howard's chair capsized on the floor. But Howard's window was open, and he could not remember opening it. "Howard, what is it? Are you tired, Howard? What's wrong?"

I don't feel well. I don't feel well at all.

Dolores put her arm around him, led him out of the room. "Howard, I'm worried about you."

I'm worried, too.

"Can I take you home? I have my car in the garage downstairs. Can I take you home?"

Where's home? Don't have a home, Dolores.

"My home, then. I have an apartment, you need to lie down and rest. Let me take you home."

Dolores's apartment was decorated in early Holly Hobby, and when she put records on the stereo it was old Carpenters and recent Captain and Tennille. Dolores led him to the bed, gently undressed him, and then, because he reached out to her, undressed herself and made love to him before she went back to work. She was naively eager. She whispered in his ear that he was only the second man she had ever loved, the first in five years. Her inept love-making was so sincere it made him want to cry.

When she was gone he did cry, because she thought she meant something to him and she did not.

Why am I crying? he asked himself. Why should I care? It's not my fault she let me get a handle on her. . . .

Sitting on the dresser in a curiously adult posture was the child, carelessly playing with itself as it watched Howard intently. "No," Howard said, pulling himself up to the head of the bed. "You don't exist," he said. "No one's ever seen you but me." The child gave no sign of under-standing. It just rolled over and began to slither down the front of the dresser.

Howard reached for his clothes, took them out of the bedroom. He put them on in the living room as he watched the door. Sure enough, the child crept along the carpet to the living room; but Howard was dressed by then, and he left.

He walked the streets for three hours. He was coldly rational at first. Logical. The creature does not exist. There is no reason to believe in it.

But bit by bit his rationality was worn away by con-stant flickers of the creature at the edges of his vision. On a bench, peering over the back at him; in a shop window; staring from the cab of a milk truck. Howard walked faster and faster, not caring where he went, trying to keep some intelligent process going on in his mind, and failing utterly as he saw the child, saw it clearly, dangling from a traffic signal.

What made it even worse was that occasionally a pas-serby, violating the unwritten law that New Yorkers are forbidden to look at each other, would gaze at him, shud-der, and look away. A short European-looking woman crossed herself. A group of teenagers looking for trouble weren't looking for him—they grew silent, let him pass in silence, and in silence watched him out of sight.

They may not be able to see the child, Howard realized, but they see something.

And as he grew less and less coherent in the ramblings of his mind, memories began flashing on and off, his life passing before his eyes like a drowning man is supposed to see, only, he realized, if a drowning man saw this he would gulp at the water, breathe it deeply just to end the visions. They were memories he had been unable to find for years; memories he would never have wanted to find.

His poor, confused mother, who was so eager to be a good parent that she read everything, tried everything. Her precocious son Howard read it, too, and understood it better. Nothing she tried ever worked. And he accused her several times of being too demanding, or not demanding enough; of not giving him enough love, or of drowning him in phony affection; of trying to take over with his friends, of not liking his friends enough. Until he had badgered and tortured the woman until she was timid everytime she spoke to him, careful and long-winded and phrasing everything in such a way that it wouldn't offend, and while now and then he made her feel wonderful by giving her a hug and saying "Have I got a wonderful mom," there were far more times when he put a patient look on his face and said, "That again, mom? I thought we went over that years ago." A failure as a parent, that's what you are, he reminded her again and again, though not in so many words, and she nodded and believed and died inside with every contact they had. He got everything he wanted from her.

And Vaughn Robles, who was just a little bit smarter than Howard and Howard wanted very badly to be valedictorian and so Vaughn and Howard became best friends and Vaughn would do anything for Howard and whenever Vaughn got a better grade than Howard he could not help but notice that Howard was hurt, wondered if he was really worth anything at all. "Am I really worth anything at all, Vaughn? No matter how well I do, there's always someone ahead of me, and I guess it's just that before my father died he told me and told me, "Howie, be better than your dad. Be the top." And I promised him I'd be the top but hell, Vaughn, I'm just not cut out for it—" and once he even cried. Vaughn was proud of himself as he sat there and listened to Howard give the valedictory address at high school graduation. What were a few grades, compared to a true friendship? Howard got a scholarship and went away to college and he and Vaughn almost never saw each other again.

And the teacher he provoked into hitting him and losing his job; and the football player who snubbed him and Howard quietly spread the rumor that the fellow was gay and he was ostracized from the team and finally quit; and the beautiful girls he stole from their boyfriends just to prove that he could do it and the friendships he destroyed just because he didn't like being excluded and the marriages he wrecked and the co-workers he undercut and he walked along the street with tears streaming down his face wondering where all these memories had come from and why, after such a long time in hiding, they had come out now. Yet he knew the answer. The answer was slipping behind doorways, climbing lightpoles as he passed, waving obscene flippers at him from the sidewalk almost under his feet.

And slowly, inexorably, the memories wound their way from the distant past through a hundred tawdry exploitations because he could find people's weak spots without even trying until finally, memory came to the one place where he knew it could not, could not ever go.

He remembered Rhiannon.

Born fourteen years ago. Smiled early, walked early, almost never cried. A loving child from the start, and therefore easy prey for Howard. Oh, Alice was a bitch in her own right—Howard wasn't the only bad parent in the family. But it was Howard who manipulated Rhiannon most. "Daddy's feelings are hurt, sweetheart," and Rhiannon's eyes would grow wide, and she'd be sorry, and whatever daddy wanted, Rhiannon would do. But this was normal, this was part of the pattern, this would have fit easily into all his life before except for last week.

And even now, after a day of grief at his own life, Howard could not face it. Could not but did. He unwillingly remembered walking by Rhiannon's almost-closed door, seeing just a flash of cloth moving quickly. He opened the door on impulse, just on impulse, as Rhiannon took off her brassiere and looked at herself in the mirror. Howard had never thought of his daughter with desire, not until that moment, but once the desire formed Howard had no strategy, no pattern in his mind to stop him from trying to get what he wanted. He was *uncomfortable,* and so he stepped into the room and closed the door behind him and Rhiannon knew no way to say no to her father. When Alice opened the door Rhiannon was crying softly, and Alice looked and after a moment Alice screamed and screamed and Howard got up from the bed and tried to smooth it all over but Rhiannon was still crying and Alice was still screaming, kicking at his crotch, beating him, raking at his face, spitting at him, telling him he was a monster, a monster, until at last he was able to flee the room and the house and, until now, the memory.

He screamed now as he had not screamed then, and threw himself against a plate glass window, weeping loudly as the blood gushed from a dozen glass cuts on his right arm, which had gone through the window. One large piece of glass stayed embedded in his forearm. He deliberately scraped his arm against the wall to drive the glass deeper. But the pain in his arm was no match for the pain in his mind, and he felt nothing.

They rushed him to the hospital, thinking to save his life, but the doctor was surprised to discover that for all the blood there were only superficial wounds, not dangerous at all. "I don't know why you didn't reach a vein or an artery," the doctor said. "I think the glass went everywhere it could possibly go without causing any important damage."

After the medical doctor, of course, there was the psychiatrist, but there were many suicidals at the hospital and Howard was not the dangerous kind. "I was insane for a moment, doctor, that's all. I don't want to die, I didn't want to die then, I'm all right now. You can send me home." And the psychiatrist let him go home. They bandaged his arm. They did not know that his real relief was that nowhere in the hospital did he see the small, naked, child-shaped creature. He had purged himself. He was free.

Howard was taken home in an ambulance, and they wheeled him into the house and lifted him from the stretcher to the bed. Through it all Alice hardly said a word except to direct them to the bedroom. Howard lay still on the bed as she stood over him, the two of them alone for the first time since he had left the house a month ago.

"It was kind of you," Howard said softly, "to let me come back."

"They said there wasn't room enough to keep you, but you needed to be watched and taken care of for a few weeks. So lucky me, I get to watch you." Her voice was a low monotone, but the acid dripped from every word. It stung.

"You were right, Alice," Howard said.

"Right about what? That marrying you was the worst mistake of my life? No, Howard. *Meeting* you was my worst mistake."

Howard began to cry. Real tears that welled up from places in him that had once been deep but that now rested painfully close to the surface. "I've been a monster, Alice. I haven't had any control over myself. What I did to Rhiannon—Alice, I wanted to die, I wanted to die!"

Alice's face was twisted and bitter. "And I wanted you to, Howard. I have never been so disappointed as when the doctor called and said you'd be all right. You'll never be all right, Howard, you'll always be—"

"Let him be, mother."

Rhiannon stood in the doorway.

"Don't come in, Rhiannon," Alice said.

Rhiannon came in. "Daddy, it's all right."

"What she means," Alice said, "is that we've checked her and she isn't pregnant. No little monster is going to be born."

Rhiannon didn't look at her mother, just gazed with wide eyes at her father. "You didn't need to—hurt yourself, daddy. I forgive you. People lose control sometimes. And it was as much my fault as yours, it really was, you don't need to feel bad, father."

It was too much for Howard. He cried out, shouted his confession, how he had manipulated her all her life, how he was an utterly selfish and rotten parent, and when it was over Rhiannon came to her father and laid her head on his chest and said softly, "Father, it's all right. We are who we are. We've done what we've done. But it's all right now. I forgive you."

When Rhiannon left, Alice said, "You don't deserve her."

I know.

"I was going to sleep on the couch, but that would be stupid. Wouldn't it, Howard?"

I deserve to be left alone, like a leper.

"You misunderstand, Howard. I need to stay here to make sure you don't do anything else. To yourself or to anyone."

Yes. Yes, please. I can't be trusted.

"Don't wallow in it, Howard. Don't enjoy it. Don't make yourself even more disgusting than you were before."

All right.

They were drifting off to sleep when Alice said, "Oh, when the doctor called he wondered if I knew what had caused those sores all over your arms and chest."

But Howard was asleep, and didn't hear her. Asleep with no dreams at all, the sleep of peace, the sleep of having been forgiven, of being clean. It hadn't taken that much, after all. Now that it was over, it was easy. He felt as if a great weight had been taken from him.

He felt as if something heavy was lying on his legs. He awoke, sweating even though the room was not hot. He heard breathing. And it was not Alice's low-pitched, slow breath, it was quick and high and hard, as if the breather had been exerting himself.

Itself.

Themselves.

One of them lay across his legs, the flippers plucking at the blanket. The other two lay on either side, their eyes wide and intent, creeping slowly toward where his face emerged from the sheets.

Howard was puzzled. "I thought you'd be gone," he said to the children. "You're supposed to be gone now."

Alice stirred at the sound of his voice, mumbled in her sleep.

He saw more of them stirring in the gloomy corners of the room, another writhing slowly along the top of the dresser, another inching up the wall toward the ceiling.

"I don't need you anymore," he said, his voice oddly high-pitched.

Alice started breathing irregularly, mumbling, "What? What?"

And Howard said nothing more, just lay there in the sheets, watching the creatures carefully but not daring to make a sound for fear Alice would wake up. He was terribly afraid she would wake up and not see the creatures, which would prove, once and for all, that he had lost his mind.

He was even more afraid, however, that when she awoke she *would* see them. That was the one unbearable thought, yet he thought it continuously as they relentlessly approached with nothing at all in their eyes, not even hate, not even anger, not even contempt. We are with you from now on. We will be with you, Howard, forever.

And Alice rolled over and opened her eyes.

≋≋≋≋≋≋≋≋≋≋≋≋≋≋≋≋≋≋≋≋≋≋≋≋≋

Fantasy is by no means always about ghoulies and ghastlies; there are also unicorns, elves, the occasional friendly dragon, and others . . . including some beings best categorized as archetypes. Whether they're good or evil is sometimes open to interpretation and argument, as in this evocative story.

Greg Bear is an excellent young writer whose novels include *Hegira* and *Psychlone*. A collection of his fantasy stories will be published soon by Arkham House.

THE WHITE HORSE CHILD

Greg Bear

WHEN I WAS SEVEN YEARS OLD, I MET AN OLD man by the side of the dusty road between school and farm. The late afternoon sun had cooled and he was sitting on a rock, hat off, hands held out to the gentle warmth, whistling a pretty song. He nodded at me as I walked past. I nodded back. I was curious, but I knew better than to get involved with strangers. Nameless evils seemed to attach themselves to strangers, as if they might turn into lions when no one but a little kid was around.

"Hello, boy," he said.

I stopped and shuffled my feet. He looked more like a hawk than a lion. His clothes were brown and gray and russet, and his hands were pink like the flesh of some rabbit a hawk had just plucked up. His face was brown except around the eyes, where he might have worn glasses; around the eyes he was white, and this intensified his gaze. "Hello," I said.

"Was a hot day. Must have been hot in school," he said.

"They got air conditioning."

"So they do, now. How old are you?"

"Seven," I said. "Well, almost eight."

"Mother told you never to talk to strangers?"

"And Dad, too."

"Good advice. But haven't you seen me around here before?"

I looked him over. "No."

"Closely. Look at my clothes. What color are they?"

His shirt was gray, like the rock he was sitting on. The cuffs, where they peeped from under a russet jacket, were white. He didn't smell bad, but he didn't look particularly clean. He was smooth-shaven, though. His hair was white and his pants were the color of the dirt below the rock. "All kinds of colors," I said.

"But mostly I partake of the landscape, no?"

"I guess so," I said.

"That's because I'm not here. You're imagining me, at least part of me. Don't I look like somebody you might have heard of?"

"Who are you supposed to look like?" I asked.

"Well, I'm full of stories," he said. "Have lots of stories to tell little boys, little girls, even big folk, if they'll listen."

I started to walk away.

"But only if they'll listen," he said. I ran. When I got home, I told my older sister about the man on the road, but she only got a worried look and told me to stay away from strangers. I took her advice. For some time afterward, into my eighth year, I avoided that road and did not speak with strangers more than I had to.

The house that I lived in, with the five other members of my family and two dogs and one beleaguered cat, was white and square and comfortable. The stairs were rich, dark wood overlaid with worn carpet. The walls were dark oak paneling up to a foot above my head, then white plaster, with a white plaster ceiling. The air was full of smells—bacon when I woke up, bread and soup and dinner when I came home from school, dust on weekends when we helped clean.

Sometimes my parents argued, and not just about money, and those were bad times; but usually we were happy. There was talk about selling the farm and the house and going to Mitchell where Dad could work in a computerized feed-mixing plant, but it was only talk.

It was early summer when I took to the dirt road again. I'd forgotten about the old man. But in almost the same way, when the sun was cooling and the air was haunted by lazy bees, I saw an old woman. Women strangers are less malevolent than men, and rarer. She was sitting on the gray rock, in a long green skirt summer-dusty, with a daisy-colored shawl and a blouse the precise hue of cottonwoods seen in a late hazy day's muted light. "Hello, boy," she said.

"I don't recognize you, either," I blurted, and she smiled.

"Of course not. If you didn't recognize him, you'd hardly know me."

"Do you know him?" I asked. She nodded. "Who was he? Who are you?"

"We're both full of stories. Just tell them from different angles. You aren't afraid of us, are you?"

I was, but having a woman ask the question made all the difference. "No," I said. "But what are you doing here? And how do you know—"

"Ask for a story," she said. "One you've never heard of before." Her eyes were the color of baked chestnuts, and she squinted into the sun so that I couldn't see her whites. When she opened them wider to look at me, she didn't have any whites.

"I don't want to hear stories," I said softly.

"Sure you do. Just ask."

"It's late. I got to be home."

"I knew a man who became a house," she said. "He didn't like it. He stayed quiet for thirty years, and watched all the people inside grow up, and be just like their folks, all nasty and dirty and leaving his walls to flake, and the bathrooms were unbearable. So he spit them out one morning, furniture and all, and shut his doors and locked them."

"What?"

"You heard me. Upchucked. The poor house was so disgusted he changed back into a man, but he was older and he had a cancer and his heart was bad because of all the abuse he had lived with. He died soon after."

I laughed, not because the man had died but because I knew such things were lies. "That's silly," I said.

"Then here's another. There was a cat who wanted to eat butterflies. Nothing finer in the world for a cat than to stalk the grass, waiting for black and pumpkin butterflies. It crouches down and wriggles its rump to dig in the hind paws, then it jumps. But a butterfly is no sustenance for a cat. It's practice. There was a little girl about your age— might have been your sister, but she won't admit it—who saw the cat and decided to teach it a lesson. She hid in the taller grass with two old kites under each arm and waited for the cat to come by stalking. When it got real close, she put on her mother's dark glasses, to look all bug-eyed, and she jumped up flapping the kites. Well, it was just a little too real, because in a trice she found herself flying, and she was much smaller than she had been, and the cat jumped at her. Almost got her, too. Ask your sister about that sometime. See if she doesn't deny it."

"How'd she get back to be my sister again?"

"She became too scared to fly. She lit on a flower and found herself crushing it. The glasses broke, too."

"My sister did break a pair of Mom's glasses once."

The woman smiled.

"I got to be going home."

"Tomorrow you bring me a story, okay?"

I ran off without answering. But in my head, monsters were already rising. If she thought I was scared, wait until she heard the story I had to tell! When I got home my oldest sister, Barbara, was fixing lemonade in the kitchen. She was a year older than I, but acted as if she were grown-up. She was a good six inches taller and I could beat her if I got in a lucky punch, but no other way—so her power over me was awesome. But we were usually friendly.

"Where you been?" she asked, like a mother.

"Somebody tattled on you," I said.

Her eyes went doe-scared, then wizened down to slits. "What're you talking about?"

"Somebody tattled about what you did to Mom's sunglasses."

"I already been whipped for that," she said nonchalantly. "Not much more to tell."

"Oh, but *I* know more."

"Was *not* playing doctor," she said. The youngest, Sue-Ann, weakest and most full of guile, had a habit of telling the folks somebody or other was playing doctor. She didn't know what it meant—I just barely did—but it had been true once, and she held it over everybody as her only vestige of power.

"No," I said, "but I know what you were doing. And I won't tell anybody."

"You don't know nothing," she said. Then she accidentally poured half a pitcher of lemonade across the side of my head and down my front. When Mom came in I was screaming and swearing like Dad did when he fixed the cars, and I was put away for life plus ninety years in the bedroom I shared with younger brother Michael. Dinner smelled better than usual that evening, but I had none of it. Somehow, I wasn't brokenhearted. It gave me time

217

to think of a scary story for the country-colored woman on the rock.

School was the usual mix of hell and purgatory the next day. Then the hot, dry winds cooled and the bells rang and I was on the dirt road again, across the southern hundred acres, walking in the lees and shadows of the big cottonwoods. I carried my Road-Runner lunch pail and my pencil box and one book—a hand-writing manual I hated so much I tore pieces out of it at night, to shorten its lifetime—and I walked slowly, to give my story time to gel.

She was leaning up against a tree, not far from the rock. Looking back, I can see she was not so old as a boy of eight years thought. Now I see her lissome beauty and grace, despite the dominance of gray in her reddish hair, despite the crow's-feet around her eyes and the smile-haunts around her lips. But to the eight-year-old she was simply a peculiar crone. And he had a story to tell her, he thought, that would age her unto graveside.

"Hello, boy," she said.

"Hi," I sat on the rock.

"I can see you've been thinking," she said.

I squinted into the tree shadow to make her out better. "How'd you know?"

"You have the look of a boy that's been thinking. Are you here to listen to another story?"

"Got one to tell, this time," I said.

"Who goes first?"

It was always polite to let the woman go first so I quelled my haste and told her she could. She motioned me to come by the tree and sit on a smaller rock, half-hidden by grass. And while the crickets in the shadow tuned up for the evening, she said, "Once there was a dog. This dog was a pretty usual dog, like the ones that would chase you around home if they thought they could get away with it—if they didn't know you, or thought you were up to something the big people might disapprove of. But this dog lived in a graveyard. That is, he belonged to the caretaker. You've seen a graveyard before, haven't you?"

"Like where they took Grandpa."

"Exactly," she said. "With pretty lawns, and big white and gray stones, and for those who've died recently, smaller gray stones with names and flowers and years cut into them. And trees in some places, with a mortuary nearby made of brick, and a garage full of black cars, and a place behind the garage where you wonder what goes on." She knew the place, all right. "This dog had a pretty good life. It was his job to keep the grounds clear of animals at night. After the gates were locked, he'd be set loose, and he wandered all night long. He was almost white, you see. Anybody human who wasn't supposed to be there would think he was a ghost, and they'd run away.

"But this dog had a problem. His problem was, there were rats that didn't pay much attention to him. A whole gang of rats. The leader was a big one, a good yard from nose to tail. These rats made their living by burrowing under the ground in the old section of the cemetery."

That did it. I didn't want to hear any more. The air was a lot colder than it should have been, and I wanted to get home in time for dinner and still be able to eat it. But I couldn't go just then.

"Now the dog didn't know what the rats did, and just like you and I, probably, he didn't much care to know. But it was his job to keep them under control. So one day he made a truce with a couple of cats that he normally tormented and told them about the rats. These cats were scrappy old toms and they'd long since cleared out the competition of other cats, but they were friends themselves. So the dog made them a proposition. He said he'd let them use the cemetery any time they wanted, to prowl or hunt in or whatever, if they would put the fear of God into a few of the rats. The cats took him up on it. 'We get to do whatever we want,' they said, 'whenever we want, and you won't bother us.' The dog agreed.

"That night the dog waited for the sounds of battle. But they never came. Nary a yowl." She glared at me for emphasis. "Not a claw scratch. Not even a twitch of tail in the wind." She took a deep breath, and so did I. "Round about midnight the dog went out into the graveyard. It was very dark and there wasn't wind, or bird, or speck of star to relieve the quiet and the dismal, inside-of-a-box-camera blackness. He sniffed his way to the old part of the graveyard, and met with the head rat, who was sitting on a slanty, cracked wooden grave marker. Only his eyes and a tip of tail showed in the dark, but the dog could smell him. 'What happened to the cats?' he asked. The rat shrugged his haunches. 'Ain't seen any cats,' he said. 'What did you think—that you could scare us out with a couple of cats? Ha. Listen—if there had been any cats here tonight, they'd have been strung and hung like meat in a shed, and my youn'uns would have grown fat on—"

"No-o-o!" I screamed, and I ran away from the woman and the tree until I couldn't hear the story any more.

"What's the matter?" she called after me. "Aren't you going to tell me your story?" Her voice followed me as I ran.

It was funny. That night, I wanted to know what happened to the cats. Maybe nothing had happened to them. Not knowing made my visions even worse—and I didn't sleep well. But my brain worked like it had never worked before.

The next day, a Saturday, I had an ending—not a very good one in retrospect—but it served to frighten Michael so badly he threatened to tell Mom on me.

"What would you want to do that for?" I asked. "Cripes, I won't ever tell you a story again if you tell Mom!"

Michael was a year younger and didn't worry about the future. "You never told me stories before," he said, "and everything was fine. I won't miss them."

He ran down the stairs to the living room. Dad was smoking a pipe and reading the paper, relaxing before checking the irrigation on the north thirty. Michael stood at the foot of the stairs, thinking. I was almost down to grab him and haul him upstairs when he made his decision and headed for the kitchen. I knew exactly what he was considering—that Dad would probably laugh and call him a little scaredy cat. But Mom would get upset and do me in proper.

She was putting a paper form over the kitchen table to mark it for fitting a tablecloth. Michael ran up to her and hung onto a pants leg while I halted at the kitchen door, breathing hard, eyes threatening eternal torture if he so much as peeped. But Michael didn't worry about the future much.

"Mom," he said.

"Cripes!" I shouted, high-pitching on the *i*. Refuge awaited me in the tractor shed. It was an agreed-upon hiding place. Mom didn't know I'd be there, but Dad did, and he could mediate.

It took him a half-hour to get to me. I sat in the dark behind a workbench, practicing my pouts. He stood in the shaft of light falling from the unpatched chink in the roof. Dust motes Maypoled around his legs. "Son," he said. "Mom wants to know where you got that story."

Now, this was a peculiar thing to be asked. The question I'd expected had been, "Why did you scare Michael?" or maybe, "What made you think of such a thing?" But no. Somehow, she had plumbed the problem, planted the words in Dad's mouth, and impressed upon him that father-son relationships were temporarily suspended.

"I made it up," I said.

"You've never made up that kind of story before."

"I just started."

He took a deep breath. "Son, we get along real good, except when you lie to me. We know better. Who told you that story?"

This was uncanny. There was more going on than I could understand—there was a mysterious, adult thing happening. I had no way around the truth. "An old woman," I said.

Dad sighed even deeper. "What was she wearing?"

"Green dress," I said.

"Was there an old man?"

I nodded.

"Christ," he said softly. He turned and walked out of the shed. From outside, he called me to come into the house. I dusted off my overalls and followed him. Michael sneered at me.

" 'Locked them in coffins with old dead bodies,' " he mimicked. "Phhht! You're going to get it."

The folks closed the folding door to the kitchen with both of us outside. This disturbed Michael, who'd expected instant vengeance. I was too curious and worried to take my revenge on him, so he skulked out the screen door and chased the cat around the house. "Lock you in a coffin!" he screamed.

Mom's voice drifted from behind the louvered doors. "Do you hear that? The poor child's going to have nightmares. It'll warp him."

"Don't exaggerate," Dad said.

"Exaggerate what? That those filthy people are back? Ben, they must be a hundred years old now! They're trying to do the same thing to your son that they did to your brother . . . and just look at *him!* Living in sin, writing for those hell-spawned girlie magazines."

"He ain't living in sin, he's living alone in an apartment

in New York City. And he writes for all kinds of places."

"They tried to do it to you, too! Just thank God your aunt saved you."

"Margie, I hope you don't intend—"

"Certainly do. She knows all about them kind of people. She chased them off once, she can sure do it again!"

All hell had broken loose. I didn't understand half of it, but I could feel the presence of Great Aunt Sybil Danser. I could almost hear her crackling voice and the shustle of her satchel of Billy Grahams and Zondervans and little tiny pamphlets with shining light in blue offset on their covers.

I knew there was no way to get the full story from the folks short of listening in, but they'd stopped talking and were sitting in that stony kind of silence that indicated Dad's disgust and Mom's determination. I was mad that nobody was blaming me, as if I were some idiot child not capable of being bad on my own. I was mad at Michael for precipitating the whole mess.

And I was curious. Were the man and woman more than a hundred years old? Why hadn't I seen them before, in town, or heard about them from other kids? Surely I wasn't the only one they'd seen on the road and told stories to. I decided to get to the source. I walked up to the louvered doors and leaned my cheek against them. "Can I go play at George's?"

"Yes," Mom said. "Be back for evening chores."

George lived on the next farm, a mile and a half east. I took my bike and rode down the old dirt road going south.

They were both under the tree, eating a picnic lunch from a wicker basket. I pulled my bike over and leaned it against the gray rock, shading my eyes to see them more clearly.

"Hello, boy," the old man said. "Ain't seen you in a while."

I couldn't think of anything to say. The woman offered me a cookie and I refused with a muttered, "No, thank you, ma'am."

"Well then, perhaps you'd like to tell us your story."

"No, ma'am."

"No story to tell us? That's odd. Meg was sure you had a story in you someplace. Peeking out from behind your ears maybe, thumbing its nose at us."

The woman smiled ingratiatingly. "Tea?"

"There's going to be trouble," I said.

"Already?" The woman smoothed the skirt in her lap and set a plate of nut bread into it. "Well, it comes sooner or later, this time sooner. What do you think of it, boy?"

"I think I got into a lot of trouble for not much being bad," I said. "I don't know why."

"Sit down then," the old man said. "Listen to a tale, then tell us what's going on."

I sat down, not too keen about hearing another story but out of politeness. I took a piece of nut bread and nibbled on it as the woman sipped her tea and cleared her throat. "Once there was a city on the shore of a broad, blue sea. In the city lived five hundred children and nobody else, because the wind from the sea wouldn't let anyone grow old. Well, children don't have kids of their own, of course, so when the wind came up in the first year the city never grew any larger."

"Where'd all the grownups go?" I asked. The old man held his fingers to his lips and shook his head.

"The children tried to play all day, but it wasn't enough. They became frightened at night and had bad dreams. There was nobody to comfort them because only grownups are really good at making nightmares go away. Now, sometimes nightmares are white horses that come out of the sea, so they set up guards along the beaches, and fought them back with wands made of black-thorn. But there was another kind of nightmare, one that was black and rose out of the ground, and those were impossible to guard against. So the children got together one day and decided to tell all the scary stories there were to tell, to prepare themselves for all the nightmares. They found it was pretty easy to think up scary stories, and every one of them had a story or two to tell. They stayed up all night spinning yarns about ghosts and dead things, and live things that shouldn't have been, and things that were neither. They talked about death and about monsters that suck blood, about things that live way deep in the earth and long, thin things that sneak through cracks in doors to lean over the beds at night and speak in tongues no one could understand. They talked about eyes without heads, and vice versa, and little blue shoes that walk across a cold empty white room, with no one in them, and a bunk bed that creaks when it's empty, and a printing press that produces newspapers from a city that never was. Pretty soon, by morning, they'd told all the scary stories. When the black horses came out of the ground the next night, and the white horses from the sea, the children greeted them with cakes and ginger ale, and they held a big party. They also invited the pale sheet-things from the clouds, and everyone ate hearty and had a good time. One white horse let a little boy ride on it, and took him wherever he wanted to go. So there were no more bad dreams in the city of children by the sea."

I finished the piece of bread and wiped my hands on my crossed legs. "So that's why you tried to scare me," I said.

She shook her head. "No. I never had a reason for telling a story, and neither should you."

"I don't think I'm going to tell stories any more," I said. "The folks get too upset."

"Philistines," the old man said, looking off across the fields.

"Listen, young man. There is nothing finer in the world than the telling of tales. Split atoms if you wish, but splitting an infinitive—and getting away with it—is far nobler. Lance boils if you wish, but pricking pretensions is often cleaner and always more fun."

"Then why are Mom and Dad so mad?"

The old man shook his head. "An eternal mystery."

"Well, I'm not so sure," I said. "I scared my little brother pretty bad and that's not nice."

"Being scared is nothing," the old woman said. "Being bored, or ignorant—now that's a crime."

"I still don't know. My folks say you have to be a hundred years old. You did something to my uncle they didn't like, and that was a long time ago. What kind of people are you, anyway?"

The old man smiled. "Old, yes. But not a hundred."

"I just came out here to warn you. Mom and Dad are bringing out my great aunt, and she's no fun for anyone. You better go away." With that said, I ran back to my bike and rode off, pumping for all I was worth. I was between a rock and a hard place. I loved my folks but I itched to hear more stories. Why wasn't it easier to make decisions?

That night I slept restlessly. I didn't have any dreams, but I kept waking up with something pounding at the back of my head, like it wanted to be let in. I scrunched my face up and pressed it back.

At Sunday breakfast, Mom looked across the table at

me and put on a kind face. "We're going to pick up Auntie Danser this afternoon, at the airport," she said.

My face went like warm butter.

"You'll come with us, won't you?" she asked. "You always did like the airport."

"All the way from where she lives?" I asked.

"From Omaha," Dad said.

I didn't want to go, but it was more a command than a request. I nodded and Dad smiled at me around his pipe.

"Don't eat too many biscuits," Mom warned him. "You're putting on weight again."

"I'll wear it off come harvest. You cook as if the whole crew was here, anyway."

"Auntie Danser will straighten it all out," Mom said, her mind elsewhere. I caught the suggestion of a grimace on Dad's face, and the pipe wriggled as he bit down on it harder.

The airport was something out of a TV space movie. It went on forever, with stairways going up to restaurants and big smoky windows which looked out on the screaming jets, and crowds of people, all leaving, except for one pear-shaped figure in a cotton print dress with fat ankles and glasses thick as headlamps. I knew her from a hundred yards.

When we met, she shook hands with Mom, hugged Dad as if she didn't want to, then bent down and gave me a smile. Her teeth were yellow and even, sound as a horse's. She was the ugliest woman I'd ever seen. She smelled of lilacs. To this day lilacs take my appetite away.

She carried a bag. Part of it was filled with knitting, part with books and pamphlets. I always wondered why she never carried a Bible—just Billy Grahams and Zondervans. One pamphlet fell out and Dad bent to pick it up.

"Keep it, read it," Auntie Danser instructed him. "Do you good." She turned to Mom and scrutinized her from the bottom of a swimming pool. "You're looking good. He must be treating you right."

Dad ushered us out the automatic doors into the dry heat. Her one suitcase was light as a mummy and probably just as empty. I carried it and it didn't even bring sweat to my brow. Her life was not in clothes and toiletry but in the plastic knitting bag.

We drove back to the farm in the big white station wagon. I leaned my head against the cool glass of the rear seat window and considered puking. Auntie Danser, I told myself, was like a mental dose of castor oil. Or like a visit to the dentist. Even if nothing was going to happen her smell presaged disaster, and like a horse sniffing a storm, my entrails worried.

Mom looked across the seat at me—Auntie Danser was riding up front with Dad—and asked, "You feeling okay? Did they give you anything to eat? Anything funny?"

I said they'd given me a piece of nut bread. Mom went, "Oh, Lord."

"Margie, they don't work like that. They got other ways." Auntie Danser leaned over the back seat and goggled at me. "Boy's just worried. I know all about it. These people and I have had it out before."

Through those murky glasses, her flat eyes knew me to my young, pithy core. I didn't like being known so well. I could see that Auntie Danser's life was firm and predictable, and I made a sudden commitment. I liked the man and woman. They caused trouble, but they were the exact opposite of my great-aunt. I felt better, and I gave her a reassuring grin. "Boy will be okay," she said. "Just colic of the upset mind."

Michael and Barbara sat on the front porch as the car drove up. Somehow a visit by Auntie Danser didn't bother them as much as it did me. They didn't fawn over her but they accepted her without complaining—even out of adult earshot. That made me think more carefully about them. I decided I didn't love them any the less, but I couldn't trust them, either. The world was taking sides and so far on my side I was very lonely. I didn't count the two old people on my side, because I wasn't sure they were—but they came a lot closer than anybody in my family.

Auntie Danser wanted to read Billy Graham books to us after dinner, but Dad snuck us out before Mom could gather us together—all but Barbara, who stayed to listen. We watched the sunset from the loft of the old wood barn, then tried to catch the little birds that lived in the rafters. By dark and bedtime I was hungry, but not for food. I asked Dad if he'd tell me a story before bed.

"You know your Mom doesn't approve of all that fairy-tale stuff," he said.

"Then no fairy tales. Just a story."

"I'm out of practice, son," he confided. He looked very

sad. "Your mom says we should concentrate on things that are real and not waste our time with make-believe. Life's hard. I may have to sell the farm, you know, and work for that feed-mixer in Mitchell."

I went to bed and felt like crying. A whole lot of my family had died that night, I didn't know exactly how, or why. But I was mad.

I didn't go to school the next day. During the night I'd had a dream, which came so true and whole to me that I had to rush to the stand of cottonwoods and tell the old people. I took my lunch box and walked rapidly down the road.

They weren't there. On a piece of wire braided to the biggest tree they'd left a note on faded brown paper. It was in a strong, feminine hand, sepia-inked, delicately scribed with what could have been a goose-quill pen. It said: "We're at the old Hauskopf farm. Come if you must."

Not "Come if you can." I felt a twinge. The Hauskopf farm, abandoned fifteen years ago and never sold, was three miles farther down the road and left on a deep-rutted fork. It took me an hour to get there.

The house still looked deserted. All the white paint was flaking, leaving dead gray wood. The windows stared. I walked up the porch steps and knocked on the heavy oak door. For a moment I thought no one was going to answer. Then I heard what sounded like a gust of wind, but inside the house, and the old woman opened the door. "Hello, boy," she said. "Come for more stories?"

She invited me in. Wildflowers were growing along the baseboards and tiny roses peered from the brambles that covered the walls. A quail led her train of inch-and-a-half fluffball chicks from under the stairs, into the living room. The floor was carpeted but the flowers in the weave seemed more than patterns. I could stare down and keep picking out detail for minutes. "This way, boy," the woman said. She took my hand. Hers was smooth and warm but I had the impression it was also hard as wood.

A tree stood in the living room, growing out of the floor and sending its branches up to support the ceiling. Rabbits and quail and a lazy-looking brindle cat looked at me from tangles of roots. A wooden bench surrounded the base of the tree. On the side away from us, I heard someone breathing. The old man poked his head around and smiled at me, lifting his long pipe in greeting. "Hello, boy," he said.

"The boy looks like he's ready to tell us a story, this time," the woman said.

"Of course, Meg. Have a seat, boy. Cup of cider for you? Tea? Herb biscuit?"

"Cider, please," I said.

The old man stood and went down the hall to the kitchen. He came back with a wooden tray and three steaming cups of mulled cider. The cinnamon tickled my nose as I sipped.

"Now. What's your story?"

"It's about two hawks," I said. I hesitated.

"Go on."

"Brother hawks. Never did like each other. Fought for a strip of land where they could hunt."

"Yes?"

"Finally, one hawk met an old, crippled bobcat that had set up a place for itself in a rockpile. The bobcat was learning itself magic so it wouldn't have to go out and catch dinner, which was awful hard for it now. The hawk landed near the bobcat and told it about his brother, and how cruel he was. So the bobcat said, 'Why not give him the land for the day? Here's what you can do.' The bobcat told him how he could turn into a rabbit, but a very strong rabbit no hawk could hurt."

"Wily bobcat," the old man said, smiling.

" 'You mean, my brother wouldn't be able to catch me?' the hawk asked. 'Course not,' the bobcat said. 'And you can teach him a lesson. You'll tussle with him, scare him real bad—show him what tough animals there are on the land he wants. Then he'll go away and hunt somewheres else.' The hawk thought that sounded like a fine idea. So he let the bobcat turn him into a rabbit and he hopped back to the land and waited in a patch of grass. Sure enough, his brother's shadow passed by soon, and then he heard a swoop and saw the claws held out. So he filled himself with being mad and jumped up and practically bit all the tail feathers off his brother. The hawk just flapped up and rolled over on the ground, blinking and gawking with his beak wide. 'Rabbit,' he said, 'that's not natural. Rabbits don't act that way.'

" 'Round here they do,' the hawk-rabbit said. 'This is a tough old land, and all the animals here know the tricks escaping from bad birds like you.' This scared the brother hawk, and he flew away as best he could, and never came back again. The hawk-rabbit hopped to the rockpile and stood up before the bobcat, saying, 'It worked real fine. I thank you. Now turn me back and I'll go hunt my land.' But the bobcat only grinned and reached out with a paw and broke the rabbit's neck. Then he ate him, and said, 'Now the land's mine, and no hawks can take away the easy game.' And that's how the greed of two hawks turned their land over to a bobcat."

The old woman looked at me with wide, baked-chestnut eyes and smiled. "You've got it," she said. "Just like your uncle. Hasn't he got it, Jack?" The old man nodded and took his pipe from his mouth. "He's got it fine. He'll make a good one."

"Now, boy, why did you make up that story?"

I thought for a moment, then shook my head. "I don't know," I said. "It just came up."

"What are you going to do with the story?"

I didn't have an answer for that question, either.

"Got any other stories in you?"

I considered, then said, "Think so."

A car drove up outside and Mom called my name. The old woman stood and straightened her dress. "Follow me," she said. "Go out the back door, walk around the house. Return home with them. Tomorrow, go to school like you're supposed to do. Next Saturday, come back and we'll talk some more."

"Son? You in here?"

I walked out the back and came around to the front of the house. Mom and Auntie Danser waited in the station wagon. "You aren't allowed out here. Were you in that house?" Mom asked. I shook my head.

My great aunt looked at me with her glassed-in flat eyes and lifted the corners of her lips a little. "Margie," she said, "go have a look in the windows."

Mom got out of the car and walked up the porch to peer through the dusty panes. "It's empty, Sybil."

"Empty, boy, right?"

"I don't know," I said. "I wasn't inside."

"I could hear you, boy," she said. "Last night. Talking in your sleep. Rabbits and hawks don't behave that way. You know, and I know it. So it ain't no good thinking about them that way, is it?"

"I don't remember talking in my sleep," I said.

"Marge, let's go home. This boy needs some pamphlets read into him."

Mom got ino the car and looked back at me before starting the engine. "You ever skip school again, I'll strap you black and blue. It's real embarrassing having the school call, and not knowing where you are. Hear me?"

I nodded.

Everything was quiet that week. I went to school and tried not to dream at night, and did everything boys are supposed to do. But I didn't feel like a boy. I felt something big inside, and no amount of Billy Grahams and Zondervans read at me could change that feeling.

I made one mistake, though. I asked Auntie Danser why she never read the Bible. This was in the parlor one evening after dinner and cleaning up the dishes. "Why do you want to know, boy?" she asked.

"Well, the Bible seems to be full of fine stories, but you don't carry it around with you. I just wondered why."

"Bible is a good book," she said. "The only good book. But it's difficult. It has lots of camouflage. Sometimes—" She stopped. "Who put you up to asking that question?"

"Nobody," I said.

"I heard that question before, you know," she said. "Ain't the first time I been asked. Somebody else asked me, once."

I sat in my chair, stiff as a ham.

"Your father's brother asked me that once. But we won't talk about him, will we?"

I shook my head.

Next Saturday I waited until it was dark and everyone was in bed. The night air was warm but I was sweating more than the warm could cause as I rode my bike down the dirt road, lamp beam swinging back and forth. The sky was crawling with stars, all of them looking at me. The Milky Way seemed to touch down just beyond the road, like I might ride straight up it if I went far enough.

I knocked on the heavy door. There were no lights in the windows and it was late for old folks to be up, but I knew these two didn't behave like normal people. And I knew that just because the house looked empty from the outside didn't mean it was empty within. The wind rose up and beat against the door, making me shiver. Then it opened. It was dark for a moment and the breath went out of me. Two pairs of eyes stared from the black. They

230

seemed a lot taller this time. "Come in, boy," Jack whispered.

Fireflies lit up the tree in the living room. The brambles and wildflowers glowed like weeds on a sea floor. The carpet crawled, but not to my feet. I was shivering in earnest now and my teeth chattered.

I only saw their shadows as they sat on the bench in front of me. "Sit," Meg said. "Listen close. You've taken the fire and it glows bright. You're only a boy but you're just like a pregnant woman now. For the rest of your life you'll be cursed with the worst affliction known to humans. Your skin will twitch at night. Your eyes will see things in the dark. Beasts will come to you and beg to be ridden. You'll never know one truth from another. You might starve, because few will want to encourage you. And if you do make good in this world, you might lose the gift and search forever after, in vain. Some will say the gift isn't special. Beware them. Some will say it is special and beware them, too. And some—"

There was a scratching at the door. I thought it was an animal for a moment. Then it cleared its throat. It was my great-aunt.

"Some will say you're damned. Perhaps they're right. But you're also enthused. Carry it lightly, and responsibly."

"Listen in there. This is Sybil Danser. You know me. Open up."

"Now stand by the stairs, in the dark where she can't see," Jack said. I did as I was told. One of them—I couldn't tell which—opened the door and the lights went out in the tree, the carpet stilled, and the brambles were snuffed. Auntie Danser stood in the doorway, outlined by star glow, carrying her knitting bag. "Boy?" she asked. I held my breath.

"And you others, too."

The wind in the house seemed to answer. "I'm not too late," she said. "Damn you, in truth, damn you to hell! You come to our towns, and you plague us with thoughts no decent person wants to think. Not just fairy stories, but telling the way people live, and why they shouldn't live that way! Your very breath is tainted! Hear me?" She walked slowly into the empty living room, feet clonking on the wooden floor. "You make them write about us, and make others laugh at us. Question the way we think. Condemn our deepest prides. Pull out our mistakes and

231

amplify them beyond all truth. What right do you have to take young children and twist their minds?"

The wind sang through the cracks in the walls. I tried to see if Jack or Meg was there, but only shadows remained.

"I know where you come from, don't forget that! Out of the ground! Out of the bones of old, wicked Indians! Shamans and pagan dances and worshiping dirt and filth! I heard about you from the old squaws on the reservation. Frost and Spring, they called you, signs of the turning year. Well, now you got a different name! Death and demons, I call you, hear me?"

She seemed to jump at a sound but I couldn't hear it. "Don't you argue with me!" she shrieked. She took her glasses off and held out both hands. "Think I'm a weak old woman, do you? You don't know how deep I run in these communities! I'm the one who had them books taken off the shelves. Remember me? Oh, you hated it—not being able to fill young minds with your pestilence. Took them off high school shelves, and out of lists—burned them for junk! Remember? That was me. I'm not dead yet! Boy, where are you?"

"Enchant her," I whispered to the air. "Magic her. Make her go away. Let me live here with you."

"Is that you, boy? Come with your aunt, now. Come with, come away!"

"Go with her," the wind told me. "Send your children this way, years from now. But go with her."

I felt a kind of tingly warmth and knew it was time to get home. I snuck out the back way and came around to the front of the house. There was no car. She'd followed me on foot all the way from the farm. I wanted to leave her there in the old house, shouting at the dead rafters, but instead I called her name and waited.

She came out crying. She knew.

"You poor, sinning boy," she said, pulling me to her lilac bosom.

The folklore of many nations has provided rich material for fantasy writers: hidden in the shadows of barrios and backwoods are innumerable strange creatures, blessings and curses. Here's one of the latter . . . and a purely mortal woman who undertakes to lift it.

Since he began full-time writing fifty years ago, Manly Wade Wellman has produced nearly seventy books and hundreds of stories ranging from fantasy and science fiction to biographies, regional histories and mainstream fiction. Some of his most famous books are *Twice in Time*, *Who Fears the Devil*, and his most recent novel, *The Old Gods Waken*.

TRILL COSTER'S BURDEN

Manly Wade Wellman

AFTER EVADARE CAUGHT UP WITH ME ON that high mountain, her poor feet were worn so sore that we stayed there all next day. I snared a rabbit for dinner and dried its sinews by the fire and sewed up her torn shoes with them. Our love talk to one another would have sounded stupid to air other soul on earth. Next morning we ate our last smoked meat and corn pone, and Evadare allowed, "I can walk with a staff, John." So I bundled our two packs behind my back and slung my guitar on top. Off southwest, we reckoned, was another state line. Across that, folks could marry without a long wait or a visit to the county seat.

For hours we made it slantways down the mountain side and then across rocks in a river. We climbed a ridge beyond, midway towards evening, and saw a narrower stream below. There was a wagon track across and cabins here and yonder and, on the stream's far side, a white steepled church and folks there, little as ants.

"We'll head there," I said, and she smiled up from under the bright toss of her hair. Down we came, Evadare a-limping with her staff. At the stream I picked her up like a flower and waded over. Not one look did the folks at the church give us, so hard they harked at what a skinny little man tried to say.

"Here's sixty dollars in money bills," he hollered, "for who'll take her sins and set her soul free."

I set Evadare down. We saw a dark-painted pine coffin among those dozen ladies and men. Shadow looked to lie on and around the coffin, more shadow than it could cast

234

by itself. The man who talked looked pitiful, and his hair was gravel-gray.

"Who'll do it?" he begged to them. "I'll pay seventy-five. No, a hundred—my last cent." He dug money from his jeans pocket. "Here's a hundred. Somebody do it for Trill and I'll pray your name in my prayers forevermore."

He looked at a squatty man in a brown umbrella hat. "Bart, if—"

"Not for a thousand dollars, Jake," said the squatty man. "Not for a million."

The man called Jake spoke to a well-grown young woman with brown hair down on her bare shoulders. "Nollie," he said, "I'd take Trill's sins on myself if I could, but I can't. I stayed by her, a-knowing what she was."

"You should ought to have thought of that when you had the chance, Jake," she said, and turned her straight back.

In the open coffin lay a woman wrapped in a quilt. Her hair was smoky-red. Her shut-eyed face had a proud beauty look, straight-nosed and full-lipped. The man called Jake held out the money to us.

"A hundred dollars," he whined. "Promise to take her sins, keep her from being damned to everlasting."

I knew what it was then, I'd seen it once before. Sin-eating. Somebody dies after a bad life, and a friend or a paid person agrees the sin will be his, not the dead one's. It's still done here and there, far back off from towns and main roads.

"I'll take her sins on me, John," said Evadare to me.

Silence then, so you might could hear a leaf drop. Jake started in to cry. "Oh, ma'am," he said, "tell me your name so's I can bless it to all the angels."

Somebody laughed a short laugh, but when I turned round, nair face had nair laugh on it.

"I'm called Evadare, and this is John with me."

"Take it." Jake pushed the money at her.

"I wouldn't do such a thing for money," Evadare said. "Only to give comfort by it, if I can."

Jake blinked his wet eyes at her. The squatty man shut the coffin lid. "All right, folks," he said, and he and three others took hold and lifted. The whole bunch headed in past the church, to where I could see the stones of a burying ground. Round us the air turned dull, like as if a cloud had come up in the bright evening sky.

Jake hung back a moment. "Better you don't come in," he mumbled, and followed the others.

"I do hope I did right," said Evadare, to herself and me both.

"You always do right," I replied her.

We walked to where some trees bunched on the far side of the wagon road. I dropped our bundles under a sycamore. We could see the folks a-digging amongst the graves. I got sticks and made us a fire. Evadare sat on a root. Chill had come into the air, along with that dimness. We talked, love talk but not purely cheerful talk. The sunset looked bloody-red in the west.

The folks finished the burying and headed off this way and that. I'd hope to speak to somebody, maybe see if Evadare could stay the night in a house. But they made wide turns not to come near us. I looked in my soogin sack to see if we had aught left to eat. But nair crumb.

"There's still some coffee in my bundle," said Evadare.

"That'll taste good." I took the pot to the stream and scooped up water. Somebody made a laughing noise and I looked up.

"I didn't get your name," said the bare-shouldered woman, a-smiling her mouth at me.

"John," I said. "I heard you called Miss Nollie."

"Nollie Willoughby."

Her eyes combed me up and down in that last light of day. They were brown eyes, with hard, pale lights behind them.

"Long and tall, ain't you, John?" she said. "You nair took Trill Coster's sins—only that little snip you're with did that. If you've got the sense you look to have, you'll leave her and them both, right now."

"I've got the sense not to leave her," I said.

"Come with me," she bade me, a-smiling wider.

"No, ma'am, I thank you."

I walked off from her. As I came near the trees, I heard Evadare say something, then a man's voice. Quick I moved the coffeepot to my left hand and fisted up my right and hurried there to see what was what.

The fire burned with blue in its red. It showed me the Jake fellow, a-talking to Evadare where she sat on the root. He had a bucket of something in one hand and some tin dishes in the other.

"John," he said as I came up, "I reckoned I'd fetch youins some supper."

"We do thank you," I replied him, a-meaning it. "Coffee will be ready directly. Sit down with us and have a cup," and I set the pot on a stone amongst the fire and Evadare poured in the most part of our coffee.

Jake dropped down like somebody weary of this world. "I won't stay long," he said. "I'd only fetch more sins on you." He looked at Evadare. "On her, who's got such a sight of them to pray out the way it is."

Evadare took the bucket. It was hot squirrel stew and made two big bowls full. We were glad for it, I tell you, and for the coffee when it boiled. Jake's cup trembled in his hand. He told us about Trill Coster, the woman he still loved in her grave, and it wasn't what you'd call a nice tale to hear.

She'd been as beautiful as a she-lion, and she'd used her beauty like a she-lion, a-gobbling men. She could make men swear away their families and lives and hopes of heaven. For her they'd thieve or even kill, and go to jail for it. And not a damn she'd given for what was good. She'd dared lightning to strike her; she'd danced round the church and called down a curse on it. Finally all folks turned from her—all but Jake, who loved her though she'd treated him like a dog. And when she'd died on a night of storm, they said bats flew round her bed.

Jake had stayed true to her who was so false. And that's how come him to want to get somebody to take her sins.

"For her sins run wild round this place, like foxes round a hen roost," he said. "I can hear them."

I heard them too, not so much with my ears as with my bones.

"I promised I'd pray them away," Evadare reminded him. "You'd best go, Jake. Leave me to deal with them."

He thanked her again and left.

Full dark by then outside the ring of firelight, and we weren't alone there. I didn't see or hear plain at first, it was more like just a sense of what came. Lots of them. They felt to be a-moving close, the way wolves would shove round a campfire in the old days, to get up their nerve to rush in. A sort of low crouch of them in the dark, and here and there some sort of height half-guessed. Like as if one or other of them stood high, or possibly climbed a tree branch. I stared and tried to reckon if there were shapes there, blacker than the night, and couldn't be sure no way or the other.

"I'm not about to be afraid," said Evadare, and she knew she had to say that thing out loud for it to be true.

"Don't be," I said. "I've heard say that evil can't prevail against a pure heart. And your heart's pure. I wish mine was halfway as pure as yours."

I pulled my guitar to me and touched the silver strings, to help us both.

"They say there are seven deadly sins," said Evadare. "I've heard them named, but I can't recollect them all."

"I can," I said. "Pride. Covetousness. Lust. Envy. Greed. Anger. Gluttony. Who is there that mustn't fight to keep free from all of them?"

I began to pick and sing, words of my own making to the tune of "Nine Yards of Other Cloth":

> "And she's my love, my star above,
> And she's my heart's delight,
> And when she's here I need not fear
> The terror in the night."

"Who was that laughed?" Evadare cried out.

For there'd been a laugh, that died away when she spoke. I stopped my music and harked. A different noise now. A stir, like something that tried not to make a sound but made one anyway, the ghost of a sound you had to strain to hear.

I set down my guitar and stood up. I said, loud and clear:

"Whoever or whatever's in sound of my voice, step up here close and look at the color of my eyes."

The noise had died. I looked all the way round.

Deep night now, beyond where the fire shone. But I saw a sort of foggy-muddy cloud at a slink there. I thought maybe somebody had set a smudge fire and the wind blew the smoke to us. Only there was no wind. The air was as still as a shut-up room. I looked at the sky. There were little chunks of stars and about half a moon, with a twitch of dim cloud on it. But down where I was, silence and stillness.

"Look at those sparks," said Evadare's whispery voice.

First sight of them, they sure enough might could have been sparks—greeny ones. Then you made out they were two and two in that low dark mist, two and two and two, like eyes, like the green eyes of meat-eating things on the look for food. All the way round they were caught and set by pairs in the mist that bunched and clotted everywhere, close to the ground, a-beginning to flow in, crowd in.

And it wasn't just mist. There were shapes in it. One

or two stood up to maybe a man's height, others made you think of dogs, only they weren't dogs. They huddled up, they were sort of stuck together—jellied together, you might say, the way a hobby of frog's eggs lie in a sticky bunch in the water. If it had been just at one place; but it was all the way round.

I tried to think of a good charm to say, and I've known some, but right then they didn't come to mind. I grabbed up a stick from the pile for whatever good might come of it. I heard Evadare, her voice strong now:

"Thou shalt not be afraid for the terror by night."

The dark things churned, the eye-sparks blinked. I could swear that they gave back for the length of a step.

"Nor for the arrow that flieth by day," Evadare said on. "Nor for the pestilence that walketh in darkness."

They shrank back on themselves again. They surrounded us, but they were back from where they'd been.

"What did you say to them?" I inquired Evadare, still with the stick ready.

"The Ninety-first Psalm," she said back. "It was all I could think of that might could possibly help."

"It helped," I said, and thought how I'd stood like a gone gump, not able to call up one good word to save us. "If those were sins a-sneaking in," I said, "there was a sight of them, but good words made them wait."

"How long will they wait?" she wondered me, little and huddled down by the fire. She was scared, gentlemen; and, now I reckon about it, so was I.

Those many sins, a-taking shape and hungry to grab onto somebody. One might not be too bad. You'd face up to one, maybe drive it back, maybe get it down and stomp it. But all of those together all sides of you, gummed into one misty mass. Being scared didn't help. You had to think of something to do.

Think what?

No way to run off from Trill Coster's sins, bunched all round us. Maybe the firelight slowed them some, slowed the terror by night, the pestilence in darkness. Evadare had taken them on her, and here they were. She kept whispering prayers. Meanwhile, they'd pulled back some. Now their eye-sparks showed thirty or forty feet away, all directions. I put wood on the fire. The flames stood up, not so much blue in the red now.

I took up my guitar and dared sit down. Old folks allow the devil is afraid of music. I picked and I sang:

239

"The needle's eyes that doth supply
The thread that runs so true
And many a lass have I let pass
Because I thought of you.

"And many a dark and stormy night
I walked these mountains through;
I'd stub my toe and down I'd go
Because I thought of you."

Then again a loud, rattling laugh, and I got up. The laugh again. Into the firelight there walked that bare-shouldered woman called Nollie Willoughby, a-weaving herself while she walked, a-clapping her hands while she tossed her syrupy hair.

"I call that pretty singing, John," she laughed to me. "You aim to sleep here tonight? The ground makes a hard bed, that's a natural fact. Let me make you up a soft bed at my place."

"I musn't go from here right now," said Evadare's soft voice. "I've got me something to do hereabouts."

Nollie quartered her eyes round to me. "Then just you come, John. I done told you it'll be a soft bed."

"I thank you most to death," I said, "but no, ma'am, I stay here with Evadare."

"You're just a damned fool," she scorned me.

"A fool, likely enough," I agreed her. "But not damned. Not yet."

She sat down at the fire without being bid to. There was enough of her to make one and a half of Evadare, and pretty too, but no way as pretty as Evadare—no way.

"All the folks act pure scared to come near youins," she told us. "I came to show there's naught to fear from Trill Coster's sins. I nair feared her nor her ways when she lived. I don't fear them now she's down under the dirt. All the men that followed her round—they'll follow me round now."

"Which is why you're glad she's dead," Evadare guessed. "You were jealous of her."

Nollie looked at her, fit to strike her dead. "Not for those sorry men," she said. "I don't touch other women's leavings." She put her eyes to me. "You don't look nor act like that sort of man, John. I'll warrant you're a right much of a man."

"I do my best most times," I said.

"I might could help you along," she smiled with her wide lips.

"Think that if it pleasures you," I said. I thought back on women I'd known. Donie Carawan, who'd sweet-talked me the night the Little Black Train came for her; Winnie, who'd blessed my name for how I'd finished the Ugly Bird; Vandy, whose song I still sang now and then; but above and past them all, little Evadare, a-sitting tired and worried there by the fire, with the crowd and cloud of another woman's sins she'd taken, all round her, a-trying to dare come get hold of her.

"If I'd listen to you," I said to Nollie. "If I heeded one mumbling word of your talk."

"Jake said you're named Evadare," said Nollie across the fire. "You came here with John and spoke up big to take Trill's sin-burden and pray it out. What if I took that burden off you and took John along with it?"

"You done already made John that offer," said Evadare, quiet and gentle, "and he told you what he thought of it."

"Sure enough," Nollie laughed her laugh, with hardness in it. "John's just a-playing hard to get."

"He's hard to get, I agree you," said Evadare, "but he's not a-playing."

"Getting right cloudy round here," Nollie said, a-looking over that smooth bare shoulder of hers.

She spoke truth. The clumpy mist with its eye-greens was on the move again, like before. It hung close to the ground. I saw tree branches above it. The shapes in it were half-shapes. I saw one like what children make out of snow for a man, but this was dark, not snowy. It had head, shoulders, two shiny green eyes. Webbed next to it, a bunch of the things that minded you of dogs without being dogs. Green eyes too, and white flashes that looked like teeth.

Those dog things had tongues too, out at us, like as if to lap at us, Evadare was a-praying under her breath, and Nollie laughed again.

"If you fear sin," she mocked us, "you go afraid air min-ute of your life."

That was the truth too, as I reckoned, so I said nothing. I looked on the half-made hike of the man shape. It molded itself while I looked. Up came two steamy rags like arms. I wondered myself if it had hands, if it could take hold; if it could grab Evadare, grab me.

One arm-rag curled up high and whipped itself at us. It threw something—a whole mess of something. A little rain of twinkles round the root where Evadare had sat since first we built the fire.

"Oh," she whispered, not loud enough for a cry.

I ran to her, to see if she'd been hit and hurt. She looked down at the scatter of bright things round her. I knelt to snatch one up.

By the firelight, I saw that it was a jewel. Red as blood, bright as fire. I'm no jeweler, but I've seen rubies in my time. This was a big one.

Evadare bent with both hands out, to pick the things up. From the mist stole out soft noises, noises like laughter—not as loud as Nollie could laugh, but meaner, uglier.

"Don't take those things," I said to Evadare. "Not from what wants to give them to you." I set myself to throw that big ruby.

"No," said Evadare, and got up, too. "I must do it. I'm the one who took the sins. I'm the one to say no to them."

She made a flinging motion with her arm, underhand, the way girls are apt to throw. I saw those jewels wink in the firelight as they sailed through the air. Red for rubies, white for diamonds, other colors for other ones. They struck in among the misty shapes. I swear they plopped, like stones flung in greasy water.

"Give me," she said, and took the big ruby from me. She flung it after the others. It made a singy sound in the air. Back from the cloudy mass beat a tired, hunting breath, like somebody pained and sorrowed.

"All right," said Evadare, the strongest she'd spoken since first we'd made out camp. "I've given them back their pay, refused all of it."

"Did you?" Nollie sort of whinnied.

"You saw me give them back," Evadare said. "All of them."

"No, not all of them, look at this."

Nollie held out her open palm. There lay a ruby, big as a walnut, twice the size of the one I'd taken up.

"How many thousands do you reckon that's worth?" Nollie jabbered at us, her teeth shining. "I got it when it fell, and I'm a-going to keep it."

"Miss Nollie," I said, "you should ought to have seen enough here tonight to know you can't keep it air such a thing."

"Can't I?" she jeered me. "Just watch me, John. I'll

take it to a big town and sell it. I'll be the richest some-body in all these parts."

"Better give it to Evadare to throw back," I said.

"Give it to little half-portion, milky-face Evadare? Not me."

She poked the ruby down the front of her dress, deep down there.

"It'll be safe where it's at," she snickered at us. "Unless you want to reach a hand down yonder for it, John."

"Not me," I said. "I want no part of it, nor yet of where you put it."

"John," said Evadare, "look at how the cloud bunches away."

I looked; it drew back with all its shapes, like the ebb tide on the shore of the sea.

"Sure enough," I said. "It's a-leaving out of here."

"And so am I," spoke up Nollie. "I came here to talk sense to you, John. You ain't got the gift to know sense where you hear it. Come visit me when I get my money and put up my big house here."

She swung, she switched away, a-moving three direc-tions at once, the way some women think they look pretty when they do it. She laughed at us once, over her shoul-der so bare. Evadare made a move, like as if to try to fetch her back, but I put my hand on Evadare's arm.

"You've done more than your duty tonight," I said. "Let her go."

So Evadare stood beside me while Nollie switch-tailed off amongst the trees. I reckoned the misty shapes thick-ened up at Nollie, but I couldn't be dead sure. What I did make out was, they didn't fence us in now. I saw clearness all the way round. The moon washed the earth with its light.

Evadare sat down on the root again, dead tired. I built up the fire to comfort us. I struck a chord on the guitar to sing to her, I don't recollect what. It might could as well have been a lullaby. She sank down asleep as I sang. I put my soogin sack under her head for a pillow and spread a blanket on her.

But I didn't sleep. I sat there, awaiting for whatever possibly happened, and nothing happened. Nothing at all, all night. The dawn grayed the sky and far off away I heard a rooster crow. I put the last of our coffee in the pot to brew for us, all we could count on for breakfast.

While I watched by the fire, three men came toward us. Evadare rose up and yawned.

"John," said Jake in his timid voice, "I bless the high heavens to see you and your lady all safe here. This here is Preacher Frank Ricks, and here's Squire Hamp Dolby, come along with me to make your acquaintance."

Preacher Ricks I'd met before. We shook hands together. He was thin and old, but still a-riding here and there to do what good was in his power. Squire Dolby was a chunk of a man with white hair and black brows. "Proud to know you, John," he said to me.

"I hurried in here just at sunrise," said Preacher Ricks. "I'd heard tell of poor Trill Coster's death, and I find she's already buried. And I heard tell, too, of the brave, kind thing your lady agreed to do to rest her soul."

"I hoped it would be merciful," said Evadare.

"How true you speak, ma'am," said Squire Dolby. "But the sins you said you'd take, they never came to you. They fastened somewhere else. Nollie Willoughby's gone out of her mind. Round her house it's all dark-shadowy, and she's in there, she laughs and cries at one and the same time. She hangs onto a little flint rock and says it's a ruby, richer than all dreams on this earth."

"Isn't it a ruby?" I inquired him.

"Why," he said, "the gravelly path to my house is strewed with rocks like that, fit for naught but just to be trod on."

"I fetched these folks here on your account, John," said Jake. "You done told me you and Evadare hoped to be married."

"And we can do that for you," allowed Preacher Ricks, with a smile to his old face. "Squire Dolby here has the legal authority to give you a license here and now."

"It's sure enough my pleasure," said Squire Dolby.

He had a pad of printed blanks. He put down Evadare's name and mine, and he and Jake signed for the witnesses.

"Why not right now, under these trees and this sky?" said Preacher Ricks, and opened his book. "Stand together here, you two. John, take Evadare's right hand in your right hand. Say these words after me when I tell you."

Authors who attempt to write in dialect run the risk of being incomprehensible, boring or "cute." But sometimes a writer can produce dialect prose that comes close to poetry, as in this irresistibly comic and surprising story of an Australian who loved fire a bit too much. . . .

This tour de force is, amazingly, the very first story Kevin McKay ever wrote. He's sold several more since, of course: the man is talented.

PIE ROW JOE

Kevin McKay

I DON'T WANTA FINISH UP IN THE COLD, MATE, so scuse me if I don't get up to shake 'ands.

I know what's wrong with you; I seen 'em bring you in with a busted leg, 'n I 'eard the doc and the nurses talkin' about you fallin' orf a tractor. I'm dyin' for a smoke— spose ya wouldn't 'ave one on ya? No—the big dame woulda taken em offa ya.

This ain't a bad 'ospital for a little country joint like this, 'cept for them two: the whoppin' big sheila like a white-painted paddle steamer, and the skinny dried-up little dame like a nole thistle ready to blow away, or burn up. Starchy 'n Husk, I call 'em. Got them names from the TV down the pub.

Bloody freezin' in 'ere. Ya'd think they'd 'ave a bit o' fire. You like fires? I do. Always 'ave done, ever since I can remember, even before I went to school. We 'ad wood fires in them days. My ole man usta cut 'is own firewood; usta put on big logs and stumps. I usta sit, watchin' 'em burn. They all made diffrunt pikshers like.

Big long logs, they go in grey colour, with long wavy cracks right down 'em. 'N at first, ya think they never gonna burn, cos the pale yella flame is breathin' over 'em, and nothin' 'appens. 'N then, grey smoke starts comin' out the cracks, and they start, real slow, sorta goin' black. 'N then little red glow worms starts creepin' over the surface, just like when a dry leaf starts to catch.

Y'ever start a camp fire out in the bush? with a handful uv dry leaves fer kindlin'? Ya start 'er up, 'n ya think she's not gonna go, but then them little red worms starts crawlin', and the wind huffs on 'er and she flares and crackles, and ya say 'she's right now' and ya put on some bigger stuff.

Look—pay a-bloody-tention when a man's talkin' to ya. Stick ya bloody book away, 'n ya might learn somethin'. Wish I 'ad a smoke. Any'ow, I know where I can get one.

Them big logs, once they was really goin', they'd give orf grey smoke, and then clear bright yella flames. 'N then —pfft—a little pocket of gas or sumpin ud burst out, and send out a clear jet of flame, clean as anything ya ever see. But she wouldn't last, she'd die out, like the arse end o' one o' them moon rockets I seen on telly; then she'd fizzle. Like everything a man ever tries to do.

I done lotsa things in me time; I've worked up and down this river all me life. I've picked t'bacca up Myrtleford and t'maters at Shepparton; I've snatched grapes every summer year after year, on me knees in red dirt, with burnin' sun on me bare back and cuts all over me bloody 'ands. I've shore sheep up the Darling, till I never want to smell that stink o' sheep shit and wet wool again. They can shove their wool . . .

Y'ever see wool burnin'? It don't burn proper, like wood. Kind of comes up in black bubbles, and stinks, and crawls over itself like.

Got a cig? No, I ast ya that. 'N I told ya, taint polite to read when a man's talkin' to ya. What was I sayin'? Yeah, about fires.

Funny 'ow a log goes into the fireplace all of one piece like, but after she's burnt a bit she starts to cut up into little squares, like snake skin. Ya can watch them little bits, and they go grey outside, but in the cracks in between it's red as guts, like when ya butcher a bunny.

'N finally, she gets a crawly kinda grey ash all over, and ya start askin' yaself, will she fall this second? the next? the one after that? But she always beats ya; just when ya thinks she's never gonna fall, away she goes.

Up go the sparks, like the souls of all the inseks what ever lived in the wood when she was alive—termites, ants, grubs. Where do they go? Up the chimney, sure, but after that?

Bugger it, listen, willya? I'm tryin' to tell ya how to start a fire. You're like the young bucks up the pub, know every bloody thing. I gave up tryin' to watch TV after they put in the pool table. Man couldn't hear 'imself think for smart alecks yellin' and shoutin' out what shots they gonna play next—and then missin' 'em.

I seen Walter Lindrum play up The Cliffs once. You wouldn't even know who 'e was, mate. Only the best player 'Stralia ever 'ad, that's who—'e could play all these young sods on a break with both 'ands tied be'ind 'im.

Talkin' about 'ands, I can still shut me eyes and see Gerald's 'and the day that schoolteacher bastard 'it 'im. It was in the winter time, cos I remember we 'ad a fire in the classroom, and I was watchin' it, in between doin' my school work, 'cos I like fires. When I was real young, before I went to school, I usta go out in the bush and start me own fires.

When me old man went farmin', only land 'e could afford was way out in the never-nevers, where a bloody lizard couldn't live unless 'e 'ad 'is own lunch 'n waterbag. The ole man 'ad to clear the bush, with two 'orses. 'Nuther thing you wouldn't know nothin' about, 'cept 'ow it runs at Flemington. We 'ad two great big Clydesdales, Punch and Judy. 'Itch a chain to 'em, and the other end round a tree stump. Never 'ad to use the whip, just yell out to 'em, and they'd belly down and 'eave, 'n out she'd come clean as a whistle. We'd burn orf the small branches 'n keep the logs and big stumps fer firewood fer the winter. She could get real cold out there in that Mallee country.

You still listenin', mate? I'll go and get us both a smoke, when I finish what I wanta tell ya. Any'ow. . .

When I was three or four, the ole man was still clearin' the land. Much good it did 'im. Bloody sand country it was; only thing 'eld it together was the scrub what 'e was doin' 'is best to get rid of. When 'e took it all orf, and got the paddicks plowed, the first good breeze sent the topsoil airmail to Noo Zealand.

That Husk, the nurse, she's like a bloody dried-up thistle, all grey and skinny and prickly. I seen thistles like that out in the Mallee. In the middle of a paddick, one lousy little thistle, maybe only a foot 'igh, what stopped the grains o' sand when the wind blew, and built up a sand'ill three foot 'igh and sx foot long downwind of itself.

I seen fences, mate, built on top o' one another. The first'd stop the sand, and evenchally get buried, then the poor bastard farmer'd afta build another, nailin' the new

droppers to wotever was left stickin' up. 'N they reckoned it was wheat land!

Ever seen a fire in a paddick uv ripe wheat? She really
goes; not much smoke then, mate, only whirls of orange-
red fire, goin' maybe forty miles a nour if there's a good
wind be'ind 'er.

Any'ow, I was tellin' ya, I like fire. Before I went to
school, and me dad and mum was busy on the farm, I
usta go walkabout in the scrub. 'N I usta siddown and
look at a patch of dry grass, and think 'ow nice it'd be if I
'ad a little fire, like, I didn't want it for warmth, y'understand, just wanted to look at 'er, 'n maybe play with 'er a
bit.

'N a coupla times, or maybe more—I dunno, I'm
talkin' about fifty year ago—I started some fires which
burnt through into where the ole man was workin', or
maybe towards the hut, cos I can remember 'im sayin' to
me mum: 'Girl, I dunno where 'e gets them matches, but
for Gawd's sake keep the things away from 'im, cos 'e is a
pie row maniac.' 'N me mum said, 'I swear I have every
match in this house in my apron pocket.'

Any'ow, I was tellin' ya about me friend Gerald. 'E
was me best school mate, although I got along with the
other kids alright, speshly when I usta start a bit uv a
camp fire for em after school. We 'ad a real nice lady,
Miss Sims, for a teacher. It was only a bit of a country
school like, with little and big kids all mixed up together,
but it was all OK till I was in sixth grade, when they sent
Miss Sims orf to another school, and we copped this bastard Searce.

'E was a washed-out gingernut, hair like a dead fox,
eyes like a dead codfish, eyelashes like dead fishes' bones.

'DISSIPLINE!' he says. 'That is what is needed here.
When I come into the room, you all sit at attention' 'e
says. 'Ow can ya *sit* at attention, mate? But 'e knew. When
'e come in, we was all sposed to sit upright, feet together,
backs straight, eyes front, 'ands joined be'ind backs. 'N ya
dare not look sideways, cos 'e 'ad this great big strap.

It was made, I reck'n, from draft 'orse 'arness—double-
sided leather, with a packing piece in between, stitched all
round, and weighin' about a pound and a 'alf. 'E always
carried it, and 'e could be quicker on the draw than Tom
Mix.

Me and me mate Gerry sat in the desk right next to
the door. Like I told ya, I was writin' a bit, and lookin' at

the fire, and thinkin' to meself 'I'll make that log bust in half NOW' when I look from the fire to dead in front of me, and there 'e is, Searce, the sod. Rubber soles, 'e wore, 'n sneaked round like a blackfella creepin' on plovers. Outa the corner of me eye I see all the other kids sit at attention, and so do I.

Poor ole Gerald, 'e was a good kid, 'e's still workin', con-she-enshus like. Got 'is left 'and 'oldin' down the left page of 'is ecker book, 'n the pen in 'is right 'and, and so wrapped up in what 'e's doin' that 'e wouldn't wake up if a dunny fell on 'im.

I dare not look up in case I meet them fish eyes. I stare straight in front at the leather buttons on the sports coat, and the end o' the strap stickin' outa the pocket. I think as hard as I can to Gerald: 'Wake up, mate, wake up!' but I never was any good at thinkin' at people. I'm frightened to give 'im a poke with me knee, cos Fisheyes can see me legs. So I sit like a statchoo, tryin' to think at Gerald. No good. That's one of the few things in me life, mate, that I'm sorry for.

Fisheyes stan's there for what seems like 'alf a nour. Then 'e slowly pulled out the strap, slowly, as if 'e's lickin' 'is chops. And BANG! 'e gets Gerald right acrost the back of the left hand.

Poor Gerry nilly shit 'imself. Up 'e jumps, and mita gorn through the ceilin' 'cept that 'is knees comes ker-runch up against the bottom of the desk. Back of 'is 'and goes white, and then red, and starts palpitatin'. 'N Fisheyes says, 'That's for not sitting to attention when I come in.'

Searce goes over to warm 'is arse at the fire. I knew 'e smoked, 'n kept a tin o' wax matches in 'is 'ip pocket, cos I'd seen 'em. 'N I thought: wouldn't it be beaut if 'is matches caught fire?

All uv a sudden 'e screamed, 'n jumped 'igher than Gerry, 'n grabbed at 'is pocket. I 'ope those bloody matches burned a foot into 'im. 'Is pants caught fire, and 'e whacked at 'em like a wheat lumper with a mouse up 'is leg.

Talkin' about legs, yours is bust in two places, I 'eard Starchy say. So I'll be outa 'ere afore you, mate. I'm only burnt a bit, that's all; be right as rain soon. I'll tell ya 'ow I come to be in 'ere if you'll put that book away. It's all bullshit any'ow.

Any'ow, as I was sayin', I'm burnt a bit. It was me own fault, so I gotta take me medicine.

I didn't leave meself a way out, see? That was me trouble. But 'e never shoulda sooled them dorgs onto me; that's when 'e really arst for it. 'E was worse than Starchy, 'n she's bad enough. What's more, even ya bed ain't ya own in this bloody 'orspital. I got outa mine a while ago, and bugger me, when I tries to get back in, there's some other joker in it!

I felt like goin' to 'ave a pee, see, 'n when I turn round and look back, 'eres this other bastard in me bed. Real crook 'e 'is—looks like a roast duck. 'Is skin's nicely browned all over, 'e's got choobs stuck up 'is snout and other places, 'n Starchy 'n Husk is messin' round 'im like crows round a dead lamb.

'Strike me 'andsome' I says to meself, 'a man better go back or 'e'll finish up out in the cold' so I moved in again, and some'ow they got this other joker out.

Any'ow, what was I sayin'? Aw yeah, out.

That's 'ow I moved out uv school. Searce's pants were on fire, see, and 'e's jumpin' up and down like a frill-neck lizard. I 'adn't learnt then to keep me face closed, and I dunno 'ow 'e guessed, but 'e looked straight at me and picked me for settin' fire to the wax matches. 'E just went plain berserk, comin' at me with the strap up.

I raced fer the door 'n out I went, straight for 'ome. When I get there I kep' goin' into the scrub, but I 'ung around the edges of the bush to see what'd 'appen. Presently, up 'e comes in 'is 1928 Ford, 'n I could see 'im layin' down the law to me ole man.

'N I got to thinkin', what if 'is petrol tank 'sploded?

BLOOOOM! Fisheyes and the ole man are runnin' for their lives. Fisheyes walked orf, offa our property, me ole man come lookin' for me. 'Venchally, of course, 'e caught me.

'But 'e hit Gerry, Dad' I said. 'Fer nothin'. Nothin' a tall!'

'I believe you, son' me dad said. 'But you know I'm gonna hafta hit you for somethin'. You got this pie row mania, and I gotta try to cure it.' So 'e cut a four-foot len'th of whipstick Mallee, and 'e let me have it. That night I left, in the dark.

Soon as it gets a bit darker in 'ere, I'm gonna go 'n get a smoke, and I ain't forgot ya. Getcha one too. Smoke's a funny thing. Ever noticed 'ow, no matter what side of a camp fire ya sits on, the smoke always seems to come your way? One of the laws o' Nachur, I reckon. Wind's from the south, so ya sits on the south, and still ya cop it, because she goes and switches.

That's what buggered me. She switched from the north to the south, and I didn't leave meself no way out.

I did leave me mum a note. I said I loved 'er and dad, and I'd come back when the schoolteacher bizness died down. Well, ya know what they say 'bout good intentions. I never did get back there before me mum and dad died. I've seen the old 'omestead, but it's like what I told ya, mate, just all sand blowin'.

Any'ow, I was tellin' ya, camp fires. I've sat round thousands of 'em, Myrtleford to Renmark, Mildura to Bourke. I never carried matches; wasn't no need to. I c'd always rake up a few dry leaves 'n sticks, and think 'ow nice it'd be if I 'ad a little fire. 'N next thing ya know, there she was, cracklin' away like a beauty. Sometimes, even, if I was real tired, I wouldn't even bother to carry the bigger bits of wood; I'd just think 'em over to the fire, like.

'N sometimes, if I'd been on the booze and I was showin' orf, I'd do me little tricks for me mates, wantin' to show 'em how to start a camp fire, 'n bring some wood, without matches or sweat. But they was mostly dopey, they could never catch on to the way of it. Some of 'em knew the same words as me old man, and that's why they call me 'Pie Row Joe'.

Good mates, they was. I never 'urt nobody after that schoolteacher bastard, till just afore I got shoved in 'ere.

That Starchy can shove—she could push Jack Dempsey round. 'Turn Mister Burns over' she says. 'Mister Burns'—strike me lucky, that's me! I never been called that afore in me life. The doc is talkin' some garbage about critical loss of fluids. 'E could lose some 'imself, 'e's still wet be'ind the ear'oles.

I'm still cold. It was bloody hot that day. I was humpin' me swag, comin' down through Karamull. On the hoof, 'opin to 'itch'ike a bit, when I sees a short cut acrost the paddicks. I been there before, so I knows the owner is a bastard, and a lucky one at that. In the drought, when 'is neighbors was flat out like a lizard drinkin', every bloody thunderstorm, the only rain in it would fall on *his* paddicks, but 'e wouldn't help nobody.

But I didn't want nothin' from 'im. I was just takin' a short cut. 'Is wheat was four foot tall, and ripe, 'n Blind Freddy could see 'e was gonna get twenty bags to th'acre while the other poor sods wasn't even gonna get their seed back.

The road went a mile that way, and then a mile back, 'n all the time I could see the pub only two 'undred yards acrost the crop. It was buh-luddy 'ot. 'Undred and twenty in the shade, cept there wasn't none, and a 'owlin' north wind right in me face. I was chewin' sand between me teeth, it was in me eyes, I was 'angin' onto me 'at, 'n them dry roley-poleys, big as sheep, was bowlin' along and stingin' me in the face like flyin' barb wire. I kep' thinkin' of a big cold beer, so I decides to risk it, through the fence.

Well, 'e'd ploughed a fire break right along the wire, so I does the right thing, I sticks to the break 'stead o' trampin' down the ripe crop. Next thing I knows, 'e's yellin' 'Get to buggery outa there' and soolin' his bloody dorgs on to me. Bastards, they was, like 'im. Yellow, like dingoes, like Fisheyes' hair. So I runs, and scrambles through the other fence, and rips me last decent pair of strides.

The pub was just up the road, so I got a beer, and then some more. One led to another, like. Was just the day fer it—'undred and twenty, and red 'ot wind like a furnace blast, and dust and dirt and the sky fulla curlicue clouds.

Any'ow, where was I? Yeah, 'ow I got into 'orspital.

So, the sun went down, like a ball o' fire, 'n I got to thinkin': oo's that bastard to sool the dorgs on to me? Never done 'im no 'arm. Be nice if 'is wheat caught fire.

So I started back up the track, in the dark. Dark in 'ere; soon be safe to go and pinch some smokes, even if we can't find no booze.

Boy, was I boozed that night. I c'n just remember wheat paddicks each side of the gravel road, 'n scrub and dry grass between the wire fences right up to the edge of the gravel.

I leaned on the top wire of 'is north fence, 'n thought about a little fire. Only a little 'un. Lovely little yellow flames, lickin' round the bottoms of the wheat stalks. Next thing I knows, it's roarin' through the crop, yellow and red and orange and twistin' in the dark, with wriggly burnin' stalks flyin' up in the air and droppin' back ahead of the main fire to start new 'uns. 'N the north wind, still blowin' a red 'ot gale, right be'ind the lot.

Beautiful, she was. Beautiful, mate. You never seen nothin' so lovely.

'N the farmer's out there, like a madman, with a little squirt 'stinguisher on 'is back, 'n when that's done, with green boughs ripped offa the scrub trees beside the road. 'N I'm laughin'. Laughin' fit to kill.

Kill? I never meant to kill the sod. Jus' made a bit o' a mistake, that's all. 'N I know where I made it.

All uv a sudden I felt that the hot northerly had dropped. Died stone dead, it 'ad, and there was a smell like wet dirt, like maybe a few spots o' rain in the air. Just all kinda quiet for a minute, with this earthy smell, 'stead o' the stink o' burnin' grass. I knew what I'd forgot.

But I shoulda known it. The signs 'ad been there all day—the northerly, the curling-up long white clouds. There was gonna be a cool change, with a roarin' southerly buster. 'N there I was, with dry grass, dry scrub 'n dry wheat all round me, and the fire on me wrong side. I starts to run, for me life.

I knew e-zackly where I was goin'. Back two 'undred yards along the road was a stormwater drain, a three-foot concrete pipe under the gravel. It 'ad white posts, so people wouldn't drive cars into it, and there was some kind o' notice board. If I was lucky, I might get to it. 'F I was real lucky, might even be water in it.

The wind shifted, bang! from north to south. The flames came back on theirselves; the wheat crackled and twisted in corkscrews of fire. The Mallee scrub along the sides of the road was lit up for two 'undred yards, red like, and balls uv burnin' wheat and roley-poleys like Catherine wheels was jumpin' the road, and startin' up flames on the other side. The tops of the trees was burnin', too.

A rabbit ran acrost the road. 'S fur was smokin'. 'S eyes was lit up, orange. They reckon rabbits can see backwards as well as forwards. What was you lookin' at then, little fella? Your past life? I never meant to get ya, pal.

I c'd see the signpost at the drain. 'Twas one of them stupid things the fire brigades puts up, ter try to stop people from startin' bushfires. It was white paint, shinin' orange; it said FIRE IS A GOOD SERVANT BUT A BAD MASTER.

I was lookin' at it in a funny way, like, from face down

in the gravel. The white paint was all bubblin' and blis-
terin', and so were me 'ands 'n arms.

So that's 'ow I come 'ere, and that's all I can remember, mate, till I woke up in this 'orspital. But I'll soon
be out, be out afore you, pal. Getcha that smoke now.
The doc keeps 'is in 'is desk. I don't like 'is brand—
they're them brown things, like little cigars, like rolled-up
used crap paper. But I'll getcha one.

I gets outa me bed. Bit wobbly on the old pins, like. I
floats down the corridor, and I grabs one of the quack's
smokes. I goes back to the ward, and bugger me! Starchy
has done it again. The ole roast duck is back in me bloody
bed.

'Bugger you, mate' I says. 'Move over.'

'E don't move; 'e's still got all this junk shoved up 'is
snout, and what's more, 'e looks bloody near dead.

'OK' I says, 'I'm comin' back in' 'n so I do.

I think how it'd be (cos I got no matches, ya know) if
this stinkin' little cigar had a red end on it, glowing like.
'N I take a draw.

Next thing I knows, the young joker with the busted leg
is yellin' 'Nurse, nurse' 'n Starchy steams in with Husk in
tow. 'His bed clothes are on fire!' the young fella yells.
Sure enough, the old roast duck has set me bed on fire,
and Starchy makes a great thing of chuckin' water round.
The silly old sod; some people just can't manage fire at
all. Starchy pulls the choobs outa me nose, and draws
the curtains round me bed.

I mean, the old roast duck's bed. So, whatta I care,
any'ow? This joint is only for sick people. Sooner I'm outa
'ere the better.

So I wander back down the corridor, out the front door.
Over the other side of the road, there's some kind of bar-
becue or picnic, with camp fires 's far 's I can see. Lovely
fires. They're chuckin' on big logs, 'n the coals are shinin'
red and orange, 'n the flames are leapin' up towards
'eaven. There's lots of me old mates there.

'Come on, Joe' they're shoutin'. 'Over 'ere, mate!'

So, I starts to go acrost the road.

Then. Then. I sees two bastards I never wanted to
lay eyes on again. Fisheyes the schoolteacher, and the
Karamull farmer. Last time I seen 'im, 'e was rollin' in
the dirt, tryin' to put out 'is burnin' clothes. But they was

255

wool, and kept bubblin' and crawlin' like big black cater-pillars.

Fisheyes 'n the farmer are wavin' their arms, too, for me to come over their way.

Be damned to 'em.

I'll see them in Hell first.

The legend of the vampire continues to fascinate people—in fact, in recent years it's become more popular than ever, as our perception of Count Dracula and his kin has changed from pure horror to the addition of tragedy and intense sexuality. "The Ancient Mind at Work" is perhaps the most believable depiction of a vampire to date.

Suzy McKee Charnas quickly became a highly popular author with the publication of her novels *Walk to the End of the World* and *Motherlines*. The present story is the first of a series that will eventually comprise a book.

THE ANCIENT MIND AT WORK

Suzy McKee Charnas

ON A TUESDAY MORNING KATJE DISCOVERED
that Dr. Weyland was a vampire, like the one in the
movie she'd seen last week.

Jackson's friend on the night cleaning crew had left his
umbrella hooked over the bike rack outside the lab building. Since Katje liked before starting work to take a stroll
in the dawn quiet, she went over to see if the umbrella
was still there. As she started back empty-handed through
the heavy mist, she heard the door of the lab building
boom behind her. She looked back.

A young man had come out and started across the
parking lot. Clearly he was hurt or ill, for he slowed,
stopped, and sank down on one knee, reaching out a hand
to steady himself on the damp and glistening tarmac.

Behind him, someone else emerged from the building
and softly shut the heavy door. This man, tall and gray-
haired, stood a moment touching to his mouth a white
handkerchief folded into a small square. Then he put the
handkerchief away and walked out onto the lot. Passing
behind the kneeling figure, he turned his head to look—
and continued walking without hesitation. He got into his
shimmering gray Mercedes and drove off.

Katje started back toward the lot. But the young man
pushed himself upright, looked around in a bewildered
manner, and, making his way unsteadily to his own car,
also drove away.

So there was the vampire, sated and cruel, and there
was his victim, wilted, pale, and confused: although the

258

movie vampire had swirled about in a black cloak, not a raincoat, and had gone after bosomy young females. Walking over the lawn to the Club, Katje smiled at her own fancy.

What she had really seen, she knew, was the eminent anthropologist and star of the Cayslin Center for the Study of Man, Dr. Weyland, leaving the lab with one of his sleep subjects after a debilitating all-night session. Dr. Weyland must have thought the young man was stooping to retrieve dropped car keys.

The Cayslin Club was an old mansion donated years before to the college. It served now as the faculty club. Its grandeur had been severely challenged by the lab building and attendant parking lot constructed on half of the once-spacious lawn, but the Club was still an imposing place within.

Jackson was in the green room plugging leaks; it had begun to rain. The green room was a glassed-in terrace, tile-floored and furnished with chairs of lacy wrought iron.

"Did you find it, Mrs. de Groot?" Jackson said.

"No, I'm sorry." Katje never called him by his name because she didn't know whether he was Jackson Somebody or Somebody Jackson, and she had learned to be careful in everything to do with blacks in this country.

"Thanks for looking, anyway," Jackson said.

In the kitchen she stood by the sinks staring out at the dreary day. She had never grown used to these chill, watery winters, though after so many years she couldn't quite recall the exact quality of the African sunlight in which she had grown up. It was no great wonder that Hendrik had died here. The gray climate had finally quenched even his ardent nature six years ago, and she had shipped him back to his family. Katje had possessed his life; she didn't need his bones and didn't want a grave tying her to this dark country. His career as a lecturer in the Sociology of Medicine here and at other schools had brought in a good income, but he funneled all he could of it into the Black Majority Movement back home. So he had left her little, and she had expected that. To the amazement and resentment of certain faculty wives, she had taken this job and stayed on.

Her savings from her salary as housekeeper at the Cayslin Club would eventually finance her return home. She needed enough to buy not a farm, but a house with a garden patch somewhere high and cool—she frowned, trying to picture the ideal site. Nothing clear came into her mind. She had been away a long time.

While she was wiping up the sinks Miss Donelly burst in, shrugging out of her dripping raincoat and muttering, "Of all the highhanded, goddamn— Oh, hello, Mrs. de Groot; sorry for the language. Look, we won't be having the women's faculty lunch here tomorrow after all. Dr. Weyland is giving a special money pitch to a group of fat-cat alumni and he wants a nice, quiet setting—our lunch corner here at the Club, as it turns out. Dean Wacker's already said yes, so that's that."

"Why come over in the rain to tell me that?" Katje said. "You should have phoned."

"I also wanted to check out a couple of the upstairs bedrooms to make sure I reserve a quiet one for a guest lecturer I'm putting up here next month." Miss Donelly hesitated, then added, "You know, Mrs. de Groot, I've been meaning to ask whether you'd be willing to be a guest lecturer yourself in my Literary Environments course—we're reading Isak Dinesen. Would you come talk to my students?"

"Me? About what?"

"Oh, about colonial Africa, what it was like growing up there. These kids' experience is so narrow and protected, I look for every chance to expand their thinking."

Katje wrung out the sink rag. "My grandfather and Uncle Jan whipped the native boys to work like cattle and kicked them hard enough to break bones for not showing respect; otherwise we would have been overrun and driven out. I used to go hunting. I shot rhino, elephant, lion, and leopard, and I was proud of doing it well. Your students don't want to know such things. They have nothing to fear but tax collectors and nothing to do with nature except giving money for whales and seals."

"But that's what I mean," Miss Donelly said. "Different viewpoints."

"There are plenty of books about Africa."

"Try getting these kids to read," Miss Donelly sighed. "Well, I guess I could get the women together over at Corrigan tomorrow instead of here, if I spend an hour on the phone. And we'll miss your cooking, Mrs. de Groot."

"Will Dr. Weyland expect me to cook for his guests?" Katje said, thinking abstractedly of the alumni lunching with the vampire. Would he eat? The one in the movie hadn't eaten.

"Not Weyland," Miss Donelly said drily. "It's nothing but the best for him, which means the most expensive. They'll probably have a banquet brought in from Borchard's."

She left.

Katje put on coffee and phoned Buildings and Grounds. Yes, Dr. Weyland and six companions were on at the Club for tomorrow; no, Mrs. de Groot wouldn't have to do anything but tidy up afterward; yes, it was short notice, and please write it on the Club calendar; and yes, Jackson had been told to check the eaves over the east bedrooms before he left.

"Wandering raincoat," Miss Donelly said, darting in to snatch it up from the chair where she'd left it. "Just watch out for Weyland, Mrs. de Groot."

"What, a fifty-year-old widow like me? I am not some slinky graduate student trying for an A and the professor also."

"I don't mean romance," Miss Donelly grinned. "Though God knows half the faculty—of both sexes—are in love with the man." Honestly, Katje thought, the things people talked about these days! "To no avail, alas, since he's a real loner. But he will try to get you into his expensive sleep lab and make your dreams part of his world-shaking, history-changing research that he stole off poor old Ivan Milnes."

Milnes, Katje thought when she was alone again; Professor Milnes who had gone away to some sunny place to die of cancer. Then Dr. Weyland had come from a small Southern school and taken over Milnes's dream project, saving it from being junked—or stealing it, in Miss Donelly's version. A person who looked at a thing in too many ways was bound to get confused.

Jackson came in and poured coffee for himself. He leaned back in his chair and flipped the schedules where they hung on the wall by the phone. He was as slender as a Kikuyu youth—she could see his ribs arch under his shirt. He ate a lot of junk food, but he was too nervous to fatten on it. By rights he belonged in a red blanket, skin gleaming with oil, hair plaited. Instead he wore the tan shirt, pants, and zip-up jacket of an "engineer" from Buildings and Grounds, and his hair was a modest Afro, as they called it, around his narrow face.

"Try and don't put nobody in that number-six bedroom till I get to it the end of the week," he said. "The rain drips in behind the casement. I laid out towels to soak up the water. I see you got Weyland in here tomorrow. My buddy Maurice on the cleaning crew says that guy got the best lab in the place."

"What is Dr. Weyland's research?" Katje asked.

"'Dream mapping,' they call it. Maurice says there's nothing interesting in his lab—just equipment, you know, recording machines and computers and like that. I'd like to see all that hardware sometime. Only you won't catch me laying out my dreams on tape!

"Well, I got to push along. There's some dripping faucets over at Joffey I'm supposed to look at. Hans Brinker, that's me. Thanks for the coffee."

She began pulling out the fridge racks for cleaning, listening to him whistle as he gathered up his tools in the green room.

The people from Borchard's left her very little to do. She was stacking the rinsed dishes in the washer when a man said from the doorway, "I am very obliged to you, Mrs. de Groot."

Dr. Weyland stood there, poised, slightly stoop-shouldered, slightly leonine somehow. At least that was the impression Katje got from his alert stance, his still, stern masklike face from which the wide eyes looked out, bright with interest. She was surprised that he knew her name, for he did not frequent the Club.

"There was just a little remaining to be done, Dr. Weyland," she said.

"Still, this is your territory," he said, advancing. "I'm sure you were helpful to the Borchard's people. I've never been back here. Are those freezers or refrigerators?"

She showed him around the kitchen and the pantries. He seemed impressed. He handled the accessories to the Cuisinart as if they were artifacts of a civilization he was studying. The thing was a gift to the Club from the Home Ec staff. Many parts were missing already, but Katje didn't mind. She couldn't be bothered, as she told Dr. Weyland, getting the hang of the fancier gadgets.

He nodded thoughtfully. Was he condescending to her, or really in sympathy? "There's no time to master the homely technology of these times, all the machines, what they mean to a modern life . . ."

He was, she realized, unexpectedly personable: lean and grizzled, but with the hint of vulnerability common among rangy men. You couldn't look at him long without imagining the gawky scarecrow he must have been as a boy. His striking features—craggy nose and brow, strong mouth, square jaw—no doubt outsized and homely then, were now impressively united by the long creases of experience on his cheeks and forehead.

"No more scullions cranking the spit," he remarked over the rotisserie. "You come originally from East Africa, Mrs. de Groot? Things must have been very different there."

"Yes. I left a long time ago."

"Surely not so very long," he said, and his eyes flicked over her from head to foot. Why, the man was flirting!

Relaxing in the warmth of his interest, she said, "Are you from elsewhere also?"

He frosted up at once. "Why do you ask?"

"Excuse me, I thought I heard just the trace of an accent."

"My family were Europeans. We spoke German at home. May I sit down?" His big hands, capable and strong-looking, graced the back of a chair. He smiled briefly. "Would you mind sharing your coffee with an institutional fortune hunter? That is my job—persuading rich men and the guardians of foundations to spend a little of their money in support of work that offers no immediate result. I don't enjoy dealing with these shortsighted men."

"Everyone says you do it well." Katje filled a cup for him.

"It takes up my time," he said. "It wearies me." His large and brilliant eyes, in sockets darkened with fatigue, had a withdrawn, somber aspect. How old was he, Katje wondered.

Suddenly he gazed at her and said, "Didn't I see you over by the labs the other morning? There was mist on my windshield, I couldn't be sure . . ."

She told him about Jackson's friend's umbrella, thinking, Now he'll explain, this is what he came to say. But he added nothing, and she found herself hesitant to ask about the student in the parking lot. "Is there anything else I can do for you, Dr. Weyland?"

"I don't mean to keep you from your work. One thing: would you come over and do a session for me in the sleep lab?"

Just as Miss Donelly had said. Katje shook her head.

"All information goes on tapes under coded I.D. numbers, Mrs. de Groot. Your privacy would be strictly guarded."

His persistence made her uncomfortable. "I'd rather not."

"Excuse me, then. It's been a pleasure talking with you," he said, rising. "If you find a reason to change your mind, my extension is one-sixty-three."

She found herself obscurely relieved at his abrupt departure. She picked up his coffee cup. It was full. She realized that she had not seen him take so much as a sip.

She was close to tears, but Uncle Jan made her strip down the gun again—her first gun, her own gun—and then the lion coughed, and she saw, with the wide gaze of fear, his golden form crouched, tail lashing, in the thornbrush. She threw up her gun and fired, and the dust boiled up from the thrashings of the wounded cat.

Then Scotty's patient voice said, "Do it again," and she was tearing down the rifle once more by lamplight at the worn wooden table, while her mother sewed with angry stabs of the needle and spoke words Katje didn't bother to listen to. She knew the gist by heart: "If only Jan had children of his own! Sons, to take out hunting with Scotty. Because he has no sons, he takes Katje shooting instead so he can show how tough Boer youngsters are, even the girls. For whites to kill for sport, as Jan and Scotty do, is to go backward into the barbaric past of Africa. Now the farm is producing, there is no need to sell hides to get cash for coffee, salt, and tobacco. And to train a girl to go stalking and killing animals like scarcely more than an animal herself!"

"Again," said Scotty, and the lion coughed.

Katje woke. She was sitting in front of the TV, blinking at the sharp, knowing face of the talk-show host. The sound had gone off again, and she had dozed.

She didn't often dream, hardly ever of her African childhood—her mother, Uncle Jan, Scotty the neighboring farmer whom Uncle Jan had begun by calling a damned *rooinek* and ended treating like a brother. Miss Donelly's request for a lecture about Africa must have stirred up that long-ago girlhood spent prowling for game in a landscape of yellow grass.

The slim youngster she had been then, brown-skinned

and nearly white-haired from the sun, seemed far distant. A large-framed woman now, Katje worked to avoid growing stout as her mother had. In the gray New England climate her hair had dulled to the color of old brass, paling now toward gray.

Yet she could still catch sight of her child-self in the mirror—the stubborn set of her firm, round jaw and the determined squint of her eyes. She had not, she reflected with satisfaction, allowed the world to change her much.

Miss Donelly came in for some coffee the next afternoon. As Katje brought a tray to her in the long living room, a student rushed past, calling, "Is it too late to hand in my paper, Miss Donelly?"

"For God's sake, Mickey!" Miss Donelly burst out. "Where did you get that?"

Across the chest of the girl's T-shirt where her coat gapped open were emblazoned the words SLEEP WITH WEYLAND HE'S A DREAM. She grinned. "Some hustler is selling them right outside the co-op. Better hurry if you want one—Security's already been sent for." She put a sheaf of dogeared pages down on the table beside Miss Donelly's chair, added, "Thanks, Miss Donelly," and clattered away again on her high-heeled clogs.

Miss Donelly laughed and said to Katje, "Well, I never, as my grandma used to say. That man certainly does juice this place up."

"Young people have no respect for anything," Katje rumbled. "What will Dr. Weyland say, seeing his name used like that? He should have her expelled."

"Him? He wouldn't bother. Wacker will throw fits, though. Not that Weyland won't notice—he notices everything—but he doesn't waste his super-valuable time on nonsense." Miss Donelly ran a finger over the blistered paint on the windowsill by her chair. "Pity we can't use some of the loot Weyland brings in to fix up this old place. But I guess we can't complain; without Weyland Cayslin would be just another expensive backwater school for the not-so-bright children of the upper-middle-class. And it isn't all roses even for him. This T-shirt will start a whole new round of backbiting among his colleagues, you watch. This kind of stuff brings out the jungle beast in even the mildest academics."

Katje snorted. She didn't think much of academic infighting.

"I know we must seem pretty tame to you," Miss Donelly said wryly, "but there are some real ambushes and even killings here, in terms of careers. It's not the cushy life it sometimes seems, and not so secure either. Even for you, Mrs. de Groot. There are people who don't like your politics—"

"I never talk politics." That was the first thing Hendrik had demanded of her here. She had acquiesced like a good wife; not that she was ashamed of her political beliefs. She had loved and married Hendrik not because but in spite of his radical politics.

"From your silence they assume you're some kind of reactionary racist," Miss Donelly said. "Also because you're a Boer and you don't carry on your husband's crusade. Then there are the ones who're embarrassed to see the wife of a former instructor working at the Club—"

"It's work I can do," Katje said stiffly. "I asked for the job."

Miss Donelly frowned. "Sure—but everybody knows the college should have done better by you, and besides you were supposed to have a staff of people here to help out. And some of the faculty are a little scared of you; they'd rather have a giggly cocktail waitress, or a downtrodden mouse of a working student. You need to be aware of these things, Mrs. de Groot.

"And also of the fact that you have plenty of partisans too. Even Wacker knows you give this place tone and dignity, and you lived a real life in the world, whatever your values, which is more than most of our faculty have ever done." Blushing, she lifted her cup and drank.

She was as soft as everyone around here, Katje thought, but she had a good heart.

Many of the staff had already left for vacation during intersession, now that new scheduling had freed everyone from doing mini-courses between semesters. The last cocktail hour at the Club was thinly attended. Katje moved among the drinkers unobtrusively gathering up loaded ashtrays, used glasses, crumpled paper napkins. A few people who had known Hendrik greeted her as she passed.

There were two major topics of conversation: the bio student who had been raped last night leaving the library, and the Weyland T-shirt, or, rather, Weyland himself.

They said he was a disgrace, encouraging commercial

266

exploitation of his name; he was probably getting a cut of the profits. No he wasn't, didn't need to, he had a hefty income, no dependents, and no appetites except for study and work. And driving his beautiful Mercedes-Benz, don't forget that. No doubt that was where he was this evening —not off on a holiday or drinking cheap Club booze, but roaring around the countryside in his beloved car.

Better a ride in the country than burying himself in the library as usual. It was unhealthy for him to push so hard; just look at him, so haggard and preoccupied, so lean and lonely-looking. The man deserved a prize for his solitary-bachelor-hopelessly-hooked-on-the-pursuit-of-knowledge act.

It was no act—what other behavior did people expect of a great scholar? There'd be another fine book out of him someday, a credit to Cayslin. Look at that latest paper of his, "Dreams and Drama: The Mini-Theatre of the Mind." Brilliant!

Brilliant speculation, maybe, like all his work, plus an intriguing historical viewpoint, but where was his hard research? He was no scientist; he was a mountebank running on drive, imagination, great personal impressiveness, and a lucky success with his first book. Why, even his background was foggy. (But don't ever suggest to Dean Wacker that there was anything odd about Weyland's credentials. Wacker would eat you alive to protect the goose that laid the golden eggs.)

How many students were in the sleep project now? More than were in his classes. They called his course in ethnography "The Ancient Mind at Work." The girls found his formality charming. No. he wasn't formal, he was stiff-necked and old-fashioned, and he'd never make a first-rate contribution to anthropology. He'd simply appropriated poor Milnes's beautiful adaptation of the Richman-Steinmolle Recording System to the documentation of dreams, adding some fancy terminology about cultural symbols to bring the project into his own field of cultural anthropology. And Weyland thought he knew all about computers too—no wonder he ran his assistants ragged.

Here was Petersen leaving him because of some brouhaha over a computer run. Charming, yes, but Weyland could also be a sarcastic bastard. Sure, he was temperamental—the great are often quarrelsome, nothing new in that. Remember how he treated young Denton over that scratch Denton put on the Mercedes' fender? Gave him a tongue-lashing that could warp steel, and when Denton threw a punch Weyland grabbed him by the shoulder and just about flung him across the street. Denton was bruised for a month, looked as if he'd been on the bottom of a football pile-up. Weyland's a tiger when he's roused up, and he's unbelievably strong for a man his age.

He's a damned bully, and Denton should have gotten a medal for trying to get him off the roads. Have you seen Weyland drive? Roars along just barely in control of that great big machine . . .

Weyland himself wasn't present. Of course not, Weyland was a disdainful, snobbish son-of-a-bitch; Weyland was an introverted scholar absorbed in great work; Weyland had a secret sorrow too painful to share; Weyland was a charlatan; Weyland was a genius working himself to death to keep alive the Cayslin Center for the Study of Man.

Dean Wacker brooded by the huge empty fireplace. Several times he said, in a carrying voice, that he had talked with Weyland and that the students involved in the T-shirt scandal would face disciplinary action.

Miss Donelly came in late with a woman from Economics. They talked heatedly in the window bay, and the other two women in the room drifted over to join them. Katje followed.

". . . from off campus, but that's what they always say," one of them snapped. Miss Donelly caught Katje's eye, smiled a strained smile, and plunged back into the discussion. They were talking about the rape. Katje wasn't interested. A woman who used her sense and carried herself with self-respect didn't get raped, but saying so to these intellectual women wasted breath. They didn't understand real life. Katje went back toward the kitchen.

Buildings and Grounds had sent Nettie Ledyard over from the student cafeteria to help out. She was rinsing glasses and squinting at them through the smoke of her cigarette. She wore a T-shirt bearing a bulbous fish shape across the front and the words SAVE OUR WHALES. These "environmental" messages vexed Katje; only naive citified people could think of wild animals as pets. The shirt undoubtedly belonged to one of Nettie's long-haired, bleeding-heart boy friends. Nettie herself smoked too much to pretend to an environmental conscience. She was no hypocrite, at least. But she should come properly dressed to do a job at the Club, just in case a professor came wandering back here for more ice or whatever.

"I'll be helping you with the Club inventory during intersession," Nettie said. "Good thing, too. You'll be spending a lot of time over here until school starts again, and the campus is really emptying out. Now there's this sex maniac cruising the place—though what I could do but run like hell and scream my head off, I can't tell you.

"Listen, what's this about Jackson sending you on errands for him?" she added irritably. She flicked ash off her bosom which was pushed high like a shelf by her too-tight brassiere. "His pal Maurice can pick up his own umbrella, he's no cripple. Having you wandering around out there alone at some godforsaken hour—"

"Neither of us knew about the rapist," Katje said, wiping out the last of the ashtrays.

"Just don't let Jackson take advantage of you, that's all."

Katje grunted. She had been raised not to let herself be taken advantage of by blacks.

Later, helping to dig out a fur hat from under the coat pile in the foyer, she heard someone saying, ". . . walk off with the credit; cold-bloodedly living off other people's academic substance, so to speak."

Into her mind came the image of Dr. Weyland's tall figure moving without a break in stride past the stricken student.

Jackson came down from the roof with watering eyes. A damp wind was rising.

"That leak is fixed for a while," he said, hunching to blow on his chapped hands. "But the big shots at Buildings and Grounds got to do something better before next winter. The snow will just pile up and soak through again."

Katje polished the silver plate with a gray flannel. "What do you know about vampires?" she said.

"How bad you want to know?"

He had no right to joke with her like that, he whose ancestors had been heathen savages. "What do you know about vampires?" she repeated firmly.

"Not a thing." He grinned. "But you just keep on going to the movies with Nettie and you'll find out all about that

269

kind of crap. She got to have the dumbest taste in movies there ever was."

Katje looked down from the landing at Nettie, who had just let herself into the Club.

Nettie's hair was all in tight little rings like pigs' tails. She called, "Guess what I went and did?"

"Your hair." Katje said. "You got it done curly."

Nettie hung her coat crookedly on the rack and peered into the foyer mirror. "I've been wanting to try a permanent for months, but I couldn't find the spare money. So the other night I went over to the sleep lab." She came upstairs.

"What was it like?" Katje said, looking more closely at Nettie's face; was she paler than usual? Yes, Katje thought with sudden apprehension.

"It's nothing much. You just lie down on this couch, and they plug you into these machines, and you sleep. They keep waking you up in the middle of your dreams so you can describe what's going on, and you do some kind of tests—I don't remember, it's all pretty hazy afterwards. Next morning there's a sort of debriefing interview, and you collect your pay and go home. That's all there is to it."

"How do you feel?"

"Okay. I was pretty dragged out yesterday. Dr. Weyland gave me a list of stuff I'm supposed to eat to fix that. He got me the day off, too. Wait a minute, I need a smoke before we go into the linens."

She lit a cigarette. "Really, there was nothing to it. I'd go back for another session in a minute if they'd have me. Good money for no work; not like this." She blew a stream of smoke contemptuously at the linen-closet door.

Katje said, "Someone has to do what we do."

"Yeah, but why us?" Nettie lowered her voice. "We ought to get a couple of professors in there with the bedding and the inventory lists, and us two go sit in their big leather chairs and drink coffee like ladies."

Katje had already done that as Hendrik's wife. What she wanted now was to sit on the *stoep* after a day's hunting, sipping drinks and trading stories of the kill in the pungent dusk, away from the smoky, noisy hole of a kitchen: a life that Hendrik had rebelled against as parasitical, narrow, and dull. His grandfather, like Katje's, had trekked right out of the Transvaal when it became too staid for him and had started over. Katje thought sometimes that challenging his own people about the future of the land, the government and the natives had been Hendrik's way of striking out afresh. For herself, she wished only to return to her old country and its old ways.

Nettie, still hanging back from the linen closet, ground out her cigarette on the sole of her shoe. "Coming to the meeting Friday?"

Dr. Weyland was giving a lecture that same evening, something about nightmares. Katje had been thinking about attending. Now she must decide. Going to his lecture was not like going to his laboratory; it seemed safe enough. "No union meeting," she said. "I've told you, they're all Reds in those unions. I do all right for myself. I'll be going to Dr. Weyland's open lecture that night."

"Okay, if you think it's fine to make what we make doing this stuff." Nettie shrugged. "Me, I'll skip his lecture and take the bucks for sleeping in his lab. You ought to go over there, you know? There's hardly anything doing during intersession with almost everybody gone—they could take you right away. You get extra pay and time off, and besides Dr. Weyland's kind of cute, in a gloomy way. He leaned over me to plug something into the wall, and I said, 'Go ahead, you can bite my neck any time.' You know, he was sort of hanging over me, and his lab coat was sort of spread, like a cape, all menacing and batlike—except white instead of black, of course—and anyway I couldn't resist a wisecrack."

Katje gave her a startled glance. Nettie, missing it, moved past her into the closet and pulled out the step stool. Katje said cautiously, "What did he say to that?"

"Nothing, but he smiled." Nettie climbed up onto the step stool. "You know how his mouth turns sort of down at the corners? It makes him look grim all the time? Well, real serious anyway. When he smiles you'd be amazed how good he looks; he could really turn a girl on. We'll start up top in this closet, all right? I bet all the guys who work nights at the labs get those kind of jokes all the time. Later he said he was hoping you'd come by."

Taking a deep breath of the sweet, sunshine-smell of the clean sheets, Katje said, "He asked you to ask me to go there?"

"He said to remind you."

The first pile of blankets was handed down from the

top shelf. Katje said, "He really accepts anyone into this project?"

"Unless you're sick, or if you've got funny metabolism or whatever. They do a blood test on you, like at the doctor's."

That was when Katje noticed the little round Band-Aid on the inside of Nettie's elbow, right over the vein.

Miss Donelly was sharing a jug of cheap wine with three other faculty women in the front lounge. Katje made sure the coffee machine was filled for them and then slipped outside.

She still walked alone on campus when she chose. She wasn't afraid of the rapist, who hadn't been heard of in several days. A pleasurable tension drove her toward the lighted windows of the labs. This was like moving through the sharp air of the bushveldt at dusk. Awareness of danger was part of the pleasure.

The lab blinds, tilted down, let out only threads of light. She could see nothing. She hovered a moment, then turned back, hurrying now. The mood was broken, and she felt silly. Daniel from Security would be furious to find her alone out here, and what could she tell him? That she felt herself to be on the track of something wild and it made her feel young?

Miss Donelly and the others were still talking. Katje was glad to hear their wry voices and gusts of laughter, equally glad not to have to sit with them. She had never been comfortable among Hendrik's highly-educated colleagues.

She had more on her mind than school gossip, too, and she needed to think. Her own impulsive act excited and astonished her: sallying forth to the lab at dusk at some risk from the rapist (her mind swerved neatly around the other, the imaginary danger), but for what? To sniff the breeze and search the ground for tracks?

The thought of Dr. Weyland haunted her: Dr. Weyland as the charming, restless visitor prowling the Club kitchen, Dr. Weyland thrusting young Denton aside with contemptuous strength, Dr. Weyland as the heartless predator she had at first thought him that morning in the parking lot of the lab building.

She was walking to the bus stop when Jackson drove up and offered her a lift. She was glad to accept. The lonesomeness of the campus was accentuated by darkness and the empty circles of light around the lampposts.

Jackson pulled aside a jumble of equipment on the front seat—radio parts, speakers and wires—to make room for her. Two books were on the floor by her feet. He said, "The voodoo book is left over from my brother Paul. He went through a thing, you know, trying to trace back our family down in Louisiana. The other one was just laying around, so I brought it along."

The other one was *Dracula*. Katje felt the gummy spot where the price sticker had been peeled off. Jackson must have bought it for her at the discount bookstore downtown. She didn't know how to thank him easily, so she said nothing.

"It's a long walk to the bus stop," Jackson said, scowling as he drove out through the stone gates of the college drive. "They should've fixed it so you could stay on in faculty housing after your husband died."

"Our place was too big for one person," Katje said. Sometimes she missed the house on the east side of campus, but her present lodgings away from school offered more privacy.

He shook his head. "Well, I think it's a shame, you being a foreign visitor and all."

Katje laughed. "After twenty-five years in this country, a visitor?"

He laughed too. "Yeah. Well, you sure have moved around more than most while you been here: from lady of leisure to, well, maid work." She saw the flash of his grin. "Like my aunt that used to clean for white women up the hill. Don't you mind?"

She minded when she thought working at the Club would never end. Sometimes the Africa that she remembered seemed too vague a place to actually go back to, and the only future she could see was keeling over at the end while vacuuming the Club rugs, like a farmer worn to death at his plow. . . .

None of this was Jackson's business. "Did your aunt mind her work?" she snapped.

Jackson pulled up opposite the bus stop. "She said you just do what it comes to you to do and thank God for it."

"I say the same."

He sighed. "You're a lot like her, crazy as that sounds. There's a bunch of questions I want to ask you sometime, about how it was when you lived in Africa; I mean,

273

was it anything like in the movies—you know, *King Solomon's Mines* and like that?"

Katje had never seen that movie, but she knew that nothing on film could be like her Africa. "You should go to Africa and see for yourself," she said.

"I'm working on it. There's your bus coming. Wait a minute, listen—no more walking alone out here after dark, there's not enough people around now. You got to arrange to be picked up. Didn't you hear? That guy jumped another girl last night. She got away, but still. Daniel says he found one of the back doors to the Club unlocked. You be careful, will you? I don't want to have to come busting in there to save you from some deranged six-foot pre-med on the rampage, know what I mean?"

"Oh, I take care of myself," Katje said, touched and annoyed and amused all at once by his solicitude.

"Sure. Only I wish you were about fifteen years younger and studying karate, you know?" As Katje got out of the car with the books on her arm he added, "You told me once you did a lot of hunting in Africa when you were a kid; handling guns."

"Yes, a lot."

"Okay. Take this." He pulled metal out of his pocket and put it in her hand. It was a gun. "Just in case. You know how to use it, right?"

She closed her fingers on the compact weight of it. "But where did you get this? Do you have papers for it? The laws here are very strict—"

He yanked the door shut and said through the open window, "You going to holler 'law' at me, you can just give the damn thing back. No? Okay, then, hurry up before you miss your bus."

Dracula was a silly book. She had to force herself to read on in spite of the absurd Van Helsing character with his idiot English—an insult to anyone of Dutch descent. The voodoo book was impenetrable, and she soon gave it up.

The handgun was another matter. She sat at the formica-topped table in her kitchenette and turned the shiny little automatic in the light, thinking, How did Jackson come by such a thing. For that matter, how did he afford his fancy sports car and all that equipment he carried in it from time to time—where did it all come from and where did it go? He was up to something, probably lots of things, what they called "hustling" nowadays.

A good thing he had given her the gun. It could only get him into trouble to carry it around with him. She knew how to handle weapons, and surely with a rapist at large the authorities would be understanding about her lack of a license for it.

The gun needed cleaning. She worked on it as best she could without proper tools. It was a cheap .25 caliber gun. Back home your gun was a fine rifle, made to drop a charging rhino in its tracks, not a stubby little nickle-plated toy like this for scaring off muggers and rapists.

Yet she wasn't sorry to have it. Her own hunting gun that she had brought from Africa years ago was in storage with the extra things from the old house on campus. She had missed the presence of that rifle lately. She had missed it because, she realized now with a nervous little jump of the heart, she had become engaged in stalking a dangerous animal. She was stalking Dr. Weyland.

She went to sleep with the gun on the night table next to her bed and woke listening for the roar so she would know in what direction to look tomorrow for the lion's spoor. There was a hot, rank odor of African dust in the air and she sat up in bed thinking, He's been here.

It was a dream. But so clear! She went to look out the front window without turning on the light, and it was the ordinary street below that seemed unreal. Her heart drummed in her chest. Not that he would come after her here on Dewer Street, but he had sent Nettie to the Club, and now he had sent this dream into her sleep. Creatures stalking each other over time grew a bond from mind to mind.

But that was in another life. Was she losing her sanity? She read for a little in the Afrikaans Bible she had brought with her from home but so seldom opened in recent years. What gave comfort in the end was to put Jackson's automatic into her purse to carry with her. A gun was supposedly of no use against a vampire—you needed a wooden stake, she remembered reading, or you had to cut off his head to kill him—but the weight of the weapon in her handbag reassured her.

The lecture hall was full in spite of the scarcity of students on campus this time of year. These special talks were open to the town as well.

Dr. Weyland read his lecture in a stiff, abrupt manner. He stood slightly cramped over the lectern, which was low for his height, and rapped out his sentences, rarely raising his glance from his notes. In his tweeds and heavy-rimmed glasses he was the picture of the scholarly recluse drawn out of the study into the limelight. But Katje saw more than that. She saw the fluid power of his arm as he scooped from the air an errant sheet of notes, the almost disdainful ease with which he established his dominion over the audience. His lecture was brief; he fulfilled with unmistakable impatience the duty set every member of the faculty to give one public address per year on an aspect of his work, in this case "The Demonology of Dreams."

At the end came questions from the audience, most of them obviously designed to show the questioner's cleverness rather than to elicit information. The discussions after these lectures were reputed to be the real show. Katje, lulled by the abstract talk, came fully awake when a young woman asked, "Professor, have you considered whether the legends of supernatural creatures such as werewolves, vampires, and dragons might not be distortions out of nightmares at all—that maybe the legends reflect the existence of real, though rare, prodigies of evolution?"

Dr. Weyland hesitated, coughed, sipped water. "The forces of evolution are capable of prodigies, certainly," he said. "You have chosen an excellent word. But we must understand that we are not speaking—in the case of the vampire, for example—of a blood-sipping phantom who cringes from a clove of garlic. Now, how could nature design such a being?

"The corporeal vampire, if he existed, would be by definition the greatest of all predators, living as he would off the top of the food chain. Man is the most dangerous animal, the devourer or destroyer of all others, and the vampire preys on man. Now, any sensible vampire would choose to avoid the risks of attacking humans by tapping the blood of lower animals, if he could; so we must assume that our vampire cannot. Perhaps animal blood can tide him over a lean patch, as sea water can sustain the castaway for a few miserable days but can't permanently replace fresh water to drink. Humanity would remain the vampire's livestock, albeit fractious and dangerous to deal with, and where they live so must he.

"In the sparsely settled early world he would be bound to a town or village to assure his food supply. He would learn to live on as little as he could—perhaps a half liter of blood per day—since he could hardly leave a trail of drained corpses and remain unnoticed. Periodically he would withdraw for his own safety and to give the villagers time to recover from his depredations. A sleep several generations long would provide him with an untouched, ignorant population in the same location. He must be able to slow his metabolism, to induce in himself naturally a state of suspended animation. Mobility in time would become his alternative to mobility in space."

Katje listened intently. His daring in speaking this way excited her. She could see he was beginning to enjoy the game, growing more at ease on the podium as he warmed to his subject. He abandoned the lectern, put his hands casually into his pockets, and surveyed his listeners with a lofty glance. It seemed to Katje that he mocked them.

"The vampire's slowed body functions during these long rest periods might help extend his lifetime; so might living for long periods, waking or sleeping, on the edge of starvation. We know that minimal feeding produces striking longevity in some other species. Long life would be a highly desirable alternative to reproduction; flourishing best with the least competition, the great predator would not wish to sire his own rivals. It could not be true that his bite would turn his victims into vampires like himself—'"

"Or we'd be up to our necks in fangs," whispered someone in the audience rather loudly.

"Fangs are too noticeable and not efficient for blood-sucking," observed Dr. Weyland. "Large, sharp canine teeth are designed to tear meat. Polish versions of the vampire legend might be closer to the mark: they tell of some sort of puncturing device, perhaps a needle in the tongue like a sting that would secrete an anticlotting substance. That way the vampire could seal his lips around a minimal wound and draw the blood freely, instead of having to rip great, spouting, wasteful holes in his unfortunate prey." Dr. Weyland smiled.

The younger members of the audience produced appropriate retching noises.

Would a vampire sleep in a coffin, someone asked.

"Certainly not," Dr. Weyland retorted. "Would you, given a choice? The corporeal vampire would require physical access to the world, which is something that burial customs are designed to prevent. He might retire to a cave or take his rest in a tree like Merlin, or Ariel in the cloven pine, provided he could find either tree or cave safe from wilderness freaks and developers' bulldozers. Locating a secure, long-term resting place is one obvious problem for our vampire in modern times."

Urged to name some others, he continued, "Consider: upon each waking he must quickly adapt to his new surroundings, a task which, we may imagine, has grown progressively more difficult with the rapid acceleration of cultural change since the Industrial Revolution. In the last century and a half he has no doubt had to limit his sleeps to shorter and shorter periods for fear of completely losing touch—a deprivation which cannot have improved his temper.

"Since we posit a natural rather than a supernatural being, he grows older, but very slowly. Meanwhile each updating of himself is more challenging and demands more from him—more imagination, more energy, more cunning. While he must adapt sufficiently to disguise his anomalous existence, he must not succumb to current ideologies of Right or Left—that is, to the cant of individual license or the cant of the infallibility of the masses—lest either allegiance interfere with the exercise of his predatory survival skills."

Meaning, Katje thought grimly, he can't afford scruples about drinking our blood. He was pacing the platform now, soundless footfalls and graceful stride proclaiming his true nature. But these people were spellbound, rapt under his rule, enjoying his domination of them. They saw nothing of his menace, only the beauty of his quick hawk-glance and his panther-playfulness.

Emrys Williams raised a giggle by commenting that a lazy vampire could always take home a pretty young instructor who would show him any new developments in interpersonal relations.

Dr. Weyland fixed him with a cold glance. "You are mixing up dinner with sex," he remarked, "and not, I gather, for the first time."

They roared. Williams—the "tame Wild Welshman of the Lit Department" to his less admiring colleagues—turned a gratified pink.

One of Dr. Weyland's associates in Anthropology pointed out at boring length that the vampire, born in an earlier age, would become dangerously conspicuous for his diminutive height as the human race grew taller.

"Not necessarily," commented Dr. Weyland. "Remember that we speak of a highly specialized physical form. It may be that during his waking periods his metabolism is so sensitive that he responds to the stimuli in the environment by growing in his body as well as in his mind. Perhaps while awake his entire being exists at an intense level of inner activity and change. The stress of these great rushes to catch up all at once with physical, mental, and cultural evolution must be enormous. These days he would need his long sleeps as recovery periods from the strain."

He glanced at the wall clock. "As you can see, by the exercise of a little imagination and logic we produce a creature bearing superficial resemblances to the vampire of legend, but at base one quite different from your standard strolling corpse with an aversion to crosses. Any questions on our subject—dreams?"

But they weren't willing to drop this flight of fancy. A young fellow asked how Dr. Weyland accounted for the superstitions about crosses and garlic and so on.

The professor paused to sip water from the glass at hand. The audience waited in expectant silence. Katje had the feeling that they would have waited an hour without protest, he had so charmed them. Finally he said, "Primitive men first encountering the vampire would be unaware that they themselves were products of evolution, let alone that he was. They would make up stories to account for him, and to try to control him. In early times he might himself believe in some of these legends—the silver bullet, the oaken stake. Waking at length in a less credulous age he would abandon these notions, just as everyone else did. He might even develop a passionate interest in his own origins and evolution."

"Wouldn't he be lonely?" sighed a girl standing in the side aisle, her posture eloquent of the desire to comfort that loneliness.

"The young lady will forgive me," Dr. Weyland responded, "if I observe that this is a question born of a sheltered life. Predators in nature do not indulge in the sort of romantic mooning that humans impute to them. Our vampire wouldn't have the time for moodiness. On each waking he has more to learn. Perhaps someday the world will return to a reasonable rate of change, permitting him some leisure in which to feel lonely or whatever suits him."

A nervous girl ventured the opinion that a perpetually self-educating vampire would always have to find himself a place in a center of learning in order to have access to the information he would need.

"Quite right," agreed Dr. Weyland drily. "Perhaps a university, where strenuous study and other eccentricities of the active intellect would be accepted behavior in a grown man. Even a modest institution such as Cayslin College might serve."

Under the chuckling that followed this came a question too faint for Katje to hear. Dr. Weyland, having bent to listen, straightened up and announced sardonically, "The lady desires me to comment upon the vampire's 'Satanic pride.' Madame, here we enter the area of the literary imagination and its devices where I dare not tread under the eyes of my colleagues from the English Department. Perhaps they will pardon me if I merely point out that a tiger who falls asleep in a jungle and on waking finds a thriving city overgrowing his lair has no energy to spare for displays of Satanic pride."

Great God, the nerve of him! Katje thought, torn between outrage and admiration. She wanted him to look at her, to see knowledge burning in one face at least, to know that he had not flaunted his reality tonight only before blind eyes. Surely he sensed her challenge, surely he would turn—

Williams, intent on having the last word as always, spoke up once more. "The vampire as time-traveler—you ought to be writing science fiction, Weyland." This provoked a growing patter of applause, signal of the evening's end.

Katje hurried out with the crowd and withdrew to stand aside under the portico of the Union Building while her hot heart cooled. Dr. Weyland's car was across the street, gleaming in the lamplight. To him, she thought, it was not just a car but his access to physical mobility and a modern mechanical necessity that he had mastered. That was how he would think of it, she was sure. She knew something of his mind now.

With the outwash of departing audience came Miss Donelly. She asked if Katje needed a lift. Katje explained that a group of women from the staff cafeteria went bowling together each Friday night and had promised to swing by and pick her up.

"I'll wait with you just in case," Miss Donelly said.

"You know, Wild Man Williams is a twerp, but he was right: Weyland's vampire would be a time-traveler. He could only go forward, of course, never back, and only by long, unpredictable leaps—this time, say, into our age of what we like to think of as technological marvels; maybe next time into an age of interstellar travel. Who knows, he might get to taste Martian blood, if there are Martians, and if they have blood.

"Frankly, I wouldn't have thought Weyland could come up with anything so imaginative extempore like that—the vampire as a sort of leftover saber-tooth tiger prowling the pavements, a truly endangered species. That's next term's T-shirt: 'SAVE THE VAMPIRE.' "

There was no point consulting Miss Donelly. She might banter, but she would never believe. It was all a joke to her, a clever mental game invented by Dr. Weyland to amuse his audience. She could not perceive, as Katje could, that he was a monster amusing himself by toying with his prey.

Miss Donelly added ruefully, "You've got to hand it to the man, he's got tremendous stage presence, and he sure knows how to turn on the charm when he feels like it. Nothing too smooth, mind you—just enough unbending, enough slightly caustic graciousness, to set susceptible hearts abeating. You could almost forget what a ruthless, self-centered bastard he can be. Did you notice that most of the comments came from women?

"Is that your lift?"

It was. While the women in the station wagon shuffled themselves around to make room, Katje stood with her hand on the door and watched Dr. Weyland emerge from the building with admiring students at either hand. He loomed above them, his hair silver under the lamplight. For overcivilized people to experience the approach of such a predator as sexually attractive was not strange. She remembered Scotty saying once that the great cats were all beautiful, and maybe beauty helped them to capture their prey.

Dr. Weyland turned his head, and she thought for a moment that he was looking at her as she got into the station wagon.

Fear filled her. What could she do to protect herself from him, how could she alert others to the truth without people thinking she was simply crazy? She couldn't think amid the tired, satisfied ramblings of the bowling friends, and she declined to stay up and socialize with them. They didn't press her.

Sitting alone at home, Katje had a cup of hot milk to calm herself for sleep. To her perplexity, her mind kept wandering from thoughts of Dr. Weyland to memories of drinking cocoa at night with Hendrik and the African students he used to bring to dinner. They had been native boys to her, dressed up in suits and talking politics like white men, flashing photographs of black kids playing with toy trucks and walkie-talkie sets. Sometimes they had all gone to see documentary films of an Africa full of cities and traffic and black professionals exhorting, explaining, running things, as these students expected to do in their turn when they went home.

She thought about home now. She recalled clearly all those indicators of change in Africa, and she saw suddenly that the old life there had gone. She would return to an Africa largely as foreign to her as America had been at first. Reluctantly she admitted that one of her feelings while listening to Dr. Weyland talk had been an unwilling empathy: if he was a one-way time-traveler, so was she. She saw herself cut off from the old life of raw vigor, the rivers of game, the smoky village air, all viewed from the heights of white privilege. To lose one's world these days one did not have to sleep for half a century; one had only to grow older.

Next morning she found Dr. Weyland leaning, hands in pockets, against one of the columns flanking the entrance to the Club. She stopped some yards from him, her purse hanging heavily on her arm. The hour was early, the campus deserted-looking. Stand still, she thought; show no fear.

He looked at her. "I saw you after the lecture last night and, earlier in the week, outside the lab one evening. You must know better than to wander alone at night; the campus is empty, no one is around—anything might happen. If you are curious, Mrs. de Groot, come do a session for me. All your questions will be answered. Come over tonight. I could stop by here for you in my car on the way back to the lab after dinner. There's no problem with scheduling, and I would welcome your company. During intersession the lab is empty. I have no volunteers. I sit alone over there these nights hoping some impoverished youngster, unable to afford a trip home at intersession, will be moved by an uncontrollable itch for travel to come to my lab and earn his fare."

She felt fear and excitement knocking heavily in her body. She shook her head, no.

"My work would interest you, I think," he added, watching her. "You are an alert, handsome woman; they waste your qualities here. Couldn't the college find you something better than this job after your husband died? You might consider coming over regularly to help me with some clerical chores until I get a new assistant. I pay well."

Astonished out of her fear at the offer of work in the vampire's lair, she found her voice. "I am a country woman, Dr. Weyland, a daughter of farmers. I have no proper education. We never read books at home, except the Bible. My husband didn't want me to work. I have spent my time in this country learning English and cooking and how to shop for the right things. I have no skills, no knowledge but the little that I remember of the crops, the weather, the customs, the wildlife of another country —and even that is probably out of date. I would be no use in work like yours."

Hunched in his coat with the collar upturned, looking at her slightly askance, his tousled hair gleaming with the damp, he had the aspect of an old hawk, intent but aloof. He broke the pose, yawned behind his large-knuckled hand, and straightened up.

"As you like. Here comes your friend Nellie."

"Nettie," Katje corrected, suddenly outraged: he'd drunk Nettie's blood, the least he could do was to remember her name properly. But he was walking away over the lawn toward the labs.

Nettie came panting up. "Who was that? Did he try to attack you?"

"It was Dr. Weyland," Katje said. She hoped Nettie didn't notice her trembling.

Nettie laughed. "What is this, a secret romance?"

Miss Donelly came into the kitchen toward the end of the luncheon for the departing emeritus. She plumped herself down between Nettie and Katje, who were taking a break and preparing dessert respectively. Katje spooned whipped cream carefully into each glass dish of fruit.

Miss Donelly said, "In case I get too smashed to say this later, thanks. On the budget I gave you, you did just great. The Department will put on something official with Beef Wellington and all the trimmings over at Borchard's. But it was really important for some of us to give Sylvia our own alcoholic farewell feast, which we couldn't have done without your help."

Nettie nodded and stubbed out her cigarette.

"Our pleasure," Katje said, preoccupied. Dr. Weyland had come for her, would come back again; he was hers to deal with, but how? She no longer thought of sharing her fear, not with Nettie with her money worries or with Miss Donelly whose eyes were just now faintly glazed-looking with drink. Weyland the vampire could never be dealt with by a committee.

"The latest word," Miss Donelly added bitterly, "is that the Department plans to fill Sylvia's place with some guy from Oregon; which means the salary goes up half as much again or more inside of six months."

"Them's the breaks," Nettie said, not very pleasantly. She caught Katje's eye with a look that said, "Look who makes all the money and look who does all the complaining."

"Them is," Miss Donelly agreed glumly. "As for me, the word is no tenure, so I'll be moving on in the fall. Me and my big mouth. Wacker nearly fainted at my prescription for stopping the rapes: you entrap the guy, disembowel him, and hang his balls over the front gate. Our good dean doesn't know me well enough to realize that it's all front. On my own I'd be too petrified to try anything but talking the bastard out of it; you know, 'Now, you just let me put my dress back on and I'll make us each a cup of coffee, and you tell me all about why you hate women.' " She stood up.

"Did you hear what happened to that girl last night, the latest victim? He cut her throat. Ripped her pants off, but didn't even bother raping her. That's how desperate for sex he is."

Katje said, "Jackson told us about the killing this morning."

"Jackson? Oh, from Buildings and Grounds. Look out, it could even be him. Any of them, damn them," she muttered savagely as she turned away, "living off us, kicking our bodies out of the way when they're through—"

She stumbled out of the kitchen.

Nettie snorted. "She's always been one of those libbers. No wonder Wacker's getting rid of her. Some men act

284

like hogs, but you can't let yourself be turned into a man-hater. A man's the only chance most girls have of getting up in the world, you know?" She pulled on a pair of acid-yellow gloves and headed for the sink. "If I want out of these rubber gloves, I have to marry a guy who can afford to pay a maid."

Katje sat looking at the fruit dishes with their plump cream caps. It was just as the Bible said: she felt it happen—the scales fell from her eyes. She saw clearly and thought, I am a fool.

Bad pay is real, rape is real, killing is real. The real world worries about real dangers, not childish fancies of a night prowler who drinks blood. Dr. Weyland took the trouble to be concerned, to offer extra work, while I was thinking . . . idiot things about him. Where does it come from, this nonsense of mine? My life is dull since Hendrik died; so I make up drama in my head, and that way I get to think about Dr. Weyland, a distinguished and learned gentleman, being interested in me.

She resolved to go to the lab building later and leave a note for him, an apology for her reluctance, an offer to stop by soon and make an appointment at the sleep lab.

Nettie looked at the clock and said over her shoulder, "Time to take the ladies their dessert."

At last the women had dispersed, leaving the usual fog of smoke behind. Katje and Nettie had finished the cleaning up. Katje said, "I'm going for some air."

Nettie, wreathed by smoke of her own making, drowsed in one of the big living-room chairs. She shook her head. "Not me. I'm pooped." She sat up. "Unless you want me along? It's still light out, so you're safe from the Cayslin Ripper."

"Don't disturb yourself," Katje said.

Away on the far edge of the lawn three students danced under the sailing shape of a Frisbee. Katje looked up at the sun, a silver disk behind a thin place in the clouds; more rain coming, probably. The campus still wore a deserted look. Katje wasn't worried. There was no vampire, and the gun in her purse would suffice for anything else.

The sleep lab was locked. She tucked her note of apology between the lab door and the jamb and left.

As she started back across the lawn someone stepped behind her, and long fingers closed on her arm. It was Dr.

Weyland. Firmly and without speaking he bent her course back toward the labs.

"What are you doing?" she said, astonished.

"I almost drove off without seeing you. Come sit in my car, I want to talk to you." She held back, alarmed, and he gave her a sharp shake. "Making a fuss is pointless. No one is here to notice."

There was only his car in the parking lot; even the Frisbee players had gone. Dr. Weyland opened the door of the Mercedes and inserted Katje into the front passenger seat with a left, powerful thrust of his arm. He got in on the driver's side, snapped down the automatic door locks and sat back. He looked up at the gray sky, then at his wristwatch.

Katje said, "You wanted to say something to me?"

He didn't answer.

She said, "What are we waiting for?"

"For the day-man to leave and lock up the labs. I dislike being interrupted."

This is what it's like, Katje thought, feeling lethargic detachment stealing through her, paralyzing her. No hypnotic power out of a novelist's imagination held her, but the spell cast on the prey of the hunting cat, the shock of being seized in the deadly jaws though not a drop of blood was yet spilled. "Interrupted," she whispered.

"Yes," he said, turning toward her. She saw the naked craving in his gaze. "Interrupted at whatever it pleases me to do with you. You are on my turf now, Mrs. de Groot, where you have persisted in coming time after time. I can't wait any longer for you to make up your mind. You are healthy—I looked up your records—and I am hungry."

The car smelled of cold metal, leather, and tweed. At length a man came out of the lab building and bent to unlock the chain from the only bicycle in the bike rack. By the way Dr. Weyland shifted in his seat Katje knew that this was the departure he had been awaiting.

"Look at that idiot," he muttered. "Is he going to take all night?" Weyland turned restlessly toward the lab windows. That would be the place, Katje thought, after a bloodless blow to stun her—he wouldn't want any mess in his Mercedes.

In her lassitude she was sure that he had attacked that girl, drunk her blood, and then killed her. He was using the rapist's activities as cover. When subjects did not come to him at the sleep lab, hunger drove him out to hunt.

She thought, *but I am myself a hunter!*

Cold anger coursed through her. Her thoughts flew: she needed time, a moment out of his reach to plan her survival. She had to get out of the car—any subterfuge would do.

She gulped and turned toward him, croaking, "I'm going to be sick."

He swore furiously. The locks clicked; he reached roughly past her and shoved open the door on her side. "Out!"

She stumbled out into the drizzling, chilly air and backed several hasty paces, hugging her purse to her body like a shield, looking quickly around. The man on the bike had gone. The upper story of the Cayslin Club across the lawn showed a light—Nettie would be missing her now. Maybe Jackson would be just arriving to pick them both up there. But no help could come in time.

Dr. Weyland had gotten out of the car. He stood with his arms folded on the roof of the Mercedes, looking across at her with a mixture of annoyance and contempt. "Mrs. de Groot, do you think you can outrun me?"

He started around the front of his car toward her.

Scotty's voice sounded quietly in her ear: "Yours," he said, as the leopard tensed to charge. Weyland too was an animal, not an immortal monster out of legend—just a wild beast, however smart and strong and hungry. He had said so himself.

She jerked out the automatic, readying it to fire as she brought it swiftly up to eye level in both hands, while her mind told her calmly that a head shot would be best but that a hit was surer if she aimed for the torso.

She shot him twice, two slugs in quick succession, one in the chest and one in the abdomen. He did not fall but bent to clutch at his torn body, and he screamed and screamed so that she was too shaken to steady her hands for the head shot afterward. She cried out also, involuntarily: his screams were dreadful. It was long since she had shot anything.

Footsteps rushed behind her, arms flung round her pinning her hands to her sides so that the gun pointed at the ground. Jackson's voice gasped in her ear, "Jesus Christ!"

His car stood slewed where he had braked it, unheard

by Katje. Nettie jumped out and rushed toward Katje, crying, "My God, he's shot, she shot him!"

Breaking off his screaming, Weyland tottered away from them around his car and fetched up leaning on the front. His face, a hollow-cheeked, starving mask, gaped at them.

"It's him?" Jackson said incredulously. *"He* tried to rape you?"

Katje said, "No, he's a vampire."

"A vampire!" Jackson exploded. "Have you gone crazy? Jesus!"

Weyland panted, "Stop staring, cattle!"

He wedged himself heavily into the driver's seat of his car. They could see him slumped there, his forehead against the curve of the steering wheel. Blood spotted the hood of the Mercedes where he had leaned.

"Mrs. de Groot, give me the gun," Jackson said.

Katje clenched her fingers around the grip. "No."

She could tell by the way Jackson's arms tightened that he was afraid to let go of her and grab for the gun.

A siren sounded. Nettie cried in wild relief, "That's Daniel's car coming!"

Weyland raised his head. His gray face was rigid with determination. He snarled, "The door—one of you shut the door!"

His glaring face commanded them. Nettie darted forward, slammed the door, and recoiled, wiping her hand on her sweater. Weyland drove the Mercedes waveringly past them, out of the parking lot toward the gateway road. Rain swept down in heavy gusts. Katje heard the siren again and woke fully to her failure: she had not made a clean kill. The vampire was getting away.

She lunged toward Jackson's car. He held her back, shouting, "Nothing doing, come on, you done *enough!*"

The Mercedes crawled haltingly down the middle of the road, turned at the stone gates, and was gone.

Jackson said, *"Now* will you give me that gun?"

Katje snapped on the safety and dropped the automatic on the wet paving at their feet.

Nettie was pointing toward the Club. "There's people coming—they must have heard the shooting and called Daniel. Listen, Jackson, we're in trouble. Nobody's going to believe that Dr. Weyland is the rapist—or the other thing either." Her glance flickered nervously at Katje. "Whatever we say, they'll think we're crazy."

"Oh, shit," said Jackson tiredly, letting Katje go at last. He picked up the gun. Katje saw the apprehension in his face as he weighed Nettie's assessment of their situation: a wild story from some cleaning people about the eminent professor.

"We've got to say something," Nettie went on desperately. "All that blood . . ." She fell silent, staring down.

There was no blood. The rain had washed the tarmac clean.

Jackson faced Katje and said urgently, "Listen, Mrs. de Groot, we don't know a thing about any shooting, you hear?" He slipped the gun into an inside pocket of his jacket. "You came over to make an appointment at the sleep lab, only Dr. Weyland wasn't around. You waited for him, and Nettie got worried when you didn't come back, and we drove over here looking for you. We all heard shooting, but nobody saw anything. There was nothing to see. Like now."

Katje was furious with him and with herself. She should have chanced the head shot, she shouldn't have let Jackson hold her back.

She could see Daniel's car now, wheeling into the parking lot.

Jackson said tightly, "I got accepted to computer school in Rochester for next semester. You can bet they don't do vampires over there, Mrs. de Groot; and they don't do Blacks with guns either. Me and Nettie got to live here, we don't get to go away to Africa."

She grew calm; he was right. The connection had been between herself and the vampire all along, and what had happened here was her own affair, nothing to do with these young people.

"All right, Jackson," she said. "There was nothing to see."

"Check," he said. He turned toward Daniel's car.

He would do all right, Katje thought; maybe someday he would come visit her in Africa, in a smart suit and carrying an attaché case, on business. Surely they had computers there now, too.

Daniel stepped out of his car into the rain, one hand on his pistol butt. Katje saw the disappointment sour his florid face as Nettie put a hand on his arm and talked.

Katje picked up her purse from where she had dropped it— how light it felt now, without the gun in it. She fished out her plastic rain hood, though her hair was already wet. Tying the hood on, she thought about her old .350 magazine rifle, her lion gun; about taking it from storage, putting it in working order, tucking it well back into the broom closet at the Club. In case Weyland didn't die, in case he couldn't sleep with two bullets in him and came limping back to hunt on familiar ground—to look for her. He would come next week, when the students returned, or never. She didn't think he would come, but she would be ready just in case.

And then, as she had planned, she would go home to Africa. Her mind flashed: a new life, whatever life she could make for herself there these days. If Weyland could fit himself to new futures, so could she. She was adaptable and determined—like him.

But if he did sleep, and woke again fifty years from now? Each generation must look out for itself. She had done her part, although perhaps not well enough to boast about. Still, what a tale it would make some evening over the smoke of a campfire on the veldt, beginning with the tall form of Dr. Weyland seen striding across the parking lot past the kneeling student in the heavy mist of morning . . .

Katje walked toward Daniel's car to tell the story that Buildings and Grounds would understand.

RECOMMENDED READING

Orson Scott Card: "Deep-Breathing Exercises." *Omni*, July 1979.

C. J. Cherryh: "The Dreamstone." *Amazons!*

Jack Dann: "Camps." *Fantasy and Science Fiction*, May 1979.

Samuel R. Delany: "The Tale of Gorgik." *Asimov's SF Adventure Magazine*, Summer 1979.

David Drake: "The Red Leer." *Whispers II.*

Harlan Ellison: "All the Birds Come Home to Roost." *Playboy*, March 1979.

Randall Garrett: "The Napoli Express." *Isaac Asimov's Science Fiction Magazine*, April 1979.

Bruce Gillespie: "The Wide Waters Waiting." *Transmutations.*

Paul Halpine: "The Wizard and Death." *Fantastic*, January 1979.

T. E. D. Klein: "Petey." *Shadows 2.*

Tanith Lee: "The Murderous Dove." *Heroic Fantasy.*

Bob Leman: "Loob." *Fantasy and Science Fiction*, April 1979.

Susan C. Petrey: "Spareen among the Tartars." *Fantasy and Science Fiction*, September 1979.

Paul Theroux: "White Lies." *Playboy*, May 1979.

Fantasy Novels
from
POCKET BOOKS

_____ 83217   THE BOOK OF THE DUN COW
Walter Wangerin, Jr. $2.50
*"Far and away the most literate and intelligent
story of the year."—The New York Times*

_____ 43131   THE WHITE HART
Nancy Springer $2.50
*"It has everything; a believable fantasy world...
a lovely, poignant book."*
—Marion Zimmer Bradley

_____ 82912   BEAUTY Robin McKinley $1.95
*"The most delightful first novel I've read in
years...I was moved and enchanted."—Peter S.
Beagle, author of THE LAST UNICORN*

_____ 83281   CHARMED LIFE $2.25
"An outstanding success."—Andre Norton

_____ 83294   ARIOSTO
Chelsea Quinn Yarbo $2.25
*"Colorful and exciting...a vivid tapestry come
to life...superb!"—Andre Norton*

_____ 82958   THE ORPHAN
Robert Stallman $2.25
*"An exciting blend of love and violence, of
sensitivity and savagery."—Fritz Leiber*

POCKET BOOKS Department FAN
1230 Avenue of the Americas, New York, N.Y. 10020

Please send me the books I have checked above. I am enclosing $_____
(please add 50¢ to cover postage and handling for each order, N.Y.S. and N.Y.C.
residents please add appropriate sales tax). Send check or money order—no
cash or C.O.D.s please. Allow up to six weeks for delivery.

NAME_____

ADDRESS_____

CITY_____ STATE/ZIP_____